TEAM THIRTEEN

NN COLE

To my family for all their love and support.

www.mascotbooks.com

Team Thirteen

Cover and map designs by Jasmine R. White

For more information, please contact:
Mascot Books
620 Herndon Parkway #120
Herndon, VA 20170
info@mascotbooks.com

Library of Congress Control Number: 2018900804

CPSIA Code: PRFRE1218A
ISBN-13: 978-1-68401-822-2

Printed in Canada

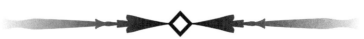

LOCATION:

HYBRID MILITARY COMPOUND

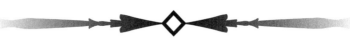

Above Ground

TRAINING CENTER

LABS & RESEARCH

INFIRMARY

TESTING CENTER

CAFETERIA

BOMB
SHELTER

NO1

NO2

NO3

BUILDING CENTER,
TRUCKS, & STORAGE

NO4

HOUSING UNITS

FRONT GATE

Level 1
Level 2   Storage
           BLOCKED

Level 1   Firearms
Level 2   Blades
Level 3   Hand-to-hand

Level 1   Labs
Level 2   Research

Level 1   Locker Rooms/Test Rooms
Level 2   Team Simulation

Level 1   Surgery

Level 2   Intensive Care

Level 1   Bomb Shelter

NO1

NO2

Level 1   Commander's Office

Below Ground

Level 3   Team Thirteen

They are a new species meant to save our world.

CHAPTER ONE

The hybrids were supposed to be a secret, but everyone knows now. They started a year ago, making them in the east, going to high schools, injecting teenagers with who knows what, making them different. Stronger. Faster. Terrifying, perfect soldiers. Slowly, they're moving west, creeping across the United States, trying to make enough hybrids to form an army. At least, that's what Layla keeps hearing.

But no one knows where the teenagers and the people who inject them go after that. There are rumors, of course. They go to the abandoned, destroyed cities. They go underground. They get shipped out of the country. Some even say they just wander around, hunting members of the Black Sun.

Wherever they go and whatever they do, Layla knows it's better than sitting at an old desk learning about geometry. Looking up from her mess of small animal doodles, Layla scowls at the back of Mr. Tanner's head. His gray curls are so messy it's a wonder how they even got like that. With the faulty lighting in the room, they throw weird shadows on the board, obstructing part of the equation from Layla's view. The closer to the front of the school building, the worse the lighting is. The Black Sun is known for bombing large cities and being this close to one of their largest has made the power and plumbing sketchy in parts of their town.

Layla tucks a wayward strand of hair behind her ear and squints at the equation on the board. She should have skipped school today and dragged Courtney with her. They could have gotten pizza, or maybe snuck around town, or watched one of those cartoon movies Courtney loves. Courtney's parents would have yelled at them, but, right now, even that sounds better than this class.

Last year they wouldn't have cared if Layla went to school or stayed in bed all day. Besides giving her sad smiles and grief filled glances, Mr. and Mrs. Jones never had any idea of what to do with her. In fact, Courtney's parents let her stay at their house for months, never going to school, randomly leaving in the middle of the night. She and some other students would meet up to talk about the Black Sun. What were they doing? How could they help in the fight against them? Where will they attack next? And, most important, what were the whispers about something called "hybrids"?

But that was before those whispers turned into well-known fact. "They do it when you're in school," Courtney's mom had said. "So, you're going to be there every day. The both of you are. And no more sneaking around, Layla. We don't need more trouble than we've already got."

Layla loves Courtney's parents. They took her in without a second thought two years ago, but they're still not her parents. And no matter how grateful she is to Courtney and her family, it took months for her friend to convince Layla to listen to Mrs. Jones.

It's not that Layla was avoiding the idea of the becoming a hybrid. In fact, it was quite the opposite. All those months spent in bed, she couldn't stop think about it, wishing for it. The problem was that it just took so much energy to get up, go to school, pretend everything was normal. There are still times when Courtney drags her out of bed, and they show up an hour late to school.

The intercom crackles, interrupting Mr. Tanner's lecture about the different types of triangles. Pencils stop scratching at paper, and an anxious undercurrent fills the classroom. Layla grips her pencil hard enough to snap the thin plastic. Announcements at school are never good. For the last four years, more often than not, Layla found out about terrorist attacks from her principal.

"Students of Preston High," the principal's hoarse voice says. "It is our honor to be selected to donate our bodies and hearts to the United States Army, Special Force Team: Hybrid." There's a too-long pause here where he clears his throat. Mr. Tanner drops his marker, and the sound of it snapping against the tiled floor startles a few students into standing straight up. No one looks half-asleep now. Slumped bodies are stiff in their seats. Sleepy eyes are wide with panic. Finally, the principal continues in a rush, "Boys, please make your way to the south gymnasium. Girls, please gather in the west gymnasium. Leave your belongings behind. Thank you, and good luck."

The announcement ends in a short burst of static before the entire school appears to go silent. Layla uncurls her fingers from her pencil, and slips her hand into her jean pocket, feeling the smooth picture folded in there. It's an image of her and her parents, taken a few months before the bombing that took them from her. She carries it everywhere and has looked at it so many times that she can visualize it in her head. Her mom's dark but graying hair and wide, wrinkle-framed smile. The glint of her dad's glasses obscuring his eyes. His tongue sticking out in a goofy way. It's perhaps the biggest reason for Layla to want to fight, but despite the reminder to become a soldier in this war, trepidation curls in her stomach.

She glances past her classmates' figures to Fisher a few desks down. He was one of the people who came to the meetings almost every night she did. He's already looking at her, mouth quirked up at the corner. Layla chews at her lip, and he nods. *Good luck.*

"Up you go," Mr. Tanner says, motioning with his wrinkled hands. His small frame is shaking. Layla doesn't need to be in the front row to see the glazed, tearful look in his eyes. He's been their teacher for almost four whole years, and now he's watching them leave to become soldiers. A nauseous swooping feeling fills her stomach. Excitement and nerves.

She has only a second to wonder why they must be separated between boys and girls before she's being shoved out of the geometry classroom with the rest of the students. The hallways are jammed. There's nothing orderly about it. Boys rush in one direction while Layla and the other girls squeeze past to go the opposite way. Her school is big, but it's old. The rusted, paint-chipped bluish lockers squeak when you open and close them. There are dents in the walls and on the tiled floors. The hallways and classrooms are built skinny and small, so no matter where you go it feels like you're always pressed in tight, shoulders rubbing against another's.

She pushes through, straining her neck to see if she can spot Courtney, but it's impossible for her to see anyone who isn't right in front of her. The double doors to the gymnasium are already propped open when Layla passes through. The only reason she doesn't come to a complete stop at the sight that greets her is because the girls behind her won't stop pushing. Still, she pauses for a second before there are hands on her back, and a hissed cry of *"move!"* gets her feet going again.

This is it. Every nerve in her body vibrates with the knowledge.

Having not seen Courtney in the bleachers, she takes a seat in the first row, front and center, making it easy for her friend to find her and even easier for Layla to see everything. Five people in white lab coats set up and fiddle with their supplies. They're all middle aged and slightly grumpy looking. Never-changing frowns pull down their lips. Their brows are furrowed, eyes downcast like they can't stand to look at all the students filing in. But they're apparently normal for all that she can tell. Do hybrids look any different from normal people? Do adult members of the Hybrid Force get injected? That was something the rumors never addressed.

Right in the middle of the gym floor are several large chests on wheels. The covers are off, allowing everyone to see the tubes of dark red liquid. On the side of each chest is a gun-shaped object. Layla's guts twist at the sight. She doesn't think they're real guns, but it looks like the small tube of red liquid would be able to fit perfectly in the ammunition slot.

They're going to inject the red liquid into them, she realizes. The liquid in those tubes is the secret to becoming a hybrid.

More girls file into the gym at a steady stream, and Layla raises her hand when she spots Courtney. Her friend's usual easy smile is replaced by a painful-looking grimace. Her short hair is puffed out in random places, so different from its usual sleek look. She must have been running her hands through it.

"You look way too excited for this," Courtney says after scanning Layla's face, and settling into the spot next to her.

"Maybe," Layla says. "You okay?"

Courtney huffs, her eyes flittering over the scientists and their supplies. She looks back at Layla and rolls her eyes. "I'm ready to pee myself," she says. "You know, like the rest of us normal people. Not everyone is as insane as you are."

Chuckling, Layla once again studies the scientists, the red vials, the gun-like injectors. She and Courtney have been best friends since Layla was old enough to know what a friend was. They grew up together, as close as sisters. Courtney was there when her parents died in the bombing, never letting go of her hand all day, never letting Layla out of her sight for weeks. They have always had each other's backs, and now it's time for their roles to be reversed. For Layla to watch over her friend.

"There's no use being afraid," Layla says. "Nothing we do can to change this."

That's the biggest issue people have with the hybrids—there's no choosing to become one. The people in charge of the military program choose when, where, and who is changed into hybrids. People whisper about their rights being taken away, and every time

Layla hears those whispers she shakes her head and laughs joylessly in their faces. The truth is they lost their rights when the terrorists took their country, and she has no problem telling them that if it were an option, she would have signed up for the Hybrid Force the second she heard about it.

"If I had known it was going to happen today, I wouldn't have come in the first place," Courtney says, voiced hushed as she eyes a passing scientist. "I don't care how mad my mom would've been."

Layla isn't surprised. Half the school is probably thinking the same thing right now. Courtney never wanted to get involved with the hybrids or the Black Sun. She and her family survived the war so far, and she doesn't want to give the terrorists any reason to turn their weapons back here. But Layla has been itching for this day to come, for a chance to have some revenge or closure for her parents' death, and for a chance to fight back.

Whereas Layla has always been ready for a fight, Courtney has been the calm shadow, pulling her back and settling her down. Maybe that's why, months ago, Mr. and Mrs. Jones insisted that Layla needed to be going to school again, every single day. Not because they believe Layla should get the chance to fight, but because they know Courtney can't do this on her own.

Raising her eyebrows teasingly at her friend, Layla says, "But then I would be all alone." Courtney, seeing right through her joking attitude, takes Layla's hand in her sweaty one, holding tight.

"Thank you for waiting." The gymnasium lapses into silence at the sound of the man's voice, booming so loud, he doesn't require a microphone. His white lab coat is unbuttoned, showing a simple dress shirt and pants underneath. The fuzzy gym lights cast shadows over his face, turning the hollows of his eyes and at his cheeks into dark pits. "And thank you for being here with us today. I know some of you are far from ready, but your time has come to help your country. There will be losses here today, but there will also be imperative gains.

Those of you who can withstand the Hybrid Serum will come with us and be trained to fight for our country and end the suffering caused by the terrorist organization called the Black Sun."

Layla's next breath hitches in her throat. The words replay through her head, "Those of you who can withstand..." *Not everyone survives the serum?* She had never heard any rumors about that. The amount of anxiety buzzing through the gym has the hair on her arms and the back of her neck standing on end. Courtney's grip tightens to the point of pain. Her nails dig into the skin on the back of Layla's hand.

The serum will kill some of her classmates. It could kill her.

"Some bodies won't accept the serum," the man continues. "Instead of binding your DNA with another animal's like it is supposed to, it will eat away at your cells in a matter of minutes."

"How many?" The question leaves Layla's mouth before she can stop it. She feels it as every head in the room turns to look at her, but she focuses on the man, forces her gaze to stay on him. From the bleachers, a few other girls chime in. Layla straightens her spine. "How many has this serum killed?"

Hesitance lightens his stony expression. He surveys the girls in the bleachers, and, as one, they all hold their breath. "Half," he says, eyes landing back on Layla. "In most cases, fifty percent of those injected with the serum do not survive."

Layla closes her eyes, just for a second, as a sickening amount of distress fills her heart. Her free hand reaches for the picture in her pocket, and she wills her mind to calm as her fingers glide over the smooth surface. It does little to help. When she looks at Courtney, the expression on her friend's face, of outright panic, has her own eyes prickling with terror-induced tears.

The hybrids who are changed disappear, and no one ever sees them again. She knew that, but she thought it was to a secret base, not to a grave. These scientists started making hybrids all the way on the other side of the country. There could be thousands of people dead from this serum. Millions. And she could be joining them shortly. Courtney could be joining them shortly.

"Now, once you have been injected, you might feel some discomfort and pain. This serum is intended to make you not only stronger and faster but enhanced in almost every way. That can include your sight, you sense of smell, your hearing…"

Layla zones out. People are going to die in this room. In just a few short minutes, possibly. And this man and these scientists are acting like it's nothing. How many times have they done this? How many teenagers have they watched die and been responsible for it?

Layla eyes the gymnasium doors, now firmly shut, trapping them in.

The speaker is now pacing back and forth between the chests of serum, his long lab coat floating behind him. "You will be essential to bringing down the Black Sun, and gaining our country back, but all these enhancements may have side effects: heightened emotions, lack of emotions, oversensitivity to sound, smell, and sight, and aggression to name a few."

And death.

The scientists don't seem to have any weapons, but still, they could be hiding some in their coats. If she tried to take Courtney and make a run for it, there would be too many of them. They'd just grab them and take one of those gun-like injectors to their necks, and that would be it. There's no way Layla can get Courtney out of this.

The man turns around, nodding at the scientists gathered behind him. A small puddle of sweat is starting to pool between her and Courtney's hands. Layla squeezes tighter as the men and women roll the chests forward. The gym is so quiet, she can hear the hundreds of glass vials tinkling against each other.

When one of the scientists, a woman with dull red hair and

even duller brown eyes, stops with the chest in front of her, Layla begins to regret picking a front row seat. The scientist's kind smile does nothing to calm Layla's nerves. Nobody says a word as the scientist picks up a vial and loads it into her injector. Across the room, other scientists do the same. A cold tingle runs down Layla's spine when the woman's cold hand cups the side of her neck. Out of the corner of her eye, Layla looks to Courtney for reassurance, but the woman's steady hand pushes her head firmly in place, not allowing Layla to see her.

The tip of the injector is hot on her neck, like they intend to burn it through her skin. At this point, her body is frozen, unable to draw a single breath. Then there is the painful sting of a needle pushing into her skin. She expects to feel something, to feel the red liquid being pushed into her veins, but she feels nothing but a slight pain. The injector leaves her skin a moment later, and the scientist wipes up the drop of blood that trickles down her neck.

A whooshing sound fills her ears, making her head feel floaty. She doesn't know if it's from the serum or the knowledge that from this point on she can never go back to being who she was a mere second ago. She's different now; whether it be for years or only minutes is the question. A weight settles on her chest, large and unmoving.

If she thought she was scared when the woman brought the injector to her neck, watching her tilt Courtney's head to the side is terrifying. Layla can see it now: how the red liquid would get sucked up, and how, with a press of her finger, the woman would shoot it into her friend's neck.

There's horror in Courtney's wide brown eyes.

"She doesn't want it," Layla says, glancing between the injector and the scientist's unreadable face. Not like the angry boys who hollered in the hallway, racing past each other to get to the gym first. Not like her.

And even though it would have torn her apart, Layla regrets not finding Courtney and sneaking her out of the school when she had the chance.

The scientist doesn't meet her gaze. "It can't be helped," she says under her breath.

Layla cringes when Courtney's nails dig in hard enough to draw blood. Tears travel down her cheeks. Layla wants to roll her eyes at her friend and smile, act like this is all a joke, but her mouth stays in a frown, her eyes locked steady. She watches the tears fall and feels how each pump of her rapidly beating heart pushes the red liquid through her veins.

She can imagine it. The dark liquid swarming around the cells, surrounding them, then eating them up. She sees it devouring everything in its path. Dissolving the very walls of her veins and causing her blood to spill out everywhere.

She shakes her head, hoping that will dissolve the thoughts, but they still linger. Even when she starts squeezing Courtney's hand just as hard as she's holding hers. Layla says just loud enough to be heard over the sound of shocked gasps, shrieks, and silent panic, "It's okay. We can do this, Court. We have to."

More tears flow down her friend's face, mixing in with mascara and tinting her tears black. "You can. Not me."

"Remember what your dad told us? We're meant to do this. Both of us." She takes Courtney's other hand, unwinding it from where her fingers are twisted in her bright shirt.

Her friend's brown, watery eyes dart between Layla's. After a few seconds, she releases a long, heavy breath and smiles. It looks forced enough to cause Layla's throat to tighten. Taking her own deep breath, she smiles back. "See? Not so hard."

But it was hard, and soon both their smiles turn into pained grimaces. The heat traveling through every part of Layla's body is like a live flame, painful and searing. She pulls Courtney's shaking hands to her chest. Her head falls to Layla's shoulder, too heavy to hold up. And then her entire body spasms, shaking Layla with the force of it. She plants her feet firmly on the gym floor to avoid slipping off the bleacher bench.

Panic hits her like a gong to the head—hard enough to clear the heavy haze of pain away. This can't be normal. Scientists still mill around the gym injecting students. None of them spare a glance back at the people they have injected. The man, the speaker from before, mills through the bleachers, monitoring everyone's movements, but he, too, pays no mind to the girls like Courtney. Or like the girl on the opposite side of Layla who is doubled over in pain, panting so loud Layla can hear it over all the shrieks and moans.

Layla hisses through her teeth as the pain flares hotter, but Courtney is quiet in her arms so far, holding her breath against the pain.

Suddenly, another girl, this one behind her, lunges forward, knocking into Layla's back. The girl pushes against her. Layla grips Courtney even tighter to prevent her from spilling onto the gym floor. She still hasn't stopped shaking. If anything, it has gotten worse. Then the girl from behind pitches forward to land on the gym floor in front of Layla's feet. She's in Layla's grade. Hannah with short, blond hair and big, blue eyes. Layla watches in horror as Hannah's eyes roll back into her head. The acidic taste of bile fills Layla's mouth, but she can't look away.

It's not until two people in white coats drag Hannah away that Layla notices Courtney has stopped moving, too.

I take a step. And then I take another.

CHAPTER TWO

*T*he pain from the hybrid serum is gone, only to be replaced by a cool calm. No, not calm. A sheet of white where Layla feels nothing. Maybe it's shock, she muses, or the deadly quiet before the first sound of thunder ripples through the air.

She stands among her surviving classmates, dripping water onto the already soaked floor. The room is hot and so humid that Layla finds it hard to draw a full breath. Or maybe that's a result of the reality of her morning crashing down on her. Scientists and serums. Hybrids and the Black Sun. Death and never feeling more alive.

The fogged mirror shows her face.

Or, at least, what's supposed to be her face. It's the first time she has seen it clearly since she was injected with the hybrid serum. The blurry glimpses of it in the subway window were not enough, and she was too focused on the man speaking at the front of the cart she couldn't catch a good enough look.

Layla wipes at the mirror, clearing away the condensation. She doesn't have her mother's eyes anymore. That was the first thing she noticed. Even through the fog on the glass, she can see her former brown eyes are now a softly glowing amber. The strange colored iris takes up the whole of her eyes, leaving no whites and making her eyes appear larger than they really are. There is a thick line of black around them, like a too heavy eyeliner, that refuses to go away no matter how much she wipes at it.

If she were to guess, she would say they're feline or canine eyes. The eyes of something fierce, of something feared. That's what she wants the terrorists to see.

Not to mention her teeth. Her gums still ache from where her canines grew long and wide. She runs her tongue over them, something she has been doing for hours now. Then she closes her mouth, seeing how her lips jut out and struggle to hide the four large teeth.

Layla isn't the only one looking at their new features in the mirrors, but even more of her classmates are huddled close to each other, their faces smudged and red from crying. Whether it's from the fear of what's to come or what they went through during the injection, Layla doesn't want to know. She rubs at her own prickling eyes and hikes up her damp towel. Crying won't help anything. When the mirror fogs up again, Layla leaves the bathing rooms to look for the issued clothing she was told to wear.

She scans each face she passes, seeing who made it and who didn't. With how small her school is, she knows them all. Sarah from algebra is pushing her face into the mirror next to her friend with the blonde hair that's always tied up in two long braids. Candace is crying in one of the corners, refusing to get up as Asha and Jane encourage her to get in the shower. They all look like a sad bunch. She wonders if the guys are doing any better.

She weaves through them all, straining on her tip toes and ducking under elbows. They let her keep her shoes, a pair of old blue converse, and she fought to keep her faded jean jacket. The shoes dangle at her side from where she carries them by their worn black laces. She keeps her jacket slung over her one of her shoulders. The locker room is big, made for a multitude of people. She clutches the towel tight around her chest, peeking around corners until she finally sees the piles of neatly folded clothes. She takes a set from one of the dark blue piles, letting it unfold as she holds it up. Immediately, she scowls at the jumpsuit. It looks like something a prisoner should be wearing, and the fabric scratches at her skin when she pulls it on.

Once dressed, she slips the picture she has been carefully holding into the red and white striped breast pocket.

There are a few others changing into the jumpsuits, but the girl next to her, Steph, is shaking, letting off so much fear, Layla swears she can smell it over the strong sent of body wash that seems to cloud the bathroom in a thick haze. She huffs out a sigh and prepares to wait for the testing assistant.

Every new hybrid that enters the hybrid military compound takes a placement test to see what section of the Hybrid Army they will be a part of: planning, building, research, labs, or teams. From the brief explanation Layla was given on the bus, she knows she wants to be part of a team. They're the ones who fight the Black Sun in person. According to the scientist on the bus, it's also the hardest section of the Hybrid Army to get into.

When more girls leave the mirrors and showers, the entry room gets so crowded that Layla's forced to stand with her back flat against the wall. Looking at them all, she can't help but wonder why they made it through the hybrid serum while Courtney didn't. The frown on her face deepens, making her teeth stab into the inside of her lip. What makes these girls strong enough to survive when they look ready to pass out any minute?

Layla can still feel Courtney shaking in her arms as her body rejected the serum. Her silent screams still echo through Layla's head.

Steph meets her stare and just like that, anger scorches up her throat. There's a small amount of satisfaction in her gut as the girl's eyes widen in surprise before quickly flicking away. Her eyes are a washed out green color with horizontal pupils. A sheep? A goat?

"W-what?" the girl stutters.

Layla tilts her head to the side in question. She watches closely as the hair on the girl's arms stands up, so light it could be called translucent. Disbelief rushes away the rest of her anger like a quick, cold wind.

She turns from the girl to carefully look around the room, seeing stitches and folds in everyone's matching jumpsuits, the individual strands of wet hair plastered to shoulders, and the sweat trickling down faces. Enhanced sight is one of the abilities a person can get from the hybrid serum. What other abilities has she acquired? They can appear slowly, the scientists told them. A new ability every hour.

The door opens minutes later, and Layla forces her wandering eyes away from the crowded room. The testing assistant stands in the doorway, dressed in pristine black dress pants and a neat white top. Her hair is yanked into a bun so tight it pulls the wrinkles around her face back into her hairline. It's a shock to Layla that the woman is, well, *normal*. Some part of her expected everyone here at the hybrid military compound to be a hybrid.

The formerly loud bathroom now watches the woman in silence.

"Is everyone ready?" she asks. Her voice is low and clear. Some of the girls nod their heads. Even more remain unmoving, but the assistant doesn't seem bothered. "Each one of you will be given a series of tests," she continues. "But before that, you will line up behind one of our scientists, so they can add you to the registry and identify what kind of animal DNA merged with yours." She scans the room twice, her gaze landing on Layla both times. "Follow me, and please keep your voices down."

Layla's not close enough to the door to be one of the first to exit the locker room, but the nearer she gets, the easier it is to hear the others in the hallway. A group of people, it sounds like. When she squeezes through the door beside three other girls, her suspicions are confirmed. The guys from her school, the ones that survived the serum, are silently waiting.

Layla takes in every face she can, noting who's missing, but not allowing herself to think about it too deeply. *Later,* she tells herself. She will think about it all later when she's on a Hybrid Team and when no one can see her tears.

Just like in class this morning, Layla's eyes find Fisher's. She only catches a glimpse of black eyes before the group of her classmates sweeps her away, but the glimpse is enough to ease some of the weight from her shoulders.

Once everyone is in the hallway and beginning to walk, Layla pushes her way to the front with ease. To her amazement, no one makes a sound as they march through the halls. Everything from the ceiling to the floor is the same drab grey color. No use or time for decorating. Excitement and dread mix inside her chest. This is real. No more waiting or beating around the bush.

There's nothing much to see in the hallways, but that changes when they turn into an open room. The scientists are spread out around the space, each with a younger assistant next to them. Hybrid assistants, she realizes as she steps further into the room. Layla goes to the first one she sees, a tall woman with long blonde hair and latex gloves already covering her hands. The scientist's assistant is a hybrid around her age. His pink eyes are framed by white lashes that match his short hair.

The woman gives Layla a curt nod. "State your full name and date of birth," she says, sounding bored. She has probably done this a hundred times before. Layla and her classmates are nowhere near being the first hybrids.

"Layla Adeline Wilson. April 15, 2098." It's the first time she has tried talking since she was injected, and Courtney was taken from her. But she pushes that thought down along with the anger and pain, and she focuses on the strange feeling of her large canines moving against her lips when she talks.

The scientist takes a blood sample and does an eye scan in the matter of a minute. Then the assistant's pad beeps, signaling the results are ready. He looks it over with a quick sweep of his pink eyes. "Mountain lion," he says.

"Is…" Layla's voice gets stuck behind her teeth. She pushes past them, cheeks slightly warm. "That's what I am? A mountain lion?"

"Mountain lion, puma, cougar," he says with more than a hint of sass. "That is what DNA locked into yours; yes."

Layla's eyebrows rise at his tone. Her teeth peek out from behind her lips, and he quickly looks away, lips pressed firmly shut.

"Now I need you to take a seat somewhere behind me." The scientist gestures with a freshly gloved hand to the group of large, round tables, eyes darting between the two teenagers. "You are officially in our records, and ready to begin your tests. There is a stack of electronic pads at each table. Turn one on and begin your first test."

I'm not who I used to be. And I never will be.

CHAPTER THREE

Jax remembers when this city was bombed. It was around four years ago when the real war was just beginning. The terrorists gave everyone a warning that time. They played it on repeat over televisions, phones, and computers for hours, but it still wasn't enough to save the city or the millions of people who lived in it.

Jax remembers sitting in his living room with his brother and mom, trying to hide his shaking hands from them. There was a shelf above the television, still is for all he knows, with a picture of his dad, looking proud and a little imposing in his military uniform. He left only a week before, and then Jax was the protector of their family.

He had been furious watching the bomb warning flash across the screen. Furious and terrified.

And now, those old feelings return as if brand new. Being this far above the city, Jax feels like he's looking at the end of the world, the end of civilization. There are no people, just dull, ruined buildings and broken blacktop. Everything is dead. Ruined. A mess of gray and black and brown with only hints of stubborn green vegetation.

After adjusting the pollution mask that covers his nose and mouth, Kyrin salutes Jax, and jumps off the edge of the building. Jax watches, waiting for him to land with bent knees and a muffled sound of victory before he follows. His stomach lurches in excitement as he freefalls. The rushing air stings at his dark squinted eyes. Three hundred feet. Two hundred. One hundred. He lands next to Kyrin on crouched legs, his bones jarring, a wide smile stretching behind his own mask, and ankle deep in mud.

Freefalling is something he doesn't get to do often, not anymore, but both Jax and Kyrin love it. The weightless feeling of freedom, then the sudden landing leaves him with the feeling that he could do anything. Maybe it's because he and Kyrin are bird hybrids. Or maybe it's because they're just plain crazy.

The towering buildings on either side block the afternoon light, but Jax's eyesight is good enough that he has no problem seeing in the dimness. Usually, he and the team would wait to start their mission until the sun had faded, allowing more shadows to form for them to hide in, but this area is deserted. The only living creatures Jax has come across are themselves and the occasional stray animal.

Without needing any instructions, Kyrin strides to the right. His dark, shaggy hair curls against his nape, wet with sweat. They've been running around this city for hours now, coming up empty handed again and again. No signs of the Black Sun terrorists that were supposedly seen in this area. No signs of anyone or anything. He gave the scanner to Celia and Mick when they left to search the other half of the city, but they still came up with the same amount of nothing as he and Kyrin. Jax knows the team is angsty and disappointed.

His boots stick in the thick layer of mud caking the ground and make a sick squelching noise with every step. The mud swallows up every footprint, making it impossible to slink silently down the alley. There are a couple low windows decorating the buildings on either side of the alley. Most of them are broken. Sharp pieces of Plexiglass stick out from the frames. The walls are cracking in places and a thick sheet of dark green moss covers most surfaces.

"Nothing," Kyrin says. He's at the end of the alley when Jax looks back, leaning against the brick wall that cuts the passageway off from the neighboring houses.

Sighing, Jax continues the short distance he has left. He swore he heard something, but maybe it was a rat or a dog or his imagination.

Even he has been desperate for something lately, but Helland insists on giving the team low risk missions, claiming they're not ready for anything more. At first, Jax was relieved. His new team wouldn't be in danger. He wouldn't lose anyone. But at this point, he's itching for more.

He gets to the end of the alley and turns back with disappointment choking his throat. "Nothing."

"We should get out of here then," Kyrin says, unsticking his boots from the mud with an annoyed glance. "Find Mick and Celia."

"The newbies should be getting in anyway." He types out a quick message on his watch to Celia, then takes another careful look at the alley, not seeing anything except insects crawling and zipping around.

Kyrin pats Jax on the shoulder. "Maybe there'll be a good one," he says. "We can add a new member. Get the commanders' attention, you know?"

Jax leans his head back to look at the blue sky. Another teammate. Another person to look after. No matter how necessary it is to add new members, Jax doesn't think he will ever get used to the fear of losing one of them.

Him and Kyrin make their way out of the alley, ending up on a destroyed and empty street. Celia and Mick are meeting them due west, where they parked the truck at the edge of the city. It would take thirty minutes to get there if they ran. Jax checks his watch. The newbies won't be starting the team testing for another four hours. They probably just made it to the compound now. Jax sets them at a walk.

They keep their weapons tucked away, but they're ready to draw them at a moment's notice. In the past, he's learned that you can never be too careful in these types of situations. The terrorists didn't get this far because of luck. It wouldn't be the first time Jax has been snuck up on. It usually doesn't end well for them, the terrorist soldiers. Usually.

Kyrin speeds ahead, then turns to walk backwards in front of him. A streak of mud paints his forehead from pushing his hair back with dirt-covered gloves. His onyx eyes search Jax's face before he says, voice a little muffled from behind his mask, "I know you're scared, Jax, after what happened to your old team." Jax balls his hands into fists, hard enough he can feel each one of his nails push through the material of his gloves and puncture his palms. Kyrin grabs his hands, unclenching them. There's a crease between his eyebrows, and he doesn't let go.

"I get that you want to keep us safe. All of us get that. But the world—our world—is screwed." Kyrin lets his hands go and throws his own in the air, motioning to the bombed-out city they're walking through.

Despite the realness of it, Jax chuckles. "Completely and utterly screwed."

"We can help to fix it." Kyrin says and turns to walk side by side with him. "Team Thirteen saving the world." Jax glances down at him with a small smile. "We just have to be brave enough."

He thinks about it as they climb over a fallen building in the road. That's why he worked so hard to get on a Hybrid Team, to become a leader, isn't it? To save the country. A new determination sets it, making him move faster. With a hidden grin at Kyrin, he jumps down a wrecked building, and sprints along the broken blacktop that used to be a road. Behind him, Kyrin curses and hurries to catch up.

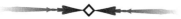

They are the last team to get there, still dressed in their gear, and, from the looks the others in the room sent them, in need of long showers. Jax leads the way to the section labeled "13," making sure to reach up and slap the number with the palm of his hand. The first time he came here after what happened with his old team, he was just appointed leader of his own team by the commanders. There was someone on a ladder, painting a number one in front of the three that was already there. The grief that plagued him for weeks was instantly replaced by anger. He ended up pushing the man out of the way to paint it himself.

He has been here a total of ten times since then, and now he's not alone. He found Kyrin first, then Celia, and only a month ago, he found Mick. But with only the four of them, the commanders have stuck to giving them scouting and intel missions. Most of them leave his team empty handed and feeling completely useless.

Newbies are brought in every week, usually no more than one batch depending on how many survived. In the beginning, they used to bring new hybrids in every few days, but times have changed since then. People are aware of what's happening now. They have to be more careful.

Living in the east, Jax was part of one of the first schools injected with the serum and brought here. It was less than a year ago, ten months to be exact. His memory of it is distant and fuzzy, like a dream he can't fully remember—terror, and pain, and a resigned feeling that he will do this for his family and for his country.

The four of them file into the small cubby room, their attention immediately focusing on the large screen. The team test takes place in the simulation room which has cameras everywhere. As soon as the test begins, the screen will split into multiple camera views, allowing them to watch everything that goes on. Right now, it's just a plain grey room with seven newbies standing in a line. Five boys. Two girls.

Jax presses the little microphone picture in the corner of the screen, allowing the testing assistant's familiar speech to fill their room. Jax knows the words by heart. She's almost finished with it; they made it just in time.

"There are seven Hybrid Teams as of right now. Team four, five, seven, ten, twelve, thirteen, and fourteen. Some have died. Some have quit." The newbies glance at each other with varying degrees of apprehension and excitement. Next to him, Mick draws closer to screen only to have Celia push him out of the way with a hiss.

"As you know," the assistant continues, "this is your last test. There is no guarantee that one of the seven teams will pick you, so give it your all." A short growl follows her statement. Jax's spine straightens, alert. He tries to pinpoint the source. The guy with thick blonde hair gives it away, shifting nervously on his feet while sending quick glances at the girl next to him. The assistant clears her throat. "This is a simulation room. Once I leave, the test will begin. You will get your mission, and you must carry it out. The teams, as well as myself, will be watching you."

The newbies' heads turn in unison, watching her as she leaves the room. As soon as the door shuts behind her, a count rings out, making a few of them jump in surprise. They all look at each other with some form of familiarity. Jax has been trained in many things from his previous leader and the human soldiers who used to help around here and from every experience he has had at the compound and in the field. It's easy to see they all know each other. It must have been a small school.

Most noticeable are the two guys at the end, seemingly best friends already. The girl with dark hair and sharp teeth, the one who growled, knows the smirking guy who stands so causally, one would think he has done this before. Everyone else must be acquaintances. Same classes. Same small town.

At the last second, before the countdown hits one and the room shifts, the girl with dark hair flicks her eyes up to one of the cameras. In that short moment, Jax understands why the boy next to her looked so frightened.

Better. Faster. Stronger. Smarter.
That's what we are. That's what they made us.

CHAPTER FOUR

*L*ayla doesn't know whose idea it was to make the testing landscape look like Denver, but she's going to find out. From what she can tell, the city is in a quiet type of chaos: the aftermath of a terrorist attack. A bombing. The ground is littered with rubble: chunks of concrete and debris from the buildings around them. The picture painted isn't a new one, but it's the first time she has seen it quite like this.

Up close. Personal.

Weeks after it happened, Layla tried to sneak into the city just to get a peek of the real thing. Sure, she had seen the news footage and the pictures, but she needed more. She only made it as far as the highway before a police officer pulled up and demanded to give her a ride home. Layla didn't have the nerve to tell him she didn't have a home anymore.

Now, as she looks around the broken city, she's even more angry at the policeman. If she could have seen it then, maybe it wouldn't hurt as much as it does now. The landscape is so destroyed, Layla barely recognizes it. But as she and the others walk in their little group, Layla in front, she can still make out some street signs, and the bakery, and the park from years ago.

Behind her, Carrie, the only other girl in her group, whispers, "Denver."

She knows that they picked this city for the testing simulation because it was the closest bombing to their home. They could have picked any place the Black Sun left their mark on: Austin, Detroit, Boston. But this is a test, so they put them in the city that would have the most effect on them. To rile them up. To see if they can handle it.

"Keep your weapons ready." Layla doesn't know when or where the terrorists will come from, but she knows they will come. It's their mission. Defeat the terrorists. Save the hostage.

"Says the girl with no weapon," Fisher says, charging past her. He knocks his shoulder into hers, sending her toppling to the side. Her foot catches on something, but she rights herself before she falls. Looking down, Layla shrieks when she sees what caught her foot.

"What is it?" Cam asks, coming up beside her.

"That's a body."

Cam's head tilts to the side. "No. That's an arm. There's nothing attached to it." He says it clinically, like he's stating the most unsurprising fact there is. Layla glares at him. "Besides, this isn't real, Layla."

She dislodges her foot from the appendage. "It was. It will be."

With one last look at the dismembered arm, she moves on. Fisher is leading the group now, not having stopped to see what she yelled about. His wide shoulders block the view of the road ahead. Scowling at his back, Layla charges past the others to be at the front with him.

"I have a weapon," she says, lips pulling back over her teeth. She hasn't been able to stop doing that. The feeling of the large canines is just too weird. Fisher responds with his trademark smile, all amusement and uncaring grace. Fisher's not a bad guy, but he's not the nicest either.

The weapon she picked is a knife, about the length of her forearm. It feels heavy in her hand, but it couldn't weigh more than a pound. The others' weapons are more impressive. Cam and Carrie have basic guns. Fisher has a bow and arrows. Conner has an axe, and Milton holds a knife much bigger and more impressive than Layla's. She likes her knife, though. It's easy to picture how to use it, unlike most of the other weapons.

It's not until they get five miles into the city that the terrorists make an appearance. Some she can see in high windows or peering over the edges of rooftops. Others she can hear hidden in shadows and between buildings. That's something that happened around the third test; the enhanced hearing. One second, she was punching in her answer on the tech pad, the room silent, and the next a harmony of heartbeats, breathing, and the gentle taping of fingers on screens filled her ears.

The terrorist targets are rarely on the ground in range of her knife, but Layla hides her confusion by helping Cam. He looks only slightly awkward with the gun he chose. Layla realized he's a bad shot in minutes, but she does her best to instruct him where to shoot when a target evades him. She needs to do something to get noticed by the teams.

Some of the newbies, like Fisher, are easy to guess what type of hybrid they are. Fisher has sharp, jagged teeth and pitch-black eyes that gleam with a predatory look. He's a shark, anyone could guess that. But others, like Cam, could be close to anything. The only feature that has changed are his eyes. She doesn't remember what color they used to be, but now they're brown with rounded pupils, and like hers, there don't have any whites.

One thing Layla does know is that his hearing isn't as good as hers. The target simulations make noise like any human would, and she can point them out faster than the others.

"At the top of that building, Cam" she says, and watches him fire. The shot misses. Another gun goes off seconds later, and the target drops. Cam curses, eyeing Carrie a few feet away.

Carrie, Cam, and Fisher continue shooting at the targets high in the buildings, but the deeper into the city they get, the more terrorists come out. Soon Layla leaves Cam's side to face off with her own targets, jabbing and slashing with her knife, aiming for vital parts. The targets are strong and fast, able to land blows that hurt like they're real. Sweat drips down Layla's back. Will the injuries stay after the test is over?

The simulation doesn't hold back on the blood or gore and the *smell*. The only thing keeping her from expelling the bile in her stomach is constantly reminding herself that they're not real.

"How do we find the hostage?" one of the guys, Milton maybe, asks.

"Up!" Fisher hollers in her ear.

Knife gripped tight, Layla looks up, expecting an attack, but there are no targets up there that she can see. "What?"

Fisher points at a building. "Get up high. You'll get a better view. Me and Cam will cover you. Try to find where the hostage would be."

Inwardly, Layla cringes at the thought of Cam covering her, but she stows her knife anyway. The building Fisher pointed to is missing three large chunks of the walls, like something came along and took a few bites out of it. As she runs toward it, she listens for any hidden terrorists, not fully trusting Cam and Fisher. Overall, the building looks steady. At least, more so than any others on that street. Not stopping her sprint, she jumps. When her hands smack a window ledge, she digs her nails into the hard concrete and hoists herself up. The jagged bricks make good handholds and footholds, but they cut painfully into the skin on her fingers and palms. Gritting her teeth, she pushes past the pain. She only stops her ascent at the sound of a bullet whizzing past.

"Keep going!" Glancing over her shoulder, she sees Cam standing almost right below her, gun aimed up.

"I swear to god, Cam!" Layla yells, grasping at a small crevice in the wall.

Another bullet zings past her. "There's someone up there!"

Gritting her teeth, she reaches for the next handhold. Her canines dig small holes in her lips, but she only unclenches them enough to say, "Then shoot at them. Not at me."

A few feet behind him is Fisher, a wicked smile on his face as he fires arrows. "Don't worry, Wilson!" he says. "I'll catch you if you fall!"

She's almost to the top, having covered the distance fast enough to surprise herself. A giddy feeling rushes through her. She huffs out a laugh. "I'll be sure to kick you in the face." Chuckles follow, blending with the sound of battle. She grabs onto the bitten-off concrete and pulls herself higher. Layla doesn't dare look down. It's not that she's afraid of heights. It's that if she looks down and sees Fisher under her, following her every move, the urge to drop on him would be too great to resist. It would serve him right for pushing her around.

Or that's what she's telling herself.

More shots are fired, so many that she can't tell who they're coming from. The closer she gets, the clearer it becomes that Cam still hasn't been able to hit the target. Layla can hear their movements above her: steady breathing, a gun being reloaded, and then the deafening sound of gunfire, so loud it makes her ears ring.

Hands slippery with sweat, she grabs the edge of the roof and pulls herself up. The rooftop is flat, mostly clear of rubble, except for the blocks of concrete that have been pushed into a single pile. The target hides behind it for cover. Their large gun rests on the top of the pile, shooting bullet after bullet. The empty casings fly to the ground to join the hundreds already there.

Layla has a brief moment of panic. Did one of her schoolmates get hit? By the looks of it, the odds aren't in their favor. With a shake of her head, she pushes the fear down. This is a simulation, she reminds herself. Their injuries aren't real, right? They can't really die.

The target hasn't looked away from aiming the gun, and with a burst of speed, Layla runs across the roof straight at them. They turn their hooded head at the last second, right before Layla crashes into them. Narrowly missing the sharp edges of the makeshift barrier, they land on the hard concrete. Layla doesn't waste any time as she gets on top of the target and throws her fist into their cheek.

Their head snaps to the side. The dark green hood slips down. It's a girl. Layla hadn't been able to tell before. Her head is shaved—no, it's bald. The target's head snaps back around, her small brown eyes filled with a blankness that makes Layla feel a little better about the hit.

The target reaches out for the gun, but Layla pushes it to the edge of the roof before her fingers can touch it. She grapples with the girl, struggling to stay on top. Every couple of seconds, a bullet hits close by. Layla growls out in annoyance when one hits close to her leg, distracting her enough to get a hard knee to the stomach.

If she and Cam both make it on a team, they'd better not be on the same one.

Prying her hand free of the target's stone-like grip, Layla meets her emotionless eyes, then brings her first up to deliver another blow to the head, this time as hard as she can. Her fingers connect with a sickening crunch, a combination of Layla's knuckles cracking and the target's nose breaking. The target slumps, unconscious or worse, Layla isn't sure. Not taking the time to check, she moves to the edge of the roof, ignoring the target's large and heavy looking gun on the way. It would be an impractical weapon for scouring the city.

She's only a foot from the edge when a burning pain rips its way through her side. Shrieking, she falls to her knees and clutches at her side. Her hand comes away wet with blood. Sucking in deep breaths, Layla crawls the remaining distance to the edge and glowers down at Cam.

She wants to jump straight off the building, snatch his gun out of his hands, and hit him in the head with it. Instead, she settles for chucking a block of concrete at his stunned face. "Cam!" she yells. "When this is over, you are going to pay for that!"

He says something, probably "Sorry," or, "But you just hit me with a rock," but Layla is already turning away. The roof is huge, so she jogs to the far end to look at the surrounding area. The familiar ache in her chest returns at seeing Denver. Seeing the real thing is terrifying.

She remembers when she first brought up the attacks to her parents. At first, they told her not to be worried. That everything would be handled. Of course, she believed them. But then, they wouldn't let her go to the city—to Denver. After that, they didn't let her leave their small, safe town at all. Long story short, Layla started to worry.

Hand clenched over her wound, Layla forces the overbearing sound of gunfire and yelling to the back of her mind. There are hundreds of targets moving around the city, looking like little dark green bugs. She can't discern any pattern in their movements. They're not moving towards her and her classmates or away to where the hostage would be. They're just waiting for them to come.

The wind whips her hair around her face and neck. The screaming sounds of constant battle dwindle down. They must be gaining the upper hand, not that they will be for long, what with all the targets waiting for them. Is this how it's going to be on a team? The odds stacked against them at impossible numbers with only their enhanced abilities as an advantage?

Layla grabs at her hair, forcing it out of her eyes and mouth. Then she holds it at her shoulder as she paces the roof, stretching her neck to see more of the city. The building is one of the highest, another reason why Fisher picked it. The masses of targets get thicker to the east of the building. Lifting onto her tip-toes, her side burning in agony, Layla finally sees it.

The mall, surrounded by so many bug-like targets that there might as well be a big neon sign pointing to it with the words HOSTAGE THIS WAY. More than half of it is destroyed, resembling a mountain of crumbling rubble more than the building Layla remembers.

She tries to get a read on how many targets there are to give her classmates an idea of what they're up against. Clenching her side, she laughs. A crap ton, she decides. That's how many.

This is going to be fun.

It feels like she has fought for hours by the time they get to the hostage. He's tied up in a stiff wooden chair, bald head bare and brown eyes unseeing. He can't be more than twelve years old, making the blank expression on his face even harder to look at.

Singed clothes and overturned clothing racks are strewn across the floor. They're in one of the larger department stores, probably so that they have more room to fight, but there aren't any targets that Layla can see or hear. Still, when she approaches the boy on aching feet, she keeps her knife ready.

The building is strangely quiet after all the screaming and fighting. The sounds of her feet echo in the large room. Layla wipes her small knife on her filthy pants, cleaning it of the caked-on blood. Then she gently pulls the rope far enough to stick the blade under. She begins to cut.

She eyes the boy for a reaction, but he doesn't flinch away or make a sound. It's almost as if he's a life-sized doll, so inanimate compared to the other simulated people. Whatever the reason, it makes goosebumps run down Layla's spine.

It takes long enough to cut through the thick ropes that Layla's attention strays to her arms. They're covered in an alarming amount of blood, fingers to biceps. Out of all of them, she looks the least banged up. Fisher has been holding his ribs in a one-armed hug since before they made it to the mall. Cam's right arm swings unnaturally at his side, dislocated and broken. The other two guys lean heavily against each other, limbs shaking, and gaze only halfway focused. Carrie is covered in so much red, she makes Layla look clean in comparison.

With a final saw of her blade, the last of the ropes fall to the ground. Layla steps back, expecting the room to change back into the plain, empty grey it started as, but it remains the same.

She throws her hands up, only to growl at the pain that flares up her side. The gun shot has stopped bleeding. Cam just grazed her, but with the constant movements from fighting, she would be surprised if she didn't split open her whole side. "What now?" she says. They found the hostage. The terrorist simulations all lay at their feet.

The answer comes when two more targets race out on either side of their group.

Knife still in her hand, Layla reacts faster than the others. She switches her grip, draws it back, and lets it fly. She aims for the chest, a quick and easy kill, but the blade hits the target right in the center of its neck. Even though it should be a killing shot, the target keeps coming, undisturbed by the knife in its throat.

Cringing, Layla rushes forward, jumping over a clothing rack and smacking into its cold body. Disgust makes her stomach a tight knot, but she has gotten this far without throwing up. She forces the uneasy feeling down. With a growl, she rips the blade out of its neck and stabs down where she meant to in the first place: the heart.

When she pulls herself off the lifeless target, two of her teammates are on the second terrorist simulation. Fisher and the rest of her team guard the boy. Even with his legs and arms free of the rope, he still hasn't moved.

Layla pulls at her wet, sticky shirt, and slides up next to Fisher. Sharp teeth bare, and crouched over his broken ribs, he slips his hands under the hostage boy's legs, lifting him off the chair. "Maybe we have to…"

But before he can finish, the department store shimmers around them. As the bright walls turn to grey and the bodies and clothes littering the floor disappear, Layla breathes a sigh of relief. Even knowing that none of it was real, it was all still hard to deal with. How long will it take after she gets on a team for it to stop being hard? She can't picture it ever being easy.

Within seconds, they're back in the same testing room that they started in. It's only when the walls stop shimmering that she manages to look around. Her gear is gone, as well as everyone else's, replaced by the dark, loose jumpsuits given to them in the locker rooms. All the weapons are gone too, making her feel unprepared for what's going to happen next.

There's not a speck of blood on any of them. All the injuries were a part of the simulation, but still Layla's hand cramps from how hard she gripped her knife. Her side still burns with the phantom pain of getting shot. Layla spreads her hands over her thighs to stop their shaking. She's not the only one worse for wear. Without a gun in his possession, Cam looks like he could keel over any second.

Layla knocks into him gently as they line up. She gives him what she hopes is an encouraging look. A loud gulp is his only response.

"Breathe," she hisses. It might have been meant for him, but as he takes a large, gasping breath, she does too.

Fisher chuckles on her other side, and Layla turns to glare at him. She knows him well enough that even with his new terrifying eyes she can see the mocking glint that covers his face like a veil. Unlike when the simulation was playing, she can now hear the cameras buzzing. The teams and whoever else are still watching.

The sound she makes comes out instinctively: a low growl that rumbles in her throat. She stops the noise, all but choking it. Another thing she will have to get used to.

"Careful, little lion," Fisher says, eyes gleaming. "You might need a friend here."

"Then I will make some," she says, pushing away the heat that floods her cheeks. Then she turns from him, signaling the end of the conversation. She doesn't need Fisher riling her up in front of the cameras. Already, she can feel her prickly anger ready to burst in retaliation.

But she can't think about that now. In just a short amount of time she could be on a Hybrid Team, which means she will be trained and out there fighting against the Black Sun. It's what she has wanted since before the rumors of the hybrid program even started. She doesn't want to think about what would happen if she's not picked for a team. Would she be able to try again? Can she train herself, and come back to the Hybrid Teams with enough skill that they see their mistake?

The seconds tick by like hours. Layla fiddles with her jacket tied around her waist before loosening the knot completely and throwing it over her shoulder with a huff. The guys have taken to pacing back and forth while Layla and Carrie remain unmoving in line. Layla tracks the guys' movements to pass the time. No one talks. She doesn't know why, but she wishes someone would.

Conner and Milton glide easily past each other. They're friends. They were in her grade, in some of her classes. She remembers seeing them sit next to each other in class and at lunch. They would yell down the hallways to each other. It sends a strong burst of hatred through her, making her throat itchy and raw. It must feel nice, she thinks, to go through all this with your best friend. To not have to hold them as they convulse, their body rejecting the serum.

Layla wants to lash out at them to stop moving—to leave, to just not be here—but the door opens. It's the testing assistant. After a heavy pause, everyone lines back up.

"The teams have decided." She looks at each of them in turn, her expression giving nothing away. "But just remember what I told you," she says. "There is not a guarantee that you have been picked."

Heart pounding, Layla clenches her fists. Like she needed reminding of that.

"Carrie. Team Seven." She waves her hand toward the door, and Carrie slowly walks out with a satisfied smirk on her face. "Conner and Milton, you both will be joining Team Fourteen." Side by side they hurry past Layla and out the door. "William. Team Four." Throwing a wink at Layla, Fisher exits the room.

Layla takes a moment to glare at him. When he slips out the door, she catches a glimpse of a tall girl. She's looking over Fisher's shoulder, right at her. Her bright yellow eyes filled with a crude kind of judgement. Layla's lips pull over her teeth in a snarl. The door closes with a soft clicking sound.

Forcing her eyes away from the door, Layla takes in the assistant's expression. Carefully blank, but tense. Layla can hear the woman's heart pounding. An unsettling feeling clenches her stomach in knots. "Now," the assistant says slowly, like the next words are painful for her to speak. Terrified, Layla's throat tightens to the point that it's difficult to breathe. "The two of you will be taken into further testing to find where you will be most helpful to our cause."

No.

To be honest, this is not what I was expecting.

CHAPTER FIVE

S he must have said it out loud, because the assistant flinches as if Layla went to hit her. But she did no such thing. Her body is petrified: stiff with shock. She thought she was prepared for this, but she's not. Being on a team, fighting, is what she's meant to do in this war. She's not meant to be in a lab, or making weapons, or helping the injured. Even though she knows those jobs are important and vital in any war, to her it would feel like hiding. And Layla's done hiding.

The assistant's face remains emotionless, but Layla can see the way she trembles all over. And that more than anything ignites the flame of anger in her, because she's not afraid like this woman is. She survived the serum. She held her best friend as she died. She sat there among her dying and changing classmates without one wish to change herself back.

"Listen," Layla says, ready to say something, do anything that will get her on a team, but before she can find the words, a strange sound fills the room, distracting her enough that she looks around for the source.

Next to her, Cam shakes wildly. Layla can picture tufted up hair along his spine. He must be as mad as she is that he wasn't picked for a team. But no, that's not right, because when he finally meets Layla's gaze, his eyes are wide with fear. Fear of *her*. That's when she realizes that the noises are coming from her.

A constant stream of growling leaves her throat. She made the noises before, of course, in the simulation and a few other times, but this time it's different: louder and deeper than any of the sounds she has made previously. But what's worse is that she didn't realize that she was doing it. Shock and a hint of embarrassment snap her mouth shut.

Each one of them jump when the door softly clicks open. Whipping her head around, Layla takes in the man who enters the room. He's big—huge, really. A foot taller than Layla, with thick, corded arms, a shaved head, and dark skin. But, his black white-less eyes give him away, and considering he's a hybrid, he couldn't be much older than herself. He wears gear like she wore in the simulation, but his is covered in a thick layer of dirt, and the stale smell of sweat surrounds him like a fog. Layla wrinkles her nose at the strong scent.

Before she can start to worry that he was sent in as a guard to subdue her, he says, "Sorry to interrupt, Jane." His gaze sweeps over the three of them, a quick assessment. When he steps closer, Layla can see his eyes are actually very dark brown, not black. "Is everything all right?"

Jane. That's the assistant's name. Layla can't remember her ever mentioning it. She looks relieved to have this man here. After clearing her throat, she says, "Yes. Yes, of course. What do you need?"

Layla gets the feeling not many people interrupt this, or any, part of the Hybrid Testing. The man straightens himself, somehow looking even more like the solider he must be.

"My team changed their minds. We want the girl."

For the first time, his eyes land on Layla, and hold her surprised stare. There's no need to look at the assistant or Cam. She can feel them watching her, too. Relief, the first hint she's felt since this morning, sooths the uneasy feeling under her skin. But she cuts her eyes away to look at Cam. He has stopped shaking, the easy expression on his face slowly returning. The two of them worked well together in the simulation, even if he does need more practice with a gun.

Facing the man once more, Layla asks, "What about Cam?"

His dark eyebrows raise, causing small lines appear on his forehead. He hardly spares a glance at Cam. "Just you."

Layla shakes her head. She shouldn't be risking her chances of him and his team changing their minds again, but she can't seem to help it as she says, "He just needs a little practice. He——"

Cam lays a hand on her shoulder, effectively stopping her. "It's all right, Layla," he says. A small smile tugs at his mouth in appreciation. "I'll be fine somewhere else."

Confusion makes her eyebrows furrow. Doesn't he want to join a Hybrid Team, too? The question must show on her face, because Cam gives her a subtle shake of his head. A bit reluctantly Layla nods.

The assistant, Jane, claps her hands once as if settling a deal. "That is very good news, Jaxon," she says, sounding almost relieved as Layla feels. "Now, please take Ms. Wilson to meet your team."

If Layla wasn't so eager to leave, she would've been insulted by how enthusiastic the assistant was to get her out of the room. Even so, she makes sure to give Jane a dirty look. Jaxon nods towards the door, motioning for Layla to follow. With one last look at Cam, she goes, trailing in the shadow following the soldier's tall frame.

With each step forward, her heart thrums faster inside her chest.

The rest of the team is waiting for her in the hallway. She knows it's them because, like Jaxon, they all wear the same dirty gear. They must have just gotten back from something. Layla wants to ask what they saw, what they heard, what they did. With how lively they look, it couldn't have been as exhausting as the hybrid testing simulation. But before she can ask, the girl, the only girl in the small group, struts up to Layla with a wide grin on her face. Her short black hair swings around her shoulders when she moves, and her bright green eyes are hard to miss. She spreads her hands out wide, arms raised as if she's going to give Layla a hug, but a foot away from her, she claps them down on her thighs with a loud sound.

"Hi," she says, white teeth gleaming even in the low lighting. Layla can't help but to study them. They're sharp and long, a little like her own, but thinner. "I'm Celia. I've been waiting for another girl to join us. Welcome to Team Thirteen."

Jaxon chuckles as he flawlessly finds his place in the group between two others; a guy with shaggy black hair, and another with dirty blonde. "Don't worry," Jaxon says, already sounding more at ease than he did in the simulation room. "She's not always this happy." Celia moves her intense gaze from Layla to give Jaxon a look. "Call me Jax. Team Leader." Layla shakes the hand he offers her. "Welcome to the team."

She notes that he does not say *my* team.

"Thanks," she says, eyeing the two other members of the group.

The one to the left of Jax with dark hair that shines blue in the fluorescent lights squints his black eyes at her, taking her in, assessing her. He is about half a foot shorter than Jax, but even with the dirt smudged across his forehead, he looks even more intimidating. If that's possible. He stands so close to Jax that their boots touch. "Kyrin." He says it almost unwillingly, like he hates Layla already.

His tone combined with the sneer on his face make anger bubble up in her once again. She can feel it in the tips of her fingers and in the pit of her stomach. Layla's eyes narrow slightly at him.

Jax brushes up against him, a gesture so natural and quick that if she wasn't so fixated on Kyrin, she wouldn't have noticed. Some of the tension leaves Kyrin, making him look only slightly softer, but, still, his gaze remains fixed on Layla.

Then the last member of the team steps forward with a roll of his eyes. "I get the whole needing to prove your dominance, or whatever, but I don't think she's going to steal your man, Kyrin."

Kyrin finally looks away only to give the other man a very rude gesture. Not that he seems to mind. His long blonde hair is pulled loosely from his face. His eyes, shining with amusement, are two different colors; one blue and one brown. His smile is more of a showing of teeth—white gleaming canines that are long, thick, and dangerously pointed.

He keeps his arms crossed across his chest as he introduces himself. "I'm Mick."

Adrenaline still courses through her from the testing simulation. A forced smile pulls unpleasantly at her cheeks. She has been through a lot today. Way too much to even want to begin thinking about. "Nice to meet you, guys," she says. "Thanks for giving me a chance. I'm Layla."

They're still in the hallway outside the simulation room, so when the door opens, Layla automatically looks back to see Cam come out after the assistant.

A sour taste coats her mouth. That was almost her.

"Cam," Layla says stepping toward him only to shut her mouth when she can't find the words to say.

The assistant watches her like a hawk, eyes squinted, and mouth pursed. What did Cam say to make her look like that? With a shake of his head, Cam offers her a slight smile. "It's okay. I don't really think it was my place, anyway, you know?"

"Yeah," she says even though she disagrees. Cam definitely needs more practice, but he could've done well on a team. "Keep in touch."

"Sure thing."

Layla watches him until he turns down the hallway out of sight. She's tired down to her bones, but she agrees to the tour Jax proposes. So far, she has only seen the large gated entrance and parts of the testing building: the locker rooms, multiple testing rooms, and the simulation room.

They forgo stopping in any rooms, leading her straight to the exit, and when they step outside, Layla gulps down the fresh air with greed. The scent of pine and dirt overwhelm her senses. The subway let them off miles outside the compound, and then they road trucks for what felt like hours through the forest to get to the front gate, but Layla couldn't complain at the time. She was just relieved they weren't hiding out in one of the destroyed cites like the rumors said.

Towering trees block most of her view of the sky, but Layla would guess it's sometime in the evening when the sun still hasn't fully set. She felt like she had been taking the placement tests for days, but how long was it really? Shivers rake up her spine, her new jumpsuit not doing much to protect her from the chilly fall air, but she keeps her jacket thrown over her shoulder, not minding it after being in the testing building for hours.

Is she even in Colorado anymore? Since most of the ride here was in the fast underground subway, Layla has no idea where she is. "Where am I?" she asks. "In the country, I mean."

"Somewhere in Montana. We aren't allowed to know the exact location for everyone's safety," Celia says.

Layla's steps falter on the grass path. She's never been this far from home, not since she was too small to remember. When Celia sees her frowning at the gaps in the tree canopy, trying to get a better look at the sky, she says, "Yeah, the tests don't take as long as you think."

"When I got out, I thought it was the next day," Mick says.

A few steps in front of her, Jax snorts. "It took us forever to convince him only a few hours passed."

She tucks her hands as deep into her pockets as she can. Her eyes dart around them, never settling on one thing. There are other hybrids here, hundreds of them, maybe even thousands, walking around in groups or alone. Among them, Layla spots older men and woman with features that are perfectly normal. More helpers like the assistants and scientists?

The buildings are situated in a kidney-shape, all dark in color and settled relatively low into the ground so as not to be seen from above unless you know where to look. Layla listens to her new team banter as they walk across the trampled grass that acts as a path around the compound. Both hybrids and humans give them a wide berth. Some going far enough as to step off the path to avoid them. When Layla points this out to Celia, all she does is roll her eyes and turns around to make a rude gesture at their backs.

Jax points the next building out, one smaller than the testing building, and instead of a garage-like door there's a regular one that blends in almost perfectly with the brick wall. "Labs," Jax says, coming to a stop in front of the building. "We don't usually go in there, and they like it that way."

"What are they studying? There couldn't be much with the war going on, right? The government scientists already made the Hybrid Serum. Now the main priority is to use us to end the war."

Jax only shrugs in response. "All I know is that they do tests with the serum, trying to find out why only half of us survive it."

Layla's guts clench at the sudden reminder of what happened this morning—of Courtney. With no small amount of difficulty, she pushes those thoughts away.

The next building is a shade lighter than the lab. A wooden sign outside reads "Infirmary." Jax offers the slight explanation of, "When someone gets injured." Next to the building is a dirt trail that leads into the forest, its path winding away between the trees. "The training center is down that path. We spend a lot of time there."

"Like eighty percent of the day there," Celia intones.

Layla's not the least bit surprised by this. "When do I start?"

Chuckling, Celia bumps none too gently into Layla's shoulder. "Oh, I like her already!"

"Tomorrow," Kyrin says. It's the first thing he has said since introducing himself back in the testing building. The smirk that pulls at his lips doesn't do much to comfort her. "We start out with firearms training. I'm the teacher."

Layla takes in his closed-off stance with apprehension. "Great."

Jax might be the leader of this team, but she feels that Kyrin is the one she'll need to impress. With his closed-off demeanor and the sour scowl he keeps sending her way, it's not hard to guess he doesn't want Layla on the team.

Jax and Kyrin lead her past the rest of the buildings, never going far enough to show her inside them. She's both annoyed and thankful at that. She wants to explore as much as she can, but she's not sure how much longer her trembling legs will carry her. Besides, she'll see the inside of them soon enough.

They stroll past a crowded cafeteria, Layla's ears straining to hear Jax over the commotion inside. Then they stop between four numbered buildings. Housing units, Jax calls them. Layla follows her new team into the building with a large *2* above the door. She pictures thin cots lined up against the walls, limited space between them, and maybe just enough room to store a few possessions. To her surprise, none of those things greet her behind the door. In fact, the front door doesn't open into a room at all, but to an elevator.

With the five of them crammed in the small space, Layla ends up smashed between Mick and Kyrin. Celia, being the closest to the door, presses the button for the third floor. From the outside, the building doesn't look like it has any upper floors, and her suspicions are confirmed when the little lights on the panel don't blink up, but down.

"This building houses all the teams," Jax says. He points over Celia's shoulder to a colorful poster above the buttons. "This tells everyone what level each team is on. It's mostly for messengers and what not. I don't recommend barging onto anyone's level. It usually doesn't end well."

"What's that mean?"

Layla can only see the one side of his face, Mick's shoulder blocking the other half from view, but she thinks he rolls his eyes. "Teams can be, *um*, territorial of their space, I guess. Mostly, it ends with the intruders in the infirmary."

Just then, the elevator door slides open, cutting the conversation off. Layla's feet meet a tattered rug as she steps into a basic kitchenette. Even here, the floors are concrete, interrupted only by another larger rug. It's the most colorful thing Layla has seen in the whole compound so far with bright reds and blues crisscrossing each other. On top of it, a small table and two worn chairs are nestled close together. It's cleaner than anything she's seen in a while, not even the thinnest layer of dust can be seen. The only thing that seems to be out of place are a few dirty mugs on the kitchen counter.

Again, she was expecting a room with bunks or cots for them to sleep on, maybe a water dispenser, and a few places to store belongings. This was way more than that. Since they're underground, there aren't any windows, but a few lights scatter the kitchen and living room area, casting a dim, warm glow. It looks like a home. Lived in and made to be as comfortable as possible.

"We usually clean before we leave to go on a mission," Jax says, striding into the kitchenette to lean against the counter. He eyes the mugs, then turns to glare at Mick and Celia. "I hate coming back to a mess."

Layla gets the unsaid message; she needs to clean up after herself or there's going to be a problem. She can do that. It's one of the rules at Courtney house... Layla stops that though in its tracks.

"Got it," she says with a nod.

Celia lays hand on Layla's shoulder, and inclines her head towards the hallway branching off to the left of the small living room. "Your room is down there. Third door on the right. Bathroom is the second door on the left." She squeezes Layla's shoulder and smiles. "I'll go get us some food, yeah?"

Mick is already heading back towards the elevator, a hand placed over his growling stomach. "I'll help."

Seconds after Celia and Mick leave to get everyone food, Kyrin is calling out dibs for the shower. Considering what all of them smell like—sweat, dirt, and the faint smell of something burning—Layla almost thanks him.

"I'm sure you have a lot of questions," Jax says. He has taken off his dusty camouflage jacket and is staring at Layla like he's trying to dig into her mind to find out how she works. She wrings the fabric of her own jacket in her hands.

"That's putting it lightly." Layla skin still tingles with leftover adrenaline from the simulation. A million questions race up her throat, trying to make it past her teeth. Through it all, images of Denver plague her mind.

Keen chocolate colored eyes bore into her, their intensity unsettling. "Perhaps tomorrow will be a better time for answers," Jax says. "It's been a busy day for all of us. You should check out your room. Try to get comfortable. Knowing Mick and Celia, they'll be awhile with dinner. They get distracted easily when it comes to food."

The easy smile on his face falls when instead of turning for the hallway, Layla steps forward instead. Maybe she doesn't want to be alone yet—doesn't want everything to crash down on her so fast. Her hands open and close rhythmically at her sides. Her voice isn't quite as steady as she wants it to be when she asks, "Is there any way I can leave? Just for a day or two?"

Almost immediately, the apprehension lining his face gives way to a look of understanding. "You have family."

Layla recoils at the word 'family'. Unbidden, her hand reaches up to pat at the picture in her breast pocket. "Something like that," she says.

Courtney is—was like her sister. Mr. and Mrs. Jones need to know what happened. They won't know how it all went. They'll have no way of knowing that Courtney is never coming back home, and Layla, no matter how terrified the idea is, wants to be the one to tell them.

Her hopes fall when Jax gently shakes his head. "We're only allowed to leave for missions. The trucks and subways would need to be redirected, taken off their path to get supplies or transfer more hybrids and personnel. Not to mention the risk of being seen by anyone. The commanders never allow it. I'm sorry, Layla."

"What if I call them?" she pushes. "Is there any way I can send them a letter or a message?"

"Listen," he says, hands splayed out before him in a placating gesture. "I've been where you are. We all have. I've asked a hundred times to contact my family. It's not going to happen."

She looks down at her scuffed converse. Tears of frustration glisten at the rims of her eyes. She wipes them away harshly. She should've known that would be the answer. The risk is too great for anyone, let alone her, to contact someone outside the compound. Yet, she still feels like cold hands are wrapping around her heart, digging in with nails made of ice.

"Third door on the right," Jax says. "It's all yours now."

There's no pity in his gaze when Layla turns and walks away.

The first thing Layla notices about her new room is that it smells like someone else had been living in it. It's faint and a little stale, but it's not something she can ignore. There are a few small dents along the cement walls, and a brownish stain in the corner of the small room. Despite all that, Layla's not going to complain. She has her own room with a single bed, a chest for her belongings, and enough spare room to not feel like the walls are closing in on her.

After taking a minute to search the room, Layla stores the jean jacket she's been carrying around in the trunk. Then she takes a seat on the thin mattress and toes off her shoes. Courtney's parents must have already figured out what happened. That the military people came to their school and took them away. From their town. From the state. From the universe. She knows the scientists won't bring Courtney's body back to her parents. If they did that, all the deaths wouldn't be a secret. They don't tell anyone who can spread the knowledge about half the teenagers dying for their country before they even get a chance to fight.

Layla springs up from the bed when the door flies open so hard it bangs against the wall. It's Celia, still dirty and dressed in her gear. A wide smile lights up her face when she meets Layla's surprised stare. Jax said she wasn't always happy, but Layla is beginning to doubt that. Celia swiftly steps around the bench at the end of the bed and holds out a small foam container to Layla. She can already taste the enticing smells on her tongue.

"Thanks," Layla says as she takes the food. "I'm starving."

"It's a little more than regular portion size since you probably haven't eaten in forever," she says, plopping down beside Layla on the bed and opening her own container of food. Layla follows her lead, appreciating the sight of roasted chicken, rice, and salad. Sure enough, she has lightly larger portions than Celia. "I convinced the guys to leave us alone for the night."

Layla unwraps the plastic fork and knife, immediately bringing a piece of chicken to her mouth. She isn't sure how long she will be able to keep her eyes open after she finishes her food, so she says, "No offense to them, but I appreciate it."

"It's a lot to take in," Celia says around a mouthful of food, summing up what Layla is feeling in a few simple words. "But Jax is a great leader, and the other two aren't so bad, either. Just give it a few days, and it'll be like you've been here your whole life."

A few days. That's hard to believe. Her eyes sting as she stares down at her half-eaten food. Aside from when her parents died, this has been the longest, most emotionally draining day of her life. Overwhelming is an understatement.

Celia stretches across the narrow distance between them to lay her hand against Layla's leg. Her dark green eyes shine with sincerity, the marble-like pattern of them mesmerizing. "Do you want to talk about anything? The serum injection? The tests?"

Shaking her head, Layla stabs a piece of chicken with a little too much force. Indeed, the plastic prongs of the fork pierce right through the bottom of the container. Sighing, she shoves the chicken in her mouth. "No. I'd rather not."

The hand on her leg retreats like the words physically stung. "Yeah, sure. No problem," Celia says quickly and quietly. "How about your hybrid abilities? Anything new?"

"More like a lot new," she says, looking around the room to find the right words to describe the new ways she can see and hear, or the amazing strength she feels under her skin that was never there before. The plain walls don't spark up the right words. She settles with the short explanation of, "Everything is just so much at times."

Celia frowns. "What do you mean?"

"Everything is louder, brighter, *clearer.*"

Eyes bright with recognition, Celia *ahs.* "You got it all, didn't you? Mick does too, for the most part, but me, Jax, and Kyrin just have a few enhancements like that. You know aside from the strength and endurance." Celia waits for her to finish her food, hands fisted under her chin before she says, "Tell me what you can hear."

Layla carefully studies her, takes in her still-dusty gear and mysterious green eyes. Then she sends her focus in the direction of the living room, and listens. "I can hear the guys talking about that Cape person again." She squints her eyes, trying to distinguish the other, much fainter sound. "Someone is tapping on a tech pad or some type of screen."

If possible, Celia looks even more excited. She turns on the bed to face Layla and leans down over her crossed legs. "Impressive. Just wait until tomorrow. Usually after a good sleep, the enhancements fully develop. You might even end up as good as Mick."

They're not fully developed yet? How is that even possible? She stares at Celia, her eyes wide as can be, long enough to be considered insulting. But her new teammate doesn't look offended. She just sets her empty food container on the bench behind her and looks at Layla expectantly. Expectant for what, she isn't exactly sure.

Earlier, Layla had wondered what kind of hybrids her new team members were, but the tour and her exhaustion were enough to distract her. Now, her curiosity spikes again. Especially if she is to be like Mick who sounds like he has the most enhancements from becoming a hybrid.

"What kind of hybrid is Mick?" she asks, breaking the awkward silence that settled over them. "What kind are all of you?"

Celia's thin, dark eyebrows shoot up her forehead. Layla guesses that wasn't the question she was expecting. "I'm a snake hybrid. Viper to be exact."

Not in the least surprised, Layla scans her face. Those dark green eyes and a smile with two sharp canines. Celia sticks her tongue out, showing off the split in the middle. A shudder threatens to overtake Layla's body at the sight. She tries to fight it off, but it still fizzles up her spine.

The wink Celia's gives her tells Layla she didn't miss it.

"You're a mammal," she says. Her head tilts to the side. "I'm not sure what kind though."

Pride fills Layla's chests when she says, "Mountain lion."

"Yeah." Celia tugs at her earlobe. "That makes sense, but as for the others, you will have to ask them yourself. Just know that it really doesn't matter what kind someone is. Everyone's enhancements are different."

She tilts her head at that. So, there could be another mountain lion hybrid with different enhancements that she has? Interesting, but it makes sense. As for asking the guys…Layla doesn't know if she has enough energy to stand up right now, let alone make conversation with three people, one who she knows already doesn't like her. "Tomorrow," she says. She'll ask them all tomorrow and begin to get to know her teammates.

Celia leaves soon after, claiming she needs a shower and clean clothes, and complaining about how the guys probably took all the warm water. Layla flops back on the bed and reaches her hand into the pillowcase where she stored the picture of her and her parents. Her eyes begin to droop, her body sinking into the thin mattress, but not two seconds later, there's a knock on the door.

"Hey," Jax says, cautiously opening the door. His gear is gone, replaced by lounge pants and a loose shirt. He holds up the multiple bags in his hands for Layla to see. "When Kyrin was in the shower, I went and got you some stuff. It's not a lot. Just the basics. In my defense, we were not really expecting to get a new member."

Jax sets the bags on the bench. "Thank you, really." Layla climbs to the end the bed, and peeks into the bags. Clothes, a pair of heavy boots, a blanket, and some other necessities like a toothbrush, soap, and deodorant. Her chest burns along with her eyes, and after clearing the tightness out of her throat, she thanks him again.

Jax shrugs, backing away towards the door. "We take care of each other here," he says in response. "There're a couple delivery trucks that come every two weeks. You can take whatever you need from them. They should be here beginning of next week."

Layla nods, already pulling the extra blanket from a bag. She feels the prickling sensation of eyes on her and looks up. Kyrin and Mick are peeking over Jax's shoulders. She fists the blanket against her chest and meets each of their stares. From Jax's dark browns, to Mick's mismatched eyes, and then to Kyrin's blazing black gaze.

She slips off the bed to stand in front of them. "Thanks, guys. I really appreciate it. And for, you know, picking me to be on your team." Her eyes meet Jax's again. "I don't know what I would have done if you didn't walk in that door."

And she means that. Not just about her future here at the compound or in this war, but what she felt. That uncontrolled anger that made her growl and snarl at the assistant. She doesn't want to think about what she might've done. Kyrin coughs and reaches through the door way to grab at Jax's hand. The dirt is gone from his forehead, and he looks like he could drown in the oversized shirt and pants he's wearing.

"Well," he says, "I think that's enough feelings and thank yous for tonight."

With that, Kyrin drags Jax down the hallway. Layla only just manages to keep the cruel words wanting to lash out locked behind her clenched teeth. At least Mick has the decency to look embarrassed. Shaking his head, he rubs his hand across his face. Slowly, he backtracks down the hall. "Right. Uh, you'll want to get as much sleep as you can tonight. Tomorrow will be a busy day I'm sure."

Layla only nods at him before shutting her door. With a groan, she drags her heavy body back to bed and buries her face in the pillow.

Bang. Bang. And a fire begins to scream.

CHAPTER SIX

*T*he morning brings Jax a new sense of purpose. As the leader, he uses the first day of training a newbie to feel them out. It's usually easy for him to know where a new teammate will fit in, or how to make their transition into everything easier. He has a feeling this newbie is going to need as much help as she can get. Stunned and volatile: that's how she acted yesterday, and he's hoping today will bring her a new sense of calm. Jax doubts it will. It rarely does.

It doesn't help that Kyrin is still agitated about their newbie. A deep frown twists at his face ever since he woke up. He was distrustful with Celia and Mick at the beginning, too, but never like this. He acts as if she's already done something wrong. Jax tried to get him to talk about it last night, but Kyrin only grumbled a few curses and flopped down on the bed. Jax planned on asking him again, but he took one look at the other's face and clamped his mouth shut.

Jax has been waking up before the sun since he joined his first team, and he's kept his past leader's strict schedule. Many of the others at the compound are awake at this time too, and his teammates have learned not to complain about it. Jax suites up next to Kyrin in his training gear, lightweight, movable pants and a jacket over a plain shirt, and eyes the scowl on his second in command's face.

They had at least talked about some of it last night. After Mick made sure that Layla was too busy talking to Celia to hear, they huddled around the island in the kitchenette with their dinner.

Watching her in the testing simulation, Jax was positive she has enhanced hearing as well as sight, and he wasn't going to take any chances of her overhearing them. Celia confirmed his suspicions late last night. Enhancements like Mick, she said. Maybe even better.

If that was true, today is going to be interesting.

The three of them had different ideas of her, that's for sure. The whole reason it took so long for them to claim Layla for their team was because Kyrin was so strongly against letting her join, but Jax saw something in her. Something that his team needs. Maybe even something their side of the war needs. That is, as long as he and his team train her right.

They will have to be careful with her, they all at least agreed on that.

"Are you sure I should be training her first?" Kyrin asks, slowly pulling his shoes on. It's the first thing he's said all morning, his voice still gruff from sleep. "We would get a better feel for her in combat. And the gunshots alone will probably set her off."

It's not the first time he's brought it up, and Jax gives him the same answer he gave last night, "Combat is always easy for newbies to learn. Firearms will take more time. And this way I can watch from the sidelines, see how she reacts to you. And we have the headphones for her. The gunshots won't do anything." He looks up from putting on his own shoes. "She knows you don't like her."

Their room is dark. Only one lightbulb in the ceiling. It keeps their energy use to a minimum, saving it for more important things like the infirmary, testing and training simulations, and the televisions in the cafeteria. Shadows are cast across Kyrin's face, making him look haunted and older. "I don't trust her."

"She wants the same thing we do," Jax says, opening the door and leading them into the hallway. "You saw her in the simulation. She can do major damage. She can work with a team."

Jax can feel the pitch-black eyes glaring into the back of his head.

After four months of being around him, the feeling is something Jax is very accustomed to. "This isn't about some petty thing. You know what I mean, Jax," Kyrin says.

Of course, he does. They've seen it with other hybrids before, Jax even more than Kyrin. Hybrids so consumed with their past, with their own problems, that they can't control themselves, or, even worse, they don't want to control themselves. They get kicked off teams, kicked out of the labs or infirmary and sent to the single therapist at the compound. No one sees them much after that.

"Just give her some time, Kye. I remember how you were that first day."

The first week, really. He wouldn't even talk to Jax. He ran away into the woods a few times but was always stopped by the guards on constant patrols. Jax never blamed him. Kyrin wasn't at a school when they injected him with the hybrid serum. In fact, he hadn't been to school in years. The lead scientists saw him walking down a passing street, stopped the car they were in, and chased Kyrin for five blocks before another car cut him off and ended the chase.

It's a more common occurrence now with the word spreading than it was when he was injected almost a year ago.

Behind him, Kyrin huffs, the intensity of his glare prickling the back of Jax's neck. He allows his eyes to close and takes a deep breath as they reach the kitchen. When he opens them, he sees Celia with a mug full of dark black coffee stuck under her nose, breathing it in. Jax has yet to figure out a single thing that Celia loves more than coffee. The familiar sight relaxes his shoulders just the slightest bit.

That is, until he hears Layla's door swing open.

The room she was given used to belong to a member of his old team, Benji. All the rooms had been used by his old team. Team Three was one of the biggest hybrid teams formed at the compound. Not to mention, one of the most skilled. After they were killed, everything was cleared out, put into storage or given to another hybrid to use. The rooms have been empty for five months now, but every time he adds a new member, every time someone takes one of those rooms, Jax is left with mixed emotions of guilt and relief, and he doesn't know which feeling is better.

It's not until Kyrin lays his hands on his back and gives a firm but gentle push that he realizes he had stopped moving completely, frozen next to the cushioned blue chair that helps separate the kitchen from the living room. He goes with the persistent pressure, allowing himself to be moved forward, and accepts the mug of water Celia hands him when he gets close enough. He chugs it all before turning around.

Layla's already wearing the training gear he picked up for her. She's close enough to Celia's size for him to guess the measurements, but the training pants might be a little too small. Her long hair is pulled into a neat knot at the top of her head, and her jacket is zipped all the way up her neck. Her face is drawn with sleep, but she is jittery, amber eyes jumping around the room, fists clenched tight at her sides. It looks like her abilities have fully developed, and she's taken aback by the intensity of it.

Enhancements even more acute than Mick... Jax stops himself from cringing. Mick has some of the best hearing, smelling, and sight for a hybrid that Jax has ever come across. To have even more than that... Well, he can't let his teammates, or more importantly, Layla herself, know that he's almost as apprehensive as Kyrin.

When her bright amber eyes finally land on him, Jax gives her a nod. "Morning," he says, voice unintentionally rough. "Once Mick gets out here, we'll go to the cafeteria for breakfast. Then firearms training. We usually go for a run around the compound before training, but I want to get you on the firearms floor before any of the others show up."

"Yeah, okay." Her fingers twitch at her sides. Her stance is wide, knees bent like she's expecting to get jumped at. "He's putting his shoes on."

Jax looks up from assessing her tense posture in surprise. "What?"

But his question is answered when Mick's door opens. Four pairs of eyes dart to watch him step into the hallway. He freezes in place, slowly looking over his shoulder at them. "Come on, I'm not that late, am I?"

Layla heard Mick tying his shoes from a different room, about fifty feet away, behind a closed door. Jax doesn't even know what tying shoes sound like. He peeks at Kyrin out of the corner of his eye only to meet the same steady glare he's been getting all morning from him. He holds back a sigh.

He takes a second to wonder if those soundproof headphones in the firearms room will work with Layla before Kyrin says, "Maybe a run would be a good idea."

Jax is already nodding his head. Hopefully a run will ease some of the tension out of Layla. And give him and Kyrin more time to think about how they're going to help their newbie. "We'll go now, before we eat," he says. Even this early, the cafeteria is hectic, and the newbie looks like she can barely handle being around the four of them.

"What did I miss?" Mick says, looking between them all.

"Like you weren't listening," Celia says, rolling her eyes. Then she gulps down the rest of her mug, marches up to Layla, and takes her by the arm. Jax mentally curses at her forwardness, but aside from flinching the slightest amount, the newbie doesn't seem to mind. Celia pulls her towards the elevator door, motioning for them to hurry.

Next to him, Mick scoffs. "I wasn't listening." He gives Jax an incredulous look. "As if I'd willingly listen to her whispering her undying love to a mug of dirty water."

Jax shakes his head but can't help chuckling.

Layla's cheeks are flushed from the cold morning and exercise. Her head is dizzy from all the fresh forest air. She never ran so fast or long in her life, and all she wants to do is head back out there. But it only went so far in distracting her from all the sounds and the smells and the too bright colors.

Maybe that's why everything is so monotone here, she thinks as she looks over the fenced in platform at the mess of people below. To help people like her. Sensory overload, that's what her teammates called it. The only cure they offered her was that she will get used to it. She just hopes that happens fast.

When she woke up, her hands wouldn't stop shaking. She had a peaceful sleep, her mind too exhausted to conjure any dreams. But as soon as she pried her slightly swollen eyes open, images from yesterday burned behind her lids. She stared up at the ceiling, not seeing it, her hands shaking and sweat cooling her sleep warmed body until the sound of a guzzling coffee machine snapped her out of it.

It had taken her seconds to become wide awake, and for an anxious feeling to settle along her bones. She stared at the ceiling, recognizable even in the pitch dark of her room. Some old part of her ached to stay in bed, to not get up. But she couldn't be like when her parents died. She couldn't stay in bed all day. And, truth be told, she didn't want to. There was a feeling under her skin. Something crawling and itching and hot.

Still, she dressed slowly, studying the stretchy training gear Jax supplied her with. The pants a little too small and the tank top a little too big, but she's not going to complain. It was better than the jumpsuit she had been wearing yesterday. After Layla slipped the jacket on, not her own jean one, but a soft charcoal cotton, and tied her hair up, she tucked the picture of her family into the jacket pocket for good luck. But then she decided against it. After tucking it back in the pillowcase, she pushed her socked feet into the pair of boots Jax supplied her with and slipped out the door.

The cafeteria is exactly what Layla expected. Like her school cafeteria on steroids. Compared to the humming quiet on the run, the noise inside the cafeteria is enough to make Layla's head split. Thousands of people are packed in the lower level of the building, all talking, and stomping around. Silverware clashes against plastic trays and cups clash against tabletops. The sheer volume of it is almost too much. No, it *is* too much, even with the deep-seated familiarity it brought as Layla got in line and picked up a tray.

Layla takes in all that she can as she waits in line, enthralled by the different colored eyes and sharp smiles. These are hybrids. She wishes Courtney could see them, could see her. If only to prove to her that they're not monsters, and she isn't either. But Courtney is gone now.

People stare at her as they walk past, but, to her slight confusion, few of them continued to look after meeting her gaze. But that doesn't mean that she can't hear them.

"It's another one of them. I can tell by the look of her," a girl with short blond hair and startlingly blue eyes says as she leans in close to her friend. Layla stares at them as they walk away. Another one of who?

Another group walks by, looking her up and down before hurrying past. Layla can easily hear it as one of the guys says, "I already heard she was crazy. One of the helpers told me she attacked the testing assistant just to get on a team."

"Savage."

Her head wipes toward the voice, lips curling to show her canines. The girl's tray clatters to the ground, her eyes bugging out of her head. Layla watches as the girl begins to curse, shoulders shaking as she bends down to gather her tray and spilt food.

Layla will show this girl how savage she is.

Her foot moves an inch before a strong hand wraps around her upper arm, stopping her in her tracks.

"Ignore them," Mick says. "We're almost to the food, and I'm starving."

Layla huffs at him and looks back at the girl. She's already gone. Only smudges of dropped food on the floor. That's fine with her since she's soon distracted by the televisions. There must be around twenty of them, all positioned in different spots so that no matter where you sit, you'll be able to see one, if not two of them. Right now, they're turned off, the black screens reflecting the chaotic activity of the cafeteria.

Today her food portions are the same as everyone else's. Hash browns, eggs, and one small apple get plopped on her tray by hybrids who look far too awake at this time of the day. Layla fills her mug with water that smells a little stale. She had to carry the cup throughout their run. It was in one of the bags Jax gave her last night, and she took special care not to accidently break it.

Somehow, they find a table with enough seats for the five of them. She gawks around the large room, barely remembering that she's supposed to be eating. Then, when she has only just started on her eggs, Jax elbows Kyrin, who shoots him a glare. After he finishes his mouthful of food, Kyrin turns his dark gaze to Layla, and says, "Have you ever used a gun before? You didn't use any in the testing simulation."

"No." Guns were banned years ago. Only military personnel are allowed to have them. Of course, that doesn't mean that people didn't find illegal ways to get their hands on them. Layla's never seen one in real life before yesterday. She thinks back to the testing simulation. "But the gunfire didn't hurt my ears that bad in the simulation. I don't think I'll need the special headphones you guys were talking about."

It's true, in the simulation, she had gunfire ringing in her ears, most of the time from Cam just feet from her, or from the terrorist targets shooting at them. The noise was loud enough to cause discomfort, but not loud enough to where she would need soundproof headphones.

"You heard all that, huh?" Jax shakes his head. Layla lowers her eyes to her tray before shrugging. She heard all of them this morning. She wasn't trying. She just couldn't help it. He puts his fork down and rests his elbows on the table. "You're hearing is more sensitive now than it was yesterday. The gunfire is turned down in the simulation, so people like you and Mick," he points at both of them, "and whoever else don't end up with permanent hearing damage. You'll need the headphones today."

Her eyebrows draw together, and a frown pulls at her lips in thought. "And when we go on missions? What happens then?" If she wears soundproof headphones during missions, then what would be the point of enhanced hearing?

Kyrin sighs, seemingly already annoyed with her. "We have special guns where the sound is muted, but they're mostly for stealth missions." He rolls his apple between his hands. "For your first lesson, you'll need the headphones. In time, you'll need to get used to the sound, but we're not going to worry about that today."

"In time?" Layla looks at them each in turn. "Exactly how long? When do we get to go out there?"

This back and forth is starting to test her already irritable attitude. They're only giving her parts of the picture, little pieces of information at a time like she can't handle it. She takes a bite out of her apple, her canines piercing it like butter. The sweet flavor fills her mouth, more pungent than ever.

Having already wolfed down his food, Mick pushes his tray away to set his elbows on the table and steeple his hands together. "Honestly, I'm still getting used to it, Newbie, and I've been here a month. Although, I don't usually train with firearms."

"And we go out there on missions when we're called to," Jax says when she doesn't respond right away. "The commanders decide, and as a new member in training, they will have to observe you first."

Layla chews her apple with more force than necessary. "Observe," she says.

"Basically, they will watch you train with us, see if you are up to par, and go from there. We can get the kinds of missions we have been getting, which are nothing noteworthy, or they can give us higher-risk missions," Jax says.

Layla looks to Celia and does a double take. The girl who was so talkative yesterday hasn't said a word since they got to the cafeteria. Her night dark hair is puffed out in random places from their run around the compound. Her hands, covered by the long sleeves of her shirt, cling to her mug of coffee. It must be her third cup. At least.

Turning away from the odd scene, Layla faces the guys and says, "Just to get this straight, the chance of our team getting better missions, missions that can do something against the terrorist, rides on me impressing the commanders. Whoever they are."

Nodding, Jax's eyes scan the cafeteria. Layla follows his gaze, seeing only the familiar sight of teenagers grouped together, talking and eating. He must come to some conclusion, because he leans in closer to her and says, "Helland and Cape are the commanders here. The people in control of almost everything at the compound. They have been here since the beginning, and do a damn good job keeping everyone in line."

Layla wonders what else these commanders do. She would guess that they keep the whole compound running smoothly. Keep them all informed and comfortable. Keep them safe, at least while they're here.

Kyrin stacks his empty tray on top of Mick's. He nods down at

Layla's half eaten food, and says, "Eat and listen."

Her head tilts to the side, lips pulling up into a sneer. If it wasn't for Celia kicking her under the table, she would've told Kyrin where he can shove her food. Celia presses her finger to her smiling lips, eyes sparkling.

Huffing, Layla crams hash browns into her mouth. She waves her fork at Kyrin. Mouth still full of the salty starch, she says, "So, firearms."

Jax made sure the firearms level of the training center is empty for their newbie's first lesson. He'll have to be even more cautious with her than he was with Mick. It seems that each new addition to his team is riskier than the last, not that he would let anyone know that.

Mick was a risk and he turned out to be one of the greatest soldiers Jax has come across. His skills with knives far surpass Jax's own. He tries to keep that in mind as he studies Layla's tense stance and her tightly drawn lips that stretch over some of the largest canines he has seen on a hybrid. And he has seen them all.

Celia is up in the rafters, dazzling green eyes jumping out amongst the shadows. After she showed him how she can put both legs behind her head while walking on her hands, Jax has given up trying to figure out how she gets up there. It was a disturbing sight that he never wants to witness again.

Jax rolls his eyes when she glares down at him. She had been doing it on and off all morning. She wants to be the one to teach Layla how to use guns. She's good, just not as good as Kyrin. And maybe he's being biased, but Jax doubts that anyone is better than Kyrin.

So just like he did with Mick and Celia during their first lesson,

Kyrin stands with Layla next to a long table covered in guns. Some are small, smaller than Jax's hand, while others are the size of Layla's leg. The bigger ones are only kept inside the training center for safe keeping and are brought outside for target practice. More than half of the military's back up weapons are at this compound. There enough guns in this single room to win a war. They just need the right people to handle them.

Jax can't wait to see her try shooting one of the big ones. The first time he did, he got blasted to the ground by the backfire. His back was bruised for a whole day. Kyrin brings up the story so much, that Jax regrets ever telling him. Layla, as small as she is, might end up on the opposite end of the compound with broken ribs. Jax sighs. It's all part of the training. No pain, no gain. That's the best way to learn, his old team leader used to say. Not by being told what's right and wrong, but by figuring it out yourself. Sometimes it can get ugly, but Jax knows it works. He just hopes that his newest recruit can take it. And that his team can handle her in return.

"We only have basic weapons. Standard guns. Knives. None of the new stuff you'll see the terrorists using," Kyrin says.

Beside him, Mick snorts. "We *are* the new stuff, man."

Kyrin and Layla only spare him a glance. Leaning back against the wall, Jax listens to Kyrin. His voice takes on a hint of wonder and excitement when he talks about any kind of gun. Jax remembers when he dragged Kyrin into the training center for the first time. It was just the two of them then. They were headed for the combat room, but Kyrin heard gun fire and took off before Jax could stop him. When he caught up, Kyrin was staring at another recruit being taught to shoot by her teammate. The look in his eyes then is similar to how he looks now. Jax could see the dark irises shining from across the room.

It seems that even his dislike of the newbie can't put a damper on his enthusiasm.

"Pay attention, *leader*," Celia scoffs at him from above.

"I am," he says quietly enough that it won't distract Kyrin or Layla.

"To what?" asks Mick. He's crouched against the wall a few feet from Jax. One of his knives are out, a sharpening tool is in his other hand. Blade training comes next, and Mick is more than eager to get going. He stops examining his knife to meet Jax's stare and shrugs. "I've got a feeling," he says, "she's a blade person like me. Besides, it's my first time training someone. You can't blame me for being excited."

Celia grumbles something unintelligible, then says more loudly, "Don't get your hopes up, Pickles."

Jax is unable to contain his laugh, especially at the look on Mick's face.

"Pickles?"

The sound of a throat clearing has all three of their heads whipping around. Kyrin is glaring at them, his hands on his hips. Jax's mouth snaps shut. When they don't make another sound, Kyrin turns back to Layla, who has been ignoring the exchange in favor of studying the small gun given to her. Jax recognizes it as the kind he and everyone else first shot with.

The two of them move to the center of the room. After a few more minutes of instructions, Kyrin turns to look at him again. Taking it as a signal to get the targets in place, Jax lifts the panel door next to him and types in the right levels. Beginner: easy.

It only takes him a few seconds, but when he turns around, Layla has her hands positioned perfectly on the gun. Soundproof headphones now cover her ears. A fierce look shines in her eyes, one that reminds Jax of someone ready for war. Maybe Mick will be wrong after all.

Even though she can't hear him, Jax says a short, "Good luck." Moving a little more down the wall, he finds a position where he can see Layla's every movement without getting in the way of the training simulation. Celia has moved to a spot above where Layla stands, and Mick slowly comes to stand by him, headphones covering his own ears.

The rest of his teammates don't need them since their hearing never was enhanced the way Mick or Layla's is. By now, Jax is used to the slight ringing in his ears after gunshots, and thanks to their quick healing, it stops in seconds, barely affecting him or Kyrin and Celia at all.

The simulation comes to life without a sound, projecting targets for Layla to shoot at. The sound of firing bullets fills the air, making it impossible for Jax to hear anything else. Layla's stance is rigid, her shoulders loaded with tension. She fires bullet after bullet. Way too many shots for the few targets that spring up. Thrilled, Mick elbows Jax in the side, but neither of them takes their eyes off Layla and the targets.

The simulation has only been going a minute or two before the gun clicks on an empty magazine, forcing Layla to stop.

Kyrin's face is tight in a way Jax knows means he's disappointed and agitated. "Relax," Kyrin says when Layla slips her headphones down around her neck.

Layla slaps the gun into Kyrin's hand with a lot more force than necessary. Her lips draw over her teeth. The run didn't help relax her. Jax thinks she might be in shock. There's an anxious energy around her that makes his hair want to stand on end.

"I hit them," she says, voice clipped.

Kyrin's head tilts to the side, assessing her with a carefully blank face. "Yes," he says. "Good job, but you still need to relax. You're too tense, and it only takes one shot per person not seven." Returning to the assortment of guns, Kyrin picks up another that's similar to the one he gave Layla. "I'll show you."

He gives Jax a nod, both in reassurance and an order. Blowing out an exasperated breath, because Kyrin is easily falling into

Layla's bad mood, Jax goes back to the control panel without a word. He turns the levels up until they can't go any higher. Expert: professional. Then he once again steps out of the way to watch.

Layla and Kyrin switch places, and after a few seconds the simulation begins. Layla's targets were in front of her, easy to see. Kyrin's are everywhere, popping up so fast even Jax only catches the slightest movement before they're gone. Kyrin spins around and side to side. Bullet casings rain down to his feet.

Even having watched him do it countless times, Jax still can't look away. Kyrin has been training with using two guns at once, difficult but not impossible for him, but for this demonstration, he only uses the one. The only sign of exertion Jax can see is a thin line of sweat that trails down his temple.

When he's done, Layla pulls the headphones off with shaking hands.

"You can't be afraid," Kyrin says, only slightly out of breath.

Her eyes flash with enough anger that Jax tenses, ready to step in. "I'm not afraid, and I needed a demonstration, not you showing off." Her words, laced with a growl, have Jax pushing off the wall. You don't see that kind of aggression in many people. Sure, everyone is angry here for some reason or another, but her whole body shakes with it, fingers all but twitching with the need to tear the walls down with nothing but her hands.

When Kyrin steps back, just half a foot, Jax is moving, slipping between their bodies and pushing them apart.

"Layla." Her amber eyes snap to him. They're the eyes of a predator. A trapped predator, spitting with fury. He can feel heat roll off her in waves, but all he says is, "Let's try hand-to-hand."

If anyone is going to get hurt by this little cat, it's going to be him.

The anger overwhelms me and soon I am gone.

CHAPTER SEVEN

ayla kicks her feet against the floor in a useless attempt to stop Jax from dragging her away from Kyrin, and to the elevator. The others follow behind them. Her heart pounds in her chest, viciously loud in her ears. She's reminded of all the times she's had trouble controlling her anger. Not just here, but before she was injected with the serum. This feels different, though. This feels like she needs to rip her own skin off to peel the hostility away. And she doesn't know how—how to control this feeling that burns inside of her.

Inhuman sounds fly from her mouth. Snarls and curses. No matter how hard she fights against him and no matter how loud she screams, Jax doesn't let up on the painful grip around her wrists. He pulls her bodily through a new room: the combat room.

Even without her feet firmly planted on the floor, she can feel the difference of the ground. It's squishy with a give that lets her kicking heels sink down an inch. She's dragged past punching bags and dummy mannequins, rolled up mats and even a boxing ring.

Layla yells and twists in Jax's steal-like grip, but it makes next to no difference. Struggling to look over her shoulder, she sees an empty spot, the floor covered with red and yellow colored tape. Her gums sting where her canines bite into them. "Let go of me!" she says.

Jax is strong, stronger even than Layla with all her enhancements, and from what Celia explained to her on the walk here, this is Jax's domain. Hand-to-hand combat. She's gotten into a few fights before, most of them after her parents passed away, but Jax…

She's not stupid, but she's angry, and anger triumphs all.

Without warning, Jax releases her wrists. She lands hard on her butt, the matted floor cautioning her fall. In a single movement, she flips to her knees and pushes to her feet. Her team spreads around her, Jax in front, Kyrin and Celia on the sides, and Mick at her back. Pulse racing even faster, her entire body begins to tremble. No, not tremble. People tremble when they're afraid, but what she feels is not fear. She shakes with a rage her body can't contain.

Jax has that cold look in his eyes that Layla only caught a glimpse of before he decided that dragging her around the training center was a good idea. It might have frightened someone like the boy with pink eyes from the testing center or the crying girls in the locker room from her school, but Layla holds his gaze with ease.

"It's hard being told to relax," he says, voice raspy but somehow firm. "Especially when it's said by the wrong person." Her fingers start to tingle with an unknown need. All their eyes, their bright, dangerous eyes, are fixed on her. "But," Jax continues, "you do need to calm down, Layla. You can't learn if you are unable to concentrate. And I won't have you hurting anyone on this team."

She can see the challenge in every part of him. From his blazing eyes, the pupils so dilated, his eyes look black, to his wide stance. But her body continues to shake. Layla huffs a breath out her nose. "I can't," she says on a growl, and it might be one of the truest things she has ever said. She can't get ahold of her erratic breathing. Every noise around them is magnified by one hundred. The lights, dim as they may be, sear into her brain.

Jax shakes his arms out at his sides, readying to move at a moment's notice. She's hyperaware of his every breath. His steady heartbeat drums in her ears. It only adds to her anger. He should be afraid. "Giving up already?" he asks.

Teeth on display, Layla shakes her head. A few strands of

hair come loose from her bun. She blows them out of her face in annoyance.

Jax nods once. "You can either take it out on me, or you can find yourself another position, and we've already seen how many teams want you."

Layla lets the jab flow over her, lets it settle in her boiling stomach. But through the rage, is fear. Finally, fear. Not about fighting one of the most experienced hybrids in existence, but about getting kicked off this team. The others shift around her. They're nervous. She doesn't know how, but she can tell.

"Fine." She has fought before.

The others react instantly. Celia curses to her right, roughly shaking her head. Mick lets out a breath so long she can feel it on the back of her neck. And Kyrin's pulse quickens so much that it blends with hers for a second before outrunning it completely. All of it happens in a moment, but she picks up each individual thing.

Annoying. Too much.

Jax slips his shoes off and tells Layla to do the same. But when she tosses them away and stands up straight, Layla hears a strange noise. What happens next doesn't make sense. Something clicks in her head. She turns to the left, to Kyrin, to the one that got her in this situation in the first place. Her gums burn and ache.

She lunges.

In midair, a mass plows into her hard enough to knock all the air from her lungs. She flies sideways, twisting in the air to land on all fours, and comes to a stop five feet outside of the circle. Without pausing, she stands and stalks toward Jax. The fact that he's the size of three of her put together doesn't cross her mind. What does is that he dragged her here, and he cornered her between his soldiers. He challenged her, and he attacked, and he's looking at her like he will do it again.

Her world narrows down to him. His dark eyes watch her every move, and Layla thinks that if he were anything like her, his lips would be drawn over his teeth and harsh noises would leave his throat.

But he's not like her, and his lips are shut in a tight line. Not a sound comes from him besides his steady heartbeat. Her own loud pants fill the air. She charges at him. Her bare feet stick to the mat, allowing her to move even faster than she did on the run earlier this morning.

Layla plows into him at full speed. The impact jars her teeth. They crash to the floor, Layla landing half on top of his body with her knee digging harshly into his gut. She raises above him. The corners of his mouth lift into a smile, making it even more satisfying when she punches him in the side of his face.

Someone gasps. Someone barks an order, but Layla's already hitting him again. His face. His ribs. The snapping sound of a broken bone doesn't register in her brain. The whole time, he doesn't fight back.

The sounds around her fade. The whispers, groans, labored breathing, shuffling feet, Kyrin's fast heartbeat, the sound of skin hitting skin. It's all gone, and Layla can't see anything but red.

Something grabs at her minutes or seconds or hours later. A tight vice closes around her waist. There's a tug, a sense of weightlessness, and then she smashes to the ground. She's up in a second. If she was hurt from getting thrown ten feet, she doesn't feel it. Looking around, she tries to find what grabbed her, what took her away from her prey. Someone stands over a heap of brown and red. With a growl, she jumps at them, her new target, but someone else grabs her arm, yanking her back.

Planting her feet, she pulls her arm away. She almost gets out of the grip before they rush forward, taking her by surprise. They get a better hold of her, clamping one arm around her middle and a hand around her neck. They force her down. Unable to hold herself up against their strength, Layla sinks to her knees. The body that holds her doesn't stop there. It falls with her, flush against her back, pushing her flat out against the cushioned floor.

Spit flies from her mouth and lands on the cushy floor as she continues to struggle against the limbs that hold her down. Knees dig into the backs of her thighs. The hand on her neck pushes the side of her face into the ground, making her bite into her gums again. She welcomes the tangy taste of blood.

Layla tries bucking them off, but they only push at her harder. Their nails dig into the skin on her neck, and the sounds of their growls grow louder than her own. Then, all of a sudden, their weight disappears. Her body is flipped over as if she weighs nothing. It happens so fast that she doesn't have time to lift a leg to kick out at them.

Layla can see them now. Or, more accurately, she can see their eyes. So close to her face that she can't see anything else. One is blue. The other is brown.

She struggles again, hands pushing at their chest. She tries to talk, but her tongue refuses to cooperate. In response, the nails on her throat dig in deeper. Another sound fills the air, a harsh screech that cuts off the other's growls in the middle.

Layla's vision blurs, spots dancing in her eyes. It takes a minute for her to realize that the body, her target, is talking now, and it takes even longer for her to understand what the words are.

But when they register, she gasps down heaving breaths.

"Can you hear me? Layla? It's Mick. You're in the combat room of the training center."

A shudder runs through her, raising goose bumps across her skin. Like a fog being wiped away, Layla can see the rest of his face above her. Some of his golden hair has escaped from his bun. His eyes are hard, one the color of ice and one the color the fallen leaves outside. His teeth, slightly smaller than her own, glisten with spit.

Her throat is raw and scratchy from all the growling. She

doesn't think she can talk. She's panicking, rocking her head from side to side. Mick's arm moves with her, his nails like a spiked collar around her throat.

Her body feels like someone else's. Unable to control her hands, they rub up and down the floor in frantic motions. From the corner of her eye she sees specs of red glistening on the tan floor and knows without a doubt what it is.

The moment slams into her in perfect clarity. She remembers Jax, and hitting him, and all the blood. *Is he okay?* She can't see him.

Above her, Mick is making shushing sounds. He places his other hand on the side of her face. "Breathe." Layla gasps, nearly choking. Then she does it again. When she gets her lungs working normally, she thinks it will be okay, that she can get up and see what happened.

Instead, her body begins to shake. Small tremors at first, then bigger ones that shake Mick along with her.

"Layla," he says. Her eyes snap to his, away from the drops of blood, but now she can only think of Courtney and how she shook Layla's whole body while she died in her arms. Her eyes were wide with pain, not like Mick's whose are almost flat, steady. And both Courtney's were brown, almost the same shade as Layla's used to be.

Her body spasms again, her muscles locked so tight they burn. She's caught between the ground and Mick, choking on air, never seeming to get a full breath. The grip on her neck becomes so painful her eyes begin to roll back. She loses sight of Mick. Is he trying to kill her? Had she hurt Jax enough to deserve death? Her hands slip and fumble, unable to get a grip on his hands.

Mick's voice floats around her. "Layla. Stop. Breathe. Focus. You are okay."

If she could draw in enough air, she would have laughed. How is she okay when he's choking her?

"Layla, please. Stop screaming!"

Is she screaming? No, she doesn't think she is. She tries to twist and turn away from him, but something slams into her forehead, hard enough to make her gasp in pain. But it does what it's meant to: focus her.

"I need you to calm down. Relax. You're okay."

Relax.

That's why she's here. Here in the combat room where there's blood on the floor. Because Kyrin told her to relax, and something in her brain felt like it blew up. He must have known, must have seen it in her eyes because he took a step back, and Jax appeared between them faster than Layla thought possible.

Mick is close enough that his breath puffs across her face. He breathes fast and hard like he just got done sprinting a mile. Sweat shines at his temples. It's from holding her down, she notes with some satisfaction. That's all it takes for her to push through the rest of the panic and fog—the feeling of vain satisfaction at her new strength. This time she does huff a laugh.

Exhaustion creeps up heavily on her, pushing her loosening muscles even further into the spongy floor. In seconds, her body stops shaking. The ringing in her ears dies down. Mick still whispers things like "breathe," and "you're okay." His head is bent down, allowing only the top of his forehead to be seen, but the vice-like grip around her neck is gone, leaving only an unpleasant stinging sensation.

Layla's voice comes out choked and raw when she asks, "What happened to Jax?"

When Mick lifts his head, the sight of blood makes her heart clench. It's smeared around his chin and upper lip from the broken nose he's sporting. Did she do that, too? There's more on his cheeks and forehead. Looking down, she sees more on his shirt, and across her own. That's when she smells it, tangy and coppery.

"You knocked him out," he says, his own voice harsh. "Kyrin

got you off. He and Celia took Jax to the infirmary."

Layla glances over to the taped-in circle. It looks like way too much blood. A puddle of red, smears all around it, and red footprints leading past the boxing ring. She has to swallow a few times before asking, "Will he be okay?"

Lifting himself off her in one fluid movement, Mick brushes his hands across his pants and says, "He has been through worse. Give him a few hours."

Fast healing, Layla remembers, is another advantage of being a hybrid. Confusion wars with her relief and the ever-present anger. "Why did he let me do that?" He could have stopped her easily, but he didn't once try to.

Rolling his eyes, Mick offers her a hand up. Layla's hands are covered in blood, slippery with the substance. She gets up on her own, then uses her stained shirt to attempt to rub her skin clean. She has another shirt just like it that she carefully stored in the dresser in her room this morning.

"He didn't want anyone else to get hurt. It's just how he is. Probably thought letting you beat the crap out of him would help you get rid of that anger."

Is she really that transparent?

"It didn't," she says.

Mick shrugs and takes out the elastic band in his hair to redo his bun. "Can't blame him for trying."

Layla looks away, down at her feet. One of her shoes is missing. "You did," she says, "You helped." She lifts her hand to her neck, gingerly touching the inflamed skin. She can still feel the anger, but it's buried deep now. If it weren't for the enhancements that allow her to hear their heartbeats and muffled gunshots from the level below, or the sour smell of blood in her nose, she would say she almost feels like she did before the serum.

Mick's gaze follows the movement of her fingers on her neck.

"I don't know about that." She tries to find the words to explain herself, but he shakes his head and prods at his swollen nose. Layla thinks that maybe he doesn't need to know. "We should get ourselves to the infirmary, too. I don't want to have a crooked nose for the rest of my life." He ignores the blood on the floor, stepping around it with ease. Already half way across the room, he glances back at Layla with a smile. "No offense."

Guilt bleeds more than the gashes across my knuckles.

CHAPTER EIGHT

"Kyrin is going to kill me." Beside her, Mick shrugs and nods. A bubbled laugh is forced out of her sore throat. She rubs at her neck, smearing the blood around. Most of the hybrids they pass on the dirt path outside of the training center don't spare them a glance. They're most likely used to seeing bleeding and injured people making their way to the infirmary, but, still, with this much blood on them, she would have thought they earned some staring.

Mick sets a brutal pace, considering Layla's mind is still reeling. Not that he knows that. They squeeze past groups of other teams, and leap over a fallen tree in the path. He wasn't kidding about getting his nose fixed.

"Better watch out for Celia, too," he says.

Layla fails to hide her wince, but Mick isn't looking at her anyway. "At least she likes me. I think." The infirmary building comes into view, the side of it marked with a large dark red cross. "Kyrin hates me."

Mick sighs and stops by the wooden "infirmary" sign. His eyes constantly move around, looking at the woods and at the hybrids moving with more purpose Layla has seen any teenagers have. When his finally settles on her, he says, "Kyrin seems like he hates most people. He didn't like me when I got here either, but he warmed up. The same will happen with you."

Layla isn't that convinced, but all she says is, "Yeah, maybe if I didn't almost kill his boyfriend."

Mick gives her a look full of pity. "An apology might help."

Huffing out a humorless laugh, Layla continues up the short path to the building and pushes through the door. Even if the thought of apologizing to Kyrin didn't set her teeth on edge, she doubts it would help all that much. She will, however, be very much inclined to apologize to Jax, and might even resort to begging when he more than likely kicks her off the team.

With the smell of the infirmary filling her nose, Layla freezes in the doorway. Her breath stops in her throat as that thought sinks in. If she were in Jax's place, she would do it—kick her off the team. If she were Kyrin, Celia, or Mick, she would kick her off the team, too. Her palms dampen with sweat, and she once more, rubs them over her neck, this time trying to get her racing pulse to calm down.

Before she can gather herself, there's a hand on her back and she's pushed into the building. The doors close behind them with a final sweeping sound. They're in an open room, cots spread across one side, and a counter lines the other. In the corner of the room lays a single, empty desk.

Loud cursing from down one of the hallways has Layla ready to spin around Mick and sprint straight back out the door. She curses to herself. This is all her fault. She can't allow herself to run away.

She and Mick are the only ones in the room. The doctors or nurses must be either helping Jax or with other patients. Following the sound of yelling, Layla steels her nerves. She comes to a stop at the fifth door on the right but doesn't make a move for the handle.

Mick reaches past her to yank the door open without preamble. Layla's shoulders tense. She's not necessarily afraid of the people behind it. She's more afraid to see the damage she's done to Jax. Although it does help the tiniest bit knowing Kyrin isn't allowed to have guns outside of the training center.

She catches a glimpse of her team, but as soon as her and Mick pass through the doorway, Celia's small body is slamming all three of them back out. Layla lands on the floor half on top of Mick. Her muscles ripple in pain, and she bites back a groan.

"You don't want to go in there," Celia says. Her own training gear is covered in smears of blood, dark and almost dry. Had Mick and Layla really been in the combat room that long? "Trust me."

But Layla does want to go in there. She needs to see what she did to Jax and she needs to know if he will be okay. Layla springs to her feet, ignoring the wave of dizziness that passes over her and turns the room fuzzy. Her body tips to the side. As Celia reaches out to steady her, Layla ducks under her arm. Her hands smack into the door that hides Jax, and quickly stumbles through.

She doesn't bother to close the door behind her. In an instant Mick and Celia are flanking her, but it's easy to ignore them and everyone else in the room when she sees Jax.

He lays on a cot, both eyes shut, swollen and bruised against his dark skin. Purple and yellowish splotches cover his chest and torso. Cream colored bandages are wrapped around his left forearm.

Layla steps back, bumping into Mick and Celia. She couldn't have done this. She doesn't remember it. She had no reason to. But as she steps forward and touches her fist to a bruise on his side, it's the perfect size and shape.

A gasp fills the room, surprised and outraged.

Layla jumps away from Jax's unconscious form as Kyrin, arms outstretched, a murderous look on his face, rushes from around the hospital bed.

Layla's not stupid. She springs back further and rushes backwards out the door. Celia slips in front of her with ease, and plants her small hands on Kyrin's chest, stopping his approach. Cursing, Celia shoves at him, and kicks the door shut once they get out of the room.

Layla and Mick end up back in the large entrance room of the infirmary. A nurse comes a minute after Celia slammed the door, rushing down the hall, her white uniform spotless. She fixes Mick's nose, and looks them both over, claiming the bruises will heal in an hour or two. Layla's knuckles will take longer to heal, as will Mick's nose.

Layla leans against the wall between two empty cots, studying her raw knuckles, but her ears are focused on the room Jax is in. The yelling had stopped around the time their nurse left, and now the sounds of a needle plucking through skin can be heard. She knows what is being stitched up, she saw it in the second she was in there. A long cut ran across Jax's nose.

Pluck.

Pluck.

There must be more being stitched with how long it's taking. Scratches probably, from the look of her nails. Blood is clotted under and around them. It reminds her of a time when she was little. Courtney was going to do her nails; cut and paint them. She cut too far, and her finger bled forever, encrusting her nail in red. But this is not her own blood.

Mick pauses his inspection of the cabinets on the other side of the room and looks over at her. "You should wash your hands," he says, nodding at one of the sinks at the counter. "Go on."

Washing them doesn't get rid of all the blood. It's still stuck under parts of her nails and caked in the places where her skin peeled back on her knuckles. She never wants this to happen again. She never wants Mick or anyone else having to subdue her like he did. All because she couldn't get a hold of herself. The wounds around her neck hurt less every minute, but they're still bright red. Layla wonders if Mick would have gone far enough as to break her windpipe. The thought makes it hard to look at him. When Jax's door opens, Layla shuts off the water.

Celia smiles when she sees them, but her eyes linger on Layla. All she says is, "You have blood on your face. Let me help."

Layla has blood everywhere, not just on her face. "I broke

two people's noses. Head wounds bleed a lot." That's what the nurse said.

Celia blows out a breath as she approaches, looking Layla over with a quick flick of her bright eyes. She wets a clump of paper towels until they're a soggy heap in her hand, then she brings it to Layla's face, rubbing at her skin and down her neck. When she finishes, she turns away to face Mick. "Kyrin said to start blades training. They'll meet us there when Jax is all fixed up."

Mick calls this floor of the training center *sharps* and *blades* interchangeably. Like the firearms floor, a multitude of weapons are on display. Instead of guns, the room is covered top to bottom with knives, swords, axes, and many, many other sharp tools for stabbing and slicing. Some hang on the walls looking like shiny decorations while others lie in cases. Even more sit along tables throughout the room.

Layla pats down her sweaty palms on her pants. They ran back to the housing floor to change out of their bloodied clothes before coming here. Celia, deeming the blood covered clothes still salvageable, whisked them off to Layla doesn't know where. A tub of bleach, maybe. She came back an hour ago with food and drinks that the three of them devoured in minutes. Then they were back to drilling Layla through her training.

Mick began with leading her through the basics of fighting with a knife. She picked up the movements fast, already having gotten the feel for it in the simulation. To Layla's annoyance, Mick refused to go beyond the basics, saying she had had enough action for the day. Layla tamped down the bout of rage that followed the statement. She has done enough damage for the day.

Now, she picks up small throwing knifes, copying Mick's exact motions to hit the bullseye target across from her. In an hour she progressed from throwing the knives five feet away from the target to twenty feet, never moving and inch farther until she got all six knives to stick dead center.

As ecstatic as Mick and Celia are at her fast progress, she can't let herself feel the same. Her eyes keep darting to the single clock in the sharps floor. Her ears stay halfway trained on the door for any sound of the descending elevator. How long will it take for Jax to heal enough to be able to walk here? It doesn't seem possible that he would be able to by the time dinner comes around.

She, Mick, and even Celia when she gets bored, throw knives at the targets for another half hour before she finally hears something. She glances at the clock. Three hours and forty-seven minutes to heal his broken bones and beaten body.

As soon as Jax and Kyrin walk through the door, Layla sets her remaining knives on the table behind her and stands with her back rigidly straight. Her mind had been racing all through the training, thinking it was useless because obviously she's going to get kicked off the team, and after hearing what she did to her own team leader, none of the other teams would even consider adding her to theirs.

She has a second to wish she could pull a Celia and hide up in the rafters, but when Jax, partially hidden behind Kyrin, comes into view, the thought vanishes. He looks almost normal, the gash across his nose now a thin cut. All the bruising that Layla later learned from Celia meant broken ribs is hidden by his clothes. He's walking straight. His face only hints at slight discomfort.

When Kyrin moves, Layla sees it reflected on the surface of a thousand blades. He stands silent in front of Jax, reminding her of a stone-faced guard. There's an expression on his face that Layla is already familiar with. It screams a warning at her, one that she chooses to listen to this time.

Like they discussed it already, Jax doesn't interfere in anyway.

It's easy to see the differences between the two. Jax all dark and big and tall. Kyrin, slim and black and white. They are both bird hybrids. Jax a falcon and Kyrin a raven. Celia ended up telling her during their food break like she couldn't help herself.

Kyrin takes another step toward her. "If something like that ever happens again——"

Already shaking her head, Layla cuts him off. "It won't."

Dark eyes narrow at her. "We don't have the time for this."

Layla knows that he doesn't mean the conversation they're having. He means they don't have time for her and her problems. They have a country to win back. Her problems are not important. They want more higher-risk missions and she's their key to getting them, but they could easily go to the next group of newbies and find a less difficult member to work with.

A cold feeling settles deep in her gut. She forces herself to meet Jax's gaze when he steps out from behind Kyrin. "I'd like to speak with you, Layla."

Hands clenched into the fabric of her too big shirt, she says in a much quieter voice than she wanted, "Okay."

"Alone," Jax adds when none of them move. "We will meet you in the cafeteria for dinner."

Unable to help feeling like this is the last time she will see them, Layla watches them turn for the elevator. It's a ridiculous thought, she tells herself. Her stuff is on their floor, the few things Jax got her. She would have to see them again no matter what happens. Celia winks at her on the way out, and Mick gives her an easy grin. Kyrin's face stays the same, not offering any reassurance. Not that Layla thinks she deserves any from him.

By the time the door shuts behind them, Jax has cleared a spot on one of the tables to prop up against. The fingers of his right hand prod along his ribcage. "How was blades training?"

There is something about being in the room alone with him

that makes Layla feel smaller. She hates it. "It went well."

"Mick was right, then. He said this morning that you were a blades person." He picks up one of the weapons on the table next to him, a skinny knife about as long as Layla's forearm.

A strange urge to laugh overtakes her. It's the nerves. She pushes it down with a painful swallow. "I'm so sorry, Jax."

"You have nothing to be sorry for. It was my idea and I let you do it." He puts the knife back down and looks her straight on, "I should be apologizing to you." Layla tilts her head as she thinks that over, but before she can draw any conclusions, he speaks again. "I needed you to take your focus away from Kyrin. I let you dive into your emotions without thinking of how strong they would be after the serum. I admit it wasn't the right thing to do, and you shouldn't blame yourself for the consequences."

It's a nice speech, but she still blames herself, and she bets the others do as well. She should have more control, not black out with the force of her anger. Even for her, it's not normal. "How about we call it a draw and not let it happen again?"

Jax's lips stretch into a closed-mouth smile. "You got yourself a deal."

Shoulders finally sinking down from their place by her ears, she shakes out her damp hands. The target practice is still set up from when Celia, Mick, and she were using it, and Layla makes her way over. She can show him what she learned today. Try to make up for beating the crap out of him just the smallest bit.

She's pulling the knives out of the three targets they were using when Jax clears his throat. "Kyrin…" he starts, and Layla turns to him, brows drawn together. "Kyrin wants you off the team."

Just like that, the room becomes unfocused, glazed and glaring and hard to look at. Her eyes slam shut. Jax still hasn't moved from his spot against the table. More than anything, Layla wants something to lean against too because her knees begin to tremble underneath her.

Kyrin wants her off the team. Jax loves Kyrin, that's obvious. The math is easy enough that Layla can figure out the outcome even with the room spinning.

Everything comes slamming back into focus at her leader's voice, stern and deep. "Do you want off the team, Layla?"

"No!" The word explodes out of her, making her head throb.

Jax nods, pushing off the table to join her in the target station. Layla hurries to collect the last of the knives and meets him at the table. "There is a reason we picked you, and a reason we hesitated."

Layla straightens out the knives against the table, treating them like delicate feathers instead of objects meant to harm. "The team needed another member to have enough people and skill to get better missions," she says.

"Right. But that wasn't why we chose you to be our newbie."

The knives are in a straight row, an inch of space between each one, but still she fiddles with them, needing to do something with her hands. Mick told her that Jax is good with blades. He has been here long enough to get a good grip on everything. He prefers hand-to-hand combat, but has no problem using any weapon, whether it be a gun, a blade, his fists, or any random object he deems useful. Layla's stuck between terror and amazement just imagining him fighting.

"You don't have to worry," Jax says, interrupting her wild thoughts. "About Kyrin, I mean. We chose you because you did good in the simulation. You proved yourself, proved that you want to fight against the terrorists. You are a natural fighter. You are smart and resourceful, and you can work with a team." He leans against the table with a sigh. "We hesitated because of the look in your eyes."

"What look?" Layla asks.

"We've seen it here a few times. When someone is too in tune with their new animal instincts. They have a hard time controlling themselves. They lash out for seemingly no reason. If it's really bad, they see everything and everyone as a threat." He straightens up from his leaned position again, grimacing all the while. "That look."

Layla wants to tell him to sit. She will find the chair herself. Or they can go back to their floor and have this conversation on the two chairs in the living room. But Jax picks up two knives, one in each hand, and Layla tosses the thought away.

She doesn't bother to correct him about *the look* or what it means. There's no reason to. It would explain why the people at the compound, human and hybrid alike, smell and look at her with fear. It would explain the things she's heard them say. "How do I control the emotions? They come on so fast and strong at times. The anger is always there, always underneath, even before the serum." To her surprise, she has no problem telling him this. He can help, and that's all that matters to her right now. "And why did I black out when I attacked you? I don't remember any of it."

Coming to stand beside her, Jax hovers his hands over the blades she still touches with light fingers. She forces her hands still, forces her whole body still against the need to bolt away. Six knives fit into one of his fists, and he fills both his hands with the slim silver objects.

He turns his powerful body towards her. Eyes widening, she watches as Jax holds out one of his hands, offering the blades. "Why don't you show me what Mick taught you today?"

Layla nods, and with fast fingers, she swipes the knives out of his hand. He keeps the other six to himself, and Layla sees why when he lines himself up at one of the target stations. She takes the station next to him, the same one she used before.

He gives her a crooked smile before lining himself up with the target. It takes him a moment to find the right position. Then he throws his first knife, landing it straight in the middle of the bullseye. Even though she was getting good at this distance, was almost ready to move another foot back, her hands slip on the skin-warmed metal of her blade.

Eyebrows raised, Jax inclines his head toward her target. Mick said that she's a natural at blades, but she doesn't feel like it. The red and black bullseye mocks her. She feels like she is back in school, giving a presentation on a topic she only had two hours to prepare for.

Settling her nerves, she lines up, aims, and lets the blade fly. It hits and sticks with a loud *thwack* in the center of the target. A smile lights her face, stretching at her cheeks. After all that had happened today, it feels odd, like her face forgot how to do it.

"I guess he was right, huh?" Jax says. The look on his face is full of conflicting emotions: pride, relief, and a pinch of pain around his forehead and lips.

He throws another one, sticking it an inch to the right of his last. "You're pretty good, too," Layla says, gesturing to his perfect form.

He shrugs "I used to teach sharps before we got Mick. I had to get good." He stays focused on his target, his head turned away from her, but she can still see his lips pull into a smirk. "It took me weeks to get ready to teach Kyrin. He was my first recruit." Layla learned that from Celia, too. "We had to focus on hand-to-hand mostly. That is, when I could pull him away from firearms."

Layla lines up again, readying to make another throw. Jax still hasn't answered any of her questions about the anger and self-control. She throws the dagger, copying Jax's placement exactly. "I want to know how to control myself better," she says, rolling another blade between her fingers. She throws that one, too, not letting Jax have his turn. Out of the corner of her eye, she sees Jax line up to take his throw, but Layla doesn't want to play this game anymore. She throws the last three knives in quick progression, huffing out breaths through her nose with each throw.

On the target, the six knives form a perfect *L* shape; one in the center, three evenly spaced going up, and two going out to the side.

Twirling one of his knives between his fingers, Jax looks over her work. Again, she sees that look of pride in his eyes. Hybrid eyes amaze her. They're so different from what she's used to. They're all color with no space for white. They're a million different textures and shades and shapes. They're the animal forced into their blood. It has only been a day, and every time she catches a glimpse of hers, she startles at the bright amber so different from her old brown.

"Emotions and instincts are heightened when we turn," Jax says. "Everyone has a different way to control them, or in some cases, not control them."

Layla takes a minute to let that sink in. The idea that some of them don't control their crazed emotions makes her blood heat. The damage someone like her could do so out of control… She has trouble picturing it. The blood and bruises from this morning was enough.

"Why wouldn't they want to control it?" she asks.

"Sometimes, it's…" he shakes his head hard like he's trying to dislodge the right words from his brain. Finally, he settles with, "It can come in handy." A pained look crosses his face, and Layla doesn't think it's from his mostly healed injuries. "I used to know someone. I was on a team with them. They would use it to our advantage." He lets a dagger fly, and Layla wants to snatch the rest out of his hand. The fact that she can do something with these awful feelings, something to help…

"How did they do that?"

Jax sighs. "Honestly, I don't know. I've never felt that way, so out of control. But the reason they did it was because our mission took a turn for the worst, and they felt that doing it would help."

It was another thing Celia and Mick let her know during their lunch. That Jax used to belong to a different team before he became the leader of theirs. Her teammates wouldn't go into a lot of detail, and Layla didn't push for fear that they would stop talking.

Layla takes in the hard planes of his shoulders, his frown, and decides that now is not the time to ask about his past. But he did bring up this former teammate, so she asks, "Did it help?"

Jax throws one of his blades before answering. "A lot of the time it did, but not always."

Disappointment hums through her, slumping her shoulders and stinging her eyes. Nothing. She has learned basically nothing from this talk besides the fact that she won't get kicked off the team. And maybe that... maybe the anger can be used for something. But with no guarantee and no idea how to channel it, Layla has a lot of work to do.

Find out how to control, or not control herself. Impress the commanders with her training. Get her team on higher-risk missions. Take the Black Sun down.

Squaring her shoulders, she tries to smirk at Jax. She's not sure if it looks right or not. "At least we got one option out of the way today."

Jax laughs, a short burst of sound like it was surprised out of him. "I don't know. I think it might have worked some."

Not exactly. Layla can feel the anger and hurt pulsing under her skin. The only difference from this morning is that she doesn't feel threatened and doesn't feel like she's about to be attacked at any moment. Layla doesn't correct him, just gives him a small smile instead.

It has always been chaos.

CHAPTER NINE

The training center is a good mile walk from the rest of the compound, but the mass of people in the cafeteria is so loud, Layla can hear it as soon as they step out into the crisp air. When she and Jax get there, she sees why. The morning crowd was full of half-awake teenagers, all grouchy, knowing that even talking too loudly could set someone off. The evening crowd is the complete opposite.

People yell across tables and run around the packed space; the televisions are turned up loud, and food is being gobbled up like it might disappear in a flash. The sounds crash into her, making her head throb and vision go slightly unfocused.

Like he can tell, Jax sets a hand on her shoulder and guides her down the steps and into the mess of the cafeteria. He locates the team faster than Layla thought possible. They picked a table on the edge of the circular pit instead of in the middle like this morning. A choice Layla is grateful for.

Kyrin and Mick sit with their backs to them, but Layla can see Celia's face over their shoulders, already watching them approach with a big smile on her face. Layla doesn't know if Celia's so happy because Jax didn't kick her off the team, or if this is just her normal everyday level of enthusiasm.

It's probably all the coffee she consumed this morning.

Sliding into the seat Celia pats, Layla scans the tables around them. There's a tension in the air, she notices, even with all the shouting and excitement. Everyone, including Mick and Kyrin, glances up at the televisions every few seconds as if afraid to miss something. An uneasy feeling settles in her stomach.

Jax sits down more heavily than usual, and immediately takes a cup of water off the tray in the middle. He takes a log drink before asking, "What is it?"

"An announcement," Kyrin says, gesturing to the nearest television with his hand, "from the terrorist scum." Layla is used to hearing the disgust and anger in peoples' voices when talking about the Black Sun, but Kyrin somehow reaches a new level.

Resting his elbows on the table, Mick leans across Kyrin to get closer to Jax. "Of course, they didn't give a time. It could be in ten seconds or another two hours, but either way you two should get some food. Especially you, Jax. The nurse gave you some pain killers, right? Best to take them with food."

"Mother hen," Celia whispers, leaning close to Layla's ear.

Mick sends a vulgar gesture their way. "Heard that."

Before they get into it and because she really is starving, Layla leaves the table to squeeze and dodge her way to stand in line for food. She has only just gotten her tray when someone looms up behind her and a familiar voice fills her already overstimulated ears.

"You're already making a reputation for yourself, aren't you?" Fisher says, butting into her space and picking up a tray of his own.

His sharp teeth are on display in a wide smile that has Layla rolling her eyes. The news of what she did to Jax couldn't have spread that fast. "I don't know what you're talking about."

All but hustling her down the line, Fisher leans further into her space. "Funny. I was on my way to training this morning. Saw your esteemed leader getting carried away and you nowhere in sight."

Layla's amber eyes narrow to slits with how hard she glares at him. "I suppose you told anyone you came across. That's what you usually do, isn't it?"

Fisher reaches over her to get at the trays of small purple potatoes, but jerks away when Layla snaps her teeth at him. She rips the spoon from his hand. Behind the counter, an older woman watches her put five potatoes on her tray one by one with an unreadable face. Layla gives the woman credit for not flinching.

When she finishes, Fisher takes the spoon from her as if she didn't just attempt to bite his arm off a couple seconds ago. "Different place, Wilson. Different rules."

She grabs for a piece of meat three different times before it makes it to her tray. She hasn't heard those words since the last group meeting she went to. In those dark places, they were different people than they were at school or at home. They didn't need to pretend they weren't familiar with each other. They didn't have to pretend they were okay. They didn't need to pretend they weren't wishing for anything but a chance to fight. It feels like a lifetime ago.

Clearing her throat, she scoops up her vegetables: carrots and peas. "Good to know," she says.

"Unless you want me to spread the word." Excitement lights his onyx eyes, giving him a slightly unhinged look. "Crazy new hybrid on the loose! Do not engage!"

Layla doesn't stop the laugh that leaves her even when she sees the girl in front of them turn with a weird look on her face and hurry down the line. "If you start saying that, I'll never get a mission."

"Or you'll get them all," he says. Layla hurries to fill a cup of water. It's not until they're out of the line, standing off to the side, that he talks again. "Do the commanders watch you tomorrow?"

Layla blinks up at him in surprise. "I don't know." She hasn't heard anything about them, but then again, from attacking her leader, almost getting kicked off the team, and training with blades, Layla might have missed the conversation about the commanders. "Do they?"

"I wasn't the only one who saw your leader this morning. They want to keep a close eye on you." She doesn't stop to think of how he knows. He always seems to know what's happening, whether at school, in their town, or now at the compound.

"You know about the hybrids who can't control themselves?" she says. Maybe he learned something more than what Jax told her.

Dark eyes boring into hers, his lips turn down at the corners. "That won't happen to you." His head tilts to the side, and he nods behind her, towards where her team sits. "Is that what they think?"

She doesn't look back at them. "I don't know what they think." Fisher doesn't need to know about how Kyrin hates her, or that he was what set her off in the first place.

But as if he read her mind, he says, "You did good in the simulation. There wasn't any sign of you being out of control, so what happened?"

Layla grits her teeth. He doesn't need to know, she repeats to herself, and being looked down on by him... Layla would rather face the commanders with teeth bared and bloody. "Nothing I can't handle if it happens again."

His eyes flick over her face, seeing all too much. He can't help her, and Layla doesn't want him to. She leaves him without another word, like she has done so many other times. Not all their rules have changed.

"Remind me again why weapons aren't allowed outside the training center," Layla mumbles when she gets back to her team.

At the other side of the table, Kyrin props his chin on his fist and looks away from the television to give her an unimpressed look. "I think you putting Jax in the infirmary is a good example."

Layla blinks once, twice. *Right.*

Her team watches her tuck into her seat and pick at her dinner. Glancing at the television to their right, Layla makes sure she didn't miss anything. In the past, whenever the Black Sun made a special announcement the message would play on loop for hours on every channel. But their television is playing a violent looking cartoon, so she's sure she couldn't have missed it.

Eyebrows raised as high as they can go, Layla faces each of her teammates in turn. Her eyes land on Jax, who miraculously has a tray full of food. She didn't see him in line, and even if she did, he couldn't have gotten to the table before her. Her confusion gets pushed away when he starts talking.

"Helland and Cape, the commanders, are going to watch you tomorrow," Jax says, confirming that Fisher was right. Jax shoves food in his mouth, allowing her some time to digest his words.

Feigning shock, she lowers her fork, and says, "I have only trained one day." *And screwed up royally*, she silently adds.

"You did great in sharps, and that's what we'll show them," Mick says, pushing his loose hair out of his face. It seems that they've already discussed this without her, made her choices for her. She scowls down at her tray.

Nodding, Jax swallows his food loud enough that Layla can hear it even with the table next to them erupting in raucous laughter. "Getting them to watch you this early is a good thing," Jax says. "Sometimes, like with Celia, they took a few weeks to come see her train. Of course, by then she was all but perfect." Celia winks at him.

"But it took longer for you to get missions," Layla finishes for him. He says nothing about the commanders wanting to keep an eye on her, nothing about them believing she will be taken to wherever the out-of-control hybrids go. Layla doesn't know if it's because they don't want to spook her, send her into another fit of rage, or if they believe in her more than she originally thought they did.

"Right. They will be with us for no more than an hour," Kyrin says. His eyes remain on the television even when he addresses her.

One hour to prove herself to these commanders. Layla knows next to nothing about them, besides that they pretty much run the compound. Saying she feels pressured is an understatement. At least she only needs to be in total control for that one hour. The thought isn't as reassuring as she hoped it would be.

She finishes her tray of food in minutes, but she wants more. Nervous eating—a habit she's had since she was little. Her team and everyone else in the cafeteria continue sitting for almost another hour before the television screens turn blank. A steady, high note almost like a siren, like a warning, fills the sudden quiet of the building.

Layla's eyes fall shut. She breathes in, out. The last time she heard that sound, it was to inform the country that the Black Sun took Washington, D.C. Took it, made it theirs. The time before that, it was to announce that Denver was destroyed. Of course, that she already knew, could feel it in the shaking ground, could smell it in the smoking air.

"Citizens of this great country," a woman's voice says. Layla looks up at the television, body tense, fingers digging into the sides of her chair. Her pulse races in her ears. "We, the Black Sun, have a request to make." The woman on the screen is dressed in the dark green uniform all the terrorists wear, a hat covers her short hair, and a bandana is tucked around the lower half of her face.

Why she needs to hide her face, Layla can't understand. Shame, she would hope, but Layla wouldn't count on it. The room behind the woman gives no clue as to where she could be located. Wooden walls without windows, newspaper clippings taped in random places. A desk is behind her, but her body hides what's on it.

Her teammates exchange looks. Never before has an announcement been about a request. The terrorists take what they want. Dread fills her stomach and slithers up her throat like a burning poison.

"The request is a simple one," the terrorist says. "Give us your former president or give us New York City."

The cafeteria erupts in gasps and cries of outrage. Her teammates curse. Layla keeps quiet, keeps focused on the woman on the television who pauses, eyes crinkling in a way that shows them she's smiling under the checkered bandana. If only Layla could reach through the screen and use one of those sharp blades she wielded today.

Spreading her arms, the woman steps closer to the camera, until all that can be seen is her face, her gleaming, normal brown eyes. She likes this, enjoys causing fear and death. "What do you think, Mr. President? Feeling generous tonight? Or is it good night for New York City?"

The screen cuts off. The same video starts again a minute later.

Some of the hybrids leave after that first two-minute video. Layla and her team sit in silence until the tenth replay.

It's she who breaks the hypnotic state they seem to be in. "He won't do it," she says, throat tight with worry and anger. "The president. He won't give himself up."

The fact that the president was a coward came into light the day of the first bombing, and he has been in hiding since the war went to hell for them. They say he's partly responsible for them, the hybrids, being possible. They say he helped bring the scientists and remaining military personnel together. Truthfully, Layla doesn't care. Not after everything the Black Sun has done while he stays hidden away.

"He won't have a choice," Kyrin says, voice like gravel. "The people who know where he is will make him."

"And how do you know this?"

He sighs loud and long. Layla's beginning to wonder who has the real anger problem here. "I'm from Chicago," he says, and Layla all but flinches. "Yeah. That explanation enough?"

Chicago. Basically, a war zone in itself. Some of the worst members of the Black Sun took up residence there, corrupting and terrorizing the entire city, holding it hostage since the beginning of the war. Throughout the last year there has been footage on the news, meant as a warning for everyone. Just watching those segments was enough to make her stomach churn, but what Kyrin must have seen—what he had has to have done…

All she says is, "How did the scientist get in there? How did they get you out?"

His face is hard with forced indifference, but Layla can see it in his eyes, can see the memories screaming past.

"It was different from your experience," Jax says. His hand moves under the table, probably to move around Kyrin's waist. "That's all you need to know." He stands, pulling Kyrin with him. "Now let's get out of here. We've got another early day tomorrow."

When she steps out into the night and makes the short walk to their housing unit, she can't help but to watch them: her team. For the first time, true curiosity spikes. She doesn't know any of them. Where they came from. What they did. That's another thing she needs to do, she decides. Find out who these people are and find out whether or not she really belongs with them.

Don't be a fool. Control is temporary.

CHAPTER TEN

t's not until later that night, when they're all back on their floor settling down and digesting the news from the Black Sun, that Layla slips her wet hair into a ponytail and drags her tired body to search for more answers. More advice. Earlier, Mick said he used to have problems like she does, though not as intense. If the commanders are watching her tomorrow, this conversation needs to happen tonight.

And even with Kyrin feeling so confident that the president will be handed in, against his will or not, they have no guarantee what will happen, no guarantee that the people who know where the president is will succeed or fail. Layla wouldn't put it past the president to let one of their most populated cities be destroyed. He has already let so many people die without showing his face. He's more than half the reason the rest of the world refused to help them with the Black Sun. He would let the world think he was already dead if it would keep himself comfortable and safe. In fact, Layla is amazed that he hasn't done so already—faked his death and got out of the country.

She had asked her teammates on the walk back to their housing unit, but nobody at the compound has the information to where the terrorists store any of their bombs and missiles. They don't know where the weapons would be fired from to be able to send hybrids there to destroy them.

Layla didn't think it was possible to feel more useless than she did the day the ground shook beneath her feet, knowing without a doubt that her parents wouldn't be coming home. But having come this far, having been changed into a hybrid, feeling readier to fight than she has in her entire life, and not being able to...

Wiping the wetness from her eyes, she charges from her room on her own mission. Training with the four of them would be more effective. She could get all their opinions and advice, but what she heard earlier stops her from asking. She had listened to find out what her leader and second-in-command were doing, and heard them strategizing, creating back up plans and fail safes, pouring through information on the Black Sun leader, running through plays of what the president might do, what people will push the president to do... The tense tone of Kyrin's voice and the determined one of Jax's was enough to put her off the idea.

She stops before Mick's door, hesitating for a reason she doesn't understand. Celia's voice floats out of the next door on the left. She can be heard over the sound of the shower, singing a pop song that has been on the radio for years and years. Layla's not going to lie, Celia's got a pretty awful singing voice.

Taking a breath, she raises her fist to knock on the door, only to have it open at the barest scrape of her knuckles. Mick's wide shoulders take up the doorframe, blocking anything beyond it. He's in his pajamas: loose, long pants, and a plain matching shirt. Layla's outfit is similar, dull colors and all. For a moment, she lets herself wish she could have picked her own clothes, then she squashes that desire down with everything else. It's stupid to crave something so material.

"Hey," she says when he continues to stare at her with sleepy eyes. If she wasn't so tired herself, she might feel badly for keeping him awake.

He moves back some, letting Layla into his room. It's a lot like hers, but with the feeling of being lived in. From what she has been told, Mick only arrived a month before her, making the fourth member of Team Thirteen, but it looks like he has been here for far longer than that.

Drawings and writing cover the entirety of the back and right walls, sketched in pencil and pen and marker. Pictures of what looks like maps, cities, and houses, and even smaller drawings of animals and people. She recognizes the faces of their team members, but the rest, she suspects, must be people he used to know, maybe his family and old friends.

"You did all these?" Layla asks, instantly regretting it despite her curiosity. Even with her new goal of getting to know them, she didn't mean tonight. Not with the Black Sun's threat on all their minds.

Mick just gives her a tired smile. "One of the members from Jax's old team started the maps. I just expanded." Mick combs his fingers through his loose hair. "But I'm guessing that's not why you came in here. What's up?"

A large mug packed full of markers, pens, and pencils of varying lengths sits on the floor next to his bed, positioned so that, if he wanted, he could simply reach down and snag a utensil while lying in bed. Layla focuses on that when she talks to him.

"About tomorrow, with the commanders. What exactly do I need to do?" Like he didn't hear her, Mick turns, pulls down the covers on his bed, and adjusts his pillow. Layla closes her eyes, takes a deep breath, and prays for patience. It doesn't help. "I know what I need to do," she says, words all but bursting from her. "Do a good job in blades and be nice and competent and stay in control and impress them so we can get our missions." She takes a breath, holding it in for a few seconds. "But how do I do all that?"

Before he can answer, the door bangs open behind them. "You just do what you did earlier today. You know, in sharps—not the disastrous firearms incident," Celia says, walking into the room. She's dressed in clothes almost the same as Layla's. Her wet hair leaves dark patches on her shoulders. If it was anyone else, Layla would have wondered how she finished in the bathroom so fast. "You weren't in your room," she explains at Layla's surprised expression. "And I was listening at the door."

Instead of plopping down on the bed like she did last night in Layla's room, Celia takes a seat right in the middle of the floor. She pats the floor beside her. Shaking her head, Layla joins her. It's hard and uncomfortable, and the coolness of it leaks through her pants into her skin. Layla crosses her legs and frowns at her feet. "It will be different," she says. "They're going to be watching me, judging me. Kyrin will be there and—"

"Don't be bothered by Kyrin," Mick says. "He'll come around."

Layla scowls at the floor. "You keep saying that."

"It's only the second time I've said it, and it's true. Now," he slips off the bed to join them on the floor, legs crossed and leaning forward. "We know Jax's method of helping you didn't exactly work." Celia snorts, and mutters something too mumbled and quiet for Layla to understand. Mick ignores her. "His particular method helped me when I first got here. Getting my aggression out through violence."

"He did that with you?" Layla asks, interrupting him. Jax's method actually worked for Mick, unlike with her. Instead of calming her down, instead of releasing her anger, it created more. So much that she blacked out from it.

Both Mick and Celia nod. "There are other things I've tried since then. Things I still do. I think I know one of those strategies that might help you." At Layla's nod, he continues. "Focus on one thing, maybe something like a memory, that calms you down and makes you feel safe." Head shaking before she realizes, Layla pushes down all the memories that instantly float into her mind. All her good memories are packed with the awful truth that they will never happen again. Those people are gone.

"Or a steady sound," Mick amends flawlessly. "I noticed you

doing that earlier today in the infirmary."

Pluck. Pluck. Pluck. The sound of a needle sewing Jax's skin back together.

Celia stretches her legs out, bending over them in a stretch. With the three of them taking up almost the entirely of the floor, the tips of her toes poke into Layla's leg. "It would need to be something always available," she says.

"Not necessarily," Mick says. "It could be a number of things. A heartbeat, footsteps, someone's voice. Really anything that you can focus on that will distract you from the rage." He holds out his hands and wiggles his fingers until Layla sets hers on top. "You listen to it, drown everything else out so that sound is all you hear, and breathe. Then little by little let your surroundings come back."

Celia frowns, eyeing Layla with more intensity than she has seen on her face before. "It's not a permanent solution," she says. "You have to understand that."

"I just need something for tomorrow," Layla says. "Show me."

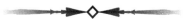

Celia watches, all but holding her breath, as Layla closes her eyes and follows Mick's instructions. She knows the two of them think she does not understand. She hasn't felt the anger Mick still has buried deep inside. She hasn't felt the anger she saw in Layla this morning, anger than she felt and smelled in the air like it was a tangible thing, but she knows that distractions only go so far in helping.

It's true, Layla is great with knives, but Celia thinks something is missing. Having watched her train with Mick all afternoon, Celia might have the answer. That is her job; to see what the others do not, but with the commanders coming tomorrow, it might have to wait.

"Try with my heartbeat," Mick says. Celia doesn't hide her eye roll, not that they are looking at her anymore.

It makes sense, of course, that Layla should focus on his heartbeat. He is the one that's going to be right beside her during tomorrow's little test. But this is Mick, and she can't stop herself from rolling her eyes at his poor attempt at flirting. Celia's far from blind. She saw Layla in the cafeteria earlier with that other newbie. William Fisher, that's his name. A shark hybrid. He was in Layla's group, someone from her school, someone she obviously knows well.

Her trained eyes notice when Mick's hands tighten. "Breathe, Layla," he says, firm and commanding. Celia expects her to growl at him like she has seen her do a handful of times already. "Don't hold your breath." It's not a growl, but the deep breath she takes is laced with a rolling crackle from deep in her throat.

She opens her amber eyes, showing how they glow in the low light. The first time she saw that, Celia had hidden her burst of excitement. *Glowing eyes.* She has seen so many hybrids here, is surrounded by more of them than regular people, but glowing eyes are something she barely ever sees. This girl… she is going to be great.

If she can get herself together, that is, and fast.

Celia watches as her newbie's awe leaves her eyes and her smile falls from her face. She has a moment to think, *Well, that didn't work*, before Layla says, "I can hear them out there. Talking about me."

Layla's hands tighten around Mick's until her knuckles turn white. Celia thinks she hears a crack. "Layla—"

"Kyrin's still trying to get me off the team." Her head tilts gently to the side like it will help her hear better than she already does. "He's saying that even without me, they can convince Helland and Cape to give you better missions."

Celia sees it as blood forms where Layla's nails dig into Mick's skin. She doesn't fight the eye roll and exasperation that comes from her actions. This girl is wound tighter than both her parents put together, and there is a good chance it will come back to bite them. Literally.

Knowing she will probably regret it, Celia clears her throat nice and loudly, causing both Mick and Layla to wince and snap their eyes open. Mick glares at her while Layla rubs at her ears. "Listen," she says, her stare not wavering when Layla's bright amber eyes swing to meet hers. "Kyrin isn't just going to roll over like a happy puppy for you. He knows you have problems. Just like the rest of us know, and just like you know." A faint blush raises to Layla's cheeks at her words. Embarrassment, not for being scolded, Celia notes, but for addressing that she has issues.

Celia waves a hand in front of her face as if to brush it aside. They all have issues. "Instead of getting all cavewoman crazy about it, prove to him that you belong on this team."

A spark lights Layla's eyes at the challenge. Celia smiles, pats Mick and Layla on their knees, and gets up to leave. The two of them have a whole night to practice, but she has done her part here.

*I've heard so much about you, and I can't say
I'm surprised to see the fear in your eyes.*

CHAPTER ELEVEN

*L*ayla is woken up before the sun is in the sky the next morning, and after grabbing a granola bar and fruit from their small kitchen, she and Mick head to the training center. She eats her merger breakfast on the way, only a little surprised to see fellow hybrids walking about. Some head to their housing units, but even more go to the labs and the testing center. From the sound of it there's at least one other team training this early, but they stay in the combat room.

Mick and she practiced for a few hours last night. She started with his pulse, focusing on it, letting it fill her head and calm her mind. Then, she found the sound of Celia's pulse, doing the same with hers. Then Jax's, and, reluctantly, with Kyrin's.

Just in case, Mick had told her, but she still felt a little weird about it, deciding to stick to Mick's instead of the other's. It was almost like an invasion of privacy for her to listen to their pulses, and, at least, Mick knew she was doing it, encouraged her to.

For the first half hour, she warms up with throwing knives and basic fighting maneuvers, keeping Mick's heartbeat in her ears the whole time. This time her opponent is a six-foot, blue and black dummy. His face has her lips curling over her sharp teeth. The material for the head is completely blank, only with dips and raises to show where the eyes and nose should be.

It could be anybody.

Right now, nervous anxiety bubbles away inside of her. The

hollow dips that make the dummy's eyes are teasing and mean, telling her that Helland and Cape will never deem her worthy enough. Just like Kyrin. In fact, the longer she practices the more the dummy's face begins to look like his.

"What's so funny?" Mick says. He has been standing close, watching every move she makes, offering both praise and instructions along the way.

Layla nods her head toward the dummy, a wicked smile stretches across her face. "Reminds me of someone," she says.

Chuckling, he runs his hand through his loose hair. A habit Layla notices more and more. "I hope it's not me."

She eyes him up and down with a smirk. "Nah."

She continues with the dummy and knives for another twenty minutes before the rest of the team shows up. Jax walks in first, half a bagel held between his teeth. As always, he looks ready for anything. He drags along a still messy-looking Kyrin who clutches a mug in his free hand. Celia, dressed in dark leggings and a tight long-sleeve shirt rushes up to her.

"I brought you guys coffee!" she says, shoving a warm cup in Layla's face. She flinches away and forces her bared teeth into a smile. Celia watches them, practically buzzing in her combat boots, until Layla takes couple drinks.

"Jax said it might be a bad idea to give you some," she says. "With your emotions and stuff, but I think it will do you some good what with the commanders coming to watch. You don't want to look like a sleep deprived sloth, you know? And you did so good with us last night. You will do great today. I know it."

Her words leave her mouth so fast that Layla isn't sure she heard them all correctly. However, she did hear enough to look questioningly at Jax, hoping he can elaborate on the whole coffee and emotion thing, but he's too busy wrestling a jelly limbed Kyrin into one of the few chairs they have in the room. Layla fights to keep the smirk off her face. If anyone is going to be looking like a sleep-deprived sloth, it's not her.

Layla drinks at least half of her coffee before handing it back to Celia, stopping her detailed story of the dream she had last night. "You can finish it off for me," she says.

Jax appears next to them in an instant, setting Layla's nerves on fire and knocking Mick's heartbeat from her ears. "No," he says, snatching the cup out of Celia's hands and giving Layla a look that suggests that she's the crazy one. "Do you see this?" He jabs his thumb at Celia's shuffling frame. "Give her more coffee and she will combust, but not before sending us all to the infirmary with brain damage."

"But, Jax…" Celia drags out his name for several seconds.

Jax groans. "Oh my gosh. Just—just go do something non-damaging, please. And you two," he points to Layla and Mick, "continue training. Start on the simulation soon. That's what the commanders are going to want to see. I need to get Kyrin functioning before they come."

"Was there any news about the president?" Layla asks before he walks away. Having started training so early, she didn't get to step foot in the cafeteria to hear any news about the Black Sun's latest threat.

Jax pauses, then sighs. "They put a picture of him on the TVs. Pretty gruesome. You're lucky you didn't see it. It was still on when we left. He turned himself in, or someone else turned him in, but you need to focus on training right now."

After making sure Celia is busy, Jax walks away, muttering darkly under his breath. Layla breathes a sigh of relief. Their president's death is nothing to celebrate, but she will gladly take it over the bombing or takeover of one of the country's most popular cities. Hopefully she will be able to catch the picture of him during lunch. No matter how gruesome it might be, she wants to see the proof for herself.

By the time the old clock positioned above the training room door ticks to the big number eight, Kyrin is up and making it his job to tip Layla off balance. He circles around the area she practices in with Mick, a frown on his face and his black eyes narrowed into slits. A steady stream of curses leaves Layla's mouth as he once again circles behind her.

It's his little test to see if she can keep her temper in check. Even she knows that she's not doing well. Mick is trying to help, offering suggestions and reminding her of what she learned last night. Right now, they're pirouetting around each other, jabbing here and slicing there. It's mostly footwork. Something she's finding both fun and challenging.

Mick juts forward. She jumps back. Kyrin's dark, lanky form appears from the corner of her eye, and Mick gets in a jab with a blunt knife. Layla growls under her breath, turning her attention back to Mick, but continuing to keep an eye on Kyrin. She can't seem to help it. Her mind refuses to ignore his circling dance.

Under the dim ceiling lights, Mick sighs and straightens from his stance. He doesn't disagree with Kyrin's test. No, he thought it was a wonderful idea. "I know it's hard," he says, moving a few pieces of hair out of his face.

Unconsciously, Layla copies his movements, and pushes her sweat-damp hair back. That seems to be all that she has been doing since she woke up this morning: copying what Mick does. She shakes her head at herself.

"I can't ignore him," she says, eyes following Kyrin as he slinks around the other side of them.

"Then don't." Layla's eyes snap back to her instructor. "Out in the field, on a mission, there are going to be times where you have multiple opponents. You aren't going to be facing off one to one. It will be one to two or three or ten."

Layla nods. "Like in the testing simulation."

"Right. So, you see them, you hear them. You know where they are, but you know where your main focus needs to be," he says. "Right now, the others are watching. You know where Jax and Kyrin and Celia are, but you are focused on me."

Just hearing that has Layla reaching out, finding her teammates, seeing what they're doing. Her eyebrows draw together, and she cranes her neck to where she hears Celia's rapid pulse. She's off to the side, picking through weapons and humming under her breath.

Layla can only see the very top of her head, her dark hair shining under the light. Feeling her stare, Celia looks up at her, green eyes peeking between the shelves of weapons.

"What are you doing?" Layla asks, all but forgetting Mick and Kyrin.

Celia comes out from behind the shelves, two different blades in her hands. "I was thinking all last night, and I finally figured it out," she says. Now the rest of the team are focused on her, too.

Jax leaves his post by the door to come closer to them. "Figured what out?" he says.

Celia holds the large, wicked blades out in front of her, looking them over. "She needs a bigger weapon. The throwing knives are good, especially for long distance since she doesn't like guns, but for close range she needs something different."

Layla takes the blades from Celia, feeling their weight in her hands. They're as long as her forearm and then some. Mick points her to the black and blue colored dummy. The rest of the team follows, watching as she tries out the motions Mick instructs her through.

The movements are different than with the smaller blades. Her whole body must be used to wield them, to control them. Layla likes them just as much as the smaller blades, but after ten minutes with the dummy, Celia clicks her tongue.

"Still not right," she says, shaking her head.

Kyrin sighs, annoyed and as frustrated as ever. "She's doing fine with them," he says. "We don't have time for this right now."

Celia turns her back on him, ignoring him completely. Hands on her hips, she surveys the weapons around them. "Come on," she says, gesturing to Layla. "If you want to impress them, you need the right weapons."

Wiping the sweat from her face, Layla follows her, casting a glance at Jax. She doesn't care what Kyrin thinks about this, but she wants to make sure it's okay with her leader. Celia can get ahead of herself, Layla knows that already. But Jax just glances at the clock and gives her a nod.

"You will do well with two," Celia says as they walk through the shelves, "and they don't have to be matching."

Somewhere along the way, Layla sets the two blades in a random spot. They search through the shelves and the tables and the walls. Celia immediately rules out any small blades, as well as any ones that are similar to the two she just tried.

Layla runs her fingers over a table of axes, looking them over as they walk by. Her eye catches a medium sized one towards the middle. Unlike the shining axes around it, this one has a matte black finish. Celia looks back at her when she stops, stares, and bends over the wide table to pick it up. She holds it out across her palms, testing the weight and the roped grip. Layla meets Celia's excited gaze and smiles, all teeth and bright eyes.

"Well," Celia says, "that's one."

They look over the axes on the table. Already decided that the shining ones could attract too much attention on a mission, she studies the axes with duller blades. Celia elbows her, showing a two-foot-long axe, double bladed, and used looking.

All Layla has to do is pick it up to know it's perfect. She would have to use two hands for it to be effective in a fight, but the different length will come as an advantage.

Taking one of her axes in each hand, Layla jiggles on the balls of her feet. Her grip adjusts perfectly to the rough handles. She can't wait to try them out. "Let's go show the boys."

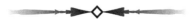

It's not until two excruciatingly slow hours later that consists of Mick and the rest of the team pushing her harder and harder with her new axes and different knives that Layla finally hears the elevator churning to a stop outside the blades room. She freezes, heart lodged in her throat, only to have Mick run into the back of her and simultaneously get decked in the head with a hard candy.

Layla tries to hold the growl building in her throat at bay, but she ends up choking on it instead. She glares up at the rafters where she can see nothing but a few strands of dark hair. "Celia!" she says in a hushed yell, worried the two commanders outside would be able to hear. Celia chuckles from her place high above them and peaks her head out so Layla can see one of her too bright eyes wink down at her. An hour ago, Celia had taken up throwing things at her as another form of distraction. Layla doesn't appreciate it.

Behind her, Mick grasps both her upper arms and gives them a short squeeze. She's not going to go into this slowly. Impress them in the first ten seconds, that's what Jax said. As soon as she and Mick take the short walk to the simulation area, the elevator doors slide open, and Jax rushes forward to meet them.

Layla doesn't dare look behind her at the sound of quiet greetings. Mick positions her stiff body at the starting mark. Chuckling, he jostles her around. "Loosen up," he says. She's so focused on the sound of approaching steps that she almost doesn't hear him.

Jax told her that the introductions will come after the two

commanders watch her practice, but she turns her nerves to steel, and turns to see them. The woman, tall and commanding, catches her eye first. Even though she wears the same type of suit as the assistant in the hybrid testing building, she looks more put together, if that's even possible. Her hair, the darkest brown and striped with grey, falls loosely around her shoulders. Her smile is easy as she quietly listens to Jax talk.

The man next to her is all but her complete opposite. The top of his balding head just reaches her shoulder, and his tight-fitting suit does nothing to hide the slight jiggle of his body when he moves. There's a strained look on his face as he flicks his eyes around the room.

Layla tenses when his eyes land on her. They are bright blue, so bright in fact that she wonders if he has the hybrid serum running through his DNA. His attention shifts from her to Mick and then to Celia high above them before landing and staying on Jax or Kyrin next to him.

Another hard candy hits Layla on the head, and before she can start growling up at Celia, like every part of her body is urging her to do, Mick tugs at the axes strapped to her hips and thighs. A silent command to take them off. To get ready. She does, turning the handles against her palms to find the perfect grip. When she settles, Mick attaches another row of throwing knives around her upper arm and grabs at her chin with his thumb and forefinger.

He ignores her warning display of teeth as he forces her head down with a not-too-soft yank. "My heartbeat," he says, voice low. "Listen to it."

Layla wants to curse at him for ordering her around, but the voices of Jax and the commanders make the words freeze in her throat. She doesn't need to turn around again to know they are watching her. Mick's eyes bore into hers, neither helping nor worsening the static anger in her head. For one panicked moment

Layla wishes she had taken the picture of her and her parents with her today, but then Mick taps his fingers where they grip against her jaw. An annoyed breath huffs out of her nose, but he ignores that too. "I'm going to turn on the simulation to an advanced level, and you are going to hit every target that appears."

A retort is building in her throat. A sarcastic one. Focus on him while probably hundreds of targets and missiles are being thrown at her? Not to mention Celia, who will probably still chuck pieces of candy at her. No big deal, right? The look in his eyes stops her from saying a single negative word.

She feels anger already bubbling in her veins, the pressure making her pulse race. She takes a deep breath and tries to gather the feelings to shove them down deep where she can't feel them. "Your heartbeat. Just like last night."

He nods, satisfied, and releases her jaw. Not a second later, his hands whip around her as she stands perfectly still. He places knives around her other arm, at her waist, and around her thighs. He's giving her time. Giving her time to find his pulse, to focus on it.

Last night, his room was all but silent. She could find his heartbeat like it was nothing. It's harder now with the conversation going on behind her, a conversation strictly about her. Mick, sensing she's having trouble, slows down his frantic knife placing. Giving her even more time.

She can feel them watching, can hear the questioning tone in their voices, but they can only see the back of her. So, like last night, she closes her eyes. Breathes in and out. Mick's hands are still on her thigh, fastening yet another sheath for a set of flat, slim daggers. He's right there in front of her.

Seconds pass, and finally, some of the tension leaks out of her. "Found you."

His heart beats in a steady rhythm, even slower than the night before. Now, she knows why he had instated she focus on his instead of her own or Celia's rapid pulse. She pushes the thought aside, needing to stay calm. She focuses harder, wrapping his sound around her like a heavy blanket until it's loud enough that her head rattles with it. The voices from behind her are all but nonexistent. There's no one here watching.

A small tap on the top of her head has her opening her eyes.

"Alright," Mick says, and Layla rocks back as his voice bashes against her skull louder than his heartbeat. He plucks something out of her hair, a yellow candy, and plops it in his mouth with an excited grin. Layla grimaces at him. "You're all ready to go. I'll be over there." He points to where Layla knows the control panel is. "Don't kill Celia."

Layla watches him walk away, keeping the sound of his steady pulse loud around her. As he fiddles with the controls, she looks down at herself, taking in the locations of her weapons. There are some she can't see, around her hips and on her back. After returning her axes to her hips, she searches for the handles and tests how they leave their sheaths. The one across her back feels long but light, for close combat. Beside her axes, the rest are smaller in size, for throwing and swift jabs.

Around her, the lights dim, and small spotlights hit the training area randomly. Already she has two knives in her hands, ready to throw.

She has done the blades simulation four times now, all at different levels, but never at advanced. She can't hear the countdown over the *lub-dub, lub-dub* of Mick's heartbeat, so she counts herself. Ten seconds, there are ten seconds between when the lights dim and flicker, and when the targets appear.

She breathes in. Breathes out.

Movement explodes around her. Human shapes pop up and out of shadows, the outlines of them changing color to blend into their background. Without her enhanced sight, Layla wouldn't be able to see them. Small, circular objects fly around in every direction. The lights flicker and move rapidly. Layla blinks, pushing the lights to the back of her mind as she spots a target. She throws the blade in her right hand, taking the target down. Then, not missing a beat, she aims for another in the corner of her eye.

She lets the sounds of bullets fill her mind along with the sound of Mick's blood pumping through his veins. They whiz by as she dodges the ones that get too close. They aren't real, they can't hurt her, but the effect is real enough to have her gritting her teeth, readying for pain.

The simulation seems to go in slow motion as the number of targets grow. Her hands are quick to find more blades on her person, and they are even quicker to throw them. The targets light up around her as she hits them. She knows from her earlier practice that if she misses they go dark. Layla makes sure she doesn't miss.

The targets get closer. They try to sneak up behind her, something they never did in the practice runs, and some new instinct is the only thing telling her they're back there. She spins around, trying to grab the sword-like blade from her back, but as she tugs on it, it stays firmly in the sheath. Her harsh breath catches in her throat. Already sweat drips into her eyes, stinging them. Even more sweat coats her hands and runs down the middle of her back.

And just like that, she's back in the hybrid testing simulation with what seems like thousands of terrorists closing in on her. Pulling at the sword harder, Layla curses. It doesn't budge. The heartbeat is still surrounding her, but it speeds up with every step the targets take. She almost looks away from the approaching forms to search him out, but she stops at the last second.

Another hard candy bounces off her head, stinging worse than the ones before. A growl rips from her throat at the pain. *Save the axes for last*, Celia said. She tries the sword one last time, but she must have put it back the wrong way when she tested it out.

Layla grabs the hilt of the shorter axe instead. The smooth, dark handle slides easily from its holder. She slashes out with it, almost too late. The two closest targets light up when the blade hits them before disappearing. Layla dodges close-range bullets from another one of the targets. The hand not busy with the axe grabs a small throwing knife from around her thigh and sends it flying toward the gunman.

The simulation continues on like this, her throwing knives and slashing with her axe, for minutes or hours more, until her lungs feel like they're bursting out of her chest, and the axe slips and slides around in her sweaty grip. One last target lights up a foot in front of her. The place where its head should be is gone in less than a second.

The lights return to normal, signaling the simulation ending. Layla sags with relief, her heart beating out of her chest, but then she remembers why she's here and exactly who is watching. She straightens her shoulders immediately and puts her weapons away on her person.

When she looks at the two commanders, their expressions give nothing away. The woman's, Helland's, mouth moves, but with Mick's heartbeat still drumming in her ears, Layla can't hear what she says.

Layla shakes her head around to bring the other sounds back. "I'm sorry?" she says.

Jax waves her over, but her legs make it difficult to move, like they're as stiff and wobbly as a newborn deer. *You did good,* she tells herself. *Better than good.* Straightening her still sweaty back, Layla moves forward until she stands right in front of them. This close, she can see that the man is definitely not a hybrid. His eyes may be a brilliant blue, but they are normal, human. Jax and Kyrin stand next to him, both looking too calm and composed for her liking.

The woman's smile doesn't reach her eyes. Light lines frame her red-painted lips. She could be Mrs. Jones' age, and maybe a few years older than the mad beside her. After being around only hybrids for two days straight, it's almost shocking how normal they look up close. The woman's voice is smooth when she says, "I said that was impressive."

"Thank you, ma'am."

"Most people just call me Helland here," she says. Helland sticks out her hand for Layla to shake. Using her pants, Layla wipes the sweat from her skin before she grabs it. "And this is David Cape. Again, we just call him Cape."

Layla shakes his hand as well, refusing to flinch at his hard grasp. "Layla Wilson," she says. "Nice to meet you."

"Yes, of course. We have already heard some interesting things about you, Ms. Wilson." His bright blue eyes turn hard as diamonds in an instant, but the closed-mouth smile stays on his face.

Ghosting her hands over the axes on her sides, Layla plants her own smile on. It must look as painful and forced as his, because he takes a small step back. Interesting, she muses, that a commander of a hybrid compound is afraid of her.

Helland clears her throat, and says, "You did very well in the blades simulation. Not to mention in the team testing, Layla—" Celia, having come down from the rafters to stand next to her, elbows her in the side, in a silent order to pay attention. "—but like Cape said, you had an incident only yesterday. Not to mention what we hear the others around the compound say about you." Heart plummeting, Layla opens her mouth at the same time Jax does, but Helland cuts them off with a wave of her hand. "Cape and I will take some time to discuss your new member and your missions before we come to a conclusion."

There is a whisper in my bones,
running wild in my veins,
racing to my heart, racing to my brain.

CHAPTER TWELVE

A week later, the team still hasn't heard any word from Helland or Cape. Even the few times Layla talked to Fisher didn't bring any hopeful news. The other residents of the compound have their opinions. Mostly surprise at her not being sent away with the other out-of-control hybrids. Celia keeps telling her to stop listening to other peoples' conversations. Which is practically impossible when it sounds like they're yelling in her face.

Her team pretends that everything's fine, says it's normal for the commanders to take a while, but Layla spends her time constantly buzzing with nerves and apprehension. She just wants to know, good news or bad. The waiting is killing her, and besides, she had waited enough back home.

She was deemed as good as Mick with knife throwing, and even better than he is with axes. After a long conversation, the team decided she was able to control her emotions enough to give the next step in physical training a try, hand-to-hand combat. And even though he didn't show any signs of awkwardness or sketchiness from their last visit there, Jax takes it slow. Excruciatingly slow with breaks in between each session to check in with her.

They've all taken to doing that: checking in with her, making sure she's not about to snap. At first, it was helpful, reassuring even, but now every time one of them looks at her with that assessing look on their face, Layla fights to not roll her eyes, fights the tingling in her fingers, the urge to knock the questions back down their throats.

They're all on their housing floor now, in the living room. With a grunt, Layla plops her sore body on the colorful rug. Next to her, Kyrin looks smug. She thinks it might me the most positive look he's thrown her way since she got here, and even if it's because she's covered in bruises from getting pushed and beaten around, Layla will count it as improvement. Jax tells her that the bruises will heal by morning, and they usually do, but at this point, Layla doesn't think the broken skin on her knuckles will ever heal over completely.

It's late at night, hours past the time they usually go to sleep, but the five of them are all wide awake. They decided that no matter what news they get from the commanders, it would be best to teach Layla everything they know about the Black Sun. So, at midnight, with mostly serious expressions, they take turns telling her about the terrorists. Some of it she knows already, but there's even more she doesn't.

All the papers she's seen Kyrin obsess over are scattered in the middle of the floor, arranged in a spider web pattern with the thinnest of strings connecting paper to paper. Kyrin points between three different pictures: a pixelated Black Sun base Jax scouted with his old team, a clear picture of the White House Layla thinks is from news coverage, and what looks like a hand drawn diagram of some of the advanced weapons the terrorists possess. Crammed, curly writing fills the margins on the pages, describing the location and details. Layla quickly reads over the small words before Kyrin dives in to explain it in more detail.

"This terrorist base is one of the biggest in the country," he says, pointing to the first picture. Across from the spread of papers, Mick hands her three more black and white pictures, and Layla looks them over carefully. They look like they're are all of the same base taken at different angles.

"The biggest we have found, at least," Celia says, eyes scanning the paper in front of her, "and it seems like more pop up every other week."

"There are teams that go on missions just to look for these bases. Scout them out and report back," Mick says across from her, answering her question before she can ask it. "Or some of our people on the outside give us the information."

Layla nods. The scientists injecting people with the hybrid serum aren't the only ones who help. There are others; former military, old government workers, and normal people who seek the Hybrid Force out, asking to join. Looking over the scattering of papers in front of her, she asks, "Have you gone on those types of missions?"

"There have been three," Jax says. He sits on one of the chairs, elevated above the rest of them to get a better look at the papers and the different ways the strings connect them. "Mostly busts."

Even more Layla understands why they need her. Why they need Cape and Helland to agree to give them higher-risk missions. They've been here for months training, learning, and strategizing, and they feel like they haven't accomplished anything to help in the war against the Black Sun.

They were brought here to fight, but the people in charge are too afraid, too cautious to let them. But their country has already lost so many people, she reminds herself. So many that they resorted to injecting teenagers with a solution that they have a fifty-percent chance of surviving, and even those who do survive might not have the strength or the guts to be fighters.

"What about before us?" Layla's eyes bore into her leader, like she can syphon the answers right out of his head. It's a topic no one has brought up, and she gets the feeling it's not something they usually discuss, but she needs to know as much as she can, and maybe she's just a little bit curious. "Before Team Thirteen. What about your old team?"

There's a second where Jax's fists clench around the arms of the chair with enough force to make the fabric squeak. Layla swears his face crumples, but when she blinks, his eyes are clear, the scrunched lines on his forehead are gone, and his hands lay gently on his knees. Still, Jax keeps his eyes firmly on Kyrin as he says, "We went on a lot of missions. We were one of the first teams made, and the best at the time."

Layla guessed as much from the rumors she collects every day. Most coming from Celia and Mick who unknowingly slip random details in their conversations. Team Three was great, one of the best. Until the mission where they were captured and killed by terrorists. Jax got away, the only one. Layla still doesn't know how that happened. She's not sure if she will ever find out.

"No matter what the commanders decide we will still be sent on scouting missions like we have been since Celia joined." His expression stays neutral, his dark brown eyes focused on Kyrin's black ones, nodding along to an unknown rhythm. Layla's eyes flicker between the two of them. "We will have to start stealth lessons soon. Maybe after a short lesson in the combat room tomorrow."

None of them mention anything about firearms and Layla can't help feeling relieved.

"Finally!" Celia jumps straight to her feet and throws her fist in the air, looking at Layla with a bright, excited smile. Stealth is her domain, like firearms is Kyrin's and sharps is Mick's. With how loud she usually is, Layla can't help but wonder how it's possible.

Layla grimaces at her. "I am not hanging around in the rafters."

"You say that now, but just you wait," she says. "You're a panther, right?"

Layla rolls her eyes. Celia knows exactly what she is. "Mountain lion."

"Yes, yes," she says in rapid procession. "You're a cat. You're going to be great at it."

Layla looks at the others—Mick's exasperated smile, Jax's eyes that don't hold an ounce of doubt, Kyrin's rumpled, shiny hair—and back to Celia. As much as she wants to take the terrorists down and save the country, she doesn't want to disappoint her team, her friends, more.

"Let's do this."

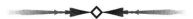

At three in the morning Layla's up and following the guys, her mind alive with excitement and curiosity. After spending hours being drilled on mission plans and every bit of information they have on the Black Sun, Layla can feel how anxious her team is.

They need a distraction. Something to clear their heads. Something fun.

At least, that's how Celia described it.

Layla's fingers twitch. Her eyes flicker over every face they pass and into the trees around them. They're far from the only ones walking down the pitch-black path to the training center. Insects create a constant melody that rings and buzzes in her ears. Despite the constant noise, she can still pick up the sound of soft boots on the leave strewn ground farther out into the forest: guards on patrol. With every step further down the path, the shouting gets louder. The clouded sky rumbles and cracks, as if wanting to add its own ruckus, make it all the louder. Bits of perspiration seem to linger around her. The forest air smells electrified and musty from the oncoming storm.

Beside her, skipping down the path, Celia says, "You're going to love it." The vicious smile on her face is convincing enough.

When they get to the doors, the three guys ahead of them turn around in perfect synchronization. Jax's eyes burn, staring hard at her. She rocks back on her heals. It's a look Layla has only seen in combat training, one that demands her to listen. She hates it.

Acting like Layla couldn't hear their entire conversation about her losing control during whatever it is they're about to do, he says, "You aren't going to fight. If you feel like you can't control yourself, you get one of us to get you out. Understand?"

Lightning cracks across the sky, highlighting Layla's gleaming teeth that are on full display in a smile even more vicious than the one Celia gave her minutes before. "I understand perfectly, *sir*."

He doesn't so much as flinch at her tone, only gives her that unnervingly steady stare, looking as though he can read her intentions on her face. Mick's head tilts to the side, looking her over, assessing her, but it's Kyrin who snarls, "If you do anything—"

"Helland and Cape still haven't decided on us yet," Layla interrupts him. She stuffs her hands into her pockets to hide how tight her fists are. "I will not risk their blessing for whatever this is."

At Jax's nod, they turn and lead her and a smirking Celia into the training center. What this is, Layla realizes as she steps out of the elevator and into the cramped floor of the combat room, is a fight. Between sweaty, jostling people, Layla can see the cage in the center of the room. Already, two hybrids are inside exchanging brutal hits.

Her team creates a line that snakes through the crowd of hybrids to get closer. People move when they see Jax, but limbs still push into her, scratching at her arms and poking into everywhere else. Layla thinks it's the first time her fellow hybrids haven't been wholeheartedly avoiding her. Never mind that they're probably too busy watching the fight to notice she's even there.

Flesh hitting flesh. Hoots and hollers. The smell of blood and sweat, of life and excitement.

Layla's heart pounds with anticipation. Her wide eyes try to take in as much as possible. This is not what she expected.

When the line that makes up her team comes to a stop, Mick pushes her in front of him, and the linked cage is inches from her face. One of the hybrids in the cage, a tall girl with dirty blonde hair, rolls to dodge her opponent's punch. The guy's fist crashes against the metal wall of the cage so hard that the entire thing rattles. Layla gapes at the display. The only hybrids she's seen fight are the ones on her team, and that was only during training. This type of fighting is different, rawer with less technique. Real. She grips the cold fence, her fingers threading through the gaps. The metal vibrates softly under her hands.

She stands, enthralled, until it's over. The blonde girl has the guy pinned to the ground, cutting off his airway until he beats at the floor in surrender. Her fingers release his throat and she springs to her feet. When the girl throws her hands up in victory, the crowd screams loud enough that Layla's head throbs. Pure excitement fills her from the tips of her toes to the hair on her head. Instead of covering her ears, Layla cheers just as loudly as everyone else.

Celia elbows her in the side and leans in close to her ear so that Layla can hear her when she says, "Told you that you'd love it."

And she does. It's the last thing she expected to see at a secret military compound. Especially when during the day, everything is so strict and controlled. They do their jobs during the day, but at night… Why did her team wait so long to show her this?

"Do the commanders know about this?" Layla asks, but Celia is already turning back to the cage, and doesn't hear her.

Mick, however, does hear her. "Helland has come and watched a few times," he says. "Cape is here at least once a week. If not more." He keeps bumping into the back of her from the wild pushing of the crowd around them. A few seconds pass where the girl in the cage continues to proclaim her victory before Mick says, "He's here now."

Layla turns to see his face, and follows the direction he nods in. True enough, Cape is there. He stands on one of the raised platforms situated outside the circle of the crowd. His gaze is trained on the inside of the cage, a slight frown on his face. There's not a trace of the forced, tight smile he wore when he met Layla a week ago.

Out of the two commanders, Cape is the quieter. The unspoken second in command. Next to Helland's professional, up front attitude, Cape is a shadow, silent and watching, only asking the questions he needs to. He's the one Layla feels she needs to be aware of, and most of all, the one she needs to impress.

Back in the ring, the two competitors shake hands, and walk out into the grabbing embraces of their friends. It's only seconds before two more appear in the cage. They were waiting right at the door, two guys, almost as big as Jax, with predatory grins stretched wide across their faces. Layla's own blood begins to race as they start the fight with brutal and wicked moves, laced with delighted laughter.

These two hybrids must be on teams. She can't picture them doing anything else but fighting. These are people in love with the fight, who were born warriors and soldiers and wouldn't have it any other way. Seeing that, seeing people like her, settles something in Layla's chest.

Her eyes follow every movement, cataloging the information for her next combat training. She raises her voice, loud enough for her team to hear her when she asks, "Are any of you going in there?" Just because Jax forbade her to fight, doesn't mean the rest of them can't.

But before they can answer the fanged hybrid lands a kick to the other's head so hard that he goes right down in a slumped heap, unconscious. Layla hisses through her teeth at the sound of his jaw breaking. Fueled by the violence, the crowd erupts, screaming and thrashing even louder than before.

The other fight lasted at least ten minutes, and it's such a surprise that this one ended so fast Layla doesn't catch herself from crashing face first into the fenced wall.

The anger comes fast, her vision slipping into a hazy, meaty red. She doesn't notice Mick's quick apology or Celia trying to catch her eye. What she does notice is Cape high up on his platform, leaning down to talk to someone. She only catches a glimpse of them through the crowd, but Layla knows who that someone is immediately. A growl rips from her throat, loud and raw enough to hurt.

"Mick," she says, not looking away from Cape or who he's talking to. Her nose and chin sting from hitting the fence. She's ready to unclench her fingers from the fence and grab onto Mick instead so he can pull her out of the training center and into the damp, open air. Jax and Kyrin, on the other side of Celia, don't seem to realize there's a problem.

His hand closes around her shoulder, turning her. Celia's pushes at her back to hurry her along, but then Cape stands, a microphone in his hand. He holds it close to his mouth, allowing it to screech over everyone's shouting. All heads swivel in his direction, and Layla forces Mick to stop pulling her through the crowd. Her breathing is hard, senses overwhelmed by the sudden silence. The need to run, to get out the door as fast as possible, courses through her. Layla can't put the team's chance of getting better missions in jeopardy. But she wants to know what will happen next, what his plan is.

"Thank you." The commander's voice rings out, echoing through her head. "We have a fighter here," he swings his hand to the cage, but Layla doesn't need to look to know who's there, "and he is looking for his competitor."

Already, Layla swears she can feel everyone's eyes on her, their sharp gazes seeing right to her racing heart. Murmurs fill the air around her. Celia curses, head swinging between the cage and Layla. She shoves hard at her back, but Layla stands firmly in place. Finally, having noticed something is wrong, Jax takes a step toward them.

"Some of you might have heard about her," Cape says, louder

now that he has the crowd hanging on his every word. "Her name is Layla Wilson."

The grip on her shoulder becomes painful, but it's the hybrid in the cage that now holds her attention. All thoughts of leaving the combat floor fade away. The roaring of the crowd is something distant. The hand on her shoulder loses its grip as she springs forward, back past her team and up to the cage wall.

He meets her there, pitch black eyes shining under the light.

"Hello, Kitty," Fisher says, jagged smile stretching wide across his face. "Want to play?"

I'm fine.

Layla concentrates on narrowing her senses down, trying to focus on what's right in front of her instead of the entire room and the soft rumbling sound of thunder. Following along the cage wall to the door, the crowd parts for her then closes in behind. Her team is no doubt going to try to stop her, so she wastes little time getting there. Her fingers slide over the cool links as she goes. Fisher walks with her on the other side of the fence, a small smile playing on his full lips.

Already in Cape's graces. Layla snorts. Of course, he is, but for exactly what reason, Layla isn't sure. Did he think that fighting her would gain him favor in the commander's eyes? His smile grows at her small laugh, and her breath catches at the sight of his wicked teeth, all of them jagged and sharp. She flashes her own. It's less of a smile and more of a warning.

Layla's only a foot away from the door when a hand shoots out from the mass of people and grabs her upper arm. A hiss escapes through her clenched teeth, but the grip only tightens. Jax emerges from the crowd, his expression enraged. His large body is close enough to Layla that it blocks out the view of the mob surrounding them.

His voice is deep, laced with an emotion Layla hasn't heard from him before. The look in his eyes is murderous. "I said no fighting," he says. "My one rule: you are not allowed to fight."

"I'm fine." And she is. The world isn't spinning anymore. The room is no longer misted in a red haze. Layla can feel the calm center of herself, like a blanket put over a fire to smother out the flame.

And maybe Jax senses it, or maybe he knows that refusing the fight isn't an option. Not with Commander Cape watching; not when he asked for it himself. Layla glances back at the man on his platform positioned above them all. He's back in his seat, hands trembling before him as he looks to her, Jax, Fisher, and the raging crowd.

Layla swears his eyebrows raise just the tiniest fraction. She swears a real smile can be seen tugging at the corners of his thin lips.

"You feel your control slipping even the slightest amount," Jax says, pulling her close so that she can focus on nothing but him, "you tap out. You get out of there. We are not sending anyone to the infirmary at death's door."

Layla turns, having heard Fisher chuckle at her leader's little speech. Before she can come up with a clever retort, she's roughly pushed towards the cage door by Jax. Layla straightens out her shirt and glares over her shoulder at him.

"I'll be right here," he says, running a hand over his shaved head. If Layla didn't know any better, she would say he's nervous. Who's she kidding? Of course, he's nervous. This could very well be the moment that Layla ruins everything. Jax throws a thumb over his shoulder. "The others are coming, too."

He opens the door for her, and Layla steps into the cage.

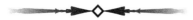

It's brighter than she thought it would be, like all the florescent lights are pointed toward the center of the cage. She and Fisher circle around. A dark, enthralling song runs through her veins, making her feel twitchy. It's different that the rage she's been feeling since she was injected. It's lighter, more exciting. Layla wants more of it. She wants it to be the only thing she feels.

They circle closer. The other participants didn't do this. They rushed right in, but Layla knows Fisher, and he's going to draw it out. Make it a show. Everything's so loud that it blends into a distant din. Through it, his voice stands out sharp and clear. "They got you on a tight leash, Wilson?"

Her head tilts to the side, and just because she knows no one can hear them over the crowd, she says, "They got you kissing the old guy's butt, Fish?"

A laugh is startled out of him. He looks beyond delighted, and Layla wonders if he feels the same twitching under his skin that she does. His voice lowers, deepens in an impression of her leader. "Stay within ten feet of one of us at all times, soldier." They circle closer, three feet between them. "Focus, soldier. Don't move unless I say, soldier."

Vision narrowing, Layla shows her teeth. He's within touching distance now, but her hands stay down, tense at her sides. She doesn't move for him, not yet. They're so close that he can lower his mouth to her ear without problem. "I remember how much you hate being ordered about." He draws back, just enough so she can meet his eyes. "Are they afraid of you?"

Yes.

The tingling stops.

And starts again a second later. It spreads across her skin like a million buzzing insects. She shivers at the intensity of it. A spike of panic slices through it, straight into her gut. What is this?

Turning to her team, to where Jax said they would be, Layla

is about to call it off. Blacking out right now in front of Cape and half the compound's hybrids would ruin them. She meets Jax's dark gaze, opens her mouth, but Fisher finally makes his move. She feels the movement of his body, the slight change in the air, and without looking behind, Layla ducks out of the way of his fist.

Fisher looks her up and down. From her bare feet to her burning eyes. He sucks on his teeth. "We have to give him a show, Wilson." He spreads his arms wide. "Want me to let you win?"

"Don't you dare." Layla stops circling around, instead shifting her weight from one foot to the other.

"Come on, then. Give me all you got."

The crowd screams louder, loud enough she wants to clutch at her head. Gritting her teeth, she spits out a curse.

And then she moves.

Fisher is right there with her, dodging her punch and dealing one of his own. She turns, feeling only the slightest contact against the loose fabric of her shirt. In a move she learned only yesterday, she grabs hold of his forearm and twists it behind his back. Then she kicks his legs out from under him.

He brings her to the matted floor with him, leaning into her to drag her down. He's fast, fast enough to spin around and pin her, but he doesn't go for the throat, he doesn't go for the easy way. Looking straight into her eyes, he punches her across the face.

Her vision is laced with black for just a moment, before everything comes into startling focus. Layla smiles, teeth coated in blood.

A show.

She can put on a show.

She gets up easily. Fisher wants her to. He doesn't make a move to try to stop her.

They're at it again. Punching, dodging, kicking, dancing around inside the cage until they're both covered in blood, their own and each other's, until their lungs feel like bursting and sweat rolls down their skin and their cheeks smart from smiling.

Until Layla thinks she loves this.

The crowd screams on, louder and rougher than ever. She catches a hard punch in the side, and gasps for air. This time it's Fisher who takes her to the ground, using the short moment of vulnerability to knock her feet out.

They roll, each trying to get on top. Locking her knees around his waist, Layla twists, forcing Fisher under her. Meeting his eyes for a split second, she bares her glistening canines, and lunges for his throat.

He surprises her with a shoving his forearm in the way of her bite, but it's too late for her to stop. Her teeth sink in to the flesh of his arm. Fisher yells a curse, and moving too fast for Layla to comprehend, he bends his knees on either side of her, plants his bare feet on her hips and kicks out hard enough that she goes flying.

And collides with the fenced wall.

Layla groans. What just happened? Her vision goes in and out of focus. Her brain pulses in her rattling skull. Fisher moves toward her and offers her a hand up. She's not sure if she will stay standing, but she grabs it anyway. His mouth moves, but Layla doesn't know what he says.

"What?"

"I said, I win."

Layla rolls her eyes, and instantly regrets it. The floor tilts under her. "I think I have a concussion," she says.

"Yeah. Probably, but I'm not saying sorry." He holds up his arm, showing off the bloody imprints from her teeth, already edged in a purplish bruise. "You bit me."

The two of them walk to the center of the cage. Their audience is screaming and stomping their feet. Layla looks to her team, to the stunned faces of the guys. She sees Celia ecstatically shrieking and waving her arms.

Fisher lifts her hand up into the air and smiles down at her. He's going to have a face full of bruises in a few minutes. Already some form, blue, black, and yellow around his eyes and mouth. "Think we did pretty good." His eyes dart to the commander on his platform. Layla's eyes follow.

Fear, that's what she sees. Then that tight, false smile.

Layla holds his gaze and bows just the smallest bit.

They say curiosity kills, but I think I'll be okay.

CHAPTER THIRTEEN

*T*he sound of her footsteps echo as she walks through the quiet white hallways. If she didn't have her enhanced hearing, she would think the building was completely empty, but she hears the nearly silent movements behind closed doors. The sounds of hundreds of heartbeats all blending together. The soft fall and shuffle of paper and objects. The place smells like strong cleaner, and it bites at her nose.

Layla tries peeking into as many rooms as possible, but most are locked. She could break the door knob with a twist of her wrist, she muses as she closes yet another door on the unassuming scientists who work between microscopes and whisper among each other. None of them bother to look up from their work to see who opened the door.

She could've ended up working here if it were not for Jax, Kyrin, Celia, and Mick. She could've been one of these bent over, tired-looking teenagers trying to find answers to questions she doesn't know. The thought is more than unpleasant, and she pushes it away.

After the fight with Fisher a few days ago, her emotions have been easier to control. Whether it was from getting into a genuine fight, being able to let the aggression out for real this time, or just being around him, she doesn't know, and she isn't going to waste the time to find out. She has felt better for days. That's all that matters.

Peeking into the next room, Layla finally finds what she's looking for. Who she's looking for. Compared to the others in the laboratory, he looks huge and out of place. Not for the first time, Layla wonders why he didn't get picked for a team. Sure, his aim wasn't great, but Layla can barely even shoot a gun. With the right weapon, he could be a strong asset on their side of the fight.

None of the hybrids look up from their work as Layla tip toes her way through the maze of laboratory tables and fragile equipment. Cam is shaking his head at a microscope when she gets close.

Layla taps him on the shoulder. "Cam."

Continuing to look at his work, he swats at her hand. "Not done," he mutters.

"Not done with what?" she asks, peeking around his shoulder. She sees neatly written notes, vials of colorful liquid, and small labeled containers.

He looks up at her question, the annoyed look on his face disappearing when he sees who it is. "Layla." A smile slowly spreads across his face. "What are you doing here?"

Layla shrugs, and casts her gaze around the room. "You said we would stay in touch."

Shifting awkwardly in his seat, Cam says, "Well, yeah. But…" He shakes his head seemingly unable to finish his thought. He distracts himself with peeling off his latex gloves.

The silence hangs in the air. Layla can hear his pulse gaining speed. Others in the room finally begin to take notice of her and stare, probably wondering why she's there, and if what they keep hearing around the compound about her is true. She's heard the gossip herself. They all must know about her by now. About how she sent her team leader to the infirmary on her first day of training.

Now it's her turn to feel awkward; she shuffles from foot to foot, searching the room for a steady heart beat to hold onto, but none of them, not even hers, is calm. Everyone, everyone in the room is afraid—and so is she—of what she might do to them if she loses control.

Layla clears her throat, tries and fails to ignore how some

of them flinch as if she yelled and lunged right for their throats. Turning on her heel, she hurriedly makes for the door. "I'm sorry," she says, avoiding Cam's eyes. "I'll just go. You're busy."

"Layla," Cam says, but his apologies are the last things she wants to hear.

Looking over her shoulder, she forces a smile, and watches how his eyes flicker from her sharp teeth, to the bruises on her cheeks and across her nose. Her smile drops. "Maybe another time," she says.

Cam makes to get up, but Layla's already out the laboratory door. Her feet are fast and silent as she storms through the too-white hallways. She wants to laugh it off, and maybe later she will. Perhaps with Celia, or maybe even Mick.

But… A monster. That's how they looked at her. Like she's a monster. As if she had blood dripping from her fanged teeth. As if she had horns protruding out of her hair.

It stings worse than the anger bubbling in her chest.

She turns a corner, dodging around a cart of laboratory equipment. Afraid. She scoffs. He wasn't afraid of her during the testing simulation. She just wanted to check in with him. See what they do in the labs. Get some time away from her team and their overbearing presence.

The door looms not ten feet in front of her when she's jerked back by a hand around her arm. With how fast she was walking and how hard the grasp is, she's surprised her shoulder didn't pop out of its socket. Still, it hurts enough to make her vision cloud, to force a small screech out of her lips.

"Let go of me," she says, lips pulled into a snarl.

The hand leaves her as if she burned it. "Sorry. Sorry," Cam says, voice soft but shaky. "I'm still not used to it. Are you okay?"

Pins and needles tingle up her arm. Rolling her shoulder, Layla sends him a glare. "I'm fine," she says. "What do you want?"

He straightens out from his hunched over position, bones

cracking with every movement. "You wanted to talk. To visit. I could use some time out of the labs."

Layla can feel the sneer take over her mouth, feel her lips stretch tight over her teeth. "Aren't you afraid of being sent to the infirmary?"

"Please, Wilson," he says, words bleeding with sarcasm. "I know you better than that."

Layla gives him an unimpressed look. They both know that's a lie. They went to school together and know each other by face and name. They might have seen each other each other every day at school, but that's as far as it goes.

Leading them out of the lab building and into the shaded, crisp air, Layla takes Cam's peace offering for what it is, and reins in her emotions. Slightly behind her, Cam takes a long breath and sighs. How long has he been in that building? It's still early in the morning, a few hours before most of the rest of the compound wakes up, but it seems like he has already been at it for hours.

They walk along the worn-down path, passing only a few blurry-eyed hybrids. Whether they're soldiers, scientists, or something else, Layla can't tell. Most of them all wear the same jumpsuit type outfit Layla did when she first got here. Having taken off his lab coat before he left the building, she can now see that even Cam wears one. Layla looks down at her own training gear. She hasn't worn the jumpsuit since that first day.

"How is the team thing going?" Cam asks. Layla expects to hear disdain or jealousy in his tone, but there is none.

A glance at his upturned face only confirms it. "Good," she says, the tension slowly leaving her shoulders. "How are the labs?"

Shrugging, Cam peers down at her. "They're okay. They have us trying to find what's wrong with the serum."

Layla's ears perk up. From the way Jax talked about it that first day, she had thought what they did in the lab was some big secret, but Cam just gave it up like it's common knowledge.

As his words sink in, Layla's steps slow before they stop altogether.

"What do you mean? What's wrong with the serum?" she asks.

Already a few paces ahead of her, Cam turns back. "Well, half the people injected die from it," he says matter-of-factly, not an ounce of emotion behind his words. Layla hands clench into fists. She breathes deeply through her nose. Cam continues, not noticing her tense up so hard her teeth ache from the force of clenching them. "The people in charge say that it's their bodies that can't take it, right? That's what they told us. That it's their DNA that won't accept the serum."

There's a flash of a shivering, heaving body in her arms before Layla pushes the image away, forces it down, down, down into the very pit of her. She draws a breath, focuses on Cam's slightly widened brown eyes. "And that's not really why they die?" she asks, voice only a little rough.

Shaking his head, Cam starts walking again, leaving Layla no choice but to follow. "It doesn't make sense," he says. "We have compared samples and tested the serum on hundreds of different peoples' DNA. The others in the lab have been doing it since before we got here. All the samples accept the serum and change to accommodate the new hybrid traits."

Layla turns the burning in her throat to steel as she says, "Courtney's dad used to tell us that it was all in our heads. That we decide if we can change or if we can't. Courtney—" Layla takes a breath, "—she didn't want to be a hybrid. She didn't want to fight in a war, no matter how much she wanted the terrorists dead and gone."

For his credit, Cam doesn't look at her like she's stupid for believing it, a superstition backed with no scientific fact. He just hums in the back of his throat, thinking it over. "So, her body rejected the serum because her mind did," he finishes for her. "I don't know, Layla, but I'm not saying you're wrong. The theory has come up before."

She had never thought of it like that, as a theory. "Are there others?" she asks. "Other theories?"

Cam snorts like *that* was the stupid question. "Twenty-five notebooks full. I had to read them all. Full of theories, and tests, and all the solid information we have."

Twenty-five notebooks full of information on the serum, and they still don't have an answer. Maybe superstition isn't so crazy an answer after all. Maybe the reason half of the teenagers given the serum don't make it through the injection is from something they can't test in their labs. Maybe it's because the people who die don't want to be changed. They refuse to let themselves be turned into soldiers, into hybrids.

But another thought comes to her mind. What about the girls who cried and cried on the subway ride to the compound? The ones that continued to cry as they showered, dressed, and lined up to get a prick on the finger and listen to the scientist announce their name and animal DNA? What about the people who sat in the bleachers, knowing what was going to come, their tears already flowing, grasping onto their friends in fear, and still made it here?

Jax jogs his way to Helland's office, traveling behind the buildings to avoid bumping into anyone. He left Kyrin still dozing in bed after he didn't so much as stir at the loud banging on the door. His team will need to get up soon, but after another late night, he decided to let them sleep in.

His fatigue is all but forgotten when he steps into the commander's building. Others stay here occasionally, military personnel mostly, but Jax suspects hybrids will soon be filling this building, too. There are so many of them, but still not enough to win against the Black Sun; not if not all of them fight.

Even though the dim lighting barely casts any light in the dark halls, Jax can see perfectly. It's one of his only enhanced senses, and it has come in handy every single day since he was changed. Kyrin has it, too. It's one of the reasons he's such a good shot. Jax doesn't wish for more, after seeing what it does to those like Mick and Layla. All the enhancements overload them.

Jax stops in front of the door with a plaque on it that reads "Commander Joan Helland." Having done this so many times, he walks right in after giving a soft knock, not waiting for her answer.

Her office is only slightly larger than the living room on his floor. The only light comes from the single window and a small lamp on her desk, causing most of the room to be cast in shadow. Jax takes in the familiar details: a dusty bookcase only partially full of books, picture frames, and a large map of the United States pinned to one of the walls.

Helland herself looks like she has not slept since the last time Jax saw her in the sharps room. Dark circles rest under her eyes, and worry lines crease her brow. There's no chair for him to sit on, not that it bothers him. At her wave forward, Jax comes to stand right before her desk.

"Good morning," he says, folding his hands behind him. "Noel said you needed to see me."

"Yes." She swipes her frazzled hair away from her eyes. "How is your new team member? Ms. Wilson."

A report. That's what she wants. Jax tries not to let his disappointment show. "Layla is doing better. There haven't been any more problems."

Helland nods, and shuffles some of her papers around. He catches a glimpse of messy, hand written notes before she closes them away in a drawer. "Cape said the fight went well a few nights ago. That she was impressive." Her lips quirk to the side as she looks up at him. "A high compliment, from him at least, as you know."

Returning her smile, Jax nods. He knows from experience that the other commander is hard to please. "I agree with him." He doesn't bother to tell her about how Layla didn't have a choice to fight, about how another hybrid lured her into it. He wouldn't be surprised if she knew already, anyway.

Resting her elbows on the desk, lacing her fingers together, Helland peers up at Jax. "And her training has been going well? Has she been improving even further in blades?"

"She exceeds in blades," Jax says, keeping his gaze level with hers. It's always a test with her keen eyes trying to see right through him. "There is not much more for us to teach her there. She is doing well in other areas, too."

"And in firearms?" the commander asks. "You know as well as I do that firearms are a skill all team members need, and you already have one member who does not use guns. Are you going to make that two?"

Jax looks down, away from her, and studies the scuffs on his well-worn boots. Every member of his old team used a gun. It wasn't a problem they had to deal with. But this new team of his, they're different. And his old team, they're gone. In the end it didn't matter what kind of weapon they used.

Helland must see the answer in his down-turned face, because she hums in what sounds like understanding. Then she says, "Only a few hours ago, a terrorist base was discovered." Jax's head shoots up in surprise. "From what they say, it's a big one, too."

Another scouting mission. It's not the higher-class mission he was looking for, but it would be good for their newbie. Ease her onto the playing field rather than throw her into chaos. Already making a mental list of things he will need to do, Jax watches as Helland hands over a mission file.

"When do we leave?"

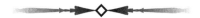

Layla knows she needs to get to training, knows her team is up by now and probably searching for her, but she and Cam continue around the compound, sometimes in silence and sometimes talking about the two weeks they've been here. In an unspoken agreement, they don't mention anything from before that.

The sun slowly creeps over and in between the trees, and it feels nice, even with the chill in the air. She spends so much time in the training building every day that the fresh air is too invigorating to leave. A couple more minutes won't hurt. Just as the thought comes to mind, a familiar voice calls out to her.

"There you are," Kyrin says, rushing his steps until he's right at her heels.

Layla can imagine her hackles rising as all her pleasant thoughts float away with the wind. Beside her, Cam is already mumbling out excuses to leave. Layla barely spares him a glance when he hurries away to the cafeteria. She doesn't blame him. Not with how Kyrin looks—the deep scowl, the hand resting over his hip like he's looking for one of his guns.

Easily keeping up with her fast pace, Kyrin says, "Everyone is looking for you, you know. Combat training started an hour ago." Kyrin grabs the sleeve of her shirt, stopping her from turning down another path. Layla spins on him with a growl, but he holds his hands up in front of her. "Lucky for you, Jax has been missing too."

That stops Layla short. "What do you mean?"

"Exactly what I said." His dark eyes scan the area around them like their leader might pop up out from behind a tree. "I haven't seen him all morning."

He doesn't sound worried, more annoyed than anything, but, Layla thinks, that seems to be his default mood. "You know where he is."

Huffing a laugh, Kyrin finally looks at her, eyes twinkling. The cheerful look is enough to make her take a step back in surprise. "Mick says he's in the commander's building. I swear he's got all of our heartbeats memorized."

Layla doesn't doubt it. If Jax is with the commanders, then that means they must have decided on her and their team's fate. Swiping her bruised, tender knuckles across her lips, Layla reins in her excitement and nerves. Even if she lost, she did well in the fight the other night, better than well if she does say so herself, but she doesn't get the impression that Cape is someone easily impressed, and in the few minutes she spent around Helland, Layla couldn't get a good enough read on her.

Kyrin interrupts her thoughts by asking, "Why were you in the labs? That's where Mick said you would be."

His arms are crossed over his chest, head tilted to the side. Layla's reminded again that this is her team's second in command, someone she should respect and listen to. Her words coming out a little forced, she tilts her head toward where Cam wondered off to, and says, "Talking to a friend."

She doesn't say she was worried about Cam or looking for someone to talk to other than her team. She doesn't say that she wanted to see someone from back home, someone besides Fisher. Layla already knows what Kyrin would say. Something along the lines of "there's no time for that."

Layla doesn't want his pity anyway. Not that she thinks he would give her any. "And I wanted to see what they do in there." It's not a lie. She has been wondering what goes on in the labs since Jax took her by the building on that first day with minimum explanations.

"And how did that go?" Kyrin says.

The lab workers' faces loom before her. Their phantom heartbeats pulse in her ears. Layla knows he can see the answer on her pinched face. Still, she puts on a forced, ugly smile, and says, "Great." Her voice matches her expression, annoyed and hostile. "All of them acted like I came to murder them. Wouldn't look at me. And the ones that did..."

Forcing herself to take a deep breath, Layla focuses on the dark-haired man in front of her and pushes the lab out of her head. Out of the corner of her eye she notices how the people in the area give them a wide berth.

All Kyrin says is, "Makes sense."

She would laugh if she weren't so surprised by his reaction. Layla's tempted to grab him by the shoulders, shake him around, and demand who this man is, because he sure isn't the same as he was yesterday. Is it because of the fight? Has she made an impression on Kyrin?

Shoulders dropping from their tense position, Layla says, "I don't want them to be afraid of me."

Eyebrows raised high, Kyrin's dark eyes roam her over. "Then put your fangs away, lion," he says. "Dull your claws and make yourself a mouse."

Layla only just stops herself from flinching at his words. She gets a picture of herself, a picture of how she once was: human, weak, and powerless. She only just got her fangs and her claws, only just got the chance to fight back in this war, get some revenge for her parents, and get a chance to rid their country of the Black Sun. Her hands clench into fists. She won't do that. She's done being a mouse, and she tells him as much.

Pulling at the sleeve of her shirt, Kyrin tugs until she begins to follow him down the worn paths. He doesn't talk for a while, not until they pass by the infirmary and the training center can be seen through the trees.

"You can't rely on Mick all the time," is what he says.

"We all rely on each other," she shoots back, not even letting his words settle in her head. "We are a team." Layla glares at the back of his head, daring him to answer. He opens the training doors without a word.

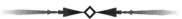

After meeting up with Mick and Celia in the combat room for one of the shortest sessions Layla has had, she and Celia walk into the forest that surrounds the compound. This is where their stealth training takes place. Unlike during the other lessons, it's just the two of them.

Surrounded by the red and gold leaves, Layla feels a familiar pang in her chest. There was a forest only a few miles away from her house. A forest she used to explore with her parents and Courtney. She has not been to it since months before the terrorist attack on Denver.

Their breaths stick in the air, white gusts that disappear in seconds. It's getting colder each day, now. Layla has seen trucks being unloaded. Boxes marked for clothes, gear, weapons, and food. Just a few days ago, she was digging through some of the boxes, searching for a few pieces of warmer clothing. Even now, she sends a silent thank you to the people, mostly former military, but not all, who brave the dangerous grounds to transport the supplies they need.

A pace in front of her, feet so silent on the crowded forest floor that Layla can barely hear her steps, Celia idly gossips about some of the others at the compound, mostly people Layla doesn't know, but she mentions Cape and Helland a few times, much to Layla's surprise.

"You did amazing," she says, changing topics so fast that it takes

Layla a moment to grasp her words. "Helland and Cape would be stupid to not let us go on higher-risk missions. We would do more good out there than in here, you know?"

Layla drums her frigid fingers against her thighs, only half-listening. There's a hybrid not too far away, pacing back and forth, a patrolling guard. The deeper they go into the forest, the more movement she hears. Tiny, quick hearts and soft paws. There isn't a second the sound of bird calls can't be heard. It reminds her of home more than Cam or Fisher ever could.

Too soon for her liking, Celia stops, but Layla quickly forgets her disappointment as she is put through drills that should be a form of torture. Celia has her climbing tree after tree, from wide, sturdy trunks, to swaying, flimsy branches. More than once, Layla eats dirt.

Then she is jumping from one tree to the next like she's training to be a monkey in a circus. They spend no less than an hour hunting and sneaking up on different animals, from small forest mice to a lone deer as big as both of them put together.

By the time they're done, leaves clutter Layla's hair, dirt and mud smear most of her clothing and exposed skin. Even in the cold air, sweat drips down her back. But her smile is genuine. Every inch of her body aches, and she feels wonderful. Stomach rumbling like it hasn't been fed in days, she's surprised she has enough energy to still be standing.

When they get to the edge of the forest, they both freeze. *Footsteps.* Looking at each other excitedly, they slow their pace, slow their breathing, and creep along like shadows. He doesn't try to hide his steps, and Layla would know that heartbeat anywhere.

Using one of the maneuvers Celia taught her, they split up. Celia takes the right, she takes the left. They practiced on some of the animals. It worked on the deer, but most of the smaller animals scurried away before they got too close.

Slowly, Layla's smile dissolves. Lips draw up over her teeth, putting her canines on display. Predator instincts, Celia called them. She has seen other hybrids do it, too. Christ, Layla has seen regular humans do it.

Peeking around a tree, Layla sees Mick looming in front of her, wearing his plain pajamas again. The sight has her glancing up. To her surprise, the moon shines between a space in the trees. They had to have been in the forest for hours if it was night already.

A shadow moves on the other side of Mick, and Layla knows it's Celia. She counts the seconds, and then together they charge, springing out of the trees and brush. Layla sees it when he tenses, sees his eyes widen, then fill with excitement and in the space of a second.

Layla has a moment to think *Crap*. She doesn't have a chance to stop her momentum before she crashes right into a much smaller body than she intended.

Celia's and her cursing can be heard over the sound of Mick's roaring laughter. Between his chuckles, he offers a hand to the both of them, and pulls them to their feet.

"What did I do wrong?" Layla says, rubbing the soreness out of her shoulder where it banged into Celia's elbow.

Hissing, Celia takes a swing at Mick, who dodges it easily. She is just as worn out as Layla is. "You weren't the problem," she says, her green eyes narrowed. "This one probably heard us before we even spotted him."

Mick chuckles one more time before he straightens. His next words have Layla's heart thumping. "Jax came back a few hours ago. He says we have a mission."

Destruction lays around me, picking at my every sense.

CHAPTER FOURTEEN

ax has been dreading and awaiting this day—when he would have to lead this new team into danger. He tossed and turned all night, plagued by nightmares starring his old team members. His lost family. Them getting hunted down and captured and tortured and killed and Jax having no way to stop it. He hadn't had the dreams in a couple months, but last night they seemed to come back with a vengeance.

So many things could go wrong today. Was the team really ready for this? Was the newbie going to black out again? Will they get ambushed and captured just like Team Three was? If that happens, he could set the newbie loose on them. No, that wouldn't be fair for her. Besides, nothing like that is going to happen. Jax stares down the length of the subway car.

After going over all the mission information with Helland yesterday, Jax left Kyrin in control of the team, and spent the afternoon getting everything ready to leave the next morning. Plans and back-up plans raced through his head as he readied and collected weapons, gear, and food for all five of them.

Last night was full of restless tension from his teammates, especially the newbie, who kept getting spooked at any and all sudden movement. Jax was lucky that Celia wore her out so much with stealth training that she ended up falling asleep right on the living room floor during his third run though of their plan. She might have been up all night otherwise.

Right now, his team is wide awake, looking over their supplies on the subway ride to the check point. There are subway tunnels starting from about a mile outside of the compound that lead to almost every state in the country. It was part of the construction of the compound. From what he could understand of it, the tunnels either don't show up on underground scans, or blend in so well with whatever else is around them that they are virtually undetectable to any terrorists looking for them. Mick understands the specifics better than he does. He's good with that kind of stuff.

Jax stands at the head of the car, swaying from side to side on the rumbling floor, running his gaze over his team. Even though it's still a scouting mission, it's different than the others they have been on. They know they are headed to a Black Sun base in Missouri, not just a random abandoned city or forest. No matter how much Helland advised to avoid them, they could encounter terrorist soldiers at any time. It wouldn't be Jax's first time. It definitely wouldn't be Kyrin's first time, but the rest of his team…

Don't hesitate. That's the advice he gave them. Don't hesitate to run and hide. Don't hesitate to kill. A few seconds could cost your life or a life of the team.

Jax calls out Layla's name a handful of times before she, as well as the rest of the team, looks up. She's nervous. It's easy to tell no matter how hard she tries to hide it. "You've done well in training, but this mission isn't going to be a set thing. We don't really know what we are going into," he says. The newbie nods. It's not the first time he has said this. "I want you to stay with Mick. No matter what."

In one of the benches not far away, Kyrin scowls. Jax knows he doesn't agree with the newbie's method of control, but it's the best they've got right now. Layla glares at Kyrin, but after a glance at Jax, Kyrin shakes his head and focuses on his guns again. In the back of the car, Mick salutes. Jax closes his eyes, takes a breath. This is going to be an interesting mission, to say the least.

He passed out the packets of information to his team as they boarded the subway. Something to keep everyone's mind occupied and focused. Even having read through it multiple times now, he takes one for himself and plops down next to Kyrin. The dark-haired man looks up from loading one of his guns, a small frown on his face.

"All right?" he asks, scanning Jax's face.

Jax nods once, looking down at the guns lying in the seat between them. He knows it's what Kyrin does when he's nervous—clean, maintain, load his guns one at a time—though none of his nerves show on his face.

Kyrin casts a disbelieving look at Jax. "They will be fine," he says, no more than a whisper. "We will all be fine."

Unsticking his own guns, Jax hands them over. "Yeah. You're right."

"Always am," Kyrin says, already taking one of Jax's guns apart to check it over.

They won't arrive at the check point for another few hours. According to the notes from Helland, this terrorist base used to be a research facility for cancer treatment. Why they would choose a building like that is beyond Jax, but the building was already cleared out, the scientists and researchers all lost to the war.

It was probably easy to steal, more than anything.

Later, when Jax's body is stiff from the jolting and bumping of the subway, and Kyrin has run out of guns to clean, they finally slow to a stop. The team is jumpy from the long ride, ready to stretch their legs and get to work. They have learned all that they can from Jax and the information packets. After they slip on their padded gear, the subway lets them off in a silent town close to the base.

The town was ambushed months ago and is abandoned now. In between the town and the Black Sun base, is a dense forest. On the other side lays overgrown cornfields and rundown houses. Jax can spot a faraway pond near a grouping of homes. The near-silence of the place is unnerving, but birds still chirp from above, creating some sense of life. The team stands close together, weapons already in hand.

Jax meets everyone's gaze, paying close attention to his newbie. "We are going to split up for now," he says. "We are a safe enough distance away from the base, but our job is to collect as much information as we can, which includes the surrounding environment." They have gone over this, too, and catching Celia roll her eyes, Jax gets on with it. "Kyrin and Celia, you will scout out the way to the base. Mick and Layla, you'll scout the town. I will scout the area for a place to set up camp, and you will all meet me there once you're done."

It's her first mission. Not as high-risk as her team was going for, but according to Jax, it's better than the other scouting mission they've went on. A good starting point for her, he said. And last night he told her she did good. That this means the commanders approve of her. If she does well on this mission, the team will likely get even better ones in the near future. She's proud of herself, she is, but right now the feeling is hidden under her nerves.

They leave her feeling too hyped up and jittery. Celia took one look at her this morning and handed her a mug of 'Relaxing Lavender" tea. It tasted disgusting and did nothing but leave a small burn on her lip that healed less than ten minutes later. She has a right to feel nervous, Layla tells herself. It's her first mission after all.

She walks with Mick, their steps too loud in the silent, beaten down town for her liking. This town isn't like Denver, that much Layla can tell. Not just because of how small it is, but because there are no signs of a bombing. Instead of crumbling buildings and crater-filled roads, bullet holes litter every door, every sign, every wall. Windows are shattered. Cars are stripped of anything useful. The place reeks of rotten food and something she's trying her hardest not to think about.

She doesn't hear one unfamiliar heartbeat except for the occasional small animal, but her hands still hover over her the newly sharpened axes on her hip and along her back, ready to pull them from their magnetic sheaths any second. So tired from all her training the day before, Layla slept hard. Now she feels too awake, too aware of everything around her. The tough material of her new gear scratches at her skin. The sun is impossibly bright. She can pick out each bullet hole that decorates every surface. Her ears twitch at the smallest sound.

She and Mick walk steadily deeper into the small town. Every dilapidated house, park, and business makes something between anger and sadness fill her. These people, these terrorists, are the real monsters. Layla wonders how many they killed just here in this town no bigger than her own. Thousands of innocents. Taking in all the damage, she lets the knowledge of what they did sink into her skin, into her mind, so she never forgets.

Beside her, Mick takes short, shallow breaths. At first, she thought it was his way of controlling his own anger at the condition of the town, but his pulse is steady, not a trace of anger lines his face. He's smelling the air, being a wolf hybrid after all. A part of her doesn't want to know what he's smelling for. Is it the decomposing long-dead bodies, the faint smell of smoke and gunfire still lingering in the air? Layla asks anyway.

"Their patrol starts sixty feet outside of the town to the north," he says, pointing his finger in the opposite direction of where she looks. A smirk lights his face, making her scowl. She knew Jax was going to put her with Mick, knew it and agreed with it, but still she can't help feeling like the team doesn't trust her yet. The feeling of resentment that follows the thought is stupid, especially when Layla doesn't entirely trust herself. "Toward the base, Layla," Mick continues. "More than likely they have a perimeter set around the building."

Layla can't comprehend how Mick can get all that from smelling the noxious air, but it would match up with the information in the packets Jax gave them all. She's supposed to be able to do that too—scent things from miles away. For her the smelling thing is harder to use than her enhanced sight and hearing. She needs to really concentrate to be able to discern one scent from another. She's been working on it though.

Her hand, damp with perspiration, settles against the rough handle of her shorter axe. "And there are five of us."

"Easier to sneak around," he says, bumping his shoulder into hers. Layla wonders if he's listening to how fast her heart is beating, how nervous about all this she is.

But if an ambush happens… They talked about it, of course. Repeatedly. Jax put them through multiple scenarios and what to do if any of them were to happen. Don't hesitate, is that main thing he stressed. Pushing down her doubt, she trudges along with her partner, and tries to pull up the familiar anger to drown out the nerves.

Besides cursing at every gruesome corpse and new despairing sight, they don't talk much after that. It's a few hours later when they finish looking through the town, and by the end of it, she has plenty to feel angry about. They don't know if the destruction and the death in this town was at the hands of the terrorists at this nearby base, but at this point she doesn't care. As long as someone pays for it.

With nothing left to see in the town, they head west towards the bordering forest to the small, makeshift camp Jax is setting up. They're a block away from the edge of the city when Layla stops dead. There's a rumbling sound in the distance. Mick, too busy sniffing at the air, trying find Jax's trail, doesn't notice it.

"Stop," she hisses. The sound is gaining fast. Mick spins around and jogs back where she stands, his eyes so wide, bits of white can be seen at the edges.

"In there," he says, pointing to a faded blue house behind them. "Hurry."

Layla doesn't need to be told twice. She's familiar enough with the same rumbling engines from the compound that she knows it's a truck. The big, bulletproof kind both the Black Sun and the Hybrid Force use. Layla hoists herself through a broken window, and Mick follows suit as soon as her feet hit the floor. They slide down the wall, so their backs are resting against the solid surface, their heads just below the window frame.

There would be no reason for anyone else from the compound to be here, and if they were, her team would have been told about it beforehand. Layla draws her knees up to her chest and pulls her axes off their holders. Mick raises a hand to her, signaling for her to wait. She's not going to risk peeking out at the road, but Layla tilts her head back, so she can see the blue sky out the window. Mick glances at his watch. A minute passes where they hold their breath, and then the truck races past, dirt flying up behind it. It passed so close to the house they're in that some of it comes through the window and settles in their hair.

"Well," Mick says a good five minutes later when they're still sitting, fixed in place, "we should probably move now."

"Holy crap," is all she says.

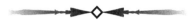

Even when the smoky, rotten smell of the town unsticks itself from her nose and the clean forest air is all she can smell, Layla's shoulders stay tensed up by her ears. Her hours of training with Celia come into use as her and Mick trek through the crunching leaves and closely packed trees. The whole time, Layla keeps one ear on the town behind them and one on Jax ahead, but another truck doesn't pass through the town. Halfway to the camp, Layla has a hand clamped over her growling stomach, constantly scolding it every time it dares to make a noise.

Kyrin and Celia must still be checking out the path to the base, because only Jax is at the camp when they arrive, his big frame wrestling a sleeping bag out of one of their packs. Layla guesses that it's Kyrin's from all the stray bullets falling out. Faster than she has ever seen him move, Jax's hand darts for one of his guns, laying on the green ground beside him.

Layla jumps back, heart lodged in her throat. There's a tree a foot away big enough for her to use as shelter, but after seeing it's only them, Jax turns back with a grunt and continues to tug the sleeping bag out of the pack. "What did you find?"

With a hand over her still-racing heart, Layla clears her throat then tells him what happened. From the surface damage of all the buildings to the reeking, shriveled corpses until finally she says, "A truck full of terrorists went through the town close to where we were."

"What?" he yells. Forgetting his struggle with the sleeping bag, Jax springs to his feet. "Did they see you? What happened?"

His dark eyes scan the nearby trees like the can see all the way to the town. If the trees weren't so tightly packed, maybe he could. Perspiration gathers along his brow and upper lip, but before he starts packing up camp in a panic, Mick steps in. He raises his hands in a calming gesture, and says, "We hid. They passed right by us without stopping."

Under his gear, Jax's shoulders visibly sag in relief. He looks skyward and rubs at his face.

On the subway, she thought his rapid pulse was from adrenaline, but without the metal tang that seemed to seep out of the walls like a heavy perfume, Layla couldn't scent what she does now. Jax is nervous. She would even say he's scared. Not for the first time, she wants to ask what exactly happened with his old team.

Giving Jax a moment, Layla gets a better look at their campsite.

It's not a big clearing. They'll have to pack in tight tonight to make room, but the ground is soft and grassy, cleared of most rocks, twigs, and leaves—anything that could make noise underfoot. She can hear running water nearby, probably a steam. They're about a mile southwest of the town, far enough away to give them some safety. Layla can picture that before the Black Sun attack, the town kids would come out here, play by the water and run through the forage. Under one of the lower standing trees three sleeping bags are already laid out in a half circle, with her, Celia's, and Mick's packs placed on the grass toward the top of each. Layla eyes the meal bars Jax must have dug out with longing. She's starving.

Instead of reaching for the food, she grabs Kyrin's forgotten pack at Jax's feet, and begins to carefully extract the sleeping bag. "The hunting dog says the guard perimeter starts about two miles out from the town," she says.

Smiling amusedly at her jab, Mick says, "So they should have scouts a mile out from the base. I expect it will be even further out once they get more troops this way."

Jax casts a thankful look at her when she successfully extracts the sleeping bag. "Good," he says. "Kye and Celia should be back soon, and we can draw up a rough outline of their base, tweak the plan if we need to, and get ready for tomorrow."

They only have the barest intel on the base, but according to the people who reported it, shipments go out every other day, and with them a good number of their soldiers. The team is supposed to wait until then to get a closer look to reduce the odds of encountering any of them. But with other trucks leaving the place randomly, they'll need to be even more careful.

Layla understands why they need to keep hidden from the terrorists, but she can't keep the irritation away. Letting the terrorists know they found the base could set them at a disadvantage for when they send in more hybrids, but Layla wonders why they don't just attack now. Destroy the base like the terrorists destroyed the town.

She had the same thought when she was looking over the mission packet, and she asked Celia earlier on the subway. "It's not how things work," she said, leaving it at that.

"There's no guarantee we would win," Mick piped up behind her, no doubt having heard their whispered conversation. "The terrorists have better weapons. The base is their territory. We don't know what we're going into. Huge disadvantages."

She had relented after that, but after scouting the town, seeing what the terrorists did, the familiar pricking under her skin began anew. Despite that, she knows she wouldn't stand a chance at swaying her leader. She decides to help him with his sleeping bag to try to chase the aggression away, and if Jax and Mick exchange knowing glances behind her back, she pretends she doesn't notice.

As they wait for Kyrin and Celia, Layla watches Mick draw up a quick but detailed map of their surroundings: the base, the town, the woods, their camp, where the subway entrance hides. The terrorist scouts and the truck path locations will have to wait until the other two get back from their scouting.

The lines across the course paper are precise, and Layla is reminded of the walls in Mick's room covered ceiling to floor in pen and marker. Long ago, before her parents died and before the war started, Layla wished she could draw, but she never had the patience to sit and practice, to be able to get the lines right or create the picture she wanted. That want was piled beneath everything else, but the longing returns as she watches his map come to life.

She doesn't know how much time passes but the sky grows steadily darker, Jax forces them to eat their meal bars and water, then takes up pacing around their cramped camp. The food helps settle her and she finally feels herself relax, but that evaporates at the sound of heartbeats and murmuring voices. Kyrin and Celia enter the camp on silent feet, and Layla's not the only one sighing in relief.

She's up, racing to Celia's side as Kyrin, not wasting any time, tells them what they learned. "Patrol starts about a mile out from their base with soldiers on duty around the entire perimeter. It's going to be hard to get a good look inside. I say it's best to keep our distance."

"Use the scopes?" Jax says, eyeing Kyrin up and down, looking for any injuries, but he and Celia look unharmed. Layla doesn't smell any blood. There's only a slight redness to their cheeks and nose from the cold.

"That would be our best shot."

The scopes, Layla learned during the mission planning last night, are what they call high powered, night vision binoculars. The compound has a supply of random gadgets stored in the commanders' housing unit. A very small supply. Over the past year, teams have been collecting what they can from their missions— fallen and lost devices from terrorists. They get handed out by Cape or Helland themselves based on what type of mission a team has.

Layla and her team test them out around their little camp as stars begin to fill the sky, and after safely storing Mick's finished maps, they settle down in their sleeping bags.

Layla's pressed between Celia and Mick. Swirly vines from the tree behind them hang down above their heads. Layla has no intention of sleeping this close to members of the Black Sun, but as she listens to the chirping bugs and her teammates quiet breathing, she begins to doze.

She snaps awake what feels like only minutes later, eyes wide and breath frozen in her throat. With the sleeping bag pulled up to her chin, Layla struggles into a sitting position. Scanning their camp, she notes nothing abnormal, but something crawls along her spine, telling her otherwise. Something is wrong.

There.

The night is quiet, every sound magnified. Something walks in the forest. Multiple somethings.

Her hand reaches out instantly, grabbing onto Mick. He shoots up as soon as she touches his shoulder. Frantically, she catches his slightly glowing eyes, points to her ear then in the direction of what must be terrorist scouts. Knowing he can hear just as well as she can, Layla turns to wake Celia. She waits only until she sees her green eyes open before she scrambles out of her sleeping bag without an explanation. She hurries the short distance to Kyrin and Jax, sleeping so close they blend together.

"What," Jax says, more of a hiss than actual words.

Inwardly cursing, she only says, "We have company."

"Grab your weapons," he says in a whisper loud enough to make Layla cringe, but his eyes are wide awake. A gun is already in his hand. Around her the others swiftly get to their feet.

Having kept her daggers on her person as per Mick's advice, Layla only needs to scoop up her axes and click them onto their magnetic holders. As quietly as they can, they roll up their sleeping bags and slip their packs on in case they can't come back. Layla's hands shake. She flexes them in the hopes that they will be steady if her blades are needed.

Or maybe curiosity will kill us all.

CHAPTER FIFTEEN

*T*hey form a line. Mick uses his hearing or smell to lead them in the right direction and Layla brings up the rear. The others fall into rank between them. If Layla didn't know that she's the most useful in the back, being able to hear anyone approaching from behind, she might have been a little pissed off.

Jax's words fill the silence, repeating his instructions over and over in her head. *We are not looking for confrontation. Don't hesitate.*

Then why are they heading straight for enemy soldiers? And Layla has no doubt that they are, in fact, enemy soldiers. Mick was the one who said they should go. They sound different, he said. They smell different, too. An uneasy feeling rolls through Layla's stomach. It's best if they know their enemy, and if Mick's trying to say what she thinks he is…

Her blood pounds through her veins, carrying the sharp bite of adrenaline with it. If it was not for her enhanced eyesight, she wouldn't be able to see Celia a few feet in front of her. The only light this far out form civilization comes from the thin crescent moon and faraway stars creating small beams of light through the densely packed trees.

She squints her eyes, looking past the tree trunks and brush, but the soldiers are ahead. Her eyes settle on Celia' s back again. Nothing about her stands out in the darkness, not even her bright green eyes. She was born to do this. Layla knows her own eyes glow in the flashes of light, just like Mick's do, just like she's seen stray cats' eyes gleaming in the headlights of a car.

Layla tries to breathe deep like Mick was doing earlier in the town to pick up any scents, but she can't differentiate anything specific between the smells of dirt, pine, and her team. She files that away to ask him about later.

Their pace picks up the closer they get, then when it sounds like the soldiers are standing right next to her, they slow down again. She listens to the enemy soldiers, waiting for them to talk, to make some sort of noise, but they are as silent as her team is. She counts seven pulses. Seven soldiers they may have to fight.

When her team gathers together, Layla's not the only one with a confused look on their face. The soldiers have stopped now, all but copying their exact placement. Only a few yards of trees separate the two groups from each other.

Mick comes to her side just as Celia mouths "up," and points with a finger to the high branches of the surrounding trees. Layla nods, and just like in training yesterday, she quickly scans the trunk and branches for the best foot and hand-holds, and beings to scale the tree. Right now, climbing feels easier than breathing does.

She can hear the slight rustle of leaves indicating the rest of her team is climbing their own trees. The one she's on is big enough for Mick to climb up on the opposite side. His brow is furrowed, and Layla almost loses her grip when she realizes the look on his face. Under the lines of confusion, his eyes are bright with terror.

They should head back, sneak back to the ground and get to the subway, but her lips stay sealed shut. She can't speak, not when the soldiers can hear her. But still, her carefully controlled breathing stutters and picks up again, faster than before. Franticly searching the area around them, Layla tries to get eyes on the soldiers, but at this height, somewhere in the middle of the tree, too many branches and leaves obscure her view. Even Celia in the tree next to her is out of her sight.

Her axes would be too bulky for combat up here, so she reaches for one of her knives instead, only to almost let out a scream of frustration when she loses her grip and slips down a foot. Mick's hand catches around her wrist, stopping her fall. His eyes blaze in the darkness, blue and gold fire. He yanks her up, pulling her to his level with next to no effort, but he doesn't stop there. Layla is pushed above him, and with each shaky inch she climbs, he pushes her a foot higher. If she was not so panicked, she might have kicked him to the ground.

When she gets pushed to one of the top branches of the tree, she can finally see them. There are seven, just like she counted. Under all their gear is the telltale mossy green color of the signature Black Sun uniforms. Unlike what she previously thought, the soldiers are talking, just not with their voices. Layla stares as their hands move rapidly in sign language, and curses in her head. She should have taken that class last year, but instead she took Spanish with Courtney.

Going to take up two of her daggers, Layla is stopped by a hard tap to the side of her head. She glares up at Mick, but he isn't looking at her. He's looking at the soldiers, and how the one facing them has bright eyes, glowing in the light being cast from their advanced weapons and equipment. Stomach clenching, Layla holds her breath, stretching her neck out to see better. Then, with a bust of movement, Mick acts too fast for her eyes to follow.

All she sees is the streak of silver sail through the leaves and branches and then into the night air. Layla's body jolts from its precarious position on the branch when the sick sound of blade piercing flesh reaches her ears. Astonished, Layla can only stare as the man's eyes roll and his body crumbles to the ground.

Mick's hands blur with how fast he throws. On the ground, the six remaining soldiers dive for cover. They look in her team's direction, raising their guns, but not being able to see them, they fire without proper aim. Layla feels the bullets cut through their tree.

A part of her wants to stop Mick, a bigger part wants to join him, but all she can focus on is the fact that the soldiers down there are hybrids and they are wearing the enemy's uniform and patrolling for the enemy base. They probably heard her team, just like Layla heard them, and were coming to take them captive or kill them right there.

It doesn't make sense.

The sight of them dropping one by one is hard to watch. Layla's hands remain grasped around the tree branch. She doesn't reach for her daggers. *Stop*, a familiar sounding voice in her head whispers. Courtney's voice.

Knives launching from the tree next to her alert her that Celia has joined the massacre. In a matter of seconds, there are only three soldiers left below them. A gun fires to her left, one shot for each of them, and before she can memorize the fear in their eyes, the hybrids slump to the ground with the others.

No matter how overwhelming her enhancements are, she has never wished them gone, but now with the smell of blood in her nose and the deafening quiet where their heats used to beat, Layla wishes she didn't have any abilities at all.

"Come on," Mick says with a growl, face set in stone and fire. He takes one look at her face before glancing away again. "Come on," he says again, softer this time.

Layla looks once more at the bodies, once more, and forces her rolling stomach to settle before she follows him down. Once they get halfway down the tree, they jump, landing on the dirt with a soft thud. Celia's already on the ground, her skin looking paler than normal. Her shaking hands find Layla's in an instant. She doesn't let go.

With muffled thuds, Jax and Kyrin land next, blending in so much with the darkness that Layla's not sure if she's looking at their eyes or their noses or at the trees above them. "We have to make sure," is all her leader says.

He leads the way, the rest of them following. Celia and Mick press close to her sides. Layla refuses to let herself wonder if it's to keep her calm or for their own comfort. Jax's nervousness from earlier is gone. The only way she can tell he's upset is from how he grasps onto Kyrin. They don't go slowly through the leaf-strewn forest anymore. They rush the short distance to where to group of hybrid soldiers are.

Mick breathes hard through his mouth. Celia's grip cracks her knuckles, and Layla cringes more at the sound than at the feeling. This close, she can smell it, all the blood. Bile forces its way up her throat, but she swallows down the acidic taste. She can see everything as they enter the clearing.

The team gathers close as Jax uses his boot to tip one of the bodies onto its back. Layla clamps her teeth hard to stop the noise that want to burst out. Her canines dig holes into her gums and lips.

It's the first one. The boy with green eyes. Mick's knife juts out of his neck, blood pools in the grass and dirt around him. Forcing herself to study his face, Layla wills her emotions to go blank. The commanders, the hybrids, and everyone else at the compound need this information. They need to know what they're up against.

With forced determination, Layla steps away from the safety of Mick and Celia. She steps closer to the body. The corpse. It's not like how it was in the town. Those corpses were months old, their faces barely recognizable as human. Disgusting, but unreal. This corpse on the ground at her feet… He's real. She watched his wild eyes turn blank.

He's young, a teenager, just like them. And when Jax shines a beam of light down at him, she stifles a scream. Even though her body is buzzing to, she doesn't back away. "I know him." Her voice is only a whisper, but in the silence after the gun shots, she might as well be yelling.

"I knew him," she says again. Turning her burning eyes to Mick, she snarls. "Why did you kill him? Why did you kill them all?"

"Be quiet. You know why," her leader says, voice strangely monotone.

She turns on him, about to spew curses, but he's pulling something off the body. The cube-shaped object is smaller than the palm of his hand. A small green circle blinks in one of the corners. A camera.

"We need to go."

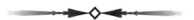

They leave the bodies, the base, and the forest behind in a rush. There is no use staying any longer. It's not safe for them to stay any longer. The cameras on the soldier's gear could have already alerted someone at the terrorist base. They will send out soldiers to see what happened, if they haven't already. To capture and kill them.

Jax keeps muttering things like "Not again." and "Just like last time." while constantly throwing glances back at her. It has got to be the most confusing and discouraging thing Layla has seen from her leader.

It's the fastest she has ever run, even with the uneven ground and her axes bumping against her thighs. Her pack is strung over her shoulders and strapped across her chest so tight that it won't budge as she leaps. In fact, it's so tight her chest fights against the straps as she gasps in air. Running isn't something she trains a lot for, maybe ten minutes each morning. It comes naturally anyway.

The thoughts rush through her head as fast as the trees fly by. The memories. Jordan. His name was Jordan. He was a year younger than her. She used to see him every day at school in the hallways or at lunch, another face in the crowd. Layla never noticed him missing from her classmates, never even thought about him at all.

Breathing gets harder with every pump of her legs, but it has nothing to do with running. What does all this mean? Even if she did have enough breath to ask, there's no time now. There's no time to do anything but run to the subway entrance where the conductor waits and get away from here as quickly as they can.

Jumping over large bushes and ducking under branches, she listens for the sounds of pursuit. While they run, Jax makes sure they don't leave a trace behind. They can't have the terrorists finding out about the subway entrance. They can't know that is how the Hybrid Force travels around.

The trees are too close together to do it any other way, so, like before, the team runs in a line with Mick at the front, but this time Layla isn't last. Every time she thinks about slowing down, she thinks of how vulnerable the rest of her team is behind her.

The burning, rotting smell of the town reaches her nose. If she had enough air to spare, Layla would've sighed in relief. All they need to do is cut through the town and the subway entrance will be a few yards away, hidden under rocks and dirt. Ten minutes, tops.

Then she hears the engines.

Kyrin and Celia also reported seeing trucks during their scouting, but these engines sound quieter than they should, nothing more than a soft purring rather than a grumbling roar. She needs to save her breath, but she curses anyway. Digging her heels into the mud and dirt, Layla braces herself for the guaranteed collision that will happen. Sure enough, Celia crashes into her a moment later. Layla grasps on to the other girl's arm, keeping them both from falling. Kyrin and Jax skid to a stop next to them, barely avoiding outrunning them.

"What are you doing?" Celia hisses. Far ahead of them Mick growls loudly and doubles back.

"They have trucks," Layla tells them. "No. Smaller. They are catching up fast. We won't be able to outrun them to the subway."

Even as she says it, lights begin to stream through the trees.

With twitching fingers, she slips out two knives. The others get their weapons out. Mick with his own knives. Celia, Jax, and Kyrin take out guns. Briefly, she wonders who was the one that shot the last three hybrids in the clearing. Jax or Kyrin.

"We're going to have to split," Jax says above the gaining sound of engines. "Try to stay out of sight. Only fight if you absolutely have to."

With that he, Kyrin, and Celia bolt, each in a different direction. If it weren't for the grip on her arm, she would be gone, too. Eyes wide in fury, she shakes the arm off with a warning show of her sharp teeth.

"Stay with me," Mick says.

The anger she usually feels at being ordered around surfaces again, joining the panic and fear and exhaustion and sorrow. Mick growls, this time in a mixture of frustration and impatience. Like in the tree, he goes to push her ahead, but she takes off in a quick bolt of speed. The only problem with this is that she has only a vague idea of where she's going. All she knows that she can't stop.

"Right more," Mick's clipped voice says. It's hard to make the words out through his constant growling. Her own lips draw over her teeth as the headlights flash in front of her. She catches sight of a motorbike, not a truck. Heading straight towards her. Not able to stop in time, she ducks to the ground in a roll. The bike rushes past, inches away from her head.

Gun fire fills the small space around them, and she scrambles behind a tree, the only kind of cover out here. There are three bikes, a soldier on each, but Layla can hear more farther out in the forest. They will be here soon. The bikes come to a stop ten feet from where Layla crouches. The tree is nowhere thick enough to cover her fully. She just hopes that the foliage around her is enough to compensate.

"What are you hiding for?" one of the soldiers says when the bullets die down. From the sound of it, it's a woman, her voice high and mocking.

Mick catches her eye from a few trees over. He shakes his head, confirming Layla's suspicions. They can't run, not with the guns trained on them, and even if they did, the soldiers would chase them down easily. More bikes rumble over. The woman or one of the others must have let them know their location.

Mick mouths something at her, but the headlights cast shadows over his face, making it impossible for her understand. But then he whispers the words, and Layla's heart clenches.

"Let go."

Oh.

On Jax's and Mick's orders she has been keeping Mick's pulse in her ears since the mission started, loud enough to be a noticeable comfort, but still quite enough to be able to hear everything around her. Ever since the night Mick showed her how to do it, they've been practicing it whenever they were able to.

The temptation to let that steady sound go is already there, has been there since this mission started, burning under her skin like a furious itch. Still hidden behind the tree, Mick hold his gloved hand up, three fingers raised. Then he lowers one.

A countdown. His flashing eyes bore into hers, willing her to understand. And she does. There's no one here to hurt besides the enemy soldiers. And when the soldiers are gone, he will bring her back. Just like in the training room two weeks ago. It feels like years and years ago.

Don't hesitate.

Her heart is a pounding, burning thing in her chest. When his last finger goes down, Layla shuts out the comforting and mildly irritating sound of Mick's beating heart.

It's like flipping a switch. Flipping the light from on to off. All the fear and grief dissolves into a fizzling anger that calms her racing mind and heart. She doesn't hide from the burning and itching. She lets it consume her, focuses it on the threat around her.

Her knife is no longer gripped in a too tight fist. It's sailing through the air, plunging into the woman on the bike. No longer crouched behind the tree, Layla sees it when the woman slips sideways off the bike seat and onto ground.

Mick springs up next to her, more of an extension of her body than a different person, but this time he lets them split up. Not only are there far too many bikes and targets not to, but he isn't safe this close to her, especially when her mind is slipping away. She might see him as a threat soon, too.

Sprinting toward the grouped terrorists, away from Mick, Layla clicks the longer of her axes off her back, and slices at the tires of an oncoming bike. It races past her, then crashes and rolls, taking the two soldiers on the back with it. One of them tries to get up, but they are quickly hit with a dagger just like the woman.

The forest is a blur around her, filled with a million sounds and smells. Headlights and the deafening sound of gunfire pounds into her head like an unforgiving train. Screams, the dying of bikes, and the smell of blood. Layla refuses to slow down, to stop moving. She doesn't stop swiping with her axe or throwing her daggers.

It takes minutes, only minutes before they are all on the ground. The quiet of the forest is deafening. No gun fire or screams, no pulses save for her own and Mick's. Some of the broken, overturned bikes shine light on the scene. Blood coats the ground, leaking from the soldiers just like the gas leaks from the crashed bikes. With no more targets, Layla blindly lets her legs carry her to Mick.

He stands in the middle of the destruction, looking like he would love to continue. It's the first time she has seen him less than his usual calm. When he looks up at her, her body tenses, preparing to strike out at him, but he moves back, gesturing for her to follow.

"We need to get out of here," he says, looking her over, assessing to see how stable she is. She feels on edge. She feels stunned. She feels a little empty. She didn't count the bodies. Should she have? "Before more of them come."

Balling her shaking and empty hands into fists, she takes off after him, sprinting all the way to the concealed subway entrance, her thoughts sluggish and painful. She tries not to think about what happened, about what she did as they board the subway, but Jax, already there with Kyrin and Celia, asks for a report and waves them onto the subway. Layla barely makes it past the door before she kneels over, emptying her stomach onto the smooth floor. Then her vision goes black.

I've heard the whispers. They think I'm a monster. Would you think that, too?

CHAPTER SIXTEEN

*H*er team left her alone only a few hours ago. Left her alone in her room so she can get some rest. They had been hovering around her since she woke up halfway to the compound strewn uncomfortably across two subway seats. Layla still doesn't know why she passed out. Was it the stress? The fear? Was it how she let whatever it is under her skin loose and killed all those soldiers? They were terrorists, she reminds herself. Black Sun soldiers. It's what she has been training for, and what she's been wishing to do since they bombed Denver and killed her parents.

Layla wonders if she could have done it without letting go of her careful control. If she could have killed a single one of them if she was in her right mind. Does it even mater?

In the dark, she can't see the picture in her hands, but she rubs her thumbs over the glossy surface. For once, it does nothing to comfort her. She can only be grateful that the team didn't mention the whole passing out thing to the commanders. It could've been a reason to hold them back from better missions in the future. She'll get used to this. This feeling of panic and guilt and terror at what she did—what she became. She's a soldier, and this is what she's supposed to be doing.

When she woke up hours ago on the subway, it was to see her teammates leaning down over her, so close their faces were all she could see. Her body ached. Her leg was blazing with pain, and when she forced herself to look down at it, her upper leg was wrapped in gauze, tinted pink from blood. She was shot. Even now, she doesn't remember at what point in the fight it happened and thinking about it brings back everything she's been trying and failing to block out: the enemy soldiers, the bikes, the screams, and the blood. The hybrid soldiers.

The burning in her thigh returns as if the thoughts are able to dull the pain medicine a nurse made her take.

Helland and Cape went ballistic when Jax told them the reason they were back from the mission so soon. Somehow, the Black Sun has hybrids of their own. One of them Layla knew, went to school with. The commanders didn't have much of anything concrete to say about it at the time, too surprised. They had her team repeat their count of the mission multiple times. Cape listened with a furrow between his brow, rocking back and forth on his heels. While Helland paced around her small office, her head shaking, unable to believe it.

Laying in her bed, Layla's hands begin to shake, gripped tight to the picture she gently sets aside so she doesn't rip it. Despite having been awake for almost two days, she knows sleep isn't coming. Images cycle through her mind at dizzying speeds. The hybrids in the clearing, clearly working for the Black Sun. The massacre with the soldiers on the bikes. Courtney shaking and dying in her arms.

But is she *really* dead?

Layla doesn't know anymore.

"I'll be down the hall if you need me," Celia had told her before she left Layla alone. But Layla doesn't want that. It's too close to how she used to search out Courtney back when her parents first died. Her shaking fists rub at her eyes hard enough to hurt, chasing the burn of tears away. She refuses to cry. She won't wake the others up and send them running back to her, but she can't stay here either, by herself and with ghosts of the people she's lost.

Uncurling from the rigid fetal position in the middle of her cold bed, Layla's body moves on autopilot. Her heart is beating too fast, but her mind is almost blank. She used to get like this back when her parents first died. Empty and searching. But Courtney, whether she's alive or not, isn't here to comfort her anymore.

So, she makes her way out of her bedroom door, past her teammates' rooms, and through the kitchen, socks slipping silently across the floor. Her leg must be throbbing, but she can barely feel it. Maybe because of the medicine, or maybe because her mind simply doesn't want to. The elevator is painfully bright compared to the complete darkness she blindly navigated through.

Her hands fumble over the button for ground level. She can still feel the sticky coating of blood on her fingers, but when she looks at them, they're clean—not a trace of the coppery smelling substance on the pale skin. Narrowing her eyes, Layla wills it to be there, for the red to appear like a stain. It would be fitting. It would be fair.

Her hands stay clean—innocent looking. The same as they've always been. Maybe if the serum in her veins didn't heal her injuries so fast there would still be traces of what she did.

The elevator doors open with a soft dinging sound, and Layla steps out into the night, not feeling the bitter cold despite only wearing a thin shirt and pants. The sounds of bugs chirping, leaves swaying and falling, her near silent steps on the warn path sooths some of her anxious thoughts. She isn't the only person awake. The labs are full of hybrids, tinkering and murmuring. The nurses in the infirmary and the workers in the cafeteria are getting ready to start the day. The soldiers who patrol the woods around the compound are alert enough that Layla can feel a few pairs of eyes on her.

She doesn't run into anyone on the paths, and not having bothered to sip on boots before she left the floor, her socked feet are soaked through from the damp grass by the time she makes it to the training center. Her axes and dagger are kept inside a special locker that the whole team uses to store their weapons, but she skips going to the small locker room and exits the elevator on level two. Firearms.

Jax and Kyrin haven't attempted to bring up training for firearms again. Jax says it's fine. That she's adequate enough with her knives and axes. That Mick doesn't use guns and she doesn't need to either. It sounds like an excuse. If she brought it up, would they try teaching her again?

The lights flicker on as she steps out of the elevator. She's probably leaving wet footprints across the tiled floor, but they'll dry soon enough. Stopping at the first table, Layla's skims her fingers over the table top an inch away from the guns laid out on the smooth wood surface. Gun are a kind of taboo; have been since before she was born. Years and years ago, they were banned from the country with the only exception being military related. She hadn't seen any in real life before she came to the compound. As a kid, the stories of people shooting up buildings full of innocent people had instilled a deep fear of the weapons. They were dangerous and abused.

And the thought of them in her hands… After what she did to the terrorists in that clearing, the thought is even more terrifying than it was at that first day of training.

She didn't tell her team this is the reason she doesn't like them. She figures they might suspect anyway.

Her hands inch closer to the guns until the tips of her fingers flutter over them. They're unloaded, but a single box of practice ammunition lays next to each. That town her and Mick scouted was loaded with bullet holes as if every surface was a target for the terrorist soldiers who were responsible for demolishing the it. Those were innocent people killed with a bullet to the head or the heart or anywhere vital.

Were the hybrid terrorist soldiers her team killed innocent too? Jordan. His name was Jordan.

They could have knocked them all out and taken them in,

brought them to the compound to be questioned. They could've done anything other than kill them. But a tiny voice whispers in her head *No, they couldn't have.* The hybrids were already looking for them, and they had cameras attached to their gear. Her team had been seen by the soldiers at the base and hunted down. If the team tried saving the hybrids, they would've been slowed down. They wouldn't have made it to the subway entrance. They would have been shot and killed trying to protect the other hybrids.

Layla blows out an uneven breath. Her fingers finally wrap around one of the smaller guns. She fumbles a little while loading it with the practice ammunition.

It had to happen. Layla knows. All of it had to happen. She knows this.

And it's all fine. It's fine.

Finished loading the gun, she bypasses the training simulation area and goes to the target range. The layout is similar to the one on the sharps floor except instead of aiming at circular bullseye targets, there are sheets of paper with human-shaped stencils on them. Layla fights against cringing at the piece of paper.

Her memory of that first day of training with Kyrin is fuzzy, overrun by what happened after he showed off his talents, so she squares up like she would for throwing daggers and positions her hands as best as she can remember. She neglects the special headphones. Being shot at in the clearing of the forest was enough to make her confident that she won't need them anymore.

Looking down the short barrel of the gun, Layla pants like she just finished her morning laps around the compound. All she needs to do is press on the little trigger. There isn't anyone she can hurt in here besides herself, and even if she does, these aren't real bullets. They wouldn't hurt like the one that cut into her thigh. At most they'd leave a nasty welt on her skin.

"Come on," she says out loud. "Just do it."

She shuffles from foot to foot before raising her arms, slightly bent at the elbows. Taking a staggering breath, she aims at the paper where the head is and presses the trigger. She jerks back at the surprising force of the small weapon and the earsplitting *bang* so close to her ears.

Her first thought is *I should have worn the headphones.*

The second is *There's someone watching me.*

She doesn't have time to feel proud or guilty at herself for shooting the gun. She spins around on her heels. When she sees who it is, she immediately lowers her arms, folding them behind her back with the gun still clutched in her hand. She resists the urge to look down at her socked and wet feet.

Commander Cape is standing in a position where he can see her shoot, but still far enough away that he would have a shot at making it to the elevator if Layla decided to maul him if he startled her. The thought would usually amuse her, but all it does is leave her feeling disheartened. What's he doing here?

"Commander," Layla says. Unlike her, he's not wearing flimsy pajamas. No, he's wearing his usual dark suit. The only thing different from when she seen him a few hours ago is that his tie is handing loose around his neck. The shimmering fabric of it reminds her of a snake.

"Good morning, Ms. Wilson. I thought you'd be getting some much-needed sleep after your mission and injury." He gestures to her leg where she was shot, but still doesn't come any closer. Now that she's not so focused on trying to shoot, she can clearly hear his rapid heart. Layla wants to shake her head at this man. Her own commander is afraid of her.

"I couldn't seem to settle down." She brings her hands from around her back, trying to show that she has nothing to hide. The gun dangles harmlessly from two of her fingers.

Cape nods. His eyes flicker around the room like he can't stand to look at her. "If it helps, Helland and I believe you did well on your mission. You are an exquisite fighter if the story is true. I don't think Team Thirteen would have made it out of there if it weren't for you, and Mr. James, of course."

Layla's eyes widen in surprise. This time she can't stop it as she lowers her eyes and glares at her thick socks. What she did isn't something she wants to be praised for, but Layla doesn't think Cape wants to hear that. "Thank you," she says, voice cracking slightly.

"You feel guilty. There's no need for that." Perplexed, Layla meets his gaze. The color of his eyes reminds her of bright, clear skies and the flowers that used to grow in Courtney's backyard. Even when they constantly flit around, they seem steady, not giving away the nervousness that drums from his heart. "I've been doing this job long enough to know when a soldier has regrets."

"I killed all those people." She doesn't say anything about blacking out, about how she let the burning, hate-fueled *thing* inside her lose. Jax already hinted at it to him and Helland earlier, not outright saying it, but Layla saw the understanding on their faces.

Cape's gaze finally settles on her, flickering to her amber eyes, rimed in black, to her teeth that push against her lips, then down to her soaking wet feet. "Yes," he says. "I know."

"I don't even know how many it was."

Cape doesn't say anything. No sympathies. No words of comfort. Would he have felt guilty if he slaughtered those people like she did? Does Mick feel anything like she does? He was right there with her, taking down half of the terrorist soldiers. What about Jax and Kyrin? How many have they killed? What about sweet, bright-eyes Celia?

Her eyes bore into the commander's, searching. She wants to reach into his brain and take what she needs, bring forth comfort and reassurance and advice. But no, there's none of that. There's only patient expectance. For what, Layla can only guess.

"It's stupid, right?" Layla says. "This is exactly what I wanted to do, and now that I've done it…"

Cape finally steps forward, his polished shoes clicking on the floor. He stops only a few feet away. Looking at him surrounded by hundreds of guns is unsettling. Even if he wouldn't be able to find a single real bullet on this floor. "You don't want to do this anymore, Ms. Wilson?"

"No! No, that's not what I meant." Restless energy is building up again from standing so still, so tense. She begins pacing the length of the shooting range, her socks making soft squelching noises with each step. "I just—the Black Sun are the reason my parents are dead. I just got the chance to fight back, and I'm not giving that up. *I'm not.* But those hybrids, that's the part I don't understand. All I can think about is that all the people I thought died from the serum are actually alive and working for them, but is that true? And why would they do that? Sure, I didn't know a lot about everyone I went to school with, but I know they all hate the Black Sun. They wouldn't work for them."

It would be the easier option, though. Layla's smart enough to see that. The Black Sun has all the advantages; power, soldiers, weapons. They practically run the country now. Many of the rumors she used to hear were about how this hybrid thing is already a lost cause. That the terrorists already won, and everyone needs to stop trying to fight. It would save a lot of lives, they said. The terrorists wouldn't have a reason to retaliate if no one fought against them.

Layla's fists tighten, only to promptly slacken again. She stares down at the gun in her hand with hatred and slams it on the nearest surface. Someone else can put it back where it belongs.

The commander hums while watching Layla stalk back and forth. "I believe that is what we are all wondering. But I have no doubt that you will play a big part in finding out." With that he heads back to the elevator doors. Layla stills, eyebrows furrowed together at his abrupt exit. She thinks that must be the end of their conversation, but before he presses the elevator button Cape turns back around. "We have all lost people because of this war, soldier. Remember that there is a much bigger reason to fight back against the Black Sun. A much bigger reason to want to win."

With that the commander leaves, leaving Layla feeling the beginnings of her accustomed anger roam under her skin. She waits until the lights above the elevator turn green before she moves. Maybe some special work with her axes will help her sort through what just happened.

I must be going insane, because I really love the rain.

CHAPTER SEVENTEEN

Feeling like he only slept for an hour at most, Jax is woken up by the deep, rumbling sound of thunder. Without a clock or window, he doesn't know what time it is, but the floor is quiet, so it must still be early. Rubbing at his swollen eyes, Jax attempts to stretch his legs out without disrupting Kyrin.

Surprisingly, he doesn't remember having any nightmares. With the mission yesterday, he thought he would be waking up constantly throughout the night. He looks over at Kyrin sleeping beside him. During the mission yesterday, after finding the other hybrid soldiers, he didn't know if the team would make it back. He figured they would be capture like his old team, but then they made it to the subway entrance and waited ten, twenty minutes where he was sure the two newest members of the team were captured or killed before Mick and Layla came sprinting towards them covered in blood and dirt.

The newbie passed out right away, but Mick explained what happened while Kyrin and Celia got the bullet out of Layla's leg and stitched her up. It's just like he would have planned it; set the newbie loose on the soldiers. His old team would have done the same with Benji if they had gotten the chance. But it still leaves him feeling a little guilty. He doesn't like treating his teammates like that; like they're only weapons. She did it on her own, he reminds himself. It was ultimately her choice, but maybe he put the idea in her head.

It was too sketchy to judge how she was handling everything last night. All of them were on edge from running into the enemy hybrids and soldiers. He hopes that today he will be able to get a better read on her.

The mission was… a lot of things. He's not sure what to call it. A failure, because they didn't get even half the information on the base that they needed to, because they encountered terrorist soldiers, and killed them all? A win, because they found out something big, something confusing and absolutely terrifying, because they all got back safe and sound?

He will need to talk with the commanders about it more as soon as possible. Try to convince them that they all need to do more. All teams should be given higher-risk missions. They need to move this war along before more people get killed. Before the Black Sun gets any more powerful.

Not to mention the hybrids. They need to stop injecting people with the serum. At least until they find out how the terrorists have them on their side. Jax will personally train the hybrids they already have in the labs and in medical and elsewhere. Train them up and get them fighting, and maybe then they will have a better chance at winning their country back.

"Jax, I can literally hear you thinking," Kyrin grumbles. Jax looks back over at his boyfriend's still-shut eyes. It must not be too early in the morning if he's awake. "Another bad dream?"

He leans his back against the wall behind the bed. "I've got a bad feeling about all this."

Kyrin peeks one of his onyx colored eyes open. "Cincinnati?"

Blowing out a breath, Jax nods. When his old team got captured, alerting the Black Sun of some of the commanders' plans, the terrorists retaliated by bombing Cincinnati. An old tactic to instill fear. An old tactic, but an effective one. He yearns to write to his brother, but what would he say?

Dear brother,

Take mom and go somewhere safe.

No. Nowhere is safe if he doesn't know the Black Suns plans. It doesn't matter. He wouldn't be able to send it anyway.

Jax blows out a long breath then looks over at Kyrin. "Something is going to happen," he says.

"Okay," Kyrin says in a soft voice, then louder, "Okay." In an explosion of movement that startles Jax, Kyrin flings the blankets into the air and rolls off the bed, landing on his feet. "Let's get the troops up and find out, then."

Jax takes one peek into the newbie's empty room and sends a look skyward in exasperation. He forces himself to close the door gently instead of slamming it into the frame like he wants to. If this becomes anymore of a common occurrence, he will need to interfere. She's not someone he wants to wander around at night.

"She's too far away. I can't hear her," Mick says when Jax walks into the kitchen. His brows are furrowed in concentration and he's sitting on one of the kitchen stools in full training gear, fingers twitching through his messy hair.

Jax takes the mug Kyrin holds out to him with a nod in thanks. "What do you think she's been doing now?"

Celia, standing close enough to the coffee machine to remind Jax of a loyal guardian, snorts. "She's probably just at the training center, or maybe she ran away. That would suck," she says, making Jax frown into his mug of tea. Kyrin shakes his head and Mick growls out a curse. "That was a joke, guys. She wouldn't run away. We should probably just meet her in the cafeteria. I'm starving."

Holding his hand up, Jax effectively stops any of them from moving. He takes a look at his teammates' tired expression before saying, "There's going to be an announcement today from the Black Sun, and possibly another terrorist attack." Celia and Mick straighten up from their slumped positions, watching him intensely, but Kyrin slowly sips from his mug, eyeing him through the dark hair that falls over his face. "They won't let what happened yesterday slip by. We found out an important bit of information; they have hybrids of their own. Ones that we injected with the serum and thought were dead."

Color slowly drains from his teammates' faces. "How bad do you think it's going to be?" Mick asks.

Jax throws back the rest of his hot tea, burning his tongue in the process. He ignores the unpleasant feeling and shakes his head. "This changes the entire war," he says. "They most likely have people on our side. Which isn't anything we didn't suspect before, but…"

"But we should probably wait for Layla to talk about this," Celia says. "And wait until we see what they actually do. And what the commanders will do." Her fingers twitch over the small packet of sugar in her hands. "No use getting ahead of ourselves, right?"

Jax hides his surprise behind his empty mug, but he can't help sending a look to Kyrin. In all the time he has known her, waiting was not something Celia ever suggested.

"All right," he says.

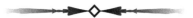

Jax is not surprised when he spots the commanders in the overcrowded cafeteria. They stand at the front of the raised platform, overlooking everyone. He could go up to them right now and tell them his thoughts on the war. In fact, his feet are already carrying him over the small distance between them, but Helland's eyes land on him like she knew exactly what he was planning. One shake of her head is enough to stop him.

Jaw ticking in annoyance, he changes his course, and nods to them as he passes. He will have to talk to them later, then.

As they sit to eat their food, Jax keeps an eye on the door, waiting for his newbie to join them. The televisions remain free of any Black Sun news, and the speakers don't scream with their warning siren, but his unease doesn't quit.

He's not that hungry, but refusing to let the food go to waste, he eats it anyway. It tastes bland and chewy, hard to swallow. The cafeteria gets fuller and fuller with every minute, and Jax catches conversations about the commanders sending out messengers to alert the whole compound of an important announcement.

He can feel the anxious energy in the air. It sets his blood tingling. Unable to sit still, he drums his fingers along the table, glancing from the door to where the commanders still stand. The team chatters around the table, but Jax barely listens.

Twenty minutes. Twenty minutes until finally the newbie walks through the door, Team Four in tow. Jax watches her in surprise as she searches through the masses of people, how her eyes stop on the commanders and narrow, how the small smile she was wearing slowing drops into a grimace. Why would she be with another team?

By the time her eyes meet his, the easy set of her shoulders is back to being tight, her hands clench and unclench at her sides, a crease has formed between her brows, and that angry, predatory quality floats from her.

Feeling the irritation at her fade, Jax sighs. No matter how much she projects those violent, confident attitudes, Jax doesn't think she can handle him telling her off after yesterday. At least not yet, and especially in front of the entire compound. Offering her a smile, he waves her over.

"Why's she with Team Four? Who's that guy?" Kyrin asks, pointing over to where she talks to the other team, hopefully saying her goodbyes.

He looks familiar, with curly hair and dark eyes. But it's the way they act together that makes him remember. They went through the team testing simulation together. Jax remembers them trading insults while working almost seamlessly together. "He was from her school," he says.

"William Fisher," Celia speaks up, bright eyes trained to their every move, and a wicked smile on her face that tells Jax she's already thinking of ways to use this against their newbie.

Mick bumps his shoulder into hers. "Why am I not surprised that you know that?"

But Celia is too busy watching Layla approach. Ignoring the slight blush on her face, Jax steps in before the overexcited Celia can get started. "The commanders are going to make the announcement about the terrorists having hybrids," he tells her, "and the Black Sun will probably have another message for us soon."

Slipping into the seat across from him, Layla looks up surprised. "How do you know?"

He's about to tell her about his old team and Cincinnati, but the commanders choose that moment to begin. All heads swivel in their direction, and at the sound of the microphones turning on, the room quiets. Televisions are switched to mute, and even the noises from the kitchen can't be heard.

"Thank you, everyone, for coming," Helland says, her voice loud and clear over the microphone. The frustration from when the team first told her the news still lingers in her tone. "One of our latest missions has uncovered some crucial information about the Black Sun."

"Many of you might find this news disheartening," Cape says, his bright eyes roaming over the cafeteria. "But just know this is not the end of this fight. We will win. We will get our country back."

Everyone waits with bated breath, even Jax, who knows what they are about to say. Fingers graze against the back of his hand and he turns it palm up, grasping Kyrin's fingers between his.

Helland speaks again. "Our enemy has their own hybrids." Jax expected yelling, but, if anything, the room gets quieter. "They are teenagers like you. From schools like yours. And you may know who they are, but they either do not know you or they do not care."

The loud sound of a *crack* echoes through the room. Jax looks over to see Layla's hands wrapped around the edge of the table. He watches with raised brows as she blows out a harsh breath and pulls her hands away, taking a piece of the table with her.

Her eyes stay down even when Cape clears his throat to regain attention. "We do not know how many they have, or exactly how they obtained and turned these teenagers to their side, but we will find out," he says, voice getting progressively harder, grittier. "Helland and I are discussing plans, and until we come to an agreement you—"

A familiar, gut-wrenching sound blasts out of the speakers, causing half of the people in the room to jump in fear. Kyrin's grip on Jax's fingers tightens enough to hurt. All the televisions turn black.

A single sentence appears one word at a time, like they are being typed out across the screen.

EVERYTHING THAT HAPPENS, YOU HAVE BROUGHT ON YOURSELVES.

*There's fire in my eyes, in my eyes,
in my eyes, in my heart.*

CHAPTER EIGHTEEN

*T*wo days later in the middle of their afternoon training, they get called down to Helland's office. A sinking feeling settles in Layla's stomach as soon as the messenger walks back out the door. To her confusion, Fisher's team was just sent out a day ago. She would've thought the commanders would wait awhile after the Black Sun's last message. And it has only been a few days since her team's last mission. Layla's leg still occasionally throbs from the gunshot wound, but no matter what she might be feeling, she doesn't let it show.

Back straight, chin high, she and her team enter Commander Helland's office, a room not much bigger than the kitchen on their floor, strewn with random books and knickknacks. It's only a slight shock when she sees that Cape is there, too. She still doesn't know what to think about their talk the other night. Shaking off the piercing stares of her commanders, Layla maneuvers herself into line, facing Helland and Cape with the rest of her team. It's a tight fit with all of them there.

Helland begins to open her mouth to speak, but Cape beats her to it. "I am glad you are all healed up, Ms. Wilson," he says. Usually that would be a nice thing to say, but his tone keeps her from so much as nodding in thanks. "Because Team Thirteen will be heading out again."

None of them are surprised. In fact, she thinks her team members smile. She doesn't look over to be sure.

Layla links her hands behind her back, waiting for their mission. Last time, only Jax was called in for the mission briefing, but this time they all were. It was a red flag in her head. She wants to tell the commanders to spit it out already, but Jax gave her explicit orders not to talk during the meeting. He'll talk for them, being the leader after all. Now that the Black Sun knows they are aware they have hybrids of their own, there's no choice but to give Team Thirteen higher-class missions.

But what Cape says has the floor tiling under her feet. "One of the teams has been captured."

"What?" Jax says, loud and snappy enough to make her flinch.

Layla's breathing picks up, her eyes darting between her leader and commanders. She has a moment to think *Please, not him.* before a slightly blurry-eyed Helland shuffles around some papers, and says, "Team Four went out yesterday. They sent a distress call thirty minutes ago. If you can get to them fast, we have a chance of getting them back."

"They should be expecting more of us to come, so ready yourselves as much as you can," Cape says with a not-at-all subtle look at Layla. "Mentally as well as physically."

"Where," Jax says, but Layla's already tuning them out, grabbing onto Mick's heartbeat fast, and letting it blare so loud in her head that it blocks out every sound around her.

Is this the Black Sun hitting back at them? Is this what their message meant? She just talked to Fisher two mornings ago, met the whole team at the training center and ran through a few drills with them for fun. The room tints red and stays that way.

After four claustrophobic hours on the subway, they get let off outside a demolished, abandoned city. A city big enough to have been attacked by the Black Sun, but small and old enough that Kyrin doesn't remember what it used to be called. Somewhere in the northern half of Wisconsin, that's all they were given about their location. But it's still close enough to Chicago that Kyrin immediately dislikes it. Anything within a states radius of Illinois sets a bad taste in Kyrin's mouth, but he's trying not to think about it.

They're at the same stop Team Four was let off at. His team is meant to follow in their steps. Without the getting captured part, of course. Find out where the other team went and follow their trail. The only problem, Kyrin thinks as he scowls up at the sky, is that it's pouring. Even with Mick's impressive sense of smell, it's very possible that the rain has already washed away all traces of the other team.

His team has been twitchy since those words left the commander's mouth, that another team has been captured. Especially Jax, though he tries to hide it, but Kyrin can tell in the way his eyes seem to burn a hole through everything he looks at, and in the way his hand is always hovering over the gun at his hip. The last team that was captured was his own.

And Kyrin can hardly stand to look at the newbie. Practically buzzing in her boots, she hasn't stood still since they left Helland's office. There's a glint in her eyes that he already hates. She sets his nerves on fire regularly, but this is just ridiculous.

"We're going to have to split up," he says to Jax. The two of them stand at the edge of the city. The dark clouds do nothing to improve the atmosphere. Already, his gear is dripping from the rain, and it won't be long before it's completely soaked through. "With all this rain, I don't know if we'll be able to find anything useful."

All Jax does is nod. Kyrin wishes they weren't all wearing filtration masks. In a bombed city like this they don't have a choice. If they weren't covering the bottom half of his face maybe, then he'd be able to get a better read on Jax.

Kyrin grabs Jax's fidgeting hand and pulls on it until he looks away from the city's remains. "You okay?" he says. Celia, Kyrin, and the newbie haven't moved from the subway entrance, giving them space, or maybe hiding from the rain. Kyrin doesn't particularly care.

"Yeah," Jax says. "It's all just hitting pretty close to home. And all this," he flings his hand to encompass the rain, the city, the situation they are in, "is shit." His eyes flick over Kyrin's shoulder, and he jerks his chin. "Round them up, yeah?"

When Kyrin looks over his shoulder, it's to see the newbie already headed towards them, no doubt having been listening, or running out of patience. Her eyes seem all the brighter with the black mask on, and with the large axes hanging at her sides, she makes a threatening sight. In fact, with her hood up, she looks like a reaper, stalking up to them with violet intent. Kyrin shakes his head. Mick and Celia still linger back, so he waves them forward.

"There are dogs in there. Somewhere. Or wolves or coyotes," the newbie says as she stops before them. "I can hear them."

"Great," he says shortly. Just what they need. "We are splitting up for this. Search your side of the city for any tracks. We'll meet up at that building straight back. Looks like one of the only ones still standing." He points out the building to everyone, so far back it's all but a speck in the dark landscape. "Mick, you're with me and Jax, and the two of you," he points between the girls, "are together."

Getting a few confused looks in return, he rolls his eyes. "Yes, Mick and the newbie aren't together for this. We need someone with their hearing and smell abilities on both teams, or we might miss something."

Celia and the newbie exchange a look, all but hidden under their masks, but Kyrin swears he sees the newbie smile, big and wide, showing off her canines like she loves to do.

"Let's get going then," Jax says.

Him and the guys take the right side, combing through the

destruction, looking for blood, or signs of struggle, or any type of footprint. Like he feared, they don't find anything, and an hour into it, Kyrin is frozen from top to bottom, barely able to feel his fingers or toes. Jax and Mick don't look much better, both as soaked as he is. The rain is letting up, but even if there was somewhere to take shelter, they don't have the time.

Anything. He would be happy with finding anything at this point.

Mick has lowered his mask under his chin, but Kyrin is beginning to doubt that it will help him find a scent. They climb up a four-story mountain of rubble, studying the rocks and debris for anything, and then they pause at the top. Looking around, Kyrin shakes his head and sighs. The sight is a reminder more than anything of why they're doing this, why they're fighting the Black Sun. But finding a foot hold to even begin taking them all down feels like eons away.

He's seen what some of the terrorists in these kinds of big cities do. The ones that make themselves out to be crime bosses and lords, so high on power and others' fear that they feel nothing can stop them. But Kyrin knows they can be stopped just as easily as anyone else. A shot to the head, to the heart, to anything vital.

"Did you see that?" Jax says. Kyrin turns around and follows Jax's outstretched finger. Nothing. He sees nothing.

"See what?" Mick asks, having come up beside them.

Before Jax can answer, the sky lights up with a flash of lightning, a rumbling of thunder, and Kyrin sees it. A glint of something shiny about ten yards away from their mountain of debris.

"It could be just a scrap piece of metal," Kyrin says. But it looked small, tiny actually. And it's the first remotely interesting thing they've seen so far.

"Let's go check it out."

They skid down the wet rocks, knees bent and arms flailing for balance. They somehow make it to the bottom without landing straight on their faces. Having memorized where the object is, Jax leads them over. Another flash of lightning illuminates the dark city for a moment, highlighting piles of rubble and chunks of concrete missing from the street before casting everything back into darkness. They stop at a divot in the road, and Jax crouches down to pick up the small object.

"A lighter," he says, using his thumb to rub the mud from the side of it.

"Does it work?" Mick asks at the same time Kyrin says, "I don't know why Team Four would have a lighter. We never take one."

After flicking at it a few times, it sparks to life, creating a small flame. "I don't think it's from the team. It looks like it has been here awhile," Jax says.

Jax puts out the light and holds it out for Kyrin and Mick to see. Sure enough, Kyrin can see the dents and worn-off paint. But if it's been in the street since before Team Four got here, then they still don't have any leads. He can only hope that Celia and the newbie found something to go on, or else they might be completely screwed.

"Hold on," Mick says in a hushed voice, raising his hand as if to shush them. "Be quiet. I think—" Mick cuts himself off, his entire body spinning to face the opposite way, the way they came from.

Kyrin and Jax freeze, knowing that if Mick hears something out there, it's best to give him the time to figure out what could be, but then Kyrin hears it too. Howling. A long, loud chorus of howls. He doesn't need Mick to confirm what it is. A pack of wolves or coyotes.

Slowly, as if the animals can hear his every movement, Kyrin extends his hand to place the lighter in one of the pockets on Jax's pack. Then he reaches for the gun strapped across his back, and says, "I guess our newbie was right."

"Of course, she was," Mick says. "I trained her." When he looks over at Kyrin, he does a double take. A snarl quickly takes over his mouth, large canines peeking out between his lips. "They are coming this way, following our scent, tracking us, but I swear to

God if you don't put that gun away, I will snap it in half."

Kyrin almost laughs; almost. "And what are we supposed to do when they start attacking us? Pet them? Play a little fetch?"

"We are not killing them," Mick says, eyes now on Jax's hand, the hand that has been hovering over his gun since before they got off the subway. "Right, Jax?"

He looks between Kyrin, Mick, and the direction the howls came from, now silent except for the slowing patter of rain on rock. "If we're not killing them, we need to move now. Head to the meeting point. We will take a few different routes to confuse them, but we're not going to find anything else over here."

Not wasting anymore time, they take off, running as quickly as they can, no longer bothering to look around for a trail. Every pile of debris looks the same as the next. Every turn they make only takes them to the same mauled road, and even with the rain now gone, the sky is still dark enough to make it impossible to tell exactly where they are going.

They take a lot of wild turns, heading vaguely in the direction of the meet-up point. Not wanting to lead the pack directly there, they turn back the way they came, and take the opposite turn. Over and over they do this, until Kyrin's feet and legs are numb, and his lungs burn with the frigid air. As soon as they get to that building, he's going to put that lighter to good use.

But all it takes is one wrong turn, and Mick's increasingly loud cursing for them all to know they messed up. Fingers itching for one of his guns, Kyrin faces the oncoming growls.

"No," Mick says. "We're going to have to run."

Just as Kyrin is about to start cussing out his idiotic team member, Jax makes for one of the halfway-destroyed buildings on their right. "Inside. Let's go!"

With a burst of speed, they follow. There's no way in hell the building is safe to go in. The doorway is crumbling and blistered. The roof is slumped into the second story. The windows all shattered, and the walls look like they're seconds away from collapsing. Inside is pitch black, allowing Kyrin to see only vague shadows of broken furniture and outlines of unknown obstacles.

"What if there's no back exit?" he asks as they pick their way across the cluttered ground.

He doesn't get an answer. The dogs are closing in. Even he can hear the distinct rumbles in their throats. Faster. They need to go faster, get some type of leverage or ground. If only Mick would let him shoot them, but then Kyrin thinks about why they're here, what they're going to run into to save Team Four. It would be a waste of bullets, he tells himself, to use them on dogs rather than terrorists.

"No. No. No," Mick says, stopping in his tracks. "They're at the back now. They've trapped us." And that's all it takes for Kyrin to toss his previous thought away in the garbage where it belongs.

The tell-tale sound of a gun being unsheathed is all that can be heard for a solid minute. "We're going to have to do it, Mick. No offense, but I'm not dying from being eaten by wolves."

"Come on guys." Kyrin knows that if he could see Mick's face, his eyes would be big, maybe even glistening with unshed tears. Puppy dog eyes. The guy does it on purpose all the time. Especially when it involves food. "There are less at the back. Only three. We can get by them and sprint all the way to the meeting point."

Kyrin tosses his head back, looking up at the darkness above them. Jax cusses. Mick's plan is crap. Kyrin's sure they all know it, but he also knows Jax doesn't like to upset anyone on the team, will do almost anything to make them all as happy as they can be in whatever situation they're in. It's one of the qualities that Kyrin loves, but it also makes him want to hit him upside the head and call him an idiot.

"Get ready then," Jax says, blending in so well with the darkness that he's only a disembodied voice. "Try to stay behind them if you can, as far away from their heads as possible."

Kyrin looks up again, fighting the urge to scream out every harsh profanity he knows. Terrorists soldiers he can handle. Crime lords and street filth, he can handle. Huge, angry canines *that he can't kill*, not so much.

When they reach the back door, Jax gives them five whispered seconds to ready themselves. Then he kicks the crooked door, and sends it flying completely off the hinges. He has a split second to see that they are, in fact, wolves, before the door crashes into two of the furry, grey bodies. Kyrin doesn't waste time watching what happens to them. He sprints out the empty doorframe and down the back alley with Mick and Jax.

The door didn't do much to distract them, and in less than a minute, the wolves are hot at their heels, barking and growling. Kyrin risks a glance back, seeing the flashing white teeth, dripping with bubbling saliva. A nauseous feeling settles in his stomach.

The hybrid serum made them all faster, stronger. They can run three times as fast as a regular human, but the wolves are just as fast, and they're not showing any signs of slowing down. Skirting around another pile of debris, he swears he can feel their hot breath on his back.

And then behind him, Mick cries out.

Skidding to a halt, he slips the gun on his back out again. What he spins around to see makes the nauseous feeling in his stomach increase tenfold. One of the wolves is on Mick, its strong legs pinning him to the concreate. Its teeth are wrapped around his left forearm. Jax is already racing back towards him, which would have eased Kyrin's mind if it weren't for the fact that his hands are empty.

Kyrin takes a moment to think, *There's no way he's going to fight a wolf with his bare hands*, before he aims his gun and fires. Not at Mick, but at the ground a few inches in front of the two other wolves.

They startle, jumping back, ears flat to their head and lips pulled over their large teeth. But the one on top of Mick doesn't get off. Kyrin aims again a foot in front of where they tussle, and fires three shots. Kyrin watches as the wolf's hackles spring up along it's back and it scrambles to get away from Mick and the bullets. After one last shot, the three wolves run off, not glancing back even once.

Putting away the gun, Kyrin helps Jax get Mick up off the ground. He's banged up a little, shaking slightly, but the most damage is from the bite on his arm. With quick precision, the three of them look it over. It's deep enough that it's going to need stitches. "I've got the medical kit in my pack," Kyrin says.

"Thanks for not killing them," Mick says. "And for saving me."

"Save it for when we get out of this city." Kyrin rifles through his pack and pulls out the white box full of medical supplies. He hands Jax the gauze to help stop the bleeding and cover the wound. He will fix it up better when they get to the meeting point. It can't be more than ten minutes away now, and hopefully the girls will have found something.

"Hey," Mick says as they begin walking, his arms thrown over Kyrin's and Jax's shoulders. "Do you think I'll finally turn into a werewolf now?"

Kyrin groans. If Mick wasn't injured, he might have pushed him into one of the mountains of rocks. But Jax laughs his first laugh all day, so Kyrin lets the awful joke slide.

The world is still clouded and grey when Layla and Celia get back to the meeting point a few hours after searching their half of the city. They sit together on the roof of the building with Celia leaning her shoulder against Layla's. Their gear is soaked from the rain, causing the already dark material to turn black. Slight shivers run through her friend's body and into hers. Even though sitting this close spreads more cold than warmth between them, they stay pressed together.

The guys are somewhere amongst the surrounding buildings, trying to find any sign of what happened to Team Four. Layla doesn't remember when this city was destroyed. From the look of things, it has been awhile. Most parts of the city are still crumbled and dirty—wasted, abandoned remains—but she and Celia skirted a part at the edge of the city being rebuilt and lived in.

The people were dirty and tired looking, adults and children alike. Some who struggled even to walk, choosing instead to kneel among piles of broken buildings, searching through the debris for anything useable. The sight of them lit a feeling in her chest. Not the burning anger, but a warm, soothing flame of hope. Maybe years from now, all the damage the Black Sun have done will be repaired.

Of course, they need to win this war first.

Layla tries to stretch out her limbs, muscles so tense from the cold that every movement is painful. "They're coming back," she says. She can hear the three heartbeats approaching, Mick's familiar one among them.

"About time," Celia says, teeth clenched tight from the icy air. Her dark, shoulder length hair is plastered to her head, and Layla knows that hers doesn't look any better. "Still don't know why Kyrin thought it was a good idea to meet at the top of a building. Especially when it's like zero degrees here."

They hadn't been waiting long for them, but it feels like time is going slower here, freezing in place just like Layla's toes are freezing under her thick socks and boots. And she wants to get going. She sniffed out a trail when she and Celia looked around, easy to smell from the blood spattered in places protected from the rain like Fisher and his team were trying to hide from the terrorists who took them. There must have been a lot of soldiers, Layla reasons. For them to overcome a group of hybrids with military training. Unless, of course, the group of terrorists had their own hybrids with them.

When the guys are seconds away, she stops fidgeting with the padded ruffles on the knees of her pants and forces herself to her feet. She drags Celia with her who grumbles, but otherwise doesn't resist. A hooded head pops around the edge of the door that leads to the stairs, and their body follows. Two more come after. Having already discarded her filtration mask from pure annoyance, Layla can't hide her grimace.

"What happened to you guys?" she asks, eyes raking over their large frames.

"You were right about there being dogs," Jax says, his voice gritty with anger or cold. He's been noticeably almost as upset about the circumstances of this mission as Layla is. But she can't bring herself to think about him when she's more focused on getting to Team Four as fast as possible.

"They weren't friendly," Celia says, letting her smirk be heard in her voice.

That much is clear. Mick and Jax's wet gear is slightly ripped and smeared with mud. Layla even spots a little bit of bubbling saliva on Jax's pant leg. Smelling blood, she runs her eyes over each of them. Mick. Mick has blood on his forearm, and bandages peek out from his ripped sleeve.

He barks out a laugh, startling Layla. "We tried to avoid them, but they weren't having it. Chased us around in circles. And when we went into a building to avoid them, they trapped us in. We had to make a run for it."

"Couldn't you have shot them or something?" Even saying the words bring a small pain in her heart, and instantly she wants to take them back. They didn't do anything wrong. They were just being wolves, protecting their territory.

Shaking his head, Kyrin digs in his pack, taking out medical supplies. "I was going to," he says, "but Wolfboy wouldn't let me, so of course, he gets bit. Probably has rabies now."

Celia, still at her side, begins jumping in place, trying to warm herself. "So, did you find anything then, because we did."

Jax holds something up, an old lighter, dented on the side and the color so faded it is unrecognizable, but when he clicks it, a small blue flame appears. "What did you find?"

Layla's already shoving food wrappers in her pack, cleaning up her mess and getting ready to leave. A couple feet away, Kyrin's stitching up the gashes in Mick's arm. "Blood. A trail over there." She points down into the city. "It leads to the highway, but I lost it there."

"The highway?" Jax says, looking out over the city, towards the abandon highway. With his enhanced eyesight, Layla doesn't doubt that he can see it a lot better than she can. "I'll send a message to the commanders, ask them if there is a base that way. In the meantime," he tosses the lighter to her, "try to start a fire. We need to get dry."

Through clenched teeth, she agrees, and asks Celia to help her.

It was Cape's idea to keep communication between the team and the commanders. Most of the time they don't want to risk the chances of the terrorists tuning in to their frequency, but they suited the team with ear pieces that link to each other and to a small radio like device back in Helland's office for them to check in with the commanders, let them know that they're not being captured, too. And since they don't know exactly where Team Four was taken, it's also for when the team needs help like they do now.

And later, according to Helland, when the other team is found and safe, they will bring backup, medics, and people to survey wherever the terrorists at the base are hiding. Layla doesn't understand why they all didn't go together in the first place.

As quickly as they can, she and Celia make a fire on the first floor of the building in case it begins raining again. Layla listens to Celia's constant mumbling as they gather random debris to add to the flames. Once the fire is big enough, the guys join them with appreciation on their lips. They lay their clothes out to dry, standing as close to the fire as they dare.

When she catches Celia bring up something about a big, warm cup of coffee for the fifth time, Layla snorts. Celia glances away from the bright flames to give Layla a surprised look, all raised eyebrows and wide green eyes. "All we need to do is send you on a mad chase through the country, stealing coffee and killing every terrorist that gets in your way," Layla says.

A wide smile takes up the bottom half of Celia's face. Her cheeks bulging around her mask from the force of it. "Not a bad idea, actually." Then a mischievous glint twinkles in her eyes. "But I think it's more like all we need to do is send you on a crazy mission to save your boy. What's his name again? Sharkboy?"

Layla's teasing mood evaporates in an instant. "That's not funny," she says.

Celia flinches back at her harsh tone and returns to staring at the fire. "Yeah, you're right. Sorry. Bad timing." She sneaks a glance back at Layla. "We'll get him back, though. All of them."

"I know," she says. She has no doubt about that. Whoever's responsible for anything that happens to Fisher and his team is going to pay.

Jax joins them minutes later, saying it might take a while for Helland and Cape to find the right information. Sitting on her pack for cushioning, Layla tucks her numb nose between her knees, and attempts to gather her patience.

If the commanders can't find the location of where the terrorists took the other team, and they're struck at a dead end, she will continue looking. She will demand for the commanders to send the backup now, to help find Fisher and his team. And if they say no, she will continue looking on her own, and she won't stop until she finds them. Fisher is her friend, and she refuses to leave him behind in the enemy's hands.

Ten minutes pass, and Layla's ready to go ahead by herself. All she needs to do, she thinks, is follow the highway, and listen for the sound of humming electricity that will lead her to people, civilization. She will ask around, she will plan as she goes.

"Hey," Celia says. Her hair is combed out and drying, and her nose is almost back to the right color. "It'll just be a little longer. Now turn away from me, I'll do your hair."

Huffing and shaking her head, Layla does what she's told. Celia tugs steadily at her hair, fighting the tangles. Layla fidgets with her tight-fitting undershirt, the only thing that remained more-or-less dry. She dares to stick her toes closer to the fire. "If they don't answer soon—"

"You're not going anywhere." Kyrin interrupts from his own place by the fire, and Layla snarls at him. He can't stop her.

Once all the tangles are out of her hair, Celia quickly braids it, starting at the top of her head and trailing down. Quietly, Layla thanks her, and begins to dress in her only slightly damp clothes.

Another five minutes later, when the team has eaten a box of meal bars, and is now mostly dressed, Jax finally walks off to speak with the commanders again. Layla throws fistfuls of dirt into the fire until she puts it out completely.

"There's a base," Jax says when he walks back over, making Layla's innards clench. "We just need to follow the highway, then turn at the pitstop point. Follow it straight back into the woods for a half a mile, and we will be there."

Of course, it's somewhere in the woods. Faster than the others, Layla gathers her axes, straps her knives around her thighs and arms. Ready. She is so ready to go.

Red as the taste of rage on my tongue.

CHAPTER NINETEEN

"**K**yrin, Celia, take the high ground if possible. If not, you know what to do. Layla you're with Mick again. Follow his lead. I'll be close by," Jax says after sending an update to Helland and Cape that they're about to enter the base.

They all have their masks off now, but Layla can still see the faint indents in their skin. More than that she can see the uncertainty on their faces. And their eagerness. Layla gazes towards the base, towards the buzz of electricity and thumping hearts. "That's it? That's the plan?" They haven't even gotten a good look at the place. They have no intel to go on. "What if there are hybrids?

"They die the same as the rest," Kyrin says with his typical sneer.

We die the same as the rest, Layla's mind unhelpfully supplies. She scrapes her fingernails against her rough pants. "Right."

Flashing her a smile, Jax takes out his gun. Layla's eyes widen. He can't be serious. But he is, and he looks *excited*. "Don't worry too much," he says. "It will distract you from what you need to do. Besides, you handled the soldiers at the last base well, and this time you're fighting to get your friend back, right? That should be enough to get you going."

Blinking, she slowly looks at her other teammates. Celia winks, Mick shrugs, and Kyrin doesn't bother looking at her. Is this how her leader is on a real, dangerous mission? The change is enough to throw her for a loop.

She shakes it off and asks the more important question. "You want me to do that again? Just let go and kill everyone?"

Jax opens his mouth but stops to press at the device in his ear. Layla can't tell what the commanders are saying on the other end, and it's more than annoying. It's too muffled, too choppy. Only his comm is linked to the radio back at the compound. The rest of the team relies on him to pass on the conversation. "Helland says to leave a few alive for questioning."

Layla throws her hands out to the side in a gesture that conveys exactly what she feels: exasperation. And mild panic. But it's the anger that she brings to the surface. She takes out two blades. Layla hates the terrorists, hates that they took Fisher and his team, but she also hates that she is beginning to feel used by her leader. The terrorists have bombs they use to spread fear, and to kill. Team Thirteen has her.

"How are you feeling?" Mick asks. They split up from the others only minutes ago. They're to come at the base from the front, while Celia and Kyrin come from the sides. Jax is going through the back, hoping the rest of the team will be distraction enough for him to enter the building quickly.

If they weren't trying to make the least amount of sound possible, Layla would have laughed. As it is, a small snort leaves her nose. "Peachy," she says, voice more like a hiss.

So far, they haven't encountered any soldiers. In fact, the base and surrounding forest seem quiet. Instead of putting her at ease, it makes her more apprehensive than if there were hundreds of enemy soldiers rushing at them. Layla can't help but feel like the terrorists at the base already know her team is there. That they are watching. But she hears no cameras, and she hears no nearby heartbeats aside from hers and Mick's.

"How's the leg?" Mick asks.

"Great." The wound from the gunshot isn't completely healed, and the trek through the city didn't help, but the throbbing is occurring less and less. Layla has a feeling that after they're done here it very well might be pounding once again.

Mick doesn't ask about her darkening mood. Not that he needs to. He was like her once, and still is somewhat—unable to control emotions, violent. He understands better than the rest, but he still doesn't do anything to stop her from being used. Maybe it's for the best. At least this way, she will move too fast to see the terrorists' faces as she ends them.

"Ready," Celia says over the device in her ear.

"Ready," Layla and Mick repeat.

Kyrin's voice follows, then after a few more seconds, Jax's.

No longer caring about the sounds their feet make on the littered forest floor, they pick up their pace until they're running through the trees. The entrance to this base is guarded by a large, solid metal gate, cameras, and four armed soldiers. Layla slips two throwing knives into her palms. When she's close enough for the soldiers and cameras to spot her, she lets the slim knives fly. Each knife finds it's mark. Instantly, two of them go down. Before the other two can raise their guns, Mick copies her movement, effectively taking them down.

The four soldiers weren't hybrids. That much she could tell from yards back. It's something Mick taught her yesterday. Hybrids have a different smell than regular humans, a tangy, almost chemical smell from whatever is in the serum. Not only that but their hearts beat slower and louder than normal humans. It wasn't something she had to worry about learning until what they found out on their last mission, and it comes in handy now.

Not a second after they rush to the gate, sirens sound, alerting the base to their presence. They climb to the top of the gate and jump to the ground on the other side. Men and women, all of them wearing the Black Sun's green uniforms, rush out of the building, armed with glowing guns and ready to fight.

But Layla has been ready for a fight since Helland gave the news.

Completely caught up in knowing that Fisher and his team are so close, Layla doesn't even flinch at the deafening sound of gunfire. She shoves Mick from her mind, and lets her senses take in everything around her.

The world tints a brighter shade as Layla watches even more enemy soldiers pour out of the building and charge towards her. Layla and Mick meet them halfway across the soon-to-be killing field. Red clashes with all the green as she exchanges her blades for axes.

There must be a hundred soldiers, if not more. As she spins, ducks, and slashes with her axes, she loses sight of Mick in the mass of bodies. They've been fighting for roughly ten minutes before a bullet catches Layla on the tip of her ear and she screeches. Not from pain, but outrage. She can feel the blood slide down her neck as she swings at the assailant. Screaming erupts from a different part of the base, and Celia's cursing is blindingly loud over the previously silent comm device in her ear.

It's easier than the last time she did this, and with fewer and fewer targets appearing, Layla decides to scan the space between the front gate and the building for Mick. If she can pinpoint where he's at, she will be able to find his steady heartbeat to bring back some of her control. Just as she spots him close to the base's front entrance, Layla notices the real reason for Celia's cursing. The green-clad soldiers are retreating into the building. Growling, she rushes after them, intent on killing them before they can make it back inside.

But then something falls from the sky.

A human. A hybrid. And there's not only one. Three more jump down from the roof after the first. Layla dodges out of the way just in time to avoid getting plowed over by four pairs of heavy boots. Every thought of regaining her control disappears, but she can't help it as she takes a moment to scan their features. Does she know them? She looks for short brown hair and a face she knows as well as her own, but she's never seen these people before. Feeling a mixture of relief and disappointment, Layla spins the hilts of her axes around in her hands, making sure she has a good grip. It wouldn't matter if she did know one of them, she reminds herself. Not if she wants to save Fisher and his team.

One of them zeroes in on her, a girl with dark skin and hair shaved close to her scalp. Her white-less eyes gleam with violence. The enemy hybrid moves as fast as Layla does, dodging her attacks in smooth, agile motions. Unlike the hybrids at the other base, these are trained well. The glint of a gun in her hand is hard to miss. The girl leaps a foot back when Layla swings her axe. Then, aiming straight at Layla's head, she fires the gun with a cold, unfeeling expression. Layla drops to the ground, hitting it hard enough to jar her bones.

Feeling the heat of the bullets above her, Layla grits her teeth and swipes her axe in an arch at the girl's legs. The blade only just reaches her shins, slicing across them, and sending her to the ground. Wasting no time, Layla's scrambles to her knees and lunges at the girl to swiftly finish the job. Then she turns as she hears another bullet whizz by her head.

"We got hybrids over here," she says into the communication device.

Then she dives at another one—big, burly, and getting ready to fire another shot at her. She pushes off the slippery grass and tackles him around the waist at full speed. The air in her lungs is punched out of her. The feeling is similar to how she imagines running into a brick wall would be, but the guy goes down under her. He doesn't give up easily. Growls rip from her throat as they roll and tussle. Her axes lay on the ground next to them, and she struggles to pull a dagger from her person.

"Take them out fast," Jax's voice says in her ear, slightly out of breath. "I'm in, but more terrorists keep coming at me."

Layla struggles to pin the guy down, looking at his face, searching again for anything familiar, but she doesn't know him. His dark eyes are blank. No anger, or hate, or panic. No emotion at all. That look, along with his shaved head, reminds her of the targets in the testing simulation.

He uses her moment of surprise to flip her over. The barrel of a gun is shoved in her face. She grips his wrist, trying to push it away, but he holds firm with that blank look on his face. Her other hand is held against the ground, and no matter how hard she tries, she can't get it loose from his hold.

Just when she thinks she's done for, a sharp sound of pain leaves the man's throat, and he slumps on top of her. Dead.

She doesn't have time to get a proper breath before Mick hauls the man off her and she rises to her feet. There's blood on his face and in his long hair. His pointed teeth gleam in the blinking alarm lights coming from the base as he talks hurriedly. "Celia and Kyrin still need our help before we can get to Jax and get the team." He cocks his head at her, a deep frown on his face. "You could have taken that guy out with a single dagger. Now isn't the time to hold back. Get your game face on, Layla. These guys still have time to do huge damage. To us and Team Four."

Looking towards the base with narrowed eyes, Layla nods. There are already so many bodies littering the ground. She can smell the blood, taste it in the air. It makes something inside her burn. Lips drawing back over her teeth, she wretches herself away from Mick. He lets her go easily. Without a word, she swoops up her axes and runs around the wall of the base to find Celia.

The faster they can get this done, the faster she can get to Fisher and get him and his team out safely.

He's missed this. The adrenaline, the fighting, the feeling that this is what he's supposed to be doing. Jax always knew that he'd be a soldier. Even before the Black Sun started terrorizing the country, he knew. *Just like your dad*, his mom would always say. But now he knows that he needs to be better than his dad.

The remaining tension since he heard about Team Four's capture raises off his shoulders. They're here, at the base. All he needs to do is get rid of these soldiers and find them. The compound won't lose another team.

Jax ducks around the door as another round of bullets comes his way. He hasn't seen any sign of the captured team, or where they are being held. The base is a maze of labs and offices. It was easy to find the scientists cowering in the lab he stands in right now, and it was even easier to knock the ten of them out, but now it seems that all the soldiers from outside are rushing back in, choosing to fight one hybrid instead of the rest of the team outside.

There's terrorist hybrids outside. At least according to Layla there are. It makes sense that these people don't want to get caught in the cross hairs of that fight. If Jax could, he would join the team outside, make sure that all of them get into the building safely, but he's got his own fight going on up here.

The hallway outside the lab room is packed with fallen terrorist soldiers, all dead because of him. Behind them, more use the bend in the wall for cover. There's no sign that they're going to turn away, not when they think they have the upper hand, but they aren't stupid. Having seen what Jax did to the others, they stay behind the wall, waiting for an opening. Jax will have to lure them closer, give them that opening. He ran out of ammo about ten minutes ago, and he's almost out of knives, having thrown and thrust them into the necks of the never-ending crowd of terrorist filth. With this many soldiers, humans and hybrids, it's no wonder why Team Four was captured. Especially if they were taken by surprise.

"Heading in," Celia's voice says through the communication device in his ear. Jax can easily pick up the sound of growling breaths, letting him know the newbie is probably with her.

"Hurry up," he says. It will only be a matter of time before his knives truly run out and he has no choice but to resort to fists, but with Celia and Layla coming, he might not have to lure them in as he planned. He can only thank the tight quarters of the hallway for the terrorist's reluctance to use their guns, but soon enough they will run out of patience hiding behind the wall just waiting for Jax to do something.

Between breaths, he gives directions to Celia. "Left. Straight. Up three flights."

Layla stops him there with a simple, "Found you."

The voices of Kyrin and Mick follow. "We're right behind you."

Jax lets out a harsh sigh of relief. His team is okay for now. He leans his shoulder against the wall by the door and glances behind him. The scientists are all still unconscious, and probably will be for a few hours. There's only one he left unharmed. He tied the man's arms and legs up with some rope he found on his way in. His grey, bushy eyebrows sit low over his eyes as he glares at Jax. Jax gives him a flat look and turns back to the hallway and waits. Two minutes later, screams begin at the end of the hallway. The soldiers become frantic, charging out from their hiding place and rushing towards him.

With his limited weapons, Jax has no choice but to let them come close. He's quick to disarm them, but one of them manages to get a punch in, straight across his face. Jax bites his tongue. Blood coats his mouth, tangy and biter. Two more soldiers grab at his arms.

Smiling a bloody red smile, Jax dislodges their weak grips and slashes out with a knife. By the time they're done, the scientist is shrieking, struggling against his bonds. Jax pushes the limp soldiers away from him. With a few steps he's in front of the scientist. Taking the man's arm in an iron grip, Jax drags him into a standing position. He's middle-aged with greying hair and a scruffy beard. Jax doesn't need enhanced senses to be able to smell the reek of him. Sweat and fear, and probably urine.

Jax meets his teammates in the hallway. They look as well as he probably does—covered in blood and sweat, wildness shining through their eyes. "I think we got them all," Kyrin says. "Did you find the team?"

Jax shakes his head. "Not yet, but I'm sure this guy can help." He props the scientist against the wall, so he won't fall over. Then he shuts and marks the lab door for the commanders to find.

It's not hard to get Team Four's location from him. All Jax needed to do was give Kyrin the signal to hold him at gun point. Now, with Kyrin at his back, the unbound scientist leads them through the building, shaking harder and harder with every bloodied hallway they cross. They go down several flights of stairs, finally ending up in the basement.

The heating must stop here too, because Jax can see his breath in the air. Despite this, his body stays warm with adrenaline. After a quick sweep of the basement, they find that the only notable thing is the one metal door. A small scanner is installed in the wall next to it, and with only a little resistance, the scientist presses his hand to it.

There's a second of silence, and then the door beeps open. His teammates crouch, readying themselves for another fight, but when Mick pushes the door wide, there's no one there. He sweeps inside, looking right and left before giving them the all clear signal.

With no more need for him, Kyrin smacks the butt of his gun against the scientist's temple, sending him crumpling to the floor, unconscious. Jax goes through the door after Mick, his nose already burning from the chemical smell of cleaner. There are three different ways to go, each one brightly lit and freezing cold.

"All right," he says, sparing a look at his teammates. Kyrin stands in the doorway, watching their backs. Mick is already starting down one of the halls. Celia is peeking down the right hall, a hand thrown over her nose, while Layla stares down the middle, nose wrinkled but twitching in a way that Jax knows means she' trying to scent the air. All five of them have blood soaking their gear. Some even drips off their weapons. "Let's find these guys."

Will I see you in my nightmares?

CHAPTER TWENTY

*L*ayla picks the way that's seeping with the nauseating smell of blood and chemicals. All but running down the hall, she tries to force her churning stomach to settle. Mick follows at a slower pace, checking behind the few closed doors even though no heartbeats sound from them. Layla knows what he's looking for—bodies, weapons, any sort of information—but that's what the others from the compound are going to do when they get here, so Layla pushes ahead.

The heartbeats are further down at the end of the hall where the light is brighter, and the smell is stronger. Two heartbeats. The other halls had multiple, but as focused as she was on this hall, Layla didn't bother to count them. The smell was enough to tell her that whoever was down this way needed help as soon as possible.

But there was something more, something that smelled too familiar to turn the other way. Fisher was down here. Some part of her knew it.

Slipping a dagger into each hand, Layla speeds up. If one of those pulses is another terrorist, whether it be soldier, scientist, or hybrid, they won't stand a chance against her. When she bursts into the open room, Layla almost breaks her promise to not throw up. Bile stings at the back of her throat.

The smell is horrid.

Gagging, Mick rushes past her frozen form, going to the machine by the metal slab and starts to frantically push buttons. Stepping closer, Layla's eyes travel along the dangling wires that come from the machine to the many places they hook into the body on the cot. If you can call the metal slab a cot. It hasn't even been a full day, but he looks like he's been here much longer.

Save for a pair of boxers, his body is bare; his eyes are shut, and his face is pale. Bruises mark his skin from head to toe. Maybe from fighting, or maybe from whatever they did to him. They remain dark purple and blue like they were given to him recently. The bruises along his ribs and around his cheeks could only be from broken or fractured bones. The bright, florescent lights make them painful to look at. Layla's head throbs as she peers closer. They don't seem to be healing. It must be from whatever is in the tubes and needles, she thinks, looking over at all the wires and the machine Mick taps at.

"Fisher," Layla says, laying a hand on his. Even in the freezing basement, his skin is burning. At the contact, his muscles strain under the wide metal bars holding him to the cot. It makes something in her mind crack, bringing on a surge of rage and fear. When he doesn't open his eyes, she says, "Will? It's Layla. We're going to get you out of here."

Slowly he opens his chapped lips, showing his jagged, pointy teeth. He whispers a curse then coughs. "You've got to be joking." Layla huffs out a laugh in surprise. Eyes peeking open, he struggles to lift his head, but with all the metal bars holding him in place, it's impossible to do so. Layla moves closer, so he can see her. "I can't believe they sent you," he says, shaking his head. The skin around his eyes is dark, like some of the veins burst, and his lips are dry and cracked. "Or did you demand to be sent here?"

Layla sighs, relieved and already slightly annoyed. "You're just upset that you're aren't the one saving me."

He shakes his head again. "Trust me," he says. "I'm not."

Before she can think about that too deeply or come up with a response, Mick says, "Got it." A second later the metal bars let out a hissing noise as they rise away from Fisher's body. "You need to get the wires out. I'll take care of whoever is in there." He nods toward a door, probably leading to a storage room.

Layla all but forgot about that other pulsing heart. She utters a quick thanks to Mick before taking a better look at Fisher. Some of the wires, mostly the ones connected to his chest and head, end in small patches, meant to monitor his heart and brain waves.

"Okay. Here we go," she says. Layla easily pulls the small patches off, relieved when it doesn't seem to hurt him. Out of the corner of her eye, she watches him. Then her hands hover over the other wires, these ones attached to needles in the creases of his arms.

"Just do it," he says, voice rough and scratchy. "Take them out."

Just as Layla begins slowly pulling the first needle out, banging starts from the closet. Hissing out a breath through her teeth, she steadies her hands and sets the freed needle on the cart by the machine. She doesn't bother to go help Mick. Whatever it is, he can handle it.

She takes another two needles out before her teammate finally exits the closet, a man slung over his shoulder. The white coat around his shoulders is enough to tell her that he is personally responsible for all these needles in Fisher. The way he is slumped, and his quiet pulse signal that the man is unconscious.

After setting him down by the door, Mick helps her remove the remaining needles from Fisher and ease him off the metal cot. Fisher is unsteady on his feet, knees weak under him. He sways from side to side, bumping into her and Mick rhythmically.

"Dehydrated," Mick says, distracting Layla from throwing murderous glances at the scientist. "Probably hasn't eaten enough or at all since he left the compound."

Fisher snarls at him, and she resists the urge to punch him on the shoulder. "He can speak for himself."

Before they start fighting, Layla speaks up with the most pressing question. "Where are your clothes?"

"What?" Fisher says. "I don't know."

The three of them search the room. For clothes, water or food, and any important information. Jax already alerted the commanders to bring backup, but it could still be a few hours before they get here, and they all left their packs back in the forest about a mile away since it's easier to fight without them strapped to their backs.

Fisher sits back down after a few minutes, exhausted. He's heavily drugged, unable to hold himself up. His eyes droop like he could fall asleep any minute. Layla's afraid to ask exactly what they did to him, to his team. She'll ask later, when they're out of this freezing, rank basement. With a cry of triumph, she finds a small fridge installed to look like just another cabinet door and pulls out a few bottles of water. After giving Fisher two and throwing one to Mick, she continues her search.

She finds another cabinet full of files. Pulling them out one by one, she places them on the counter. There's no time to look at them right now, but this will make it easier for the others to find them. If this scientist shows more backbone than the other one and refuses to give up the information on what they did to Fisher, hopefully the files will help. Mick emerges from the storage closet again, this time with clothes in his arms instead of a person.

Layla stops short on her way back to the cot at the sounds from the comm device in her ear. Yelling and banging. She and Mick exchange a look. They need to get out of here. The two of them quickly help Fisher get dressed in the boxy scrubs. Well, as much as he will let them help.

"Kye!" comes Jax's voice from the device. Layla's stomach clenches with fear. She has never heard him sound like that: panicked, wrecked.

Layla urges Fisher to get moving. "What's going on?" he asks as Mick drags the scientist onto the cot and uses a spare shirt to tie his wrist to the sides of the frame. There's no use messing with the machine to get the metal bars to trap him in. Even if he does wake up before help gets here, there's nowhere for him to run to.

"I'm not sure," she tells Fisher. Then she presses the small device harder into her ear as they start slowly down the hall with Fisher between them. "Guys, what's going on?"

Instead of Jax or Kyrin, it's Celia who answers. "I've got the team here. They say one of them was taken away."

"We have him," Layla says. She has no doubt that Celia knows exactly who it is that's missing. "Jax? Kyrin? Tell us something."

There are a couple minutes of silence where the three of them get almost all the way down the hall. Layla gets steadily more nervous before Kyrin finally answers, "Just get over here."

Once again, Layla casts a look at Mick. Whatever it is, she doesn't think one of them got hurt, but it can't be good. Next to her, Fisher growls in annoyance and pain. They are moving as fast as they can, but with him sagging between them, it could take them awhile to get to Jax and Kyrin.

"Going as fast as we can," comes Celia's voice. "We have injuries."

Jax's voice is hard to recognize when he says, "Take them up. Commanders should be arriving soon. They can help, and as soon as they arrive, start sending medics down here. We have more prisoners." The sound of screeching metal tears through her ear, cutting off Jax and making Layla hiss at the pain that radiates through her head. "Layla. Mick. We are going to need your help over here."

More time must have passed than she thought if Jax thinks the help will be here soon. The three of them are only feet from the basement door now, and when they get to the hallway intersection, Fisher props himself up against a wall, breathing labored and sweat already soaking through his borrowed clothes.

The blood from the earlier battle is now dry and crusted, pulling at the skin on Layla's face and neck when she talks. "Wait here for your team," she says, wishing she could take him with her or give him anything to help. "Celia is going to help you out, and the commanders will be arriving soon with backup."

Fisher wipes at his forehead, eyeing her up and down, no doubt taking in all the blood on her. She doesn't feel any shame at what she did out there; she refuses to. "Where are you going?"

She points down the hallway to the right where Mick hovers, waiting for her. "Jax says there are more prisoners to rescue. They need our help."

Fisher stares down the hallway, and for the first time Layla wonders if he can hear and see and smell like she can. She wonders what abilities he obtained when his DNA joined with that of a shark. Frustration lights his features. He wants to help, Layla knows, but if he came along, he would be more of a burden than anything.

"Celia says some of your team has injuries," she tells him. "They aren't far off now, but they will probably need you."

He rolls his eyes at her as if to say *Really? I'm the one who is going to need help.* He glances at Mick, who has started to pace, and then down the hall. "Just be careful," he says quietly.

Taking a step back, Layla smirks. "You know me, Fish. Always careful."

Eyebrows raised, he watches her as she continues to back up. Before she turns around, she sees him shake his head. "Idiot," he mouths. Layla can't find it in herself to disagree.

Jax stares, dumbfounded, at the sight before him. Kyrin's talking with the rest of the team over the communication devices, telling them to get down here and help. His mind is strangely numb as he listens to the team respond, but his eyes remain locked on the people in the small, filthy cell.

His feet lead him here on instinct. After all, there was nothing for him and Kyrin to go on when they got down here. The flights of stairs took them deeper and deeper under the Black Sun base, and when the stairs finally ended, there was nothing but darkness and numerous bitter cold hallways. He could sense the buzz of electricity in the air, knew there had to be lights somewhere, but they didn't dare try to turn them on. That is, until they got to the unmistakable horrid smell of filthy, unwashed bodies and waste.

When Kyrin hit the switch, and the hall flickered with dim, dusty light, Jax thought he was going to throw up. An entire hall full of barred-in cells, all of them empty save for one. If the smell wasn't bad enough, the sight of them was. They were emaciated, completely covered in all kinds of filth.

But their eyes…

When Jax saw their eyes, he yelled at Kyrin loud enough to startle the hybrids in the cell. He rushed forward until he was right in front of them, grabbing onto the frozen metal bars at the front of their cell. And then his heart plummeted to his feet, because they aren't a group of terrorist hybrids like he thought. Even with their sunken and dirty skin, he recognizes them. He would recognize them anywhere.

Glassy blue eyes stare through the bars at him, stare without understanding or hope. Emotions burn at his throat, too many for him to name. Rage, guilt, panic, pain…

The girl watches as he backs up just a few inches, her dark skin taut over the high bones of her cheeks. Five months, that's how long they've been here. Jax was certain they were all dead, but he can't worry about the why or how. Not right now. Scanning the bars, he searches for the door to the cell, but there isn't one. No door, no lock, no opening of any kind.

Fists clenched at his sides, Jax resists the urge to send his hand straight through one of the thick cell bars. From the look on their faces, it would no doubt terrify them. He breathes hard through his nose, instead focusing on what his team is saying. After a few seconds of listening, he gives his orders, tells Layla and Mick to get down here. Then he turns the devices off, and gestures for Kyrin to do the same.

He needs to send a message to the commanders, and he can't do that with the rest of the team connected. As Kyrin comes up to the cell, Jax switches the device to a different frequency for the third time that day. "Commanders," he says in a voice that shakes more than he would like it to.

It takes a minute for them to respond. A minute in which Kyrin studies Jax's face and the people in the cell, his eyes bright with understanding. That look is enough to make Jax turn to face the other way. He will not break here.

"Yes? We are coming as fast as we can." Helland's familiar voice sounds over the device.

Jax presses it harder into his ear, the slight sting of pain making it easier to breathe for a moment. "We found Team Three."

Silence. Silence, and then a platoon of questions spoken fast enough that he's unable to follow them.

"They need medical," he says, cutting her off in the middle of her sentence. "Drastically. But it's them. All six of them." Taking a shaky breath, he turns back around to look at cell. Kyrin is running his hands over the bars, no doubt looking for a way to open it. "I don't know what they did to them, what the terrorists did. They don't seem like they know who I am."

Helland says something else, a tilt to her words that Jax takes as her not believing him. He meets Kyrin's eye and clicks the device into silence. He's not going to waste time explaining, convincing them that what he's seeing is real. They'll see for themselves when they get here. Right now, he needs to figure out how to get his team out of the cell.

Thunder and lightning.
I'm stunned when I hear your breathing.

CHAPTER TWENTY-ONE

*N*either Jax nor Kyrin gave them much to go on. More prisoners. Most likely too weak to move on their own if it requires medics to come down rather than meeting them up in the fresh air. They didn't mention if they were hybrids or not, but either way, Mick and Layla don't waste any more time, sprinting down the hall away from where Fisher stands by the door.

Unlike the hallway they went down, this one doesn't end in a brightly lit medical room. It ends in a small dark staircase. Before her foot hits the first step, a shiver runs down her spine, causing her sight to lose focus for a split second. The hair along her arms raises under the thick sleeves of her gear, and she smells a faint foul scent, even worse than in the other hall.

Mick gives her a nudge, and she looks over her shoulder with a scowl. Not in a teasing mood, he only nudges her forward again. This time her foot lands on the first step. The stairwell is so dark that even with her enhanced sight, all she can see is the outline of the steps under her, nothing beyond that. How Jax and Kyrin navigated their way down here, she doesn't know.

Layla zeroes in on the sound of people, of pulses and low voices, and imagines that Mick is doing the same behind her. The stairs go on, one floor, then two, then three, until finally they hit the bottom. With how dark it is, Layla only hears it as Mick fumbles against the wall, and then there's the telltale click of a switch, and the lights flicker to life. Jax and Kyrin have better eyesight than both her and Mick. They would've seen the light switches, but they chose to leave them off. Did they think there were more terrorists down here? She doesn't smell any fresh blood, only a distant, noxious odor. The prisoners.

They encounter more hallways that twist in all directions, resembling tunnels more than anything. The cleanliness and chemical smell from upstairs doesn't extend to down here. Must, dirt, rotting, and filth fills her nose. The ceilings are lower, only a few inches higher than the top of Mick's head. Her fingers dance across her blades as they set off in silence, following the sound of pulses down the center hallway.

It's like a maze down here, Layla realizes as they pass hall after hall, all branching off the main one. How Jax and Kyrin found anything down here without being able to hear like she can, is a feat in itself, but she guesses that's why they're the leaders of their team.

They edge around a corner halfway down the main hall, hearing and smelling Jax and Kyrin right on the other side. The light is already on here, dimly shining down on two neat rows of cells attached to the walls on either side of the hall. Layla's heart pounds, eyes wide as she tries to process what she's seeing. There are six of them in the cell, huddled so close together Layla has trouble telling whose arms and legs belong to who. Startling her, Mick twists around her to approach them.

She follows at a slower pace, afraid she'll spook them. It wouldn't be surprising considering the reactions she usually gets at the compound, and the last thing she wants to do is scare these poor people. All of them are hybrids. Wide, colorful eyes stare as she and Mick get close.

The closer she gets the more her horror grows. They are filthy, all skin and bones, their heads shaved, and their scars and bruises on display under threadbare clothes. There's nothing in the cell, save for a bucket in the corner. Terror ripples off them, stinging Layla's nose and making her want to cringe back. But she pushes her need to run, and to vomit, back. Pushes it way down deep.

There's no door that she can see, but Jax and Kyrin have bent the bars of the cell back to create a wide hole big enough for them to come out one at a time. Despite this all six remain in the small cell. It's enough to show her how weak they are if they couldn't get out of the cell themselves. Or they're just too stunned, too terrified to try. Kyrin looks up from where he crouches with Jax in front of the cell. He sighs, waving at them to come closer, and says, "They won't come out."

Layla falls to her knees in front of the cell close enough to the bars that the hybrids inside flinch back. All six of them grasp onto each other with white knuckles. The hard shell of her control begins to crack. Breathing through her teeth to defuse some of the smell, Layla stands and backs up a few feet.

Six pairs of eyes follow her movements. Like she did with Cape a few nights ago, Layla spreads her hands out in front of her, trying to show them that she doesn't mean any harm. She hasn't done it since they were in the forest, but Layla grabs onto Mick's heartbeat now. If she can get her own to calm, if she can appear as unfazed as he does, then maybe that will help.

Even now, Mick is talking, whispering to the prisoners that they're safe now, and that they'll be taken back to the compound. Layla glances at Jax and Kyrin, finally noticing their current state. Half their gear is off. Their clothing not covered in blood: insulated undershirts and tight pants, are in a pile on the floor. It's frigid enough in these underground tunnels that her every breath clouds the air. They were going to give their clothes to them, but the prisoners refused. They're just as afraid of Jax and Kyrin as they are of her, but Layla can't find it in herself to be happy about that.

Jax looks devastated, head tucked down between his knees, and Layla sees the tremor in his hands, sees how tight he's clenching his jaw. Layla's own eyes widen in sudden understanding. She looks back over the huddled hybrids. Nobody told her a lot about Jax's old team, but they can't be anyone else. The missing Team Three. She thought they were captured and killed. Everyone thought that.

Layla gathers steel into her veins, forces a calm rage to enter her heart. They won't get anywhere just staring at each other. These people need to be taken out, and waiting for help, for all those people to rush down here, could set them off and terrify them even further.

"Did you try to help them out?" she asks, voice quiet, controlled. Maybe they really can't do it themselves. By the look of it, the cell isn't big enough to allow much movement, and who knows when the last time they got out of it was. Their muscles could be weak from disuse and atrophy.

Kyrin shakes his head. "We didn't want to force them." He stands up and sighs. "But that's what the others will do, won't they?"

Moving back to the front of the cell, Layla says, "Yeah. It would be best if we did it, I think." She wraps her hands around the bent bars, getting ready to widen the gap enough for two people to fit. But first she needs to make sure it's okay with her leader. They are his team, his friends, after all. "Jax?"

In answer, he rises to his feet, and moves to wrap his hands around the bars on the other side of the gap. After a quick look at the hybrids inside, Jax gives her a nod. Gritting her teeth, Layla pulls with all the restrained anger in her. The bars let out an unholy screech as they're pressured to bend under their hands.

"That's good," Mick says. He's already going to duck into the cell, but Jax holds out an arm, stopping him. Bending at the waist to avoid hitting his head on the bars, Jax enters the cell himself.

He moves as if he's approaching a scared, wild animal, but that might not be too off the mark. Layla watches, all but holding her breath, as he bends down so he's eye level with his old team. "I'm going to pick you up," he says in a voice softer than any she has heard in a long time, "and get you out of here."

Layla can't tell if they understand him, or if they believe him, but they don't give any sign of resistance save for clutching onto each other harder. Jax scoops up one of the hybrids, a man with marbled eyes, and stands back up to his full height. That gets an uneven hiss out of the woman who sat next to him. Layla steps forward, readying for the attack, but the dark-skinned girl shushes the other, and they all settle down.

It's not right, Layla thinks as Jax nods at the dark-skinned girl, not right at all. Jax carries the man out of the cell and settles him on the ground outside of the cage. As soon as he clears the opening in the bars, Mick slips through them, picking up the one that hissed. Layla waits for him to clear the opening before copying his movements.

The guy she picks up weighs next to nothing. His skin is ice cold, and his shaking breath leaves shivers across Layla's skin. How are they alive? How did they survive this long and deteriorate this fast? Months, they would have only been here months, but it looks like years of damage has been heaped on them.

Layla sits the guy as gently as she can next to the other two. Jax and Mick are already going back into the cell, but Kyrin stays crouched down in front of the three they got out. Slowly he maneuvers his and Jax's clothes onto their frail bodies. The first man is already clothed in Jax's undershirt and pants. They sag on his too-small body.

Layla doesn't think there will be enough clothes for them all, but still she begins removing her gear, stripping off the clothes meant for warmth, and piling them up before the her. Then she holds them up for the girl Mick carried out to see, hoping for some type of acknowledgment, but she just gets a wide-eyed stare in return.

Jax is already helping another to the floor. Tears line his dirty cheeks and slide down his neck. Blinking rapidly, Layla attempts to give the hybrid a reassuring smile. Jax sets the dark skinned next to her, the leader, if Layla's not mistaken. The girl eyes her, the clothes, and the hybrid next to her, before she says, in a voice ruff like sandpaper from disuse, "Go ahead."

Layla helps get the warm clothes on them one by one, wishing they didn't leave their packs in the forest. They had hats in there and extra gloves. They would've been good to put over their shaved heads, their freezing cold fingers.

Jax paces up and down the hall, waiting for the commanders again, to see how far away they are. His breathing is loud and uneven, and when he passes their group, the man on the end, the one with the marbled eyes, reaches out and takes Jax's hand in his.

He stops immediately, and Layla can feel the thickening in the air, feel it as everyone tenses and quiets for a moment. And that is when she hears it. She glances into the cell, but aside from the bucket and a few rags, it's empty. As her gums burn and her eyes widen, she reaches out to grasp onto Mick's arm. He meets her with a furious gaze.

"Seven," she says. "I hear seven."

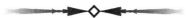

No one tells her that she needs to let go of the fraying leash on her control. She's already there, stalking down the cell-lined halls on silent feet, but she knows that no matter how quiet she might be, whoever is in these halls might hear her just as well as she can hear them.

After seeing the condition of Team Three, none of her teammates were that worried when she told them about the extra pulse. It's another prisoner they said, but Layla's not so sure about that now. With each turn she takes, with each hall she clears, they move farther away like they're listening for her and leading her deeper and deeper into the underground tunnels. This person is not weak, is not a prisoner.

"Backup arriving in ten," Jax's voice says over the comm device.

Along with Kyrin and Mick he's staying with Team Three, which is not a problem for her. The farther she gets from them, the easier it is to concentrate on the seventh prisoner, or not prisoner, that is lurking down in these hallways. It's a hybrid. She can tell now.

After the first couple turns, the cells disappeared, replaced by dirt coated brick walls. There are still lights, much to Layla's relief, but they're so old and far-between that they don't do much to brighten the way.

Whoever is down here is silent save for their heartbeat, but Layla's ears still twitch, attempting to catch any sound of movement. And that's why when she does hear something, a sliding of a shoe against the dusty ground. A grin stretches across her face. This cat and mouse game is over.

She hurries, sprinting down and around the damp halls. When she gets close, she digs her heels into the hard ground and skids to a stop just shy of slamming into one of the stone walls. This close, she can hear them breathing. Peeking around the corner, Layla can only just make out their shape. She guesses it's a girl with a small, slight frame, only slightly bulkier than her own. She stands with her back to Layla, seemingly frozen in place.

Fingers dancing over a dagger on her thigh, Layla sniffs at the air. She was right about the girl being a hybrid, but she doesn't remember ever hearing about anyone getting captured besides Team Three and Four, and Celia said nothing about a girl missing from Fisher's team. Her fingers silently remove a dagger. "Hello?" Layla says, voice laced with a growl.

When the girl doesn't react, Layla moves forward. She only just gets within arm's reach when the hybrid spins on her heel and lunges at Layla too fast for her to dodge. Layla hits the concrete floor with a painful hiss and struggles to get the hybrid off her.

Voices buzz in her ear, her teammates with news, but Layla's focus is on the hybrid. Layla gets her feet firmly planted on the ground and heaves herself up, knocking the girl off her in the process. Layla grabs at the girl's arm, but instead of soft fabric and flesh, her fingers dig into something strong and unyielding.

Layla grunts. "What?" The hybrid punches out with her arm, trying to hit Layla in the face, but with a few jerks Layla twists the hybrid's arm behind her back. Using her other hand Layla shoves the girl's head down hard enough that it presses against the floor.

The muscles in her arm strain with the force of holding the hybrid in place. Sweat races down her temples. No, this is not a weak prisoner. This is a terrorist hybrid. "You're coming with me," Layla growls out.

Squirming harder, the hybrid almost manages to dislodge Layla's grip, forcing her to dig one of her knees into the hybrid's back to hold her steady. The soldier under her huffs out a breath. "When did you learn that?" the girl asks.

Layla's hands slip in surprise. Every noise in the musty hallway amplifies as her concentration breaks. And then the hybrid is laughing, a high-pitched sound that Layla knows well. Using Layla's surprise to her advantage, the hybrid pushes up with all her strength. For a second, Layla is airborne. Then she crashes into an unforgiving, concrete wall.

Her shoulder crunches with the impact. Flames of pain race down her arm. Layla holds back a screech and gets her legs under her. The girl is standing over her now. Short hair sways against her chin. Slowly, Layla raises to her feet. Her vision swims with the movement.

"Courtney?" Cursing herself for the terror and hope that flows into her voice, Layla squints to get a better look at the girl. Ever since they found out the Black Sun has hybrids, hybrids that were thought to not have survived the serum, she has been wondering about Courtney, hoping that she was somehow alive.

Layla squeezes her eyes shut to get the room to stop swaying. When she opens them, they lock right onto the other hybrid. There is absolutely no mistaking her friend, her sister. She has the same brown eyes she's always had. The same nose. The same mouth. Not a thing about her has changed. In fact, if it wasn't for the distinct hybrid smell on her, Layla would think the serum didn't work on her friend at all.

Courtney's face goes slack. Her shoulders drop, and her feet stop their pacing. And something in Layla's chest soars at the sight.

"Courtney, hey. Do you know who I am?"

Layla reaches out her hand, going to touch her shoulder, but Courtney jerks as if she were smacked. Then her blank gaze zeros in on Layla. Her lips pull into a cruel smile, so different than anything Layla has ever seen on her face.

Layla backs up a step. "Courtney…"

She lunges.

But Layla was ready for it, saw it coming as soon as she turned her eyes on her. She ducks and weaves to the side. Spinning, she catches Courtney with a knee to the gut. Courtney doubles forward, and Layla kicks the back of her knee, taking her to the ground once again. She can bring her up with the others, with Jax's old team. Helland and Cape will know what to do.

The shouting in her ear is enough to startle her. Her mouth moves, making no noise. Layla trusts her team, but she doesn't want them to race down here. After seeing what they did to the hybrids in the forest on their last mission, she doesn't know what they would do to Courtney. *Don't hesitate.*

No. She won't be calling them down here.

"I'm fine," she says to her team.

"You don't sound fine." Even with her face being squished

against the ground, Courtney still manages to sound arrogant. "They not treating you as well as you hoped they would?"

The voice might be Courtney's, but the words aren't. The friend Layla knew didn't speak to hurt people. She didn't fight to hurt people. She was against both so much that she would have down right refused to be a part of the hybrid army if she had the option to.

Layla looks down as Courtney still struggles to get out of her iron-like hold. She gave her gloves to the hissing girl, and now her nails dig hard enough into Courtney's gear that they bend. "What did they do to you?"

A smile stretches across the side of Courtney's face, and her brown eyes turn to stare up at her. Layla's stomach clenches at the contact. She thought seeing the empty eyes of Team Three was bad, but this… "Who?"

In a rush of movement, Courtney yanks her arm out of Layla's hold, and elbows her in the face before she has a chance to react. Layla's head smacks to the side. She can feel the warm blood as it spurts from her nose. Layla forces herself up, ignoring how the floor seems to tilt under her feet. Charging after Courtney's retreating figure on shaking legs, Layla's hands go for her daggers. She won't let her get away. Not after finding her—seeing her alive.

Courtney speeds around a corner, headed in the opposite direction of where the rest of Layla's team and Team Three is. Following the sound of her, the smell of her, Layla sprints down the maze of halls until the brick walls turn to moss-coated cement and the air is heavy with moisture.

The comm device crackles in her ear, and Jax's voice comes through, slightly fuzzy with the distance between them. "Layla," he says, "what is going on?"

Layla's voice is labored when she says, "Terrorist hybrid. She got away. I'm following."

"Get back here. We need your help."

Snarling, she picks up her pace again. "I can't do that. She's—"

Jax cuts her off. "Unless she is going to blow the place up, get back here," he says in a voice that makes her gums burn. "Our hybrids are weak. They need medical now, and we need to take them up there."

Her feet slow again, but she doesn't turn from Courtney's trail. "She's my best friend."

Layla hears multiple people cursing, before Kyrin cuts in with, "They are dying, Newbie. Get over here, now."

Clenching her shaking hands into fists, Layla finally stops. She breathes in, then out. With every second, the sound of Courtney fades away. Layla sends up a silent promise to come back, to find Courtney and bring her back.

Then she turns around.

Backtracking her steps would be impossible with the lack of attention she paid to the numerous turns, so as she starts down the dark hallway at a brisk jog, Layla strains her ears for the sound of her team and Team Three.

By the time cells begin to line the walls again, Layla's gear is soaked through with sweat, but when she makes that last turn, she steadies her breathing and forces the flames burning in her throat down, down into her stomach where they will remain until she's able to release them again.

Mick, Jax, and Kyrin each have one of the weak hybrids in their arms or across their backs. Three more still sit on the cold floor, and as she approaches, Jax nods at one of them, the dark-skinned leader with big blue eyes. Layla bends down close to her.

"Her name is Jen," Jax says, adjusting the man's limbs that are wrapped around his torso and neck. "You're going to take her up, but first I need you to hand me Benji, and then give Laura to Mick."

Layla's eyebrows furrow together at his plan, but she follows his directions anyway, and lifts the guy on the ground into Jax's arms, trying not to wince at how light he is. Mick comes forward with the marble-eyed man on his back, and Layla silently scoops Laura, the smallest one, up and into his arms. Layla doesn't miss how she grasps onto the other hybrid, or how some of the tension leaves her frail body.

"I'll lead the way," Kyrin says, already moving down the hall. Mick and Jax trail after slowly, waiting for her.

When Layla looks at Jen, her eyes are staring directly into hers. The lab she found Fisher in swims before her eyes. Machines and needles. The terrorists are not above experimentation, and they are absolutely not above torture. Layla thinks she can see that in the light blue eyes.

"Come on, then," Jen says in that rough voice, and Layla swallows, wondering if that's what she told them when the terrorists hurt her. *Come on, then. Get it over with.*

Layla forces steady breaths through her mouth as she slips one arm under Jen's knees and the other around her shoulders. They don't run into anyone else as they climb up and up. By the time they make it to ground level, Jen has stopped shaking in her arms. Layla keeps her eyes locked on the hybrid clinging to Mick's back while she lets her senses stretch as far as they can, hoping to catch some sign of Courtney.

There are puddles under my feet,
and they turn my boots dark and sticky,
and they leave tracks behind me,
red as red can be.

CHAPTER TWENTY-TWO

*F*orest air penetrates her nose, tainted with blood and sweat and gunpowder. Jen shutters in her arms, and Layla tightens her grip behind the back of her knees and across her upper back. She takes in the girl's clenched jaw and greedy eyes that gaze up at the evening sky. *Saved.* Layla saved this girl, this hybrid, this person. Courtney got away but seeing the pure relief lining Jen's expression melts away some of the ache in her chest.

When Layla looks up, the first thing she notices is that the lawn is cleared of the terrorist's bodies. Blood still cakes the grass, hidden under trucks, tanks, and dirty boots. Two tents are set up, red crosses above their pinned back doors. The medics on stand-by silently swarm them, carrying stretchers and gently prying the former prisoners out of their holds.

"Keep them close together," Jax orders the people dressed in white scrubs. A few of them are Layla's age, their eyes and smell easily setting them apart. "Do not separate them for any reason."

Layla's concentration snaps back to the team. Fear leaks from them, turning the air foul and raising goose bumps along her arms. She doesn't fully let go of Jen until the medics agree and the girl's startling blue eyes narrow in expectation. Once the six of them are loaded onto the stretchers, Layla and the guys follow them to the medical tents.

There's an excited mood around the base, but her team stays somber, quiet. Her eyes sweep around the lawn as they walk, spotting Helland and Cape standing tall and giving orders. People dressed in tactical gear and wearing latex gloves make their way into the base. They're to investigate the place, turn it inside-out looking for information. A part of her doesn't want to know what they'll find. The things they must have done to Team Three ran through her mind the entire walk out of the base, and she's not sure she wants to know if she guessed any right. But as she remembers the numerous files she stacked up on the counter in the lab, a bigger part of her wants to know everything.

Celia sweeps out of one of the medical tents when they get close. Face quickly turning white, she looks over Team Three with a stunned expression. She rushes to them, effortlessly dodging between the people in her way. Mick claps a hand on her shoulder when she reaches them, and Layla slides up next to her. Layla grasps her hand. "You okay?"

Celia huffs out a breath, "*Me?*" Her eyes follow as Team Three, with Jax, Kyrin, and Mick following, enter through the white flaps that make up the medical tent door. Layla clenches her hand harder. "Team Four is already with the medics," Celia says.

Good. That's good. Fisher and his team should be alright. Layla thinks about telling Celia that Team Four wasn't the only hybrids down there, but she hasn't told her or any of her team about Courtney. No one has brought up her past or injection day since that first night at the compound. Still, she saw Courtney down in those hallways, and the words are all but ready to burst from her, but she forces them back, and asks, "How are they?"

"Nothing like that," she throws her hand towards the medical tent Team Three went through, its flimsy curtain door being pulled shut. "Scrapes, bruises, a few broken bones. Your friend, Fisher, is the worst." That gets Layla's attention. "They aren't sure what was put in him."

Layla curses. From the look of his injuries, she assumed they put something in him to weaken his ability to heal. A chemical or drug. "We left the scientist alive. He's still down there, but he will know. I'll make him talk myself if I have to."

Eying her up and down, Celia folds her arms across her chest. "I'll help," she says. "If you need it, that is. Now go check on them, okay? He has been asking for updates every ten seconds."

The medical tent was hastily set up, that much she can tell when she walks in. Thin mattresses are rolled out on the floor along with cases full of different medical equipment. A plastic-like sheet covers the floor, protecting everything and everyone from the rain-soaked, gore-stained grass. Carefully, Layla steps around the equipment towards the far corner where Fisher and his team sit wrapped in blankets, drinking water and nibbling on food. There's not much medics can do for bruised skin and tormented minds.

"Hey," she says as she stops in front of them. They look up, tired smiles on their faces when they see her. "I'm glad you guys are okay."

"All because of you and your team," Sara says. She's the leader of Team Four, has been a hybrid almost as long as Jax has. Her long blond hair sways when she shakes her head, dark eyes glistening as they meet Layla's. "They got the jump on us. They knew we were coming."

Layla freezes for a moment in surprise. "Why do you say that?" Helland and Cape didn't know the exact details of the team getting captured, only bits and pieces. There was nothing about the terrorist soldiers knowing anything about the team's mission.

Under all the exhaustion, fury drums from each of them. How many times have they tried telling someone this only to be passed off as needing rest? Briefly, she meets Fisher's stare, but after seeing the questions in his dark eyes, she looks away. Not yet.

"They ambushed us," Sara says. "There is a city nearby, an old one. We were barely halfway across it before they just came out of nowhere. On every side of us. Too many for it to be a coincidence."

She doesn't need to say more. Layla can see it playing out in her head. The five of them walking through the ruins of the city. They tried to fight back, took out a few dozen soldiers. Layla was standing where it happened. She saw the blood the rain couldn't wash away.

But if there were too many soldiers for Team Four to fight, where did the rest of them go? Sure, there was a good amount her team took out at this base, but Team Four are the compounds current top hybrids. There must be soldiers from the ambush that went elsewhere.

And if Sara is right about the terrorists knowing her team would be there, then that means there are Black Sun members in their ranks.

Carefully, Layla sits down on an empty space on the mattress. Every muscle in her body aches, and she leaves smears of blood on the blankets, but she can't find it in herself to care.

"What happened?" Fisher says. There's a blanket wrapped around his shoulders and up over his head, casting shadows on his face and making the bruises around his cheeks look so dark that they blend in with his black eyes. Eyes that bore into her with a familiar intensity.

Layla looks to the door of the tent like she can see past it and all the way into the next one with Jen and the five other tortured hybrids. "The other prisoners were Team Three," she says. "Jax's old team."

There's a strained silence. She can hear each of them stop breathing, their hearts picking up speed. Dust floats into the air when Layla picks at a blanket, each particle flying up then slowly drifting back down.

"What?" Sara barks out.

Eyes locked on the fingers that poke out of Fisher's blanket, Layla tells them of the deeper level halls, and the cells, and the team. Her voice is hard and flat, and a familiar face keeps flashing through her mind.

"What else?" Fisher asks when she's done. "There's something else."

"I saw Courtney."

There's a crackle from the comm still in her ear, stopping her from going further, but that was all she needed to say for him to understand. She can see how his body goes rigid even under his blankets. Shaking her head at his unspoken questions, Layla rises to her feet. Helland's voice rings in her ear. "Team Thirteen please meet Cape and me at the entrance to the base."

Fed up with the device, Layla yanks it out of her ear and off her gear, then tosses it into one of the equipment bins. "The commanders are calling," she says. "I have to go."

She makes it a step before there's a commotion behind her.

"Wait. Just wait," Fisher says, pushing on the hybrid next to him for balance as he rises to his feet. The blanket falls off his shoulders, showing the borrowed scrubs Mick found for him in the lab. The sight of them has her lip curling into a scowl.

He spins her around and pushes her toward the entrance of the tent. Layla goes willingly, and chances a glance out the door flap, seeing her team making their way out of the other tent. Celia points in her direction, and she briefly meets her leader's eye before she turns away.

"She's alive," Fisher says, "and she's with the Black Sun."

Layla resists the urge to bite at her nails. "She got away." Fisher looks over her shoulder, and she doesn't need to look behind her to know Celia is making her way over. "I'll tell you about it later, okay?" she says. "After this is all over and we're back at the compound."

"I'll come with you to see Cape and Helland," he says.

The door flap flies open, and Celia looks between them with narrowed eyes. "Like hell you will," she says, emerald eyes flashing. "You passed out as soon as you dragged yourself out of the base. No one wants to carry you around anymore."

Surprised, Layla looks him over, trying to find what else she might have missed. He shows his teeth at Celia, and Layla barely catches herself from slapping him across the chest. He already has enough bruises.

"Now, come on," Celia says to Layla, holding the tent flap open.

Casting Fisher an apologetic look, Layla says, "I'll see you at the compound."

"Don't do anything stupid," he says.

Layla can see the commanders as soon as she leaves the tent. No longer ordering people around, they stand waiting for her team in the destroyed grass and mud. The dark silhouette of the terrorist base outlines their tall, proud frames.

"Couldn't have walked over here," Layla growls under her breath.

Celia elbows her in the side, a slight smile on her face. Layla hisses at the sharp pain in her already aching muscles. By the look of it, her team had medical treatment themselves. Bandages peek out of their gear, and salves are smeared over exposed cuts, making their skin glossy.

She can feel the itching sensation of her own injuries healing. Blood clotting in every cut and scrape, caking around her nose. When she sees the first aid kit in Kyrin's hand, she feels a mix of annoyance and appreciation. He hands it to her as they walk past, leaving her no choice but to grab it and follow. Her injuries will have to wait until after this talk.

"Jax," Helland says when they get within a few feet. "You said you would save people for questioning."

The clipped tone of her words betrays the calm set of her face and shoulders, setting Layla's teeth on edge. Jax's face is set in stone, so different than the pained expression he wore down in those halls. He stands with his back rigidly straight, arms folded behind his back, and feet spread apart.

"Most are on the third floor. They should be unconscious. I marked the door," he says. Layla almost smiles, thinking of the bright red "SCUM" he wrote on the wooden surface of the door.

"There is a scientist in the lab behind the basement door. Down the center hallway," Layla says, capturing the commanders' attention. "He was the one with Will Fisher."

"Very well," Helland says, gesturing to a woman nearby. "Thank you, soldiers. Cape will give you the rest of your orders."

Do I got a good heart? Full of dead bugs and cavities.

CHAPTER TWENTY-THREE

*L*ayla counts it as a huge stroke of luck that the scientist is still unconscious, because she's the one set to watch him as the others rest. There's a dark red line of blood starting at his temple and training down to pool in the collar of his shirt from where Kyrin hit him, and his head bumps against the metal floor of the truck bed. Layla doesn't feel the least bit bad for him. Not after knowing some of the things he must have done.

Abduction. Experiments. Murder.

He has probably done it all.

So, no, Layla refuses to feel bad at all as she glares at him, remembering the hallways full of cages; the room full of monitors and needles and Fisher strapped to a chair; the people they thought were dead, but are really some kind of brainwashed hybrids that they can manipulate at will.

Layla refuses to believe any other explanation. Courtney is one of them, and she hated the Black Sun as much as Layla does, but she never wanted to be part of this war. She never wanted to fight or kill.

"You're going to burn a hole through his head."

Layla startles at the sound of Jax's rough voice. She thought he was sleeping like the others. Indeed, his heartrate is calm enough, and seconds ago his head was tipped back against the truck wall, eyes closed. Layla peeks at Jax from the corner of her eye, and sighs. "Doesn't sound like a bad idea," she says.

Jax chuckles, low and quiet to not wake up their teammates. "It really doesn't."

Somewhere between talking with Cape and getting on the truck, Jax had returned to his usual self. The excitement from fighting and the angst from finding his old team gone, replaced by the solid leader she's come to know. Layla would be relieved if she didn't believe he was just pushing everything away, waiting for the safety of his room or the training center to let everything out.

Just like she is.

The truck bumps along on the uneven forest ground. Taking main roads would be too noticeable, so they're stuck driving down old dirt roads and untracked paths. There's too many of them for the subway, but at the speed the driver is going, they might get to the compound in record time.

Layla turns back to the man as he groans and squeezes his eyes tight. He still doesn't wake. Eyes staying firmly on the scientist, Layla asks Jax, "Will they tell us what he says? What any of them say?"

The commanders are going to question him and the other scientist they left behind as soon as they get to the compound. If the scientists say anything about the hybrids that the Black Sun have, or about what they did to Fisher and Team Three, Layla wants to hear it.

"If it's important to the cause, they will tell everyone."

Layla tries to let this reassure her, but she can see more loopholes in his answer than bullet holes in a dummy after Kyrin is done with it. What's important to her can be thought of as useless to the commanders. They'll say it's not the main issue, or it's not what they need to be worrying about right now.

If she asked, would they tell her?

Layla could wait to find out. Get the answers in a few days, and in the meantime, form a plan with the others if they don't get the information they need. She can form a plan to get back to Courtney somehow. The man's fingers twitch. His pulse jumps faster. The compound is still miles away, and Layla has never been patient.

She does it fast so Jax won't be able to stop her until it's too late. Hauling up the semiconscious man, she slams him into the wall of the truck. It's loud enough that her sleeping teammates jump straight to their feet. The man's eyes open, watering in pain. He is unfocused, confused. Afraid.

"Layla," Jax says like he's not at all surprised, more exasperated than anything. A beat follows when his mouth opens to say more, but he must change his mind, because he snaps it closed with a resigned look. She can see the exhaustion now, both physical and emotional, from the way his eyes and posture are drooped, from the sound of his voice.

"I have to know," she says. "The commanders won't tell me about this. You know that, Jax." Layla doesn't turn to look at the others, and she doesn't bother to ask what they think. This is her decision.

"They might," he says, still not bothering to stand up. There's a pause where Layla waits with bated breath. Then he sighs. "Just don't kill him."

The truck turns onto a dirt road, no less bumpy than the forest floor. They ride another ten miles, and the team settles down again before the man starts to talk. His words are slurred, and he spits them out in hatred. Hatred not just for Layla and her team, but for the Black Sun as well.

"They made me do it." He repeats it over and over. They threatened the safety of his family, his wife and children. Layla can't dwell on that right now. She can't feel bad for him. With each mile, she gets farther away from Courtney. Who knows if the people scouring the base have found her trail and deemed her worthy enough to follow.

Slamming her hand into the metal wall of the truck an inch from the scientist's ear, Layla cuts off his pleading. He shrieks, jumps, and winces. "I need to know about the hybrids that fight with the Black Sun."

"I-I swear I didn't do it."

Hands bunching into fists, Layla wants nothing more than to slam them into the man's face, but she forces herself to take a step back. Sending this man back into unconsciousness won't help her at this point. "I don't care what you did," Layla says, beyond fed up with this man and his blabbering. "You can tell the higher ups when you go into questioning. Right now, I need you to answer me."

"Best to do as she says," Celia, sitting against the wall of the struck, says. Layla hears the quiet sound of a knife flipping in the air. Mick. They're trying to help her without interfering. Layla sends them a thankful look over her shoulder and turns back around to smile wide at the man, showing off as many teeth as she can.

"The hybrids," the man stutters, eyes locked on her teeth. Impatient, Layla steps forward, back into his space, causing his words to rush from his mouth. "They are the same as you. They were given the serum in the schools along with you."

"They are the ones who died from the serum," she says.

The man nods, a painful frown on his face. His head must be throbbing from the hit Kyrin gave him. "Yes," he says. "Half of the injections contain chemicals that make it appear as if those who have taken it have died. The members of the Black Sun who are present at the school take these students with them. When they come to, they are subjected to mind-altering chemicals and procedures that allow the terrorists to have control over them. Well, partial control."

"Partial?" Her mind reels at all the information. She was right about the dead hybrids not really being dead. She was right about the mind control. And, worst of all, she was right about the Black Sun having members on the inside.

"Well…"

A gust of wind rushes through the cracked emergency door on

the roof of the truck, just enough to blow her hair the slightest bit. The man's voice fades as her senses flare, because along with the smell of woods, the scent of people hits her. Unknown humans and a hybrid that she has already familiarized herself with.

"We need to go," she says.

Mick sheaths his knife and stands up. "There are other people out there. Two miles west," he says. "We need to tell the driver to go a different way to get safely to the compound."

But Layla's not listening. She's collecting her axes, checking over her knives. When she waited for the scientist to be carried to their truck, she and the others went around, collecting all their salvageable weapons. They didn't find them all of course, and there could be nothing done about Kyrin, Jax, and Celia's lack of ammo. The help barely brought any extra, but Layla found enough of her knives to fill up the sheath on her thigh.

Cursing under her breath, Celia stands and checks her own supply of weapons. Layla tosses her a grateful smile. Having explained to her what happened when they were collecting daggers, Celia knows what's happening and knows there's no stopping her. When she looks at Layla, all Celia does is roll her eyes.

The others are watching them, and Layla sighs. She knows gushing about how Courtney is her best friend and would never hurt anyone will do nothing to sway them, so she goes with a different route. "Guys," she says, "the hybrid I was tracking from under the base is out there. If we can get her before she gets back to the terrorists, or before our people find and kill her, we will have a huge advantage."

"What advantage?" Kyrin asks. He has one of his guns out now, reloading ammo into it. Layla takes it as a good sign.

"We bring her in for questioning like this man." She throws her hand out in the cowering scientist's direction. It's hard to say what she plans to next, but she forces the words out anyway. "We can study her, right? Find out what they are doing to them. Prove to Helland and Cape that we need to stop injecting people, because until we know how they are doing it and how to stop it, we are giving the Black Sun more hybrids. Maybe we can even find a way to reverse the brain washing."

Mick steps toward. "And this guy?" he says, nodding his head at the scientist. "What are we going to do with him?"

Jax is the one who answers. "Same as before, I guess."

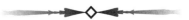

From a safe distance away, Team Thirteen watches as Courtney approaches a truck. The truck is similar to theirs, aside from the dark green color and the manned gun perched on the roof. The soldier up top doesn't look to be all that engaged with the gun, too focused on the conversation Courtney and another man are having. But that can change in an instant if they mess up.

As soon as they make their presence known to be exact.

Layla trusts Jax enough to lead her and the team on dangerous missions with every assurance that they will make it back to the compound safe, but this feels different. This is going against the commanders' orders into something potentially more dangerous than Layla originally thought it would be. The only assurance she has now, apart from her team, are their weapons and skills.

Eyes narrowed in the direction of the truck, Jax holds up his hand. His fingers are folded into a tight fist. She has never been in a situation where signals were needed, but Layla gets the idea. *Wait. Hold.*

She doesn't dare make a sound. It's a miracle that Courtney hasn't heard them yet. Jax raises from his crouch, stopping just short of his full height. Layla's placement in the forest makes it hard to have a clear view of Courtney, only allowing her to see her and the man from the chest down. Fighting the urge to do the same as Jax, Layla wiggles her cramped toes.

She doesn't have to wait long before Jax turns back around and gives them another signal. *Go ahead. Scout.*

With a nod, she begins to move forward. With her legs crouched to stay low, her muscles scream. The bullet wound on her thigh burns like it's fresh. She pushes through pain with purpose. Courtney is right there, just yards from her.

The air is still, the sky dark, and the trees and tall weeds provide decent cover. The only problem is that they're all dead from the cold of the upcoming winter, making them crunch under her feet if she isn't careful. The closer she gets, the slower her steps become. Fear growing steadily stronger, Layla holds her breath as she gets close enough to see their faces.

Courtney's familiar voice cuts at her chest like a knife. She wants nothing more than to speed up, grab her, and run. Find somewhere safe. Even if that ends up being in another country altogether. The sudden want is overpowering.

Stopping behind two trees, Layla peers through the small gap between their trunks. Her friend looks fine, unharmed and straight-faced, though that could be from the brain washing. These terrorist hybrids could be trained to not show fear or pain.

The man talking to Courtney is strangely familiar. A memory tugs at the back of her mind. He's clean-shaven, with dark, neatly combed hair. Layla's heart clenches as she listens to him talk. It's not what he says that triggers her memory of a long-ago announcement on the television, but the way he talks. Completely and utterly normal. She remembers being surprised that he didn't sound strong, gravelly, or commanding like she imagined.

Layla had also imagined she would meet him in a very different way.

She watches as Courtney extends her arm, handing over a gun

Layla didn't notice she had. The sleeve of her green jacket pulls back, revealing not smooth tan skin, but a scaled white pattern underneath. Armor. So, that's what Layla felt back in the tunnels, but why is Courtney wearing it? Layla hasn't fought any other terrorist soldiers with armor.

Abruptly, Courtney straightens her already stiff stance. Her eyes remain on the Black Sun leader, but her head tilts slightly to the side. She's listening. Layla's stomach twists. She tries to duck behind one of the trunks before Courtney's head snaps to the side, but she's not fast enough. Courtney's gaze meets hers, singling her out among the trees.

When their eyes meet, the strangest expression lights Courtney's face, and Layla could swear it was recognition, but the moment is ruined when the leader head snaps up and follows her gaze straight to where Layla is hiding.

All at once, she ducks behind the trees, draws two blades, and calls to the others. There's no time to be sneaky anymore. They need to take the leader out, get Courtney, and find a way back to the compound. Then all of this will be over.

Jax and Mick duck behind the tree next to hers just as the shots start firing. The bullets hit the tree she hides behind with enough force to shake her teeth. Layla spares half a second to fear they will shoot straight through the wood and into her back. A growl rips through her as the tree creaks, signaling the trunk is split. It won't last through the barrage of bullets much longer.

With Jax and Mick behind her, Layla runs from their cover, ducking into the tall grass. A quick glance is enough to get the positions of the terrorists and Courtney. Still running, Layla throws a knife, aiming for the one manning the gun on the roof of the truck. Another clump of trees draws near, and using the momentum from her sprint, she slides on her knees into the cover they provide. Mick, hot on her heels, crashes into her side.

"You got him," he says. His voice is clear and steady, even with the continuous gunshots and shouts. "I threw one just to be sure."

Scrambling up from the muddy ground, Layla peeks around the moss-covered tree trunk. "Where did Jax go? I thought he was following."

Narrowing his eyes in concentration, Mick tilts his head to listen, but Layla knows it's hard to hear a single heartbeat amongst constant gunfire. After a minute, he shakes his head, coming to the same conclusion as she did.

More terrorists pile out of the truck, five of them in total. One has pushed the dead man out of the way to get to the gun. The leader yells at the other four before he climbs into the truck, dragging Courtney with him. She already looks so different from when Layla saw her in the tunnels. Her eyes are wide, and her forehead is crinkled. Her movements are slow, confused. Something is wrong.

"Celia and Kyrin?" she asks.

Mick picks two more knives from his thigh. "Not sure," he says. "Probably up."

Layla looks to the surrounding tree tops, but unsurprisingly she doesn't see either of them. This spot is too far away for her or Mick to get an accurate shot, and even if they tried it would only alert the enemy soldiers of their position. With guns like those, the terrorists don't have to worry about distance.

Scanning their surroundings, she tries to find a closer place they can reach without putting them in range of the enemy. Her eyes are drawn back to the terrorists when the shots stop. In the sudden quiet, Layla can finally understand what they are screaming, but when she sees the small body wrapped around the man on top of the truck, the words fade from her mind.

Celia.

Layla doesn't think. She runs.

Knives fly from her hands towards the four remaining men around the truck. Mick races past her in a blur. Shots barrel down from a tree to her left. And then a force like a steam truck plows into her side, lifting her clean off the ground.

Layla tries to yell, but there's no more air in her lungs. She hits a tree hard enough to bend the branches and shake the entire trunk when she collides. When she opens her eyes, the forest, the road, the truck, and the people are painted in red. Gasping for air, Layla feels her blood begin to burn.

A face blurs before her, and she squints, grabbing for a knife. A hand presses to her shoulder, hard, causing pain to flare, hot and angry. Layla growls.

"Stay down," Jax says. "Just, stay down."

Layla tries to push him away, but her arms feel like lead, and he doesn't move an inch. "Move."

"I'll get them. Just say here. That's an order." She can hear the desperation in his voice, the plea. Pushing his hand off her shoulder, she growls again.

"You can't do that alone, Jax!" she yells, but he's already backing away. Layla can't see around his big frame. She can't tell what is happening back by the truck or where any of the others are. Why is he doing this? It hurts to move, but Layla forces the branches off her body and struggles to get up. She makes it to her knees before everything goes black.

And your blood is war paint.

CHAPTER TWENTY-FOUR

"**I** swear if you don't get up, I'm leaving you here."

Groaning, Layla opens her eyes. Night has fallen, turning the woods dark and eerily quiet. The smell of gunpowder is still fading into the cold air, bringing the memories of what happened to the forefront of her mind. Body burning with exhaustion and pain, she flinches as hands grab her under the arms and haul her up, causing the pain to burn worse than before.

"Stop." Her voice is hard, and even through the pain, through her spinning and blurry vision, Layla prepares for a fight.

"Calm down. You're lucky I was nice enough to get you out of that tree." Kyrin's voice is unmistakable, and Layla lets her head fall back against something solid. Another tree, from the musky smell of it. If she can just get her head to stop spinning…

"If you go back to sleep—"

"I won't," she says, shifting around, taking stock of all the aches and pains that flare at the movements. "Hurts too much."

Through her slit lids, she sees him roll his black eyes. "You'll be fine," he says. "No gunshot wounds. Nothing fatal. Your biggest injury was hitting your head again. It's a miracle you don't have a concussion. Oh, and a tree branch was slicing into your back. I got it out, cleaned it up, and stopped the bleeding."

As if his words alert her to the injury, she can feel the slight itching burn of the muscle and skin healing back together. With a painful hiss, she stretches her arm back to feel over the gash across the top of her back where her gear is torn.

"The others?"

Kyrin's black eyes seem to darken impossibly further. Layla sees so much more than anger in them, though it is present. She sees terror, sadness, and pure rage. The sight of it makes her own blood rush a little faster through her veins.

"They took them," he says in a voice that matches his dark eyes. Even though she was expecting it, her heated blood freezes over in an instant. "Tranquilizers." He tosses a small object at her, and she catches it on instinct. It's a small blue dart, the liquid chamber drained of chemicals. Turning the dart over in her hands, she feels some of her despair ease. "They're still alive."

Still alive. The Black Sun's leader didn't kill them. Not yet, at least.

"Do they have their comm devices?"

"I don't think Jax took his out, but the scum probably stripped them of anything." He points at his ears, and says, "Besides, neither of us have ours."

Gritting her teeth, Layla pushes her feet under her. Celia and Mick and Jax are still alive. And Courtney, too. All of them in the hands of the Black Sun. The leader of the Black Sun. Was it just a few hours ago that they were in the halls under one of their bases, seeing what they did to the captured hybrids, seeing the lab equipment and cells? Will they do the same to her teammates? Or will the terrorists seek revenge and end her team right there?

Her fault. This is all her fault. If she didn't make them chase after Courtney, then half of her team's lives wouldn't be in danger. Layla stands on shaking legs, the rage in Kyrin's eyes mirrored in her own. She has spent weeks with at least one of them at her side smiling, laughing, and fighting. The absence of any of them would be noticeable, but with three of them gone, it's like half of her world is, too.

She has lost too many people already. Her family. Her friends.

Not her team too.

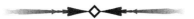

The pain streaming through every part of her body diminishes with each step down the muddy road, but the pain in her chest increases. She wants to curl back up against that tree, put her head in her hands, and cry. Her fingers slide across the rough handle of her axe, missing the glossy texture of her picture back at the compound. She wishes for her bed. Not the one back at the compound or the one at Courtney's house, but her own. In her parents' house. In her childhood home. She wants her parents sitting on either side of her, a constant comfort.

Would they be proud of what she has done?

Becoming a hybrid, fighting back against the Black Sun. Killing the people responsible for their deaths. Putting her team in danger for Courtney.

Would he parents approve of all this? Would they tell her that she's doing the right thing? She thought so at first, but Layla doesn't know anymore.

Her throat burns and clenches as tears race down her cheeks, leaving freezing trails in their wake. Kyrin knows she's crying. She's not quiet about it, but she doesn't care right now. They have been following the tracks the truck left behind well into the night. Their breath freezes in white clouds, and the tips of her toes lost feeling long ago, but the rage she continues to hold at bay is enough to warm the rest of her.

After telling him that Jax was the one to push her into the tree, Kyrin cursed for a solid ten minutes. If she were in better spirits, she would have laughed or joined him, but she longs to hurt anything she can get her hands on. If she lets go now, she doesn't know if she would have anything left to give when they reach the end of the tracks. More than that, she doesn't trust herself to let go around Kyrin. After all, he was the first thing that ever set her off all those weeks ago.

Kyrin told her he was grazed with one of the tranquilizers, and he remembers Jax forcing him to stay hidden in the trees and grass before he passed out. Kyrin spent a solid ten minutes pacing the length of dirt road, pulling at his hair, and cursing everyone from the Black Sun leader to Jax to Layla herself. Layla gave him space, choosing to do a quick but thorough search of this area of the forest, mostly to gather fallen weapons, but the bullet holes in the trees couldn't be missed.

"They wouldn't kill us," Kyrin had said when she called him over. He dug one of his fingers into the bark of a tree where a bullet went halfway through. "When they saw we were hybrids, I saw them trade their regular guns out for the tranquilizer ones."

Layla couldn't help thinking that didn't mean Celia or Mick or Jax were unharmed in the fight or weren't being held as prisoners at the end of the tracks. It was too easy to picture them as Jax's old team was: behind bars, trapped in a cell. And it's too easy for her to blame herself for it all. If she never insisted that they go chase down Courtney, then they would still be safely on their way to the compound.

She walks on the opposite side of the road than Kyrin walks on. He hasn't really yelled at her, or blamed her for anything, but she knows that he's thinking it just as she is. A part of her wants him to yell at her, to make her pay in some small way. He stays quiet, so maybe the sound of her crying is enough of a deterrent.

Their pace is steady, but the end of the road is nowhere in sight. "If we start jogging now, we can rest during the day when it's warmer. Less chance of freezing in our sleep," Kyrin says.

The air feels warmer than it did when they slipped off the truck, but that might be more from her constant movement than the actual temperature. With there not being much in their packs to keep them warm, and having given all their underclothes to Team Three, the idea of freezing in their sleep might not be too far off.

"Let's run, then," she says.

She runs hard enough for the wind to wash away her tears. Running in the darkness of the night with only the stars providing minimal light does nothing to quell the violence building under her skin. In fact, it excites it, makes it harder to ignore. Mick is maybe hundreds of miles away for all Layla can tell, not anywhere near close enough to calm her down.

It's all up to Kyrin and her now.

Kyrin keeps up, his heavy boots quiet on the damp ground. The moon shifts between the clouds, darkening the world and bringing it to light interchangeably. She is so focused on the wind in her hair and the road in front of her that she nearly misses it. An engine, loud and gaining.

"Incoming!" she says. Not wanting to get separated, she puts on an extra burst of speed to cross to the other side of the road and duck into the trees with Kyrin.

"What is it?" he asks when they get deep enough into the woods that Layla deems it safe to stop.

The rumbling is loud enough that Layla is surprised Kyrin can't hear it. "Another truck, I think."

Stupid as it may be, Layla want to get a good look at the truck when it comes by. Finding a sturdy tree to climb is easy enough. She climbs quickly, the wood under her hands cold and slick. In seconds, she's high enough to see the headlights come into view. She flattens her body as much as she can along the branch and watches the truck race down the road at a speed she would call unsafe considering the many potholes and obstacles. It's just like the truck that contained the terrorist leader and took half of her team away.

Thankfully, the gun on the roof is unmanned, but she can

hear enough people within the vehicle to know there would be no problem to have someone go up if they needed to. Layla lets out a breath as it passes, but she waits until the lights fade down the curving path before she climbs down.

"Five people inside," she says when her feet are back on the ground.

With a nod, Kyrin leads the way to the road. Layla had hoped they would be able to stay safely in the cover of the trees, but the tracks would be nearly impossible to follow as the forest gets denser.

"Are you sure it was theirs?" Kyrin says, sticking next to her instead of going to the opposite side or the road. "It could have been one of ours."

Layla shakes her head. "It was theirs. Unless we had a truck at the last base with a gun on top that I didn't see."

Layla forgets to mention the fact there was only a slim chance that the driver in the front seat noticed them leaving the truck, and even if they did, who knew if they would be out looking for the team. After all, they have two teams in need of medical attention and terrorists to question. She and Kyrin are most definitely on their own for this.

Sighing, Kyrin takes one of his guns out, checks the ammunition, then puts it back. "Was it manned?"

"No, but if there was one, there are bound to be more."

It takes an hour, in which Kyrin constantly reloads and checks his guns, and Layla arranges the few knives she has on her person in the easiest positions to grab, before they come up with a better plan. At most there would be ten people in one truck, five for each of them. It shouldn't be a problem for them. They're antsy. Ready for a fight, maybe even wishing for a bigger one.

"Use the smallest number of weapons and ammo you can," Kyrin had said. Taking commands from him is harder than taking them from Jax, but Kyrin is second in command on their team, and now isn't the time to test that.

Once again, Layla and Kyrin are on opposite sides of the road, hidden enough in the trees to prevent the soldiers in the next truck that comes by from seeing them too soon. The soldiers might have the truck providing protection, but she and Kyrin will have the advantage of surprise. Kyrin said the terrorists must not be looking for them since the top guns are unmanned, which would provide them the best chance of seeing and shooting them down.

Just when she's beginning to doubt another truck is coming, she hears it. She whistles, signaling to Kyrin to get ready. When the truck gets close enough, Layla clicks her axe off its holder, runs forward, jumps, and crashes into the passenger door. The truck veers, two of its wheels lift off the dirt road. Using all her strength, she plunges the blade of her axe into the thick window. Only a thin line appears in the glass. Her other hand slips on the metal surface of the truck, causing her to dig her axe into the crease of the door for a better hold.

Like they planned, Kyrin fires quick, precise shots, so that every bullet hits the same spot on the driver's side window, weakening the glass. Yanking the blade back out of the truck, Layla rears her arms back and crashes it against the window again. This time the glass splinters, lines streaming from the hole the axe made. With one final hit, the glass shatters and, without missing a beat, she swings her foot up to hook over the window frame.

Leftover glass cuts into the back of her knees and cuts a rip in her pants, but she forces herself inside anyway. She lands awkwardly on the stunned man in the passenger's seat. Not giving him time to grab his own weapon, Layla quickly takes him out with a hard bash to the head with the hilt of her axe.

The other two are yelling. One is trying to get a gun out of its place at his hip, and the other is trying to keep the truck from crashing into the trees. It's tight quarters inside with only a bench seat. She gives up on trying to detangle herself from the body under her and reaches for one of her smaller knives instead.

The man's screams ring out as she stabs the blade into his hand, stopping him from reaching for his gun. Then the driver's side window shatters. There's a loud bang of a gun, one last shot that takes out the two of them at once. The driver's hands slip from the wheel. Layla lunges forward, but Kyrin beats her to it.

"I got it," he says, forcing the limp body out of the way with one hand. "Get in the back. Take out the others."

She can't stop the growl that leaves her throat at the order, but she climbs back out the window. The truck is still going, the dead driver's foot must be stuck on the gas petal. Layla can hear the three people in the back shouting. At this speed, the wind is icy cold, and strong enough to make her lose her balance as she heaves herself onto the roof of the truck. Quickly, she rights herself and rushes over to the unmanned gun, finds the hatch, and lifts the door open.

She drops down into the back of the truck and draws her knives. As expected, the three passengers are human, wearing the dark green uniform of the Black Sun. Before they can react, one of her knives catches a woman in the throat, and the other two charge at her. At that moment, the tires screech to a stop, and the truck fishtails, sending them all to the floor.

Diving towards the closest man, Layla runs her knife across his throat, quick and clean. The last soldier is already slumped on the floor unconscious, having hit his head on the floor of the truck.

When Kyrin rights the truck, she has all three soldiers ready at the door. They get the bodies into the woods as fast as they can, not knowing when the next truck will come by. Still, with only the two of them, it takes a good twenty minutes. There's no way they can hide the crazed tracks the truck made from swerving, and Layla just hopes no one notices them.

As if the thought conjured it, Layla hears the unmistakable sound of an engine. Growling, she hurriedly pushes the terrorist's softly glowing guns closer to Kyrin and fastens her blood-stained seatbelt. "We should have left them all in the back," she says.

"Have you actually learned to drive?" she asks, voice high and screechy with anxiety. Wind from the broken window whips her hair into her eyes and mouth. The cold bites at her fingers and nose and forces its numbing teeth into the material of her jacket.

Kyrin drives with jerky turns and a wide variety of curses. The trees are blurs of dark shapes moving by so fast, she can barely make anything out. They don't know if there will be scouting terrorist soldiers or hybrids in the forest, but the closer they get, the more likely it is. Even if the soldiers would have no reason to be alerted by one of their own trucks, the way Kyrin is driving might raise suspicion. And maybe the broken windows, too.

"No one to teach me, and people in the city never drive," he says as he jerks the truck around another bend. "Just tell me how close they are."

Layla puts her focus on the road behind them, even going as far to look in the side mirror, but she sees nothing but her own bright golden eyes. The other truck is still miles behind them. She tells Kyrin as much, but he keeps the truck zooming at breakneck speed. From the vicious smile on his face and the gleam in his eyes, Layla's beginning to think he *likes* this.

"How many people in this one?" he asks.

She focuses on the rumbling engine again, but this time she digs deeper until the sound of a pulse reaches her ears. And another.

And another. There are too many to sort through. Too many to count. Some of them are different, though. Some beat slower, to a slightly different rhythm. Panic starts a fire in her stomach and raise to the back of her throat.

"They have hybrids," she says in a rush. "I can't count them all. When there are too many, they blend together."

Kyrin spits out a curse. "Mick can."

"I know," she all but growls.

But she's not Mick, and as much as she wants to know what her and Kyrin are up against, she still can't get a number. *Use your head, Layla. Not your fists.* All the air is punched out of her lungs, because that's Courtney's voice in her head. It's something her friend has told her more than once when she became frustrated or angry.

Layla wouldn't always listen to her, but this time she does.

Taking a breath, she tries to steady her racing pulse. When you can't outrun your pursuer, you turn and fight. But this isn't something she and Kyrin can fight, so they need to take the easy route. Sitting straighter, Layla scans the road sides.

"There," she says, pointing to a small side road. "Pull in there. We'll have to hide until they pass."

Kyrin shakes his head. One of his hands grabs at the softly glowing gun on the seat between them "They will see our tracks and wonder why we went off road," he says. But with a too-fast jerk of the wheel, he steers the truck onto the thin road.

Layla regrets the suggestion immediately. The road is far too narrow for a truck this size, or really any vehicle larger than a four-wheeler. Tree branches scrape against the sides of the truck and poke through the broken windows. Layla only just avoids getting gashed in the cheek by one of them. If Kyrin's driving doesn't kill them, nothing will.

"Stop! Stop! Stop!" she yells as she spots a large tree sitting in the middle of the road.

Kyrin slams on the brakes, causing her body to fly forward as they skid to a halt. "I saw that." Eyes wide, she wipes her sweaty hands on her pants. After clearing his throat, he says, "We didn't make it far. We need to get rid of the tracks, or there's a pretty solid chance that they are going to see our truck went off road."

Keeping both ears on the rapidly approaching truck, she and Kyrin quickly race back to where the turn started and begin to sweep the dirt and mud around to messily erase the tire tracts. Layla's eyes sweep over their word as she backtracks into the cover of the woods.

"Oh, god. Oh, god," Layla whispers. It looks exactly like someone swept over tire tracks.

Lights chase at their heels. Layla hurries to sweep over the last of the tracks then ducks into the brush besides Kyrin. They're silent, absolutely still, knowing any movement can alert the soldiers to their position. The engine of their stolen truck is shut off, silent in the dark night.

In the quiet, thoughts race through Layla's head. Are they going to see how they tried to hide the track? What if the hybrids can hear them no matter how silent they try to be? After all, Layla can hear their hearts, the chorus of their breathing, the quiet murmurs of their voices.

Her nerves are too shot to make sense of what they say. Each individual word running into one another. For all she knows, they could be speaking a different language.

The truck passes by so fast the tree branches sway with it, but she stays frozen in place, hardly breathing.

Fifteen. At least half of them hybrids. If they caught her and Kyrin it would have been real messy.

Layla turns to Kyrin, finger to her lips. There's still a chance of the soldiers hearing them. Kyrin rolls his eyes at her. He doesn't need to be warned. Ten minutes later, when the truck is so far away that she has a hard time hearing the engine, they move from behind the bushes and head towards the truck.

"I'm driving." There's not enough room to turn around, and Layla's already tensing just imagining Kyrin driving in reverse. "I can only cheat death so many times."

"Cats have nine lives," Kyrin says in his grumpy voice, but he tosses the keys over.

"I think I just lost them all to panic."

I could use some coffee, and a new, shiny gun.

CHAPTER TWENTY-FIVE

*C*elia opens her eyes to a spacious room, bright and quiet. Her head is spinning, and her mouth feels like she ate sand. She is in a heap on her side, as if someone deposited her on the floor like a bag of garbage. The floor is painfully hard underneath her, and when she raises her head, the skin on her cheek peels away from it slowly, stinging.

Mick is in front of her, his messy, blonde hair hanging limp and dirty over his closed eyes. Bruises run along his jaw, and there's a sizeable cut on his chin. Her gaze trails over the veins in his neck, bright blue against his skin, thrumming with life. She closes her eyes, allowing herself a split second of solace. Then, with a hiss of pain, she raises another inch off the floor. She can't see the other people in the room, but she can hear them. Their shuffling and tapping feet. Their murmuring voices.

It all comes rushing back to her, the forest, Layla's hybrid friend, the terrorist leader.

Celia bites her lip with the sharp points of her teeth to stop the multitude of curses from leaving her mouth. They saved two teams from a terrorist base only to get themselves captured trying to what? Save an enemy hybrid? It was true that Layla's friend, Courtney, would have been a great asset. They could have gotten tons of information from her. If she made it easy, that is. But now, they won't have that chance.

At least she's not dead, Celia thinks as she quietly runs her hands over her legs and torso, feeling numerous injuries and searching for any of her weapons, but they are all gone. Not even the small throwing knife in her boot remains. Goose-bumps trickle along her spine at the thought of these monsters touching her. Her upper lip curls in disgust.

Celia struggles to sit up, hands slippery with sweat against the smooth floor. She makes it to her knees, only to stop short at the sight of Jax. Stomach in her throat, she lurches towards him. Unlike her and Mick crumpled on the floor, her leader is seated in a chair, thick bands holding him in place around his arms and legs, around his chest and torso. His head dangles towards his chest. Franticly, her fingers gently push at his neck. She breathes a sigh of relief when she finds his pulse, slow but steady and strong. He's still unconscious. He's still alive.

"Sir," Celia hears from across the room. With a hand on Jax's shoulder, she looks over. Three men. Two of them are soldiers armed with guns. The leader stands between them. He wore a suit when she first saw him by the truck, but now he's thrown on a lab coat. Celia doesn't see any weapons on him. The soldier with a shaved head reaches for his gun, but the leader clicks his tongue at him.

Celia's face splits into a deranged smile, fangs digging into her bottom lip. They kept them alive for a reason. Information, hostages, revenge, threats, or maybe just for fun. They won't kill them, not yet. She digs her nails into the thick Kevlar of Jax's jacket and jerks his shoulder hard.

She waits a second or two, but Jax doesn't move. A flicker of movement to her left draws her attention. Mick. His mismatched eyes are full of dread, but under that there's anger. There's determination. Celia winks at him. The room is larger than she initially thought, but Layla and Kyrin are nowhere in sight. Jax's twitches under her palm. His head lifts, eyes meeting hers, full of that same solid determination in Mick's. In her own.

They just need time.

Layla and Kyrin are nowhere in sight. She can only hope that means they got away.

The clack of shoes echoes through the room. She takes it as a sign to move. Using Jax's thighs for support, Celia pushes herself to her feet. Mick has raised to his knees, fists clenched at his sides. His eyes burn holes through the men, and his face is set in stone. The dread from before is all but gone, like it was never there to begin with. Jax's muscles bulge, tendons stand out against his skin, trying to get out of the bonds, but he won't. He can't.

Celia turns and holds the leader's gaze unflinching.

"Nice to meet you," he says, and he sounds sincere. He sounds like he means it. Her fingers itch for a gun, for a knife. Coming to a stop some feet from the three of them, he offers her a half smile. "If you don't mind me saying, you have the most wonderful eyes."

CHAPTER TWENTY-SIX

*T*iny bits of sun can be seen coming through the clouds, and there's an important question on Layla's mind. On one hand, she and Kyrin can stake out wherever the trail leads. Layla hopes it's another base. At least then, her and Kyrin will have an idea on how to proceed like find its weakest points to form a plan of entry. On the other hand, they have this truck with a fully loaded gun on top, the terrorist's guns, and their own weapons. Do they charge in with guns blazing?

Kyrin has retreated to the back, and Layla can hear him messing around with the large gun on top of the truck. He could be familiarizing himself with it, dismantling it, or doing something else. When she asked, all she got was a firm warning to focus on the road both in front and behind, and on the forest on both sides.

It's weird, Layla thinks, being pretty much alone after so long. Before they came to inject her school, she lived with Courtney. She was almost never apart from her best friend, and when she was, it was only for short periods of time. After she got injected, Layla has been surrounded by her team and all the others at the compound.

If she tries hard enough she can picture herself all alone in a morning sun-lit forest driving nowhere, driving somewhere peaceful where the terrorists, the pain of losing her parents, the pain of losing Courtney, and the corruption of the Black Sun doesn't exist.

But the beautiful picture won't focus. It's blurry and broken, something that she knows isn't possible. She has no idea what they are going into. Are the terrorists going to be expecting them? Should

Kyrin and her prepare for an ambush? That seems to be what the terrorist soldiers are good at. And what state will the rest of her team be in? Images of them broken, beaten, and locked up flick through her head. What if her and Kyrin don't make it to Celia, Mick, and Jax? What if they're already too late.

A body throws itself through the open window. Knowing it's Kyrin, she only spares it a glance before focusing back on the tracks. Surprisingly, he is grinning, wide and excited, though there's also something deranged about it that lets her know whatever he was doing up there was successful.

Layla doesn't know if he'll answer, but she asks anyway, "What was all that about?"

"Improvements," he says, tucking something into one of his many pockets. Seeing her glare, he elaborates, "Let's just say we have a backup plan."

Layla checks the mirrors, hoping somehow that she can see to the top of the truck and find out what he did. But of course, she can't, and she has to fight down the urge to snarl at him. Now is not the time for mystery and secrets.

"Do we even have a plan to begin with?" she asks. "Besides, I thought I was the backup plan."

"Do you want to be the backup plan?" Kyrin checks his new, advanced guns, counts his ammunition. His hands skitter over the metal quickly and carefully not shaking one bit, unlike hers that slide over the steering wheel, slick with sweat and maybe a small amount of the previous passengers' blood.

The truth is she isn't sure anymore. Isn't sure she wants to be that last resort. So many doubts run through her head. So much can, and will, go wrong. Is she capable of killing as many people as they think will be there—at the end of this trail? Will she even care if it means getting her teammates out of the terrorists' hands?

"I say we go as quietly as possible," Kyrin says, taking her silence as answer enough. "No matter how much I'd love to run in guns blazing, we wouldn't make it. There are only two of us, and we have to assume there's going to be a lot of them if the Black Sun leader is there."

Layla nods along, hands so tight on the wheel she can feel the metal curve to fit the impression of her fingers.

"Pick them off one by one," she says. They pass over a bridge barely wide enough for the truck to fit. The soft sounds of living break through the trees. Layla takes one hand off the wheel to pat along her legs for her daggers. She glances at the seat between her and Kyrin where her axes gleam in the pale sunlight.

Kyrin cocks one of his guns and aims it out the window. "Two by two," he mumbles.

Layla barely gets to take any terrorists scouts out thanks to Kyrin shooting them down before she can spot one. They left the truck in a clear patch of woods. The space is small enough that the tail end of the truck presses flush against a tall tree, but there's a clear path back out onto the road, and enough coverage to hide the truck from anyone who doesn't get too close.

Layla keeps her hands free as they run, allowing her to go faster and dodge trees and bushes with ease. Her lungs burn with the cold, fresh air, somehow craving more even after how much they've already ran. She pushes herself to go faster, until the air rushes by so strongly it burns her eyes.

Not surprisingly, Layla's ahead of Kyrin, but that doesn't mean he gives her the chance to take any of the patrolling terrorist scouts out. Bullets hit them before she can get a clear aim to throw a knife, taking them down with only one shot. To the head. To the heart.

More than once, she finds herself eyeing the guns strapped to their fallen bodies or thinking of lagging back to ask Kyrin for one of his. But she hasn't picked up a gun since that night she talked with Cape, and that hardly counts. Layla's not sure she would know what to do with it if she had one. Especially with Kyrin taking out people that she only catches glimpses of.

Layla counts them as they pass, the scouts, almost unable to help herself. Both rage and guilt hit her at each face, as well as relief and satisfaction.

It's weird having Kyrin behind her instead of Mick or even Celia. If it were Mick, he would be besides her, attacking with knives and claws. And Layla would do the same. Celia, on the other hand, would have been anywhere, a shadow, falling bodies the only evidence that she's there at all.

She has never fought next to Jax, since he pairs himself up with Kyrin just as much as he pairs her up with Mick. That should change, because even if Kyrin is part of the same team, the second in command, fighting besides him doesn't feel natural like with Celia or Mick.

Kyrin's gun fires again, making her growl when her gut clenches at how close the bullet whistles past. She hears it hit its mark tens of feet in front of her and the thud of the falling body that follows. Leaping over the same body seconds later, Layla spares them a glance. *Twelve.*

So far, all the soldiers have been human, with no scent or sound of hybrids. Even the ones from the truck are nowhere near. They must have gotten to the base, and from what she can sense, she has no doubt now that there is a base, but the busy sounds and multitude of smells from hundreds of people coming from the distance make it impossible for Layla to tell hybrid from human.

She sprints through a gap in the trees, only to come to a sudden halt, heart in her throat. The woods end there, leaving her standing out in the open. She catches a glimpse of soldiers and a building before she hikes it back into the trees. The last thing she needs is to be spotted now when they're so close to her team.

Kyrin is slowly nearing her, but their surroundings are clear of terrorist soldiers for now. That doesn't comfort her as much as she wishes it would. She remembers what happened on her first mission when they found the hybrid terrorists. It's only a matter of time before someone at the base figures out that something is wrong. Layla flattens herself against the ground, looking over the base in the distance. It's not what she was expecting, low to the ground and relatively small. Brows furrowed, she tries listening closer. How many terrorist scum are in there? Where are the real threats—the hybrids? Where is her team?

What she hears has her cursing a string of profanities.

"What is it?" Kyrin asks, shimming himself down next to her. His own guns are strapped to his hips, out of bullets, but he lifts a glowing rifle close to his face to look through the small scope. It's not to see better. No, he can see miles away without problem. He's already taking aim at the patrolling soldiers, seeing who he can get a shot at, and who would be left for Layla to take care of.

"It goes underground. Five floors, I think," she says, ducking her head to wipe the sweat out of her eyes.

They are situated on a hill overlooking the squat base. Here, the grass is high, allowing them to crouch without worry of being spotted by those below them. Mostly men make up the routine patrol. They carry large guns held across their chests. Back and forth they walk, with an almost bored ease. But that doesn't mean they aren't doing their jobs. Layla can see their eyes scanning the tree line. Not that she expected anything less, considering the leader is most likely somewhere within the building.

"Well?" Kyrin asks, voice low but still containing that annoyed, hostile tone. "Got anything?"

This was part of the hastily made plan the two of them came

up with in the truck. If Layla could smell Celia, Mick, or Jax, then they would know exactly where to go, but with the base going underground, the scents are all but nonexistent, soaked up by the dirt.

Layla shakes her head. "We will have to get inside."

"Get ready then," Kyrin says. His gun is geared up, aimed at the few guards. His heart beats wildly, but his knees bend, ready to take off down the hill. His expression is calm and focused. "In ten."

"Wait," she says. "Can't you hit those guys from here?"

Kyrin gives her a look like she's an idiot. "Not with this gun. The bullets won't reach that far. We'd just alert them of our position, and it'll be a disaster from here on out. I'd need a—"

"Right," Layla interrupts. "I get it. Let's do this."

Layla counts down in her head, her muscles tightening and releasing in anticipation. They rise at the same time and run down the hill so fast Layla feels like she can kick off the earth and fly through the air. Still running, Kyrin's gun takes down the roaming terrorists with nearly silent blasts. This time, they don't move the bodies like they did in the woods. They only slow down when they reach a door.

There are two guards right on the other side of the door, and more just around the corner. She motions to Kyrin, loosening two of her knives. At his nod of understanding, she slips inside and quickly takes out the guards.

"This way." Layla's only just extracting her knife from one of the guard's throats when Kyrin slips past her and to the right.

She quickly wipes the blade on the man's uniform and slips it back into its sheath. There are more people in the hallway, but by the time she gets there most are already on the floor, dead or nearly there from Kyrin's bullets. She sidles up to him. He now has a gun in each of his hands, no more than extensions of his arms. Knives leave her own, aimed at the people on the right as Kyrin aims left.

Mid-throw she asks, "Where are we going?"

But he doesn't answer, and they're moving again into a stairwell at the end of the hallway. As soon as Layla steps on the first concrete step, she can smell them, her team. It's faint, made that way by the others in the building, but it's there enough that she can follow.

Kyrin's in front of her, feet blurring down the steps, but he doesn't seem to need her directions. He passes the first floor they come across, instead going down past the second and third. It's like he's able to smell their team too. Layla wants to ask him about it, but now isn't the time for those kinds of distractions.

When they reach the door to the fourth floor, the smell hits her like a fist to the gut. The smell of pain and fear and blood and bleach. And her team. Down here there miraculously aren't any guards posted along the walls, but Layla barely registers that as she and Kyrin fly past tightly closed doors, following the scent of their team.

A black rage creeps around the edges of Layla's vision, ready to consume her, to lead her. But she pushes it away. Saves it for later. She needs to focus.

She can smell Mick the most. His scent saturating the air, laced with anger and pain. If she listens hard enough, if she's able to sort through all the other pulses, she might be able to hear him, too. But she can't. Clenching her shorter axe, she forces her legs faster, faster, only slowing down to listen or smell. To find out what's going on down here and how to save their team.

Traces of Jax and Celia's scents continue down the hall, but Mick's stops and flows out of the door to her right. She catches Kyrin's arm, halting him with a growl. The door is locked, but that doesn't stop her. With a sharp twist of her wrist, Layla forces the doorknob to turn. The sound of the lock breaking echoes down the hall, and she quickly pushes the door open.

The room is small and brightly lit with mold caked in the

grooves of the tiles on the floor. The scent of old blood and fear and anger and Mick send Layla's control plummeting. She grabs onto it with bared teeth and white knuckles. Her glowing eyes find Mick immediately, but it takes her a few moments to recognize him. His long blonde hair is shaved off at his scalp, tendrils of it lying around the old tub he lays in. No. Not lays. He's chained in. Large steel links wrap around the tub and are shackled to his body to keep him in place.

"Get him out of there," Kyrin orders, but Layla's already moving, boots skidding across the damp floor as she hurries to Mick's side.

If they did this to Mick, Layla's afraid to wonder what they did to Celia and Jax. A string of curses leaves her mouth when she peers into the tub. The water is more than half way to frozen, a layer of ice resting on the surface. The water reaches almost to Mick's chin. It's a miracle that he hasn't frozen to death yet. She gently touches his bruised and puffy face only to hiss at the freezing, wet skin. His mouth moves. A whisper of her name.

"What did they do to you?" she says. Mick's eyes peek open, and something loosens in Layla's chest. Because that's burning rage, an inner fire shining out from behind blue and brown eyes. He's okay. Or he will be soon.

After a look behind her to Kyrin, who stands in front of the closed door reloading his ammo with blind efficiency, Layla gets to work on the thick chains. Five of them are strapped around the tub and circling Mick's limbs. Palming one of her axes, she takes a swing at the first chain near the base of the tub. It breaks with a loud crack. She's already hitting the next as she watches Mick slowly, so slowly, slip the chains from around his arms.

Layla curses again. "He's going to need help," she says to Kyrin.

A wicked laugh leaves Mick's mouth, and something in his eyes sparks and crackles. The sight makes a shiver run down Layla's back. It's the first time she has seen his hard-earned control slip. From the sound of his frantic pulse, she thinks he has about as little control as she does right now. Layla tugs a little harder on the leash around her emotions.

"Just tell me you have weapons to spare," Mick growls.

Layla breaks the last chain, and he rises from the tub, shaking with cold and rage. She has never seen him like this, so close to the edge of his perfect control. Layla steps back and watches as he rips his soaking wet shirt off, his blue lips pulling into a snarl.

"Faster, dammit," Kyrin says, already handing over two smaller guns that he must have picked up in the forest. She wants to snarl at him, but Mick grabs up the guns, and eyes Layla.

"I'm better with knives, you know." He already pocketed the guns in his soaked pants, and his hand is held out to her.

Without waiting for them, Kyrin opens the door, peeks left and right, then holds his gun up and heads down the hall toward where Jax and Celia are being held. Again, Layla wonders how he knows where they are. He can't smell like she and Mick can, so it must be something else.

She unfastens a row of throwing knives in a rush. There are only about eight of them left, so she hands over two rarely used larger knives as well. She's left with her axes and two throwing knives around her thigh. It's enough, she tells herself. As long as she has her axes, it will be enough.

"Are you sure you're okay?" she asks.

Mick fastens the throwing knives around his upper arm and palms the two knives in his still shaking hands. "Doesn't matter right now. Let's take care of these bastards."

Some emotions suffocate you. Like guilt. Like hate.

CHAPTER TWENTY-SEVEN

*T*he day his team was ambushed and captured was nothing like what happened to him and Team Thirteen. In fact, it was the complete opposite. His team were the ones in the truck, speeding out to a base a few hours outside of the compound. They were laughing, joking about the commanders and the other teams, flaunting that they knew best—that they were going to be the ones to win the war for their country.

And then the soldiers came, an entire army of them in trucks and on bikes and on foot. They had known his team was coming. Jax remembers how their bright smiles disappeared. Replaced by bared teeth and horrified eyes. He remembers the sound of guns clicking and screams and growls. He remembers looking at his leader's slacked face and running. Running as hard as he could until he fell over in exhaustion, throwing up everything in his stomach.

The cell is strikingly similar to the ones that his team was trapped in at the terrorist base they were in mere hours ago. Is this what they felt like then? For five months, trapped in a cell like this one. At the hands and whims of the Black Sun. Not for the first time, bile stings the back of his throat.

The only difference from their cell and his is that this one has a lock. A lock that he can't break, and no matter how hard he pulled or pushed at them, the metal bars didn't let out a single groan. That's how they got his team out of their cell, bent the bars back and slipped through the gap. Jax doesn't remember how many times he has tried, but he can't bend the bars even the slightest bit. It feels like a life-time since he's felt this weak and powerless. Maybe except for when his former team was captured, and he got away, and maybe when he laid eyes on them in that underground prison.

Seeing them today... or was it a new day? He looks up at the caged ceiling, banging his head none too softly on the bars behind him. Jax didn't know how to feel when he saw them in that cage. Surprised. Happy. Terrified. Guilty. He thinks the guilt stood out the most. They were emaciated. All because he didn't try hard enough to find them. To even *think* they were still alive.

He remembers them in the medical tents. They couldn't bear to be apart from each other. Jax told the medics at least five times, but they didn't listen. Screaming. Silent, desperate screaming when they tried to tear their hands apart from each other's. He almost broke right then at that sight alone.

Is this what they felt like in that cage? The question won't leave his head.

And then the newbie... Layla. He should have stopped her.

They're not so different, the two of them. Actions and thoughts overruled by emotions. It's not fitting for a soldier, let alone a leader. And now his new team is captured. He saved Kyrin and Layla. He saved Kyrin. But the others...

With all of his weakened strength, Jax pulls at the bars again. This is how they kept his team contained, with drugs to make their muscles feel like liquid and their brains covered in a heavy layer of fog.

The terrorist leader didn't get anything from him, Celia, or Mick in the interrogation. No matter how hard they hit or threatened, the three of them did not budge. Jax was proud, so proud of his team, his friends, for being so strong.

The things the leader asked... They were confusing to say the least.

Of course, there were the questions they all expected. Questions about the compound, their plans, who helps them. But the questions about hybrids were different. Not how many they have, or how they're getting trained, or even about the serum.

"Tell me," the leader had said. "What kind are you?"

Jax will never forget that slight gleam in his eyes. Of mania and obsession.

Even with the drugs, he can still think, still move. He can still see Celia, bruised and unconscious in a chair in the middle of the room. Wires are hooked to her, some going into her skin and others just taped to the surface for delivering drugs into her blood stream, keeping her unconscious, and monitoring her pulse and brainwaves.

They didn't do that to him. They only stuck a few needles into his neck and locked him up. He should have been able to break the bonds. He should have been able to protect Celia and Mick from them. He should have fought harder, put their focus on him. They made him watch instead.

He doesn't know where they are. Worse than that, he doesn't know where Mick is. He only saw that they dragged him out in the middle of the interrogation before he blacked out. When he woke up it was just him and Celia. The terrorist leader and his cronies that beat them senseless were nowhere in sight.

It was times like these when Jax wishes for enhanced hearing or smell like Mick, Layla, and even Celia have. As it is, the only things he can hear are the consistent beeping of the machine monitoring Celia's heart and his own harsh breathing.

Gripping the bars of the cell tightly, Jax forces himself to look over at Celia. What they did to her… When she gave him that look, Jax wanted to throw up right them. *Let them.* it told him. *Don't tell them anything.*

There's no warning before the door swings open, banging against the wall with force. Jax's eyes shoot away from the sickening sight of Celia. Expecting to see the Black Sun leader or one of his lackeys, Jax's body tenses painfully, but he forces himself to stand tall, preparing to put their attention on him instead of Celia.

But it's not the leader who charges into the room. His legs almost give out from under him, because it's Kyrin.

Jax's heart stutters. Kyrin looks rough, but alive and ready to wage war. Dried blood coats his clothes and some is crusted along his exposed skin. His black hair is slick with sweat. His fingernails are crusted with dirt, probably from Jax pushing him down during that fight, hiding him so that he, at least, would be safe. But Jax doesn't give a damn how dirty he is as long as he's okay.

In the second it takes Jax to blink, Kyrin's in front of him, his dark, familiar eyes inches from Jax's face. He watches Kyrin's eyes roam over him, taking in the blood and bruises, the useless way he slumps against the cell wall. Weak. A failure. He couldn't save Celia and Mick. He couldn't fight against the terrorists when they beat and interrogated them one after the other.

When Kyrin's eyes meet his once more, there's a blaze burning in them, alight with a rage Jax hasn't seen from him before. Kyrin spills a string of curses, and Jax can only stare as he easily pulls the lock off the cell door.

When the door swings open with a long squeal, Jax doesn't waste any time to lunge himself at Kyrin. He curls his arms around him, needing to pull him as close as he can. Jax is only given seconds before Kyrin's pushing him away into the hard bars of the cell behind them.

He places a single kiss on his lips before he says, "Not safe yet." Those three words are enough to snap Jax back to reality, but his limbs are still heavy, and his senses are still dulled. "Stick with me."

"I'm with you."

Taking a breath, Jax looks over Kyrin's shoulder at Celia. The rest of his team is there, but he doesn't get to revel in that thought because Layla has her fingers on one of the wires going into Celia's skin and she's pulling at it.

Eyes wide, Jax rushes forward, trying to get to her, to stop her. He almost loses his balance and would have toppled to the floor if Kyrin wasn't there to steady him. "Layla don't!" he shouts. Her hand freezes but doesn't let go of the needle. In a jerking movement, glowing eyes meet his. Full of hate. Full of so much anger. "Don't touch them," he says, steadying himself enough to stand upright without help. "What they put in there… it can kill her."

Layla shows her teeth, but for the first time, Jax doesn't feel that pull. The one that tells him he needs to show her that he is the one in charge. Something else the drugs are taking from him. "Then it needs to come out before it does kill her," she says.

Mick steps closer to Celia, laying his hand on her forehead. She doesn't move an inch. "I hate to disagree with you, Jax, but Layla is right. The longer the poisonous substance is in her system, the more damage it will do."

Jax shakes his head forcefully, but it does nothing to clear the fog over his mind. "One of them is the antidote. He told me, rubbed it in my face. If you pull the wrong one out, she will die."

"He's right, you know."

Do you know how to stop a heart?
Put a gun to it and count to three.

CHAPTER TWENTY-EIGHT

*T*he room Kyrin leads them into is bigger than the last. A rancid smell filling it, a smell caked on from months and months of experiments and torture. At least, that's what looks like happens in this room. There aren't any more tubs, but cages, much like the ones in the tunnels underneath the other base, line one side of the room. Layla got one glance at her leader before Kyrin burst forward, blocking her view. Puddles of blood can be seen on the tiled floor, looking like someone gave up halfway into cleaning it.

Rage. It was like her blood was lava, scorching her insides. No. not scorching them. Forging them, turning them into rock, into something solid and unyielding.

That's what she felt when she walked into the room, and the feeling only gets stronger as her eyes landed on Celia laid out on a stretcher. For a moment, Layla thought she had to be dead. There's no way someone could be that still. But when her hands settled along her friend's bruised neck, there was a pulse—faint, but there.

And then the man's voice sounds. Layla snatches her hand away from the needles, and swivels, tearing her eyes from Celia to the open door. Instinctively, her body slides over to block her unconscious friend from sight. She suspected that this was a trap after running through the near empty hallways. There had to be more soldiers at this base than the ones they fought outside. She didn't give herself time to listen for them then, too busy finding her missing team members, but now she wishes she would have. If only to prepare herself and her team.

The man who enters the room is middle aged, dark hair turning grey around his temples. His wide nose crinkles as he looks her team over. Two armed guards shadow him. Under the bright lights, it's even easier to identify him as the leader of the Black Sun. He looks just like she remembers from the old video feeds she saw years ago. Layla doesn't know his name, not his real one. No one does. Dean. Brown. Author. Dr. Hitchcock. He's called himself every one of them and more.

"It's nice to finally meet the hybrids who have been destroying my bases." His suit is pristine, but as be brings his hands from around his back, Layla sees the scrapes and bruises marring his skin. She can smell her friends' blood on him like a stain. "Cougar, right?" the man says, dark eyes locked on Layla. "Or do you prefer mountain lion?"

Layla allows a sharp, wicked smile to spread across her face, thinking of all the ways she plans to hurt this monster of a man. Her fingers brush the twin knives still strapped to her thighs. "Either will do," she says, voice low and rumbling. She will say anything to keep his attention off Celia. "I wish I could say it's nice to meet you too, but I'm not a good liar."

The leader of the Black Sun laughs, eyes shining in what looks like delight. Layla sneers. Guards flank him. Seven in total. They're muscular, obviously trained in combat, but none of them are as big as Jax. Not that it matters. Layla hears more coming down the hall, their rushing feet matching the pounding in her ears. Gripping the thin hilts of her daggers, she readies herself.

"Well, we can't have that," the leader says.

Just like that, seven guns are trained on her team. They move in fast, and Layla feels a small amount of pride when two soldiers rush toward her instead of one. She's about to start fighting back, about to grab her axe, but the tell-tale sound of a safety unlocking stalls her hand.

"You even try," one of the soldiers says, "and this bullet is going in your little monster friend, here."

Sure enough, he's pointing his gun at Celia. One glance across the room is all Layla needs to know they're stuck. Mick and Kyrin have two soldiers of their own to deal with. Already they're being forced to their knees, and Kyrin's being stripped of his guns. A few feet over another soldier does the same with Mick.

Layla growls when the stocky, bald man puts his hands on her shoulders and pushes her down, but she doesn't dare try anything else. Not with Celia at gun point. Layla drops to her knees. The soldier harrumphs at her and reaches down to click the axe off her hip.

She stops him by grabbing his wrist, squeezing it so hard she feels the tendons and bones shift under his skin. Meeting his gaze, she says, "I can do it myself."

The leader laughs, delighted. "Hurry up. Hurry up. The girl doesn't have all day."

For a second, Layla thinks he means her, but after he looks pointedly at Celia, she hurries to get her small number of weapons off and hand them over. She feels too bare, naked without them. When the man pats her down, she must force her hands to stay at her sides and not reach up to snap his thick neck. Their weapons are given to one of the soldiers, and once they're done, he hurriedly carries the guns, knives, and Layla's axes out the door.

"I've been wondering though," the leader continues, "what kind of hybrid your little friend is." A cool calm enters Layla's mind at his words, allowing her tight muscles to relax. Layla bares her teeth menacingly, but the man only looks at them with rapid interest. "People, like yourself, who have bonded with mammal DNA are quite easy to identify. On the other hand, reptiles, birds, amphibians, even insects" he ticks them off on his long fingers, "those can be a little more difficult."

Layla feels it as her lips close over her teeth, and her face falls into a blank slate. This man isn't what she expected. After seeing what the terrorists did to Team Three and Fisher, she can piece together what this man wants—information about hybrids. The real question is why. He has his own hybrids. As many as there are at the compound if half the people injected get brought to him.

She reaches behind her to ghost her hand over Celia's, making sure she's still there. She can see the gun from the corner of her eye, it's faint glow unmistakable. Layla resists checking on her teammates. But even without looking, she can hear how weak Jax is, how slow his heart is beating. The odds are that only she and Kyrin will be able to fight. She expected something like this to happen, but still she had hoped…

A stupid, foolish hope. With only two of them able to fight, they're outrageously outnumbered, and there isn't any need for Layla to search out Courtney's scent to find her. The new base is all but seeping in it. Courtney is a good fighter, that much Layla got from meeting her under the base. She would pose a threat. The only question is when will she be called in here?

The leader cocks his head to the side, eyes focused entirely on Layla. With the soldiers locked on them, there's no need for him to keep watch of the rest of her team. "Are you even listening to me?" he asks with a wide, amused smile.

Letting a predatory look cross her features, Layla takes a step forward, away from Celia on the stretcher. The soldier who isn't focused on Celia, follows her with his gun. Hatred slams through her veins, making her hands tighten into fists. She could do it. She could crush the gun out of the soldier's hand and rush at the leader. Kyrin and Mick can get the guards, and the three of them can fight their way back outside. But not without leaving Celia's life to chance.

"It isn't uncommon," he says, eyes drawn to her trembling hands. "The lack of focus. The inability to concentrate and pay attention. It's one of the things I am looking to fix."

A retort is on the tip of her tongue, but Mick beats her to it. Voice flat and cold, he says, "Fix."

And that seemed to be all it takes for the leader to get going. The words pour out of him like water from a burst dam. "Your government did a wonderful job with the serum, but it can be improved. Just small changes to make those kinds of problems go away. Just think about it. The perfect soldier."

Layla's heart flutters, light and fast. Inside her head, she screams, *NO!* If he could do that, if he could get rid of the attention problems along with peoples' very thoughts, it might be the end of their country for good.

"But, sadly," he continues, "the serum is so closely guarded that my people can only tamper with it. So, I have to work with already turned hybrids." He looks over Layla's shoulder. With his height he can easily see Celia laid on the stretcher. "A lot more difficult, let me assure you."

"I can imagine," Mick speaks again, surprising her. In spite of, or maybe because of his weakened state, Mick's tight leash on his control is slipping fast. Anger practically leaves him in waves. Layla swears she can feel the heat of it. But his voice is steady, and if she dared to look away from the leader, she would see that his face is utterly blank.

"I'll make you a deal," Kyrin's voice fills the minute of silence. Just now, Layla notices the blood dried on his face, standing out stark against his pale skin. Sweat trickles down her back. "You let our friend go. You take whatever is killing her out safely. And we will tell you what you want to know about hybrids."

Kyrin's eyes are sharp. He must have come to the same conclusion she has—that the leader is obsessed with hybrids. Next to him, Jax is barely standing, all his weight slumped against Kyrin. Layla meets Kyrin's coal black eyes, and in them she sees an order.

The leader smiles. He holds out his arms, then claps his hands together. "That sounds like a deal."

He motions to the soldier standing over Celia, shooing him along until he's standing on the other side of the cot. Layla hisses as the leader comes closer and turns to the side so she can keep him and the soldier in sight. The leader steps forward slowly. Layla notes with a great deal of satisfaction that his cautious steps are because of her.

When she doesn't move farther out of the way, he raises his eyebrows and gives her an amused smile. Mick grabs her arm from behind and firmly pulls her to the side. Her legs move with stiff jerks. The soldier moves with her, and Layla can't help to glance longingly at the door. Her axes are just beyond that door. She can hear the soldier who took them. Layla risks another glance at Kyrin.

The leader begins taking the needles out swiftly one after another, pressing at the machines every couple of moments. The set-up is different than what was attached to Fisher at the other base. He was hooked to one machine, while Celia is hooked to three. The number of needles in her body makes it hard for Layla to ignore the churning in her stomach.

Taking measured breathes, she fights to keep her body from tensing up too much. With Kyrin too far away, she will only have a split second to do what she needs to.

The leader's hands pause on the machine, and he turns to her with that raised brow expression, eyes flickering over her face. She gives him a smile of her own, all teeth and swagger, none of her internal panic to be seen. Layla puts her hands up, but she doesn't dare to back up another inch.

Clink. Clink. Clink.

The needles fall onto the small, silver side table. The seconds pass by slowly. They could have been standing there for an hour or for minutes before there are five needles left to be removed. One in the crease of each elbow and wrist. The other in the side of Celia's neck. Layla can see the veins they hook into, bulging bright and dark beneath the light skin.

"We can start with a simple question," he says, pausing to look closely at the needle he just removed. "What kind of hybrid is your lovely friend here? I'd like to know if my guess is correct."

The look on his face has Layla's skin crawling. She wants to drag this man as far away from Celia as possible, but he's watching her now, and there are still too many needles left. "She's a snake," Layla says.

"Yes, yes, but what kind? The eyes. They are remarkable. Have you seen them?" His heartbeat speeds up, excitement clear on his face, and he reaches for Celia's face, settles his fingers around one of her eyes like he's going to pry the lids open.

Layla doesn't think. She pitches forward with a growl. "Don't touch her." The two guards tense, gripping their guns hard. The leader freezes, his hand skimming over Celia's forehead. *Then tell me,* his eyes seem to say. For a moment, Layla feels like her blood is going to boil in her veins. Then she says, "A viper. She's a viper."

The leader frowns. "Really?" Shaking his head, he returns to pulling the needles out of her wrists in quick succession. With how fast he's going, Layla thinks that might be the last of his questions. At least until the needles are all removed, but then he says, "I've been wondering," his finger hovers over a button on the machine. Layla barely stops herself from snapping her teeth at him, "what kind of hybrid is the strongest. Species wise. I have always leaned toward mammal hybrids." He presses the button and turns his eyes to Layla. "Do you agree?"

The murky gray substance in the tube attached to Celia's neck retreats. Slowly, the leader pulls the long needle out.

"All of us are different," Layla says, and even if she could think of a decent lie to tell, there wouldn't be a point in trying to fool him. She doesn't plan on leaving this place with him alive. "Strength does not correlate to species. Same as with normal people. Race. Gender. Everyone is different."

"Are you sure?" He smirks, turning away from Celia's still body.

His fingers work rapidly over the buttons on the machine, and Layla focuses on the clicking sounds as she tries to think. From where she stands, she can only see part of his hand: the top of his knuckles and his thumb. But she can imagine the keys. She got a quick look at the machine before he burst into the room. So, Layla knows that when his hand reaches up, it's to hit the enter button. Then there's a glint around his wrist catches her attention.

Layla's knees weaken under her at what she sees. A tingling starts in her fingers.

The leader must notice her looking, because with a swift jerk he pulls his sleeve back down. But it's too late. Too late to hide what she saw.

"What about you, wolf? What do you think?" he says.

Mick's face is steadily growing paler from the cold and exhaustion, but there's no fear in his eyes as he says, "I've always thought that it is up to the person to decide how strong they are. If they are going to lie down and take it or stand up."

Look at me, Layla wants to yell at him, but his blazing gaze doesn't turn her way.

The leader pauses in his button pushing, humming as he thinks over the words. He spins one of the needles between his slim fingers. "Nothing to do with species? Now, that is something to think about."

There's only one more needle left, hooked into Celia's left arm. *Now*, Layla's brain screams at her. She glances at Kyrin out of the corner of her eye. He's already looking at her. Calm. Bored. He thinks she can do it. Take the leader and the two guards out. But he doesn't know what's under the leader's neat suit. And he can't hear the others. Hundreds of them, like buzzing insects roaming every floor above and below them. Waiting.

The leader sets the needle down on the metal table with a clang. The last one still needs to be removed, but Layla knows how he does it. She knows what buttons he presses and the way he slowly glides the needles out. She has watched him take out fifteen, twenty others? She lost count.

"Layla," Kyrin breathes, too quiet for anyone but her and Mick to hear.

Her fidgeting hands clench into fists. She needs to tell him there are hundreds surrounding them. There's no way out of this building. The only reason they got this far in the first place was because he wanted them to. The leader let them in. There's no way they are going to get out of here.

But when the leader opens his mouth to ask his next question, Layla moves.

She goes for the soldier first, grabbing his outstretched wrist and punching his elbow up. It breaks with a sickening crack and a painful yell, but Layla doesn't stop. She snatches the soldiers falling gun out of the air and throws it to Kyrin.

Then the room dissolves in to chaos.

Gunshots pierce her ears. Layla barrels into the soldier, knocking him down. They land next to the silver table, and Layla reaches over to pull it down. The needles rain onto the floor. She grabs two, one in each hand, and it almost feels like her daggers. Almost, but not quite. They don't run smoothly over the man's neck, but they do cut in deep enough to do the job.

It only took seconds, and when she looks up, it's to see the two soldiers who held Kyrin and Jax laying on the ground, blood seeping over their chests. Kyrin is shooting at the leader, but the bullets bounce harmlessly off his armored body. Layla swears. She can hear

Mick fighting behind her, but she needs to get to the leader. Layla rolls off the man and shoves more needles into the pockets of her pants, ignoring how some leak with unknown fluid.

She twists around the stretcher. Time seems to slow as she sees the soldier with his gun pressed to Celia's head. Layla throws one of the needles at his heart as if it was a throwing knife just as a bullet wizzes past. And hits the soldier in the head. She feels the hot wetness of his blood splatter her face, sees it splash onto Celia's form. Layla doesn't stop. She moves towards the leader before the soldier's body hits the ground. She jumps over the table, over Celia, and straight for the leader.

They crash to the floor in a mess of limbs. Her chin cracks off his armored chest, but the pain only spurs her on. His neck isn't fully covered by the armor. She could cut into his throat with a needle like she would do with a dagger, but she wants to see and feel it when he goes limp beneath her. She wants to have this moment ground into her memory. How she ended the Black Sun's leader, avenging her parents and her friends.

Mick's cursing is loud enough to pierce through the rage induced fog that has settled over her mind, but it's not loud enough to cover the sound of running. Hundreds of clomping feet rushing toward them.

The needles are scattered across the floor, having dropped them to catch herself. Instead of reaching for one, her hands find his soft, breakable throat, wrapping around the weathered skin, feeling the rapid pulse under her fingers.

This plan. This plan is going to fail. She knows that, but none of them are staying here to get experimented on, to get beat on, to be held captive.

Layla has no intention of dying here. Or letting her friends die here.

The leader struggles under her. He tries to pry her hands away, tries to push her off, and even though she has the advantage of being stronger, her hands are too busy at his throat to hold his limbs down. His armor-plated elbow jams into Layla's ribs. The sound of a crack fills her head. Pain flares, and the air is knocked from her lungs.

Mick and Kyrin are yelling, but whether it's meant for her to hear or not Layla doesn't care. She won't look away from the leader. She won't take her hands away from his vulnerable neck.

His plain, surprised brown eyes roll back, but with one last violent push of his hips, he manages to throw Layla off. His gasp of breath is one of the worst things Layla has heard in her life. He throws himself on top of her. Faster than he should be able to, he punches her straight across her face. Black spots dance across her eyes, and then he has a needle at her throat.

Layla grabs his wrist, feeling where the armor gives way to the soft flesh of his hand. She forces his hand away, but he holds strong, teeth bared with the effort to push the needle closer to her skin. She must have hit his nose sometime during the struggle because blood runs from it and trails into his mouth, grotesquely lining the spaces between his teeth.

Drawing her legs to her chest, she plants her feet on his stomach. There's armor there, too. The solid feel of it unquestionable under her boots. With a grunt, Layla pushes him off. He flies off to the side, choking for air. Layla raises to her feet in one fluid moment. The leader is on his hands and knees, shaking his head hard enough that she can see sweat fly from his hair. But then the next second he's franticly reaching under Celia's metal cot. He comes back with one of the soldier's guns. In the time it takes Layla to blink, the barrel is pressed to her sweaty forehead.

Layla freezes in shock.

Distantly, she hears the shift of the bullets and the click of a trigger. And then she moves. Only an inch to the side. She feels the bullet scrape against the right side of her scalp, a burning, stinging sensation. Tendrils of her hair flutter to the floor. Blood gushes into her ear and over her neck.

The tangy smell of her own blood fills her nostrils. She sees red.

She wanted to make this count, to draw his suffering out. Make him feel just an ounce of what she did when the bombs hit Denver, or when she thinks about Courtney. But her senses are cranked up to ten, and she can hear her team's every breath, she can hear the soldiers steadily moving closer, and the man outside the door with their weapons, hesitating with his hand on the doorknob. There isn't time for it.

So, gritting her teeth, eyes bright with fury, she grabs the gun from the leader, crushing some of his unprotected bones in the process. The metal barrel cracks in her grip. The glowing blue light flickers. She turns it on the leader, aims it straight at his head like he did to her.

His eyes grow impossibly wide. Sweat beads along hairline and upper lip. His heart stutters to work through his panic. She hears the breath catch in his throat.

"No," he whispers.

Layla doesn't have the words to tell him what he has done to her life—to every American's life. All she can do is make sure she doesn't look away when she pulls the trigger.

An explosion of red. The unmistakable silence from where the man stood. Layla wipes the warm wetness of his blood off her face and commits the sight to memory.

"Should have snapped his neck," Kyrin says, snapping Layla out of her trance. She drags her gaze away from the disturbing sight of the leader crumpled on the floor. "It would have been faster and more effective." His eyes are still dark and unreadable, but Layla can see the command in them. *Get ready. We aren't done yet.*

Mick and Jax are unstrapping Celia from the bed. Jax is moving at a much, much slower pace than normal. She tries not to feel too worried about that. The same thing was wrong with Fisher. If they make it back to the compound, the doctors at the infirmary would have already found out how to treat them. *When* they make it back, Layla corrects herself. She reaches out to help with Celia, but Kyrin all but snarls at her.

"You're with me," he says. His hand reaches out to her, offering her another one of the soldier's guns, but she shakes her head. Yeah, she shot the leader, but shooting someone point blank is different than shooting someone yards away. And her axes are just outside the door with the quivering soldier.

"I don't think now is the time to learn how to shoot," she says.

Kyrin shrugs. "You would be surprised."

He's acting nonchalant about what just happened. Layla's heart is still beating double. The tingling under her skin buzzing with a painful ferocity. Layla and Kyrin head to the door, both glancing over their shoulders at their beat-up teammates before slipping out.

The soldier is halfway down to the stair way, fleeing for his life. Kyrin shoots him down with one bullet, then turns to face her. "We're clearing a path to get Celia and Jax out. Mick can still fight, but not well enough to not get himself killed." His hair is slicked back with sweat and a darker, thicker substance. Blood, Layla realizes. But a rare hint of a real smile tugs at his lips. He nods his head to the end of the hall where the opening of the stairs is. "I'm not sure if I want to ask you how many there are."

The terrorist soldiers have been already gathering since the leader showed up in that room. There's at a standstill on the stairways. Right now, five or so squeeze through the doorway to the hall she stands in, but they don't come any closer to her, seeming to be waiting for an order. They're eyes jump from the soldier spread out on the floor, to her and Kyrin, and to the door behind them. Using just her ears, she tries to get a number on them all but loses count as sixty. Not that it matters, as the soldiers spill out into the hallway, more and more crowding into the space.

"I know you're scared, Layla," Kyrin whispers. Is she scared? Her mind is reeling too much to know what she's feeling. Panicked, maybe. Determined, absolutely. "You know the only way to get out of here is if you let go. Completely."

No surprise greets her at his words. She only nods, having already come to that conclusion long before they got rid of the leader. "I know."

Like the first mission. Like with Jax.

Layla doesn't spare Kyrin another glance as she drums up all the rage and grief she holds back every day. She thinks of Celia, Fisher, Team Three, Courtney, her parents, and everyone else hurt by the Black Sun. It's easy to let go. Not just easy, but freeing, exhilarating. Natural. This is who she is. She can smell the pine and dirt of the forest under all the bodies and blood. She can hear each of their hearts, each of their breaths.

Kyrin stays back from the massacre. He guards the torture chamber door, waiting to take down anyone who gets past the newbie. It's hard to watch her like this, but he refuses to look away. This is the reason he never wanted the wild cat on his team. And this is the reason his teammates did want her.

They're all made out to be weapons, but Layla's on a whole different level. They compared her to Mick when she first came to the compound, told her she was like he used to be, but that was a lie. Mick had control, had the will and the want to hold back. Layla doesn't have those things. She balances too close to the edge, all the while knowing that she will be readily pulled down into the fire.

He doesn't know what they would do if she wasn't willing to listen. If she decided to make her own choices. If she wanted to become a leader, challenge Jax and himself. Their team would be wrecked, and, even with the leader dead, this isn't the end of the war. Kyrin has been watching and living through this war since the first Black Sun attack. This is merely another battle.

But it is a battle he will not lose.

Aiming his gun, Kyrin pushes the thought out of his head.

One of the terrorist soldiers has gotten past Layla, and he shoots him down with one bullet, right through the head like Layla did with the leader. Kyrin has never felt good seeing someone die, no matter how bad they were. It's survival, plain and simple. Kill or be killed. But the leader's death felt different. It felt good.

Minutes pass, filled with growling, shouts, and other sounds he tries not to listen too closely to. He could throw up if he let himself. Just from watching, but that wouldn't do anyone any good. Besides, he has felt like throwing up since he woke up in the woods with Jax gone. He can hold it until they get home.

The soldiers stop coming through the stairway, but he has no doubt that there are more of them. They must have finally caught on that it will only lead to their death if they enter this hall. Kyrin keeps his eyes on Layla, his gun aimed by her feet, and doesn't turn away until she prowls down the stairs after the soldiers.

Letting out a breath, he opens the door for the rest of his team to come through. Mick carries Celia in his arms, and Kyrin is relieved when he catches her eyes moving beneath her lids. He couldn't help but worry that the Black Sun's leader lied to them, just like they lied to him, and only pretended to cooperate and take the needles out safely.

Jax trails behind them, looking tired and angry enough that Kyrin wants to carry him in his arms like Mick does with Celia. Instead, he looks them all over quickly and says, "Stay behind me. We're following the newbie."

The growls and sickening noises echoing through the narrow

stairway is enough for them to know where to follow. There are so many soldiers on the floor that Kyrin doesn't consider trying to move them, and with a sick feeling in his stomach, he, Jax, and Mick walk across the slippery bodies and down the stairs.

Mick is growling behind him. "You let her go."

"She let herself go." And he was going to leave it at that, but he's angry and impatient and done with this idea of control that Mick has. "She is not a dog and we are not holding her leash. It is time you all understand that."

Kyrin can feel the eyes glaring daggers at his back.

"Now is not the time." Jax's voice is heavy and raw. It makes Kyrin's clench he teeth, wishing he could have shot the leader himself.

"How are you doing back there?" he asks.

Jax chuckles darkly. "Wish I had a better view."

Kyrin lets out a bark of surprised laughter. Mick curses at the both of them, cradling the still unconscious Celia close.

The door at the top of the stairs bangs open, signaling Layla's at the ground floor. Kyrin's smile falls as he quickens his pace. The muscles in his legs burn from overexertion. He hasn't had any rest since they got off the subway outside the demolished city. Kyrin refuses to count being knocked out by Jax for a few hours as rest. Behind him, Mick and Jax struggle, panting and occasionally tripping down the stairs. Just when Kyrin spots the light spilling from an open door, Mick stops, grabbing at the back of Kyrin's jacket to stop him as well.

"Damn," he says. "There's a hybrid."

Kyrin motions for them to wait and sneaks up the few stairs before reaching the door. He peeks his head out. More soldiers are packed in the hallway. Too many to single out Layla, let alone another hybrid he doesn't know. After spotting where the exit door is located, he climbs back down the stairs.

"It's Layla's friend," Mick says before Kyrin can tell them a thing. He's holding Celia in the crook of one arm now. The other clicks a knife Layla left behind off his belt. "I recognize her scent from the forest."

Kyrin takes a second to close his eyes before meeting Jax's. They need to get out. Get Celia safe. He can't protect them all on his own, and if Layla's friend is in here, that's what he would have to do. Jax nods at him, agreeing to his silent explanation.

"We need to get out of the base," Kyrin says out loud for Mick to hear. "Layla can handle herself."

Hesitation flickers across his face, but Mick drops his head to study Celia curled in his arms, and then he nods.

Your eyes are empty and so is my heart.

CHAPTER TWENTY-NINE

*I*f any other feelings besides rage and heat exist, Layla has forgotten them. The monster under her skin, in her head, controls her every movement. It is freeing and exciting and terrifying. A thick, goopy substance coats her hands and slips down her face. Somewhere in the very back of her mind she knows it's blood. She knows she's hurting people. Killing people. They're bad people, but under all the hate, her brain is yelling at her to stop.

Too many people. Too much blood. Through the rage and heat, panic squeezes at her insides.

She can't stop. This is the mission. Get her team out. Don't let them down. Don't let them be the ones on the floor bleeding out or dead.

She can hear her team in the hallway across the room, their heartbeats drumming in her ears, but between one swipe of her knife and the next, her team is gone. Swallowed up by the others, or worse. The next few kills come faster, easier with the possibility that her friends might have been taken away by the terrorists.

She climbs on top of a man's shoulders and wraps her legs around his neck. She forces her nose high in the air in the hope that she can smell them over the blood and sweat and fear. The man under her grabs at her and flails around, but she squeezes her thighs tight enough around his head to hear a bone snap.

She catches the barest whiff of them, heading to the right, toward a cracked door. The exit sign above it is almost too bright for her to look at. They weren't taken. They're getting out. A rumbling sigh of relief leaves her mouth. Layla twists her body with a sharp jerk and catches herself against the floor when the man falls.

She heads to the door, her feet slipping and gliding over the slick ground. She's almost done. Almost there, and then no more slashing and stabbing with her axes. She hates the Black Sun. She hates them more than anything else, but her conscious nags at her. This is too much. Too many by her hands alone.

But she refuses to stop until they're safe. Even if it makes her a monster.

Her nose twitches with a familiar scent. One that reminds her of busy hallways, and an overstuffed couch. A scent that reminds her of home and family. With a shake of her head, Layla makes it to the other side of the room. One hand is on the door, the other rearing back her axe, and that's when she hears her. Over the screams and grunts and sounds of pain. A voice so familiar it could be her own.

"Get out of my way, you idiots."

Layla freezes in place for a second before she slowly turns around. She's not used to hearing her like that. Rude and forceful. A predator claiming her prey. A red haze still covers her vision, but Layla can see that the remaining men and women surrounding her move away, lowering their guns, and pressing themselves flat against the walls. Then, one by one, they leave the room entirely with relieved looks on their faces, happy to get away from the slaughter.

Fingers twitching over her axes, Layla watches Courtney walk towards her, stepping over and sometimes even on the bodies littering the floor. She wears the same clothes as when they met in the halls under the other terrorist base where Layla found out that she's alive—that she didn't die in the school gymnasium, gasping and shivering in her arms.

The monstrous rage slips off her body, a layer of skin being shed. It leaves Layla feeling sick, but she pushes it aside. The colors, scents, and noises all zero down to a bearable level. With the ability to focus, Layla clicks her axes back on her person and steps forward, outwardly calm and assessing.

But with the rage gone, her mind is terrifyingly blank.

Courtney meets her halfway in the cleared-out room. The place reeks of fresh blood and sweat. "Courtney?" Layla says, voice rough and throat aching like she had been growling the entire time. "Are you—"

"You followed me here," she interrupts, arms folded across her chest, and Layla remembers the armor that was under her clothes like the armor the leader wore. "You and your friends."

Even with the monstrous rage burrowed back under her skin, Layla can still feel that anger. Waiting with glowing eyes and a sharp smile. Waiting for her to unleash it once more. Layla's narrows her eyes at being interrupted. At the mention of her team. "You don't belong here. You never wanted to fight, and you definitely didn't want to fight for the Black Sun. This isn't you."

"Is your friend okay?" she says like she didn't hear a word Layla said. Layla's head swims with the change of topic. Her hands clench at her sides. It's hard. Hard to focus this early after shutting herself off from the beastly feelings and thoughts. Courtney's dark eyes are flat with a lack of emotion. "The girl."

Celia's unconscious form is something that will haunt her in nightmares for a long, long time. Her team is outside now. Waiting for her. If she takes too long, Celia will be the one to suffer. Would her team leave without her? Layla's not sure.

"You're going to come with me," Layla says, lips pulling back in a snarl. "Right now."

Pulling two knives out, Courtney smiles. "I'm going to kill you. Then I'll bring your friends back for some more fun."

Something in Layla's mind snaps. The blankness inside her mind turns into purpose. A cold rage, different than the red from before. Her heart stings with betrayal. Her two axes slide into her hands, hilts instantly covered in new blood. "The leader of the Black Sun is dead, Courtney. We killed him. You don't need to do this anymore."

Confusion crosses over Courtney's face, scrunching her nose and pulling at her eyebrows. Then it smooths out into a look of pure amusement. A bubble of laughter escapes her throat. "*Him?*" she says, pointing vaguely behind her shoulder.

Distantly, Layla can hear a horn blaring. Either Kyrin must be getting impatient, or something worse is happening. She doesn't have time for this. Celia doesn't have time for this.

Quickly, Layla scans the floor, memorizing the clear spaces between all the bodies and slippery blood. She uses an axe to wave her friend forward. "Come on, then. Let's get this over with."

Despite her bravo, weariness seeps through her being. Her arms tremble with exhaustion. If bullets had no effect of the leader's armor, her axes won't stand a chance on Courtney. Unless she went for the neck, but Layla doesn't think she can do that. Even if Courtney is a brain washed soldier for the Black Sun, she's still Layla's best friend.

Watching Courtney step forward, Layla wills the rage forth. For the room to take on a tinted red color and her mind to stop yelling at her to stop. But none of that comes. No matter what Courtney does, Layla will never want to hurt her.

They slip through puddles of red. Layla dodges a fair number of killing blows. She waits to make her move, luring Courtney closer, but the other hybrid always manages to stay out of range, twisting and jerking her body away from Layla's axes.

Courtney has more training than all the other Black Sun hybrids Layla has dealt with so far. Somehow, she was chosen for a high-ranking position in the terrorist's organization. With her armor, training, and having direct contact with the leader, there isn't another explanation.

The truck horn blares again, making Layla's heart lurch. Using one of the fallen bodies as a base, she pushes off, jumping straight at Courtney. They collide with a jarring impact. Her axes slip out of her hands. Layla clambers on top of her and fallen soldier's body. She struggles with Courtney, managing to get a couple hits in. Too full of adrenaline, the pain from the other hybrid's blows doesn't completely register.

In the corner of her eye, she sees the glint of a knife heading straight for her chest. Betrayal and rage burn anew in her veins. With a burst of speed, she pushes herself away from Courtney. The knife misses by inches, but her axes are laying on the opposite side of Courtney.

Layla hurries to her feet and backs away. She doesn't have her weapons. Guns are scattered around the floor, their soft glow making them easy to find among the bodies. But the leader's face floats before her eyes. Not full and whole and normal, but halfway gone and bloody and broken. His blood probably still coats her skin. She can't have Courtney's on her as well.

Layla's back hits a wall, and Courtney advances toward her, her dark hair swinging around her shoulders, a determined look on her face. The same look she used to have when she had to drag Layla out of bed and to school.

The first knife she throws is easy for Layla to dodge. The second is harder. It whizzes towards her chest lightning fast. When it's an inch from her chest Layla's fingers close around the sharp blade. A hiss escapes through her teeth as it slices deep into her hand. Layla chucks it back at the other girl. It sticks into the fabric of her green jacket, but instead of the soft sound if the blade sinking into flesh, there's a light pinging noise of it hitting the armor.

Layla's hope crashes. There's a stinging sensation in her eyes, and it takes her a moment to realize she's crying. There was a chance that the armor didn't cover her whole body, but now that chance is dead. Dead along with her if she doesn't do something.

"I'll admit that was impressive," Courtney says as she plucks the knife from her jacket. She's pacing back and forth now, feet away from where Layla leans against the wall. "But you're looking tired. I'm a little disappointed."

Beyond the doors, the soldiers aren't moving. Her team isn't rushing back to help her. Layla wants to sink against the wall, slide down to the ground, and stare at her crimson stained hands and arms and legs. But she wants to go home more. She wants to go back to the compound with her team, make sure Celia gets help, make sure Fisher is okay. She wants to sit in a steaming hot shower until all the blood and gore is washed from her skin—from her very memory.

"You never did like when I slept in." Layla rubs her hands up and down the sides of her legs. A tingling sound answers her.

The needles.

She forgot they were there, stuffed into her pockets for her to use on the soldiers. She doesn't know what's in them, but they are her only option.

Layla raises her wet eyes to meet Courtney's. She's frozen in place with a confused look is stuck on her face, and Layla feels like she was punched in the chest. She wants to believe that it's Courtney remembering, fighting against what the terrorists did to her, but Layla doesn't know that, and she can't take the chance.

She fishes two needles out of her pockets, pushes down the plungers of the plastic syringes, and throws them at Courtney's stunned form. They hit her in her exposed neck, one on each side, just like Layla planned. Two more are in her hands already, but she waits. Five seconds. Ten.

Courtney crumbles to the gore-filled floor and doesn't move.

Layla settles Courtney's unconscious body in the back of the truck, tucking her into the jacket Mick handed to her. Then she meets the others on the hill overlooking the base that she and Kyrin used. Her eyes land on Celia. The girl with light that shines out of her very skin. The girl whose eyes now bleed with terror and hold a kind of desperation that makes Layla wonder if she even sees her.

They should have kept the leader alive. If he even was the leader. Layla isn't so sure anymore. They should have brought him to the compound for Helland and Cape to question. Layla hopes the scientists from the last base have enough information to go on, because she doesn't plan on letting any of these terrorists live. Not after what they did to her friends.

Layla turns her back on her team.

Her feet carry her fast and hard. Her lips draw over her teeth. The last remaining terrorists stream out the doors of the base, wondering where their leaders are. They pull their guns from behind their backs, but Layla's on them before they can set their aim. Her axe in one hand, she slashes through a woman's chest. She grabs another by the neck with her free hand and yanks up and up. He goes limp. She lets him fall to the hard ground.

There are around sixty left, none of them hybrids, but she wishes there were more. In her fury, her teeth ache, dying to be used. Every inch of her is a weapon. She lets her mind go blank. She lets her rage take control.

One last time.

She's a sight to behold when she doesn't hold back. From the moment she attacked him in the combat room, Jax has known that. She's wrath and rage in human form. Neither he nor Kyrin make a move to help her. No, he can only watch with a sense of crazed satisfaction as his friend tears apart the group of remaining terrorists. Kyrin swears next to him as Layla uses her teeth to rip out another's throat.

"She's gone," Mick says. His voice surprises Jax. It's darker, heavier than it used to be. There's a glint in his mismatched eyes. Jax studies him watching Layla. It doesn't take long to figure out that he wants to be beside her, joining in the massacre. Jax can't find it in himself to blame him.

"What do you mean she's gone?" he asks.

Mick's hand is placed steadily on top of Celia's head. She still trembles on her knees in the grass, her eyes focused in the direction of Layla. "Look at her," he says, and Jax does. They are all dead, but her wrath continues. He almost cringes imagining the noises Mick can hear. Jax can see the tears rushing down her face. There are enough of them to wash away the blood caked on her skin.

Jax sees what Mick means, but still, they don't go to her.

This is for all of them.

Let her rage.

Let her tear them apart.

Let her send the Black Sun a message.

From all of them.

From Team Thirteen.

Just remember me. Whether I am down at your feet or standing at your side. Remember me.

EPILOGUE

A week. Jax has been stuck in the infirmary for a week. The effects from the drugs that man put in him are gone, and if it were not for the overbearing nurse and Kyrin, he would have escaped the place by now. Or at least left the room to visit his old team.

Even Mick is up and running, stopping in to give him and Kyrin information about Celia and Layla and the compound. Of course, Layla stops by too, and Jax tries to hide how he sees the new respect in Kyrin's eyes. It's about time he's softened up to her.

Right now, Kyrin's posted against the door frame, half in the room and half out, ignoring how Jax paces the length of the small room. Helland came to check on him twice in the week he has been here, only giving him minimal information about the Black Sun scientists they took in for questioning. Him and his team got an earful from the commanders on their return to the compound. Their biggest offense wasn't running off on their own, but not bringing the leader's body back with them. They left it there with all the others. Cape, himself, went to the base to check it out, but it was already teaming with hundreds more soldiers. There isn't a chance of them getting the body.

Despite that, Jax doesn't regret any of it. He thought he would, but no. His team got out alive, a large branch of the Black Sun was taken down, and they got valuable information. The only thing Jax would have changed is what happened to Celia.

"Layla said that she doesn't think that man was the real leader," he says for the hundredth time. Kyrin sighs, and peeks farther into the hallway. "But does that really matter? They would have just made someone else the new leader."

"Let's hope they're less of a creep," Kyrin mutters. "Guy was seriously obsessed with us. With hybrids." He comes back in the room, shutting the door behind him, and takes seat on the edge of the single cot. "They still aren't sure what happened with Celia."

Jax screws his eyes shut, only to have the image of her paint itself on the backs of his eyelids. That's one thing he can't remember. He ran through it a million times in his head—waking up with her hand on his shoulder, meeting her eyes, the questioning, the beatings, Mick getting pulled away, snarling and snapping, more beatings, a sharp prick in his arm, and blackness.

"Mick says she's eating again," Kyrin says, rubbing at his eyes. Neither of them has been sleeping much, too full of worry and restless energy.

Jax sits down next to Kyrin, slightly out of breath. He admits that he's not fully recovered, but he's well enough to leave this suffocating room. "How does she look?" Unlike him, Kyrin can visit her every day.

Red-rimmed eyes raise to meet his. "Bad," he says, voice rough with emotion. "She looks better sometimes after the newbie visits her, but…" He shrugs his shoulders.

Pulling him into the juncture of his arm, Jax swallows back the tight feeling in his throat. "We'll find her all the coffee in the trucks. That should get her up and running."

Jax doesn't know how long they sit like that, staring at nothing in particular before the door cracks open, and Mick slips through. There's a strained looking smile on his face as he holds up a small rectangular package. "Layla found chocolate," he says, "and I used a bar to bribe the nurse to let you leave the room, so let's go see our little piece of sunshine, yeah?"

Jax rushes out the door before Kyrin or Mick can move, slipping the bar of chocolate out of Mick's hand on the way. He will thank him later. Right now, all he can think about is that he can finally see his friend with his own eyes and tell her that she will be okay.

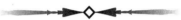

They put Courtney in the labs, not in the infirmary with Jax and Celia. For hours, Layla had watched as they tried to get the armor off her unconscious body. It wouldn't budge. They ended up having to dismantle it with sharp tools, taking it off piece by piece. It's somewhere in the commander's building now, locked up with all the other special gadgets. Layla doesn't know what they're doing with it. If they're even doing anything with it.

She's still not her old self. Whatever control the Black Sun did to her lingers, causing her to lash out at random. From what Layla and the scientists at the compound understand, Courtney doesn't have access to all her memories from before being injected with the serum, and whatever she has seen or heard with the terrorists is under lock and key. Another type of conditioning, the lead scientists told her grudgingly. To not give any information to anyone unless they know the correct words to say. Like a secret code.

Layla stopped listening to the scientist after that. She didn't want to know what kinds of torture her friend went through for that to be possible. She can't stand the nightmares. But still, her mind supplies images and scenarios of what could have happened. It's enough to keep her up and drag her tired body to check on Courtney or Celia or Jax.

She spends all her free time in the labs and in the infirmary now, refusing to take her meals in the cafeteria or send anytime alone on her housing floor. Endless questions tumble through her mind every day. The scientists explained what they're doing with Courtney, but she still cornered Cam to tell her more.

"We're finding out what is different about her," he said. "Or what is different about the serum she was injected with, and how to reverse the control they have over her."

Mind control.

Layla could have laughed if she wasn't so terrified.

She didn't get far with questioning the scientist in the truck before Courtney's scent came through the window. But what she got from his was all that there was, Layla found out from the commanders. The Black Sun is in their government, and that means it's in the Hybrid Force, too. They have infiltrated the hybrid division of the military and are hiding among them. They tampered with half the serum, turning and brainwashing the teenagers to their side.

Closing her eyes, Layla rests her head against the window looking into Courtney's room. She tried going in the small room and talking to Courtney once, and ended up sending her friend into a vicious state that had her spitting and biting at the lab assistants. It's safe to say that Layla isn't allowed to go in there anymore. Not until Courtney is better.

"Hey."

Layla doesn't turn around at the voice, already knowing who it is. She studies her knuckles, picking at the still healing scabs. Fisher has been checking up on her since she got back. She can only interpret it as some sort of payback for saving him. They're friends, yes. And with most of their other friends working for the Black Sun, they might know more about each other than anyone else, but this constant concern is new.

She just hopes it's not some type of hero worship.

"What's so funny?" he says, running a hand through his curls.

"Nothing." Layla straightens the slight smile on her face. "Nothing is really funny."

Humming, Fisher joins her at the window, looking at her closely before turning to the lab room. They're taking blood again and bringing in Courtney's lunch. "Where are your other friends?" Fisher asks.

"Where are yours?" He doesn't look at her, but Layla sees his eyebrows raise. Sees his lips pull into a smirk. "Celia, Jax, and Kyrin are still in the infirmary. Jax wants to leave. Kyrin won't leave Jax. And Celia... she still doesn't really want to talk yet." Layla looks down, staring at her scarred knuckles. "Mick and I have been trying to get her to talk, but..." Layla shrugs.

"She probably just needs time," he says.

Biting her lip, she thinks of her friend. The wax-like sheen on her skin and her dark, distant eyes. The words the nurses used like *PTSD*, *neurogenic shock*, and a too long word that they told her means fear of medical situations. Layla swallows down the lump of pain in her throat. "Yeah."

"And so does Courtney."

Layla's frown deepens, causing her teeth to pinch at her lips. "Yeah," she repeats.

After a few seconds of silence, Fisher asks, "Did you ever find out about the one scientist from the base? The one that was in the lab with me?"

She gives him a look she hopes is apologetic and shakes her head. Besides the news about the enemy hybrids, Helland and Cape have been keeping everything else as quiet as they can. "Commanders wouldn't tell me. Wouldn't let me see the guy." Layla laughs, cold and short. "They probably think I'll kill him."

"Would you?"

She thinks about it, about seeing the man's face. Seeing him standing over Fisher or Jen and the others with needles ready in his hands. She feels the familiar rush of anger ripple across her skin. "I don't know," she says. "I could."

Layla looks up at Fisher. Half-healed scrapes and bruises cover his face. She knows there're more under his shirt, bigger and so much worse than the ones she can see. Their own scientists were able to find out what the needles were putting in him, nothing lethal, nothing meant to harm him. It only temporarily weakened him and kept him subdued enough to perform tests. Like the stuff they gave Jax. Like the stuff that was in one of the needles she threw at Courtney. Fisher still spent a good couple of days in the infirmary with the rest of his team.

She hasn't been able to see Team Three at all. They are closed off in a special wing of the infirmary. Intensive care. Her team gets updates every day, but the medical terms swirl around in her head without making sense.

Every day, every hour, memories of the second base infiltrate her thoughts. What she did there.

The confusing emotions that come with losing control and killing are unexpected. Layla expected and accepted that she would be used as a weapon from the moment she was injected with the hybrid serum. Sometimes she even hoped for it—to be valuable to the team and the war against the terrorists.

She still can't put a name to how she feels about what happened after she got Courtney out of the building, about how she saw Celia and snapped. That... that monster she became...

"I don't like killing people, Will," Layla says, interrupting the comfortable silence between them. It's something she needs to say out loud. "I just want you to know that."

Fisher smiles down at her. "I know that."

But she doesn't hate it either.

ACKNOWLEDGMENTS

A massive thank you to everyone at Mascot Books. Daniel for being patient with me and helping me the whole way through editing and publication. Treva for making this possible by believing in *Team Thirteen* since coming across it on Publishizer.com.

Thank you to my mom and dad, my Uncle Chris, Amanda, Zach, and Jessica, for being there since the beginning, listening to all my crazy ideas, and pushing me through the hard spots. Thank you to all of my huge, wonderful family. There are too many of you to name but know that each one of you deserves a spot here.

Much appreciation to everyone who supported me on Publishizer.com, Kenny Ruffatto, Danielle Ruffatto, Natalie Ruffatto, Barbie Ruffatto, Eryn Ruffatto, JoAnn Ruffatto, Alan Vehrs, Sarah Jerz, Travis Peters, Lorraine Drehobl, Cheryl Kendra, Amy Lee, Andrea Reid. Without your help, publishing this book wouldn't have been possible.

ABOUT THE AUTHOR

 **NN COLE** grew up in a small town in Northern Illinois where she discovered her great love of books and reading. This love later developed into an interest of writing and creating her own stories. She began writing her first novel, *Team Thirteen*, while working towards a degree in science.